St. Helens Libraries

Please return / renew this item by the last date shown. Items may be renewed by phone and internet.

Telephone: (01744) 676954 or 677822
Email: libraries@sthelens.gov.uk
Online: sthelens.gov.uk/librarycatalogue

0 1 JUL 2021
2 2 JUL 2021

7 FEB 2022

1 9 APR 2022

 STHLibraries   sthlibrariesandarts   STHLibraries

We Are All Birds of Uganda

We Are All Birds of Uganda

HAFSA ZAYYAN

1 3 5 7 9 10 8 6 4 2

#Merky Books
20 Vauxhall Bridge Road
London SW1V 2SA

#Merky Books is part of the Penguin Random House group of companies
whose addresses can be found at global.penguinrandomhouse.com.

Penguin
Random House
UK

First published by #Merky Books in 2021

www.penguin.co.uk

A CIP catalogue record for this book is available from the British Library.

ISBN 9781529118643 (Hardback)
ISBN 9781529118650 (Trade paperback)

Set in 12/14.75 pt Dante MT Std
Typeset by Jouve (UK), Milton Keynes
Printed and bound in Great Britain by Clays Ltd, Elcograf S.p.A.

The authorised representative in the EEA is Penguin Random House Ireland,
Morrison Chambers, 32 Nassau Street, Dublin D02 YH68

Penguin Random House is committed to a sustainable future for
our business, our readers and our planet. This book is made
from Forest Stewardship Council® certified paper.

MIX
Paper from
responsible sources
FSC® C016897

For Riaz
Before I met you, I didn't know I could fly

PART I

1

It is six minutes to four in the morning. Sameer's eyelids droop, but only momentarily, rescued by his peripheral sight of the time, small and fuzzy at the bottom of the computer screen, and the overwhelming instinct to meet the goal he set for himself: send out the document by 4 a.m. Revived by a sudden rush of adrenaline, his eyes jolt open and the screen comes back into focus. He taps at the keyboard, conscious that it is the only noise in the still air around him: even the A/C gives up at midnight, the soft hum of the machine abandoning the office, leaving the air uncomfortably clammy. He hits send at exactly 4 a.m. Immediately, he reaches for the phone, orders a cab, tries to file some of the hundreds of emails crowding his inbox while waiting, but ends up dozing off until a telephone call from the cab driver rouses him. He barely remembers the journey home.

Home is a high-rise new building in the heart of Clerkenwell – a spacious one-bed penthouse apartment with floor-to-ceiling windows and panoramic views of the city skyline, rented to him for the tidy sum of £2,500 a month. The flat is roasting when he gets in: he forgot to switch off the underfloor heating before he left for work and it has been on in the empty flat for nearly forty-eight hours. As he walks unsteadily towards the bedroom, Sameer begins to strip off his clothes: grasp jacket, unbutton shirt, unzip fly. He cannot remember the last time he felt this exhausted. But this deal has been particularly brutal. He has regularly stayed in the office past 2 a.m. over the last few weeks, and yesterday evening he didn't make it home: just took a quick nap at his desk for an hour before continuing with a double espresso.

He stands in his bedroom, naked apart from his boxers. His Hackett suit (usually hung up next to neatly lined rows of white shirts immediately after being removed) lies strewn on the floor. Casting a glance at his reflection in the floor-length mirror by his bed, Sameer grimaces; he hasn't been to the gym for two weeks in a row, and he is certain it shows – his arms seem smaller, his chest softer. His face resembles the pasty colour of his body: it hasn't seen the sun in a long time. *Chand ki moorat*, his mother used to say: the pale face of the moon. He considers using the bathroom – there is a slight pressure in his bladder and he can feel plaque on his teeth – but his body makes the decision for him by collapsing onto the pillowy white sheets of the king-sized bed. He doesn't need to set an alarm: he can go into work tomorrow whenever he wakes up because he has completed a major part of his workstream – for now. Unbidden and unwelcome, the last thing that comes into his mind before he falls asleep is that his mother would be waking up to pray *fajr* at this time.

It's midday when Sameer wakes up. He doesn't remember switching off the heating when he came home, but he must have done because he never made it under the covers and now he is cold. Rubbing sleep from his eyes, he reaches for his phone and takes it with him to the bathroom, reviewing his emails while relieving himself. There is an email in his inbox from Matthew Tenver, the group head, sent at 9.03 that morning, untitled: *Sam, let me know when you get into the office (no rush – I know you were here earlier this morning). Deb and I would like to have a chat with you. Matt.*

Sameer stares at the message blankly. Deborah Hayes is the human resources manager. He wonders if they're going to talk to him about the hours he's been working, about his physical and mental health. The firm had a shock six months ago when one of the junior associates in their New York office had suddenly died of a heart attack after working a 140-hour week. Sameer did not know him personally, but after his death was announced, he'd looked him up on the firm intranet: Michael Pierce. Sameer had scrutinised his picture and read his bio, searching for any similarities between them – a black-and-white snapshot in time, smiling strongly into the camera, goofy teeth showing, thick-rimmed glasses, spiky brown hair; a Yale graduate, Harvard fellow and litigator specialising in antitrust. The announcement had made clear that Michael had an underlying heart condition, but since his death the firm had rolled out mandatory well-being training for all employees. Michael's death, which had passed through the London office somewhat impassively, had roused an image in Sameer's mind of his own mother, dressed head to toe in black, sobbing uncontrollably. But he did not mention the news to her, or to the rest of his family.

It takes him less than fifteen minutes to shower, change and leave the flat. His stomach growls, annoyed at being neglected, and he stops to pick up a coffee from the cafe on the corner of the street. The man behind the counter grins and pretends to check the time: 'Bit of a late start for you, isn't it?' Sameer responds with a faint smile, not interested in engaging. 'Ah well,' the man's red face beams as he hands over Sameer's latte, winking conspiratorially. 'It is Friday!' Although they don't know each other's names, they know each other well, as Sameer stops here nearly every morning for coffee and a bagel. There is rarely food in his house.

The flat is less than a thirty-minute walk from the office. This Friday is bright and warm for April and Sameer spots a lone cherry blossom tree bursting with spring flowers,

5

steadfast among the concrete, as he heads towards the office. For a moment, with the midday sun streaming onto his face, the coffee beginning to work its magic, assisted in its endeavours by the fact he got seven hours of sleep for the first time in several weeks, and the knowledge that he will not have much to do when he reaches the office, Sameer feels content. He is twenty-six years old, living in the centre of London. He's good at his job and – what's more – he likes it. He earns the kind of salary that allows him to spend money without thinking about it; he has everything he could need. His flat is filled with the latest gadgets: a 65-inch HD television, played through a state-of-the-art surround-sound speaker system; the latest iPad Pro, lying in a corner of his bedroom, still unwrapped a few weeks after it was delivered; a drone, drunkenly purchased after a night out. He holidays without needing to save for it (although he cannot now remember the last time he took a holiday). Among these thoughts – whenever he has such thoughts – something else niggles in the back of his mind, but he pushes it away.

As he reaches the office building, Sameer catches sight of the office managing partner, James Butcher, walking towards the office with a Pret bag in hand. Sameer tries to hurry, not wanting to be left to make awkward conversation – but the large revolving doors are automated and by the time Sameer has entered the building, James is right behind him. 'Hi, James,' he says politely as they pass through security and head towards the lifts. Their offices are on floor 24 of the building.

'Sam,' James nods. Sameer can see a baguette peeping over the top of the Pret bag. Prosciutto flops over the side of the bread as if making a half-hearted attempt to escape.

The lift arrives and Sameer moves instinctively into a corner. 'Anything nice planned for the weekend?' he begins, tailing off as a few more people enter the lift, jabbing the buttons for a series of floors below 24. James does not respond. Sameer begins to feel a small line of sweat collect on his forehead. He reaches for the safety of his phone and pretends to be engrossed in the several hundred unread emails in his inbox.

'Sam,' James says. Sameer looks up – the lift is now empty apart from the two of them. It arrives at the twenty-fourth floor with a gentle ping and James steps out. 'Don't think we haven't noticed,' James's eyes are kind. 'You've been doing a great job.'

Sameer is stunned into silence, this compliment completely unexpected. Before he has the chance to reply, James has disappeared. These types of comments are rare and a small smile surfaces in response. Well, he thinks to himself, it just goes to show how much he is valued by management. It makes all the effort he puts in worth it.

Buoyed by this interaction, he walks to his office with a slight spring in his step, passing row after row of glass doors housing his colleagues sitting behind their large computer screens, files of papers everywhere, the faint smell of coffee lingering in the air. Sameer shares an office with Ryan, an associate who has become a good friend of his over the years. Ryan is staring intently at his computer screen when Sameer walks in: a yellow-and-black banner gives away the BBC Sport domain.

'Hey man,' Ryan looks up briefly from the screen. There is a faint northern twang to Ryan's voice; it is almost lyrical. Sameer has always liked him, particularly since he had found out that – unlike the majority of their colleagues, who came from families of lawyers, doctors or investment bankers – Ryan came from a family of coal miners before the pits had closed. Sameer's father had once been a refugee. 'What time did you leave this morning?'

'Oh, I don't know,' Sameer shrugs. 'After midnight it's all the same isn't it? You didn't exactly leave early either, mate.'

'Yeah. I'm getting slammed on Project Skylight.'

'So slammed you've only got time for a few hours of BBC Sport today?' Sameer says, shedding his jacket and switching on his computer screen, which faces away from Ryan and the prying eyes of the corridor. Even though Ryan and Sameer are the same level of qualification, the roll of the dice in the human resources seat reshuffle had somehow left Sameer with the window seat and, with that, an unspoken respect – partners looked at you differently when you moved up from sitting next to the door.

'That's why I'm so slammed,' Ryan responds drily. 'Skylight is interrupting my otherwise very busy schedule . . .'

Sameer laughs and swivels his chair to face his computer. He logs on and sends a response to the email received from Matt that morning; a meeting is arranged for that afternoon. The rest of the day passes in a blur, dealing with an inbox he has ignored for several days. A few minutes before 5 p.m., he heads for Matt's office, trying to control a twitch under his left eye that he developed a few months ago.

Deb, the face of human resources, is already seated when Sameer arrives. She is grasping a file of loose papers that are spilling onto her lap; her cheeks flush as she tries to prevent the pages from falling to the floor. Matt is sitting behind his desk, squinting at the screen and slowly tapping at the keyboard, right hand only, one finger at a time. Sameer wonders how he manages.

Matt looks up, asks Sameer to shut the door, and points towards the empty chair in front of him. 'Sam,' he begins. 'I'd like to start by saying that in the five years that you've been here, you have really impressed us,' and at this, Sameer has to try to contain the smile that begins to spread across his face. 'Right from your time as a trainee, we knew you were one to watch, and you've only gone from strength to strength since then. Your written work is excellent, you've managed entire deals on your own, and you've built strong relationships with clients. I've heard nothing but good things about you from the other partners you've worked with. Really – well done.'

'Thank you, Matt,' Sameer says, and now he is unable to stop himself from smiling. 'I'm very grateful for the opportunities the firm has given me.'

Matt nods an acknowledgement. 'So, why have I called you here today? You may have heard that we've now managed to get through the minefield that is Singaporean regulation, and we'll be launching an office there in approximately six months' time.'

Sameer's breath catches in his throat. A little over a year ago, he had applied to go to Singapore to help launch the firm's newest branch in South East Asia. Only six of the firm's brightest and best associates would be picked for the job, and although it was a temporary position, with the opportunity to return after two years, there was a chance that if you stayed on and did well enough, you might make partner out there very quickly. For various reasons, however, the firm had been unable to open in Singapore at the time and the opportunity had vanished almost as soon as it had appeared. Sameer had all but forgotten about it – until now.

'Are you still interested?' Matt asks. 'Obviously, we'd be disappointed to lose you in London, but we think it's the right decision for the firm. We really think you could help us build a practice out there.'

'That sounds great,' Sameer replies, heart pounding. 'I'm really very happy to be considered.'

'Glad to hear it. Deb will sort you out with the details. If you want to go ahead, all you have to do is sign on the dotted line,' Matt says cheerfully, turning back to his computer screen.

'You don't have to make a decision right now,' Deb chimes in, flapping through her papers like a flustered bird. 'I'll send you all the paperwork on Monday and you can have a couple of weeks to think about it.'

'Thank you both very much,' Sameer rises. He feels strangely euphoric as he goes back to his desk.

'Ryan,' he says in disbelief as he walks in, 'they've offered me Singapore.'

'What do you mean?' Ryan responds without looking up. 'Singapore isn't happening.'

'Apparently it is,' Sameer says, breathless. He begins to log off his computer; he does not need to stay in the office any longer that evening. 'And I've been asked to go.'

'Wait, what?' He has Ryan's attention now. 'How did you find out?'

'Matt – I just had a meeting with Matt and Deb.'

'I applied for that too, you know,' Ryan says, his eyes flickering from left to right across his computer screen, index finger rapidly running over the scroll roller of his mouse. Sameer did not know; perhaps they had not been so close a year ago. He opens his mouth to suggest something – to indicate how happy he would be if they ended up there together – but then decides against it. Ryan's finger is still running over the scroll roller, eyes searching. He finally stops. 'Well, I'm happy for you, mate,' he says. 'You really deserve it.'

'Thanks, mate,' Sameer replies. There is a brief silence as he gets up and puts on his jacket.

'We should celebrate,' Ryan says suddenly. 'Are you out tonight? We should do something.'

'I'll be out,' Sameer nods, heading for the door. 'Come join – pre-drinks at mine?'

'Sounds good,' Ryan calls as Sameer leaves the room.

•

Most weekends – when he is not working – Sameer goes out with his former flatmates and friends from home, Jeremiah and Rahool. When they had first moved to London, Sameer, Jeremiah and Rahool had all lived together in a small flat in Bow. Four glorious years of the boys from the original Leicester crew living together, the three who had made it out, made it to London; playing football around their tiny kitchen, breaking dishes and laughing; entire weekends of just FIFA, the flat filled with pizza boxes and beer bottles, the air a stale mix of sweat and testosterone. Then, when his hours started to get longer, Sameer decided that he wanted to be closer to the office, and he moved out. The boys did not want to join him (and would not have been able to afford to); they found another flatmate and stayed in east London. Jeremiah and Rahool now come to Sameer's flat on the weekends that he is free. They have brought their new flatmate, Ed, on a couple of occasions. Ed is unobjectionable, but Sameer dislikes him as a matter of principle.

On his way home, Sameer stops at his local Chinese to pick up a takeaway. As he watches the chef prepare the order – dashing oil into a large wok, adding noodles, chicken, sauce – he wonders whether Singaporean food is like Chinese food, and then he wonders what his mother would make of it. This thought brings a tingle of nervous unease and he immediately turns to his phone for distraction: BBC News, *Body found in search for missing teen*.

At home, Sameer eats quickly, thumb flicking across his phone as he chews. He connects it to the surround-sound system and hits play on one of his playlists: Dave's 'Psycho' blares through the speakers. For a moment – as tends to happen when a deal enters a lull after a period of intensity – he is overcome with exhaustion. Maybe he will text the boys and cancel; perhaps they can rain check to the following weekend. But he has barely finished eating when the buzzer rings. Jeremiah and Rahool bounce into the flat with a bottle of vodka.

'Hey, man, long time,' Jeremiah slaps Sameer on the back. 'You look tired.'

'I *am* tired,' Sameer protests, grabbing Rahool's outstretched hand. 'How you doing? You guys are here early.'

'We've got big news,' Jeremiah begins to grab glasses from the kitchen and line them up on the counter. Rahool unscrews the bottle cap and pours a generous helping of vodka into each.

'So have I actually.' Sameer stares at the glasses of vodka. 'I don't have any mixers. I'm sorry – I forgot. Haven't really been with it.'

Jeremiah laughs. 'Fine,' he says. 'We'll do it like the Russians: just water and ice.' He starts adding water to the glasses. Rahool dispenses ice from Sameer's fridge-freezer into the glasses. Sameer accepts a glass from Rahool, but he does not feel like drinking it. 'First, can we sort out the tunes please?' Jeremiah jumps onto the sofa, getting out his phone to connect it up to Sameer's surround sound. A small amount of vodka-water-ice sloshes from his glass onto the settee. 'This stuff doesn't exactly get you in the mood for celebrating . . .'

'What are we celebrating?' Sameer asks. The music stops and then starts again; a new track, with a deeper base.

'If you want Dave, let's listen to something a bit more upbeat,' Jeremiah says, changing the track to 'Thiago Silva' and nodding his head along to the new tune. 'Rahool?'

Rahool is leaning against the wall that separates the beginning of the kitchen from the living room, drink in hand, as if he is unsure about whether or not to enter. Although Sameer has been friends with Rahool for longer, Sameer knows more about Jeremiah than he does about Rahool. Rahool is quiet. He's the sort of person who is content to just be present; part of the group, but not part of the conversation. When he does speak, it is careful, considered. Even drink does not make him open up; if anything he becomes stiffer, more awkward. Next to Jeremiah, who, by contrast, can be so loud it borders on brash, Sameer sometimes forgets that Rahool is even there.

'You first,' Rahool says, nodding towards Jeremiah.

Jeremiah's eyes are wide, brimming with excitement. 'OK,' he says, 'I've been offered a job at Beatz Studio.' There is a short silence. 'It's a recording studio in South Croydon. I'm going to be assisting the studio manager.'

'Wow, J, that's great news,' Sameer says, clapping him on the back. Jeremiah works as a DJ, playing anything from club nights to birthday parties, but he also has a bedroom studio where he makes music. He's wanted to be a music producer for as long as Sameer can remember.

'This is a really big step for me,' Jeremiah continues, taking a big slug of his drink. 'Beatz is working with some major underground artists right now, know what I mean?' He finishes his drink and moves past Rahool into the kitchen to fill another one. 'T Shawty, Riddim, Boss Man. Can you believe it – Boss Man!' Jeremiah's voice rises and crescendos with the sound of ice being dispensed from the fridge freezer into his glass. Sameer has never heard of any of these artists. He shoots a look at Rahool, who shrugs and takes a sip of his drink. 'What I'm saying, man, is that I'll get to meet these people – I'll be the face of the studio, you know, sorting things when the artists arrive, working closely with the engineer, getting the artists to grips with the studio. And the best thing?' He pauses and Sameer realises that Jeremiah expects him to guess.

'Um, you might end up producing music for one of these artists?'

'Well, no – but yes, that's a very good point –' Jeremiah shakes a finger at Sameer, grinning, 'that is one thing that might definitely, possibly, happen.' He takes a long swig from his glass. 'Guys, catch up?' he says suddenly, noticing that his friends are not drinking at his pace. 'No, the best thing – the *best* thing – is that it's part of my contract that I can use the recording studio equipment when it's not being used and when I'm not working. I'm talking state of the art – latest and best technology – I mean, half the stuff in that studio I don't even know how to use yet.' Jeremiah runs a hand over his head, as if he cannot believe the news himself.

'That's awesome. After all these years – you're finally doing it.' Sameer is pleased to hear his friend's news; it brightens him and makes the vodka-water look slightly more appealing. He takes a sip and imagines the liquid running through his veins, recharging his batteries. 'So when do you start?'

Jeremiah beams. 'Next month. Can't wait!'

Sameer motions for Rahool to come into the room. 'Congratulations, J,' he says, raising his glass. 'To following your dreams.'

'To following my fucking dreams!' Jeremiah repeats, clinking his glass against Sameer's and Rahool's. He drains the drink in one go and gets up to make another.

'So what's your news, Rahool?' Sameer turns to his other friend. He is starting to feel energised.

'You first.'

Sameer shrugs. 'OK,' he says, once Jeremiah has returned to the sofa. Jeremiah changes the track to 'All I do is Win' and starts to sing along happily. Sameer inhales. 'I'm moving to Singapore with the job.'

Jeremiah immediately stops singing. Rahool's mouth drops open slightly.

'Wait, what?' Jeremiah squints at Sameer as if he is trying to work out whether Sameer is joking.

'How long for?' Rahool asks.

'Two years to start, possibly longer.' Sameer tips the rest of his drink down his throat and stands up.

'That what you want?' Jeremiah asks.

'Well, I applied for it, so I guess, yeah,' Sameer responds, annoyed that his friends have not immediately understood the significance of the opportunity. 'I'm basically going to be involved in setting up a new office out there. It'll be intense, but rewarding. I could make partner very quickly. And tax is like 15 per cent.'

'So you're going to be super rich, eh?' Jeremiah says. 'Well, if that's what you want, I'm happy for you, man.'

'Who exactly doesn't want to be rich?' Rahool raises an eyebrow.

'It's not about becoming rich.' Sameer pulls a face and pours himself another drink. The ice dispenser groans: it is nearly out of ice. 'It's about the opportunity. I'm getting the chance to help a global firm establish its next footprint in South East Asia. There's only going to be about ten of us to start with out there, and all of us will have a role to play. I'll be directly involved in creating new client relationships. And I'm going to be living in another country for the first time in my life. A hot country!'

The boys laugh, and Sameer relaxes. 'We'll obviously come visit you,' Jeremiah says, raising his glass. 'To Singapore!'

'To Singapore!' they chorus, and drink. 'A Milli' plays from the speakers.

'So,' Rahool says eventually. 'What will your family say?'

'Don't know,' Sameer lies. He does not want to think about

this tonight. Tonight is about celebrating. He finishes his drink and pours another. 'But what's up with you anyway?'

'I'm moving too, actually,' Rahool says.

Sameer smiles. Rahool is an IT consultant and his work often requires him to spend time on-site with a client. Usually his clients are based in or around London, but Rahool has spent several months in Germany and Spain in the past. 'To Singapore?' Sameer says hopefully.

'No.' Rahool is not looking at Sameer. 'I'm leaving London. I'm moving back home. To Leicester.'

And just like that, the fun is over.

Sameer sets his glass down on the coffee table. 'Why would you do that?' he asks, voice strained in an attempt not to sound accusatory. 'You're quitting your job?'

'You know I hate that job,' Rahool shrugs. 'I've hated it for a long time. How does it make sense that I've been in it for five years and I still have no idea what I'm doing? Every project, I end up taking on things that are way above my pay grade and fumbling my way through – but they won't promote me or give me proper training. The company doesn't value me. If I really think about why I've stayed here so long – well, it was mainly because of you two,' Rahool gestures towards his friends. He still has not looked at Sameer. 'We've had a good time, the three of us, haven't we, living in London? But I'm done with it now.'

Rahool has said a lot, and Sameer struggles to digest it. He wishes he had not been drinking.

'You'll be back with our old Leicester crew,' Jeremiah drawls, raising his glass towards the ceiling. 'To the Leicester mandem!'

Sameer and Rahool do not respond. 'What are you going to do in Leicester?' Sameer asks, knowing already what Rahool is going to say.

'I'll join the family business. It's not as if my degree helped me to get a job I enjoyed, so I might as well go home.'

Sameer says nothing. Jeremiah has started to flick through the tracks on his phone very quickly, having lost interest in the conversation. Jeremiah's family do not run a business; he does not understand.

'Look, mate,' Rahool continues, 'I'm not you. I didn't go to Oxbridge and get a job as a top lawyer in the City. I don't earn enough to live alone in a flat like this.' Sameer feels heat rising in his neck, but Rahool's face is not unkind. He finally looks at Sameer, and he is sympathetic. 'What I'm saying,' he says gently, 'is that London is not to me what it is to you and J. I'm broke, I hate my job, and I'm tired of it. J is here for a reason, and he's going to make it. And you, well – you're not even staying in London yourself any more. The point is, I'm not sure what I'm doing here anyway.'

It does make sense, Sameer thinks. Or at least, he thinks it makes sense. He feels a quiet discomfort, a sense of betrayal, but he nods, perhaps a little too enthusiastically, at Rahool. Their fathers had been friends for many years, both migrants from Uganda who had arrived in Belgrave, penniless, and had gone on to become successful businessmen. Rahool's father had started out as a car mechanic, and now ran his own truck and van rental company. Sameer's family had started out selling saris, and then sold the sari shop to open a restaurant specialising in East African Asian cuisine – Kampala Nights – which now had four branches across the Midlands. Both families had invested their money wisely. Both families were very comfortable. For some reason that Sameer cannot now rationalise, he had always thought that Rahool was with him on the idea that they would not just end up working in the family business, that they would make it on their own. He finishes his drink, goes to the bottle of vodka and realises it is nearly empty.

'It's the end of an era,' he announces solemnly to his friends. He opens a cupboard near the fridge and pulls out a bottle of Veuve Clicquot that the partners had gifted the associates at Christmas. It is warm, but no matter. They must celebrate; and to do so, they must drink. 'I'm going to Singapore. Rahool, you're going back to Leicester. J, you're going to South Croydon,' Sameer starts to laugh. He unwraps the foil and begins to untwist the cage holding the cork. Before he has the chance to react, the cork flies off. Jeremiah ducks; the cork hits a mirror hanging above the sofa, but it doesn't break. Champagne erupts from the bottle, frothing over Sameer's hands and legs and onto the floor. He quickly raises the bottle to his lips and tries to suck up the foam.

The boys are laughing. They bring over their glasses, trying to catch the froth as it slips from the bottle towards the floor. When it finally subsides, the bottle is half empty. Sameer pours out what is left and the bottle is finished. They are all still laughing. Rahool raises his glass. 'To the end of an era,' he echoes.

'The end of an era!' Sameer and Jeremiah boom. Sameer looks at his friends through the film of vodka and champagne. He feels a strange urge to cry.

A few hours later, after a predictably long queue and a quick extortion at the door, Sameer and his friends are inside east London's most popular club. Sameer immediately goes to buy a round of drinks. They didn't drink anything else after the champagne and, stepping inside to see the throbbing mass of bodies moving to music, he suddenly feels horribly sober. 'Three vodka Cokes, please,' he shouts to the barman, who nods and flips three glasses onto the counter.

'Hey, mate.' Sameer feels a hand on his back. It's Ryan, with someone he doesn't recognise.

'All right?' Sameer grins. 'What can I get you?'

'I should be buying for you, my friend,' Ryan responds, muscling in between Sameer and a woman standing next to him at the bar. Ryan's finger begins to tap rapidly on the counter. His friend does not attempt to come close to the bar and stands apart, on his phone.

'You didn't make it for pre-drinks,' Sameer remembers, secretly glad that Ryan had not come. His drinks appear and he pays.

'Work,' Ryan rolls his eyes and then flashes a bright smile. 'But it's all good, man – I made it out! Shots please, mate – whatever you've got. Six of them. So, Singapore. Exciting. You must be excited. I would be so excited if I was you.'

Sameer is vaguely conscious that Ryan has taken something. The shots arrive, and Ryan knocks one back. 'For you,' he says, pushing the other five towards Sameer. Sameer can smell Jägermeister.

'Five for me and one for you?' Sameer says, pushing two back towards Ryan. 'How is that fair?'

'Singapore for you and nothing for me,' Ryan responds, laughing. 'How is that fair?'

Sameer frowns, unsure whether Ryan is joking. Ryan has already downed another shot. 'OK,' Ryan says, leaning towards Sameer. 'I've helped you out now. Come on, drink.'

'OK, OK.' Sameer takes the first shot, grimacing. In the split second that Ryan is not looking while he pays for the shots, Sameer quickly pours the other three down the side of the bar by his feet. He picks up the drinks he had ordered and moves away from the bar. Ryan follows, his friend tagging behind.

'It's funny because that's how things are now these days,'

Ryan is shouting, but Sameer cannot hear him properly over the music. 'All about being PC and all that.'

They reach Jeremiah and Rahool, and Sameer hands them their drinks. Ryan's head is bopping up and down, nodding unstoppably. 'Like, you and your mates here, you'd all do pretty well these days.'

Sameer points to his ears. 'I can't hear you,' he shouts, taking a gulp of his drink and turning away.

'You know what I mean though, right?' Ryan claps Sameer on the back, hard. 'They've got quotas to fill, haven't they?' He waves a hand in front of Sameer, as if swatting away a fly, and stumbles into the crowd. He is swallowed in seconds, followed by his friend, who is still on his phone.

'What was he saying?' Jeremiah shouts. 'That was Ryan, wasn't it?'

'Don't know,' Sameer responds, pointing again at his ears. 'Couldn't hear.'

After a few moments, Sameer turns to Rahool, who is closer to him. 'I'm leaving,' he says.

'But we only just got here,' Rahool protests.

'Yeah – you stay. Have a good night. I'll message you – we need to do something before we all go our separate ways.'

Sameer does not say goodbye to Jeremiah; he slips out of the club quietly and into the night. He has sobered up completely. Maybe he hadn't understood Ryan properly, maybe there had been some miscommunication. But something jars, instinct giving way to unease, and he knows that he will not know how to look at Ryan on Monday. He unlocks his phone, scrolls to Hannah and sends a WhatsApp.

Sameer (01.02): *Hi, you awake?*

Home is walking distance, but Sameer flags down a black cab. He does not want to walk past the other revellers tonight. He WhatsApps Hannah again.

Sameer (01.04): *Getting in a cab, can pick you up?*

Hannah was last seen at 23.58.

'Where to?' the cab driver asks. Sameer gives his address and climbs into the car. He calls Hannah, once, twice. The phone rings and rings and she does not pick up.

2

To my first love, my beloved

15th August 1945

It is my wedding night tonight. But instead of lying with my
new wife, I am sitting here in my study, writing to you. I could
not bring myself to touch her; I could barely look at her. And
now she lies in our marital bed, alone, whilst I sit here with a
pen and paper.

I know this is foolish. I know this letter will never reach you.
But I did not know what else to do. I had to talk to you.

The *nikkah* took place earlier today in the stuffy heat of our
front room. A power cut meant that the fans were not working; all the windows were open, but no breeze could allay the
stickiness that clung to us all. It was a small and rushed affair;
just Papa, Samir and Abdullah were present to witness
Muazzam Kaka confirming that Shabnam – my new wife –
agreed. The imam hurriedly recited the *fatihah* and Shabnam
appeared like a ghost through the side door, draped in a red
gauze dupatta. A small, sickly looking child in a green salwar
kameez holding a plate full of *laddoos* followed her. Shabnam
sat down beside me, accompanied by the thick scent of jasmine, and I could feel the weight of her body depress my side
of the sofa. My insides began to churn before the *laddoo* even
reached my lips. Shabnam is twenty-one years old. I am forty.

I need to explain to you how this has happened. Much like
our own wedding, I did not choose this. The news of your passing reached India before I even had the chance to shed a tear.

Do you remember Muazzam Kaka, Papa's younger brother? I am certain you do; you were always so good at remembering faces and names. He came to Uganda to visit just once, many years ago, when Samir was born. His son died last year, leaving behind a wife and two young children. When they heard the news of your passing, they appeared without a word of warning. Muazzam Kaka and Papa took me aside and explained that it was my 'duty', as the only surviving grandson of my late grandparents, to take care of my cousin's family. I had never met my cousin before he died. Muazzam Kaka was as good as a stranger to me when he arrived. But I am duty-bound.

And so here I am, on the evening of my second wedding night, writing a letter to my first wife, the one and only love of my life.

I cannot begin to describe how I miss you. The pain subsides only when I am sleeping, but then I dream of you, running through the long grass towards the Nile, dupatta waving in the wind, laughing and calling me to follow you.

When I close my eyes, our wedding night comes back to me with such startling clarity, as though it took place just yesterday. Funny how twenty-one years pass in the blink of an eye. Before we were wed, I had only ever glimpsed you outside the mosque, head covered, eyes downwards, clutching your younger sister's hand. I saw you once after our families had agreed our marriage, about a month before the *nikkah*. I was driving down Nasser Road, and I saw you walking past, holding bags of shopping spilling with fabrics, your fair skin flushed. I thought then that you were the most beautiful creature I had ever seen.

And then, before I knew it, it was the day of our wedding. Quite a contrast to the events of today: when we married, the local mosque was packed to the brim and we had the grandest of receptions in the Imperial Hotel. No fewer than a thousand guests. I must have been the most nervous I have ever been about anything in my life. The festivities passed in a colourful blur – do you remember how much you cried? – and then we were left to our own devices in the honeymoon suite.

I remember pushing back the material weighing on your head and watching your hair tumble down to your shoulders, releasing the smell of something sweet that I would wake up to every morning for the next twenty-one years of my life. Oh, to live that moment again! Before I knew you; yet, even then, knowing that I already knew all of you.

'Hasan –' you whispered so softly that I could barely hear you, and your thick lashes raised to meet my eyes for the first time. I saw something in you so vulnerable at that moment and it suddenly struck me that you were only sixteen. Do you remember what you said next? 'Hasan, I just want to talk tonight.'

And that is what we did. I helped you to unpin the heavy bridalwear attached to your shoulders, circling your waist, and chained to your wrists. You removed it all in the privacy of the bathroom, whilst I tried to quell the more basic instincts aris-ing in my groin as I waited for you in the bed. When you finally re-entered, in a long white nightgown, you looked like an angel. We sat on the bed and talked until our voices became hoarse and we could no longer keep our eyes open.

I loved you deeply from that moment, and I have never stopped loving you since.

Abdullah tells me the pain of grief will subside with time. He cradles my head gently in his arms, like he used to when I was a young boy. He tells me to trust him. He has lost siblings, par-ents, cousins, friends. He has even lost a son. But he has never lost his wife. He has been married to her for forty years now. We only reached half that time. Oh, my darling Amira. What I would not give to have even just one more minute with you.

When I close my eyes, I can picture you standing in the kitchen, back door open to allow the smell of spices to escape into the courtyard, your sleeves rolled up tightly, those slender, determined arms kneading a lump of dough. I can still taste the soft, hot *rotli* made by your hands.

It makes me smile now to think that when we first moved into this house, I wanted to employ a cook. You hated the idea. 'Hasan,' you said to me, 'what will I do all day if we have a cook? We already have Abdullah, that's enough.' We both knew that Abdullah's cooking left much to be desired. I knew it was not easy for you navigating the vast expanses of the new house, whilst managing our children, my father and our new daughter-in-law, Tasneem. That is why I hired the ayah, my dear – to give you room to breathe. And even though you were annoyed with me at first, after just a few days I saw you visibly relax. You spent more time in the kitchen, talking to Tasneem and showing her your recipes: fiery and crisp chilli mogo, green mango pickle, red chicken curry. The ayah spent more time scrubbing the floors and hanging up our laundry. It is a sign of our success, my sweet Amira, that we should have an ayah.

What satisfaction I had felt when the new house came on the market! One of the largest houses on Nakasero Hill, and the timing could not have been better, because Samir had just become engaged to Tasneem, and we needed more room for the newly married couple. This house has six double bedrooms, three en suite and two separate bathrooms, two reception rooms, a dining area, a great big kitchen that opens out into a courtyard, and a sprawling back garden with the greenest, neatest grass you have ever seen, politely lined with mango trees and frangipani. The garage can hold up to four cars. Our driver and ayah reside in the boys' quarters, which is close – but not too close – by. You were not so keen at first on moving up the hill and leaving behind the house in which our marriage had been built. But when we pulled up to the steel gates, and you saw bright pink bougainvillea bursting over the veranda to rest on the garage roof your heart softened. Bougainvillea was your favourite flower.

My heart was bursting with pride on the day that we moved in. Three weeks before Samir was to be wed: just enough time to get things in order. The sun was streaming through the windows, lighting up every room with a brightness that made my eyes water. The children were shrieking with excitement as they ran from room to room and outside into the back garden to somersault on the springy green grass. Papa was content, leaning on his walking stick with a soft smile at the corner of his mouth. You were wearing a pale blue salwar kameez, and the bougainvillea flower tucked behind your ear tickled me when I leaned in to kiss your cheek. Samir had done us all proud: he was joining the family business and marrying a girl from a very good family. The business was doing better than it had ever done before. I remember looking up to the sky, thanking Allah, and wondering how Ma would feel if she could see us now. We were moving into an old *muzungu* home, on old *wazungu* land. And it was all ours.

It is funny how one's whole life can change in a single moment. I almost despise this house now. Every room is a projection of what I thought would be a future with you and our family. Sometimes the urge to go back to our old, smaller house, just to inhale the smell in the corridors, is so strong it overwhelms me. After you passed away, your things were taken by your family. Let them, Papa said. It will help you to process her death. But I kept one of your dupattas. It still smells like you. I dig my head into the soft fabric and inhale deeply and the smell of you evokes such a forceful memory in me that I almost feel like I have travelled back in time.

It is getting late, my love, but I am not ready for sleep. Do you know that it was almost fifty years ago today that Papa first set foot in this country? I cannot imagine what it must have been like for him, leaving behind his parents, two brothers and sister in Gujarat to set sail on a dhow with an uncle he barely knew. Papa does not speak much of his life in India, but I know that it was hard. The idea was that if Papa could achieve some success, the rest of the family would be sent for and the poverty of their lives in India would be over. But by the time Papa was ready to send for them four years later, Papa's only sister had died of dysentery. Papa's younger brother, Muazzam Kaka, had married and wanted to stay in India. But Papa's parents and his older brother arrived on the shores of Mombasa in the spring of 1904, and they brought with them Papa's new wife – my ma.

Why is it that the women in my life have left me too soon? Papa says that Ma was of a weak disposition. She is shadowy behind my closed eyes; truly, I cannot remember her at all. Sometimes I wake in the middle of the night, sweating and panting, terrified I am going to lose the image of you in the same way. But I have your picture, taken just last year, smiling shyly into the camera.

I never had a single picture of Ma. When I think back to the early years of my life, I can only remember my dadi and Abdullah – although we used to call Abdullah 'Boyi' back then of course. It is as if the memory of Ma has been erased. All I can see is Dadi, standing in our tiny kitchen in a grey cotton sari, adding cinnamon bark to frying onions until the whole house was filled with fragrance; Boyi, taking our washing to the communal backyard, scrubbing green soap into our underwear and rinsing them clean.

Boyi must have been about fifteen years old when he first came to work for us, and, despite his tender age, he assumed the role of bathing me, feeding me and keeping me entertained in Ma's absence. He was all I ever had as a playmate. I used to be so envious of your large family: your three sisters, your brother. I had always longed for a sibling but none had survived: one miscarriage, one stillborn, and my little sister Zahra, who had died suddenly aged one. And Papa never remarried. You knew that was why I craved for us to have a big family. And, like the dutiful wife that you were, you bore me five healthy children: Samir, Shahzeb, Farah, Ahmed and little Aisha, who is still too young to understand what has happened to you. I never imagined that one day I would go on to adopt somebody else's children – or that I might have children with someone else.

My love. I hope you can forgive me. I truly believe that you would, if you thought of Shabnam and her young children left alone with no one to take care of them. You were always so gracious in the way you treated others less fortunate than yourself. You accepted Abdullah as a brother immediately, in spite of his African blood. You saw that Abdullah was not like other *karia*; that he was loyal, hard-working and honest, and that he had accepted Islam into his heart. You treated him with such patience and you gave him so much of your time, to the point – I must admit – that it sometimes bordered on the absurd. But, that was you: forever putting those less fortunate before others. Abdullah had always been a special case though. He had worked for five years as a boyi to a British inspector general living on the top of Nakasero Hill and I believe it was that experience which gave him the solid foundations he had when he came to us. Returning to the hill was like a homecoming for Abdullah.

My dearest Amira, despite the present successes of our business, the thought of continuing without you makes me despair. How beauty entered my life after you became a part of it! You, glowing with enthusiasm, heavily pregnant with Samir, sitting patiently as my scribe, diligently and carefully writing up the company books as I directed, until you became proficient enough to do it by yourself. You, managing the *duka* while I went to Jinja, Mbarara, Mbale to trade. You reminded me of myself when I was young, after Papa first opened the cotton ginnery and left me to manage the small shop under the house where we lived on Market Street. I used to work in that shop after school every single day; weekends spent sleeping on the shop floor and waiting for the delivery boys to come; stockpiling – food, soft drinks, soap – in the middle of the night, trying not to get behind on my schoolwork.

Amira, I do believe that you were my lucky charm. It was you who brought us our success with the cotton ginnery. It was you who really helped our shop and tailoring service to expand and grow. The world surprised me by continuing to turn in your absence. Now that you are gone, I fear for our good fortune. Whatever brilliance we possessed has been eclipsed. Now that you are gone, I cannot shake this overwhelming sense of dread.

3

It takes just over an hour to get from St Pancras to Leicester by train. In the window seat, Sameer can see the reflection of his face, floating in the glass pane, staring through him and into the distance. There is not a cloud in sight today. Green fields dotted with sheep and bordered by the blue expanse of sky roll by. He closes his eyes and rests his head against the window, but he cannot sleep. In his head, he begins to run through the different ways he might tell his family that he is moving to Singapore. It has been two weeks since he was first offered the role. He signed the paperwork last week; he didn't want to be in a position where his family might talk him out of it. The departure date has been scheduled for just under five months from now.

The train pulls into the platform and Sameer steps out. The familiar facades of the station's interior tug at him, giving him a feeling of comfort. He has not been home for six weeks and he realises, with mild surprise, that he has missed it. Singapore will only be for two years, he tells himself.

The ticket barriers are open (why did he buy a ticket? he thinks, irritated – they will probably be open when he leaves too), and he walks through their arms and out of the station, into the bright light of the day. Round the corner, in the usual meeting spot, his father is waiting for him in a white Range Rover that Sameer doesn't recognise.

'Hi, Dad,' he says, opening the passenger door and climbing up onto the seat. With one hand, Sameer throws his rucksack onto the back seat; in the other, he holds a bouquet of roses for his mother. 'New car?'

'Hi, son,' his father replies, engaging the gears and slowly pulling out onto the road. Every time he goes home, Sameer is surprised at how his father seems to have aged. 'No, it's not new – I'm just borrowing it from the Patels while the Merc goes for servicing.'

The Patels are Rahool's family. Sameer is conscious that his parents will be aware that Rahool is returning to Leicester from London. Before his father can mention it, Sameer asks: 'How are you?' They are crossing the Humberstone round-about. This is not the way home.

'I'm fine, son. I'm fine. Very busy, as always. Like you. We haven't seen you in a long time.'

'Work,' Sameer replies shortly, looking out of the window. 'It's been busy.' The car approaches Belgrave Road; it is a Saturday and the traffic is already building up. Women in saris amble past on the street; shopfronts in red, yellow, blue blare names, Lakhani, Akshar, Arshi, Krishna. Gold jewellery glints invitingly from behind shop windows; heavy, brightly col-oured fabrics pose, draped on mannequins standing to attention; street food sings and steams from a vat, *chaat, pani poori, paan*. This is the Golden Mile. 'Where are we going?'

'Your mum wanted me to pick up some samosas,' his father replies, deftly sliding the car into an available space along the crowded road. Just a few metres away, the first Kampala Nights restaurant that his family ever opened stands proudly, orange letters beating against a black backdrop. 'Come on,' his father says, glancing at his watch and getting out of the car. Sameer hesitates for a moment. They are not far from the road that they used to live on until Sameer was eight years old, and com-ing here always gives him a lukewarm feeling of nostalgia. He puts the roses down on the front seat and gets out of the car.

Inside the restaurant, they are greeted by low lighting, the soft melody of steel drums and the mouth-watering smell of spices. KAMPALA NIGHTS WELCOMES YOU, says a sign near the entrance. PLEASE WAIT HERE TO BE SEATED. They walk past the unmanned post and into the restaurant. 'Hey, boss is here,' a boy comes running out from between the tables, giving Sameer's father a cheeky grin and mock salute. 'Boss man, you here to eat?' A faint moustache lines the boy's upper lip, a pathetic straggle of hairs populate his chin: he is barely eighteen. Sameer remembers himself at that age and wonders whether the boy is at university or whether this is his full-time job.

'I'm here to pick up our order,' Sameer's father says, eyes narrowing and surveying the restaurant critically. There is an open kitchen, where the diners can see chefs dressed all in white tossing ingredients in pans over flames, sprinkling herbs over plates with a flourish, slicing red-orange peppers with huge steel knives. Tribal masks and abstract paintings are hung on walls next to zebra-print and ornamental wooden ladles. Sameer hasn't been to the restaurant at lunchtime recently, but is surprised to see that it is almost full – families, couples, groups of friends. 'Why is no one at the door?' his father says to the boy, who responds with a guilty shrug and runs off towards the front of the restaurant. More employees appear from the restaurant's depths; Sameer's father barks instructions under his breath ('Your hair is poking out of your hat,' he snaps at one of the chefs; 'Why aren't you wearing the uniform?' he asks one of the waiters, whose black T-shirt fails to read 'Kampala Nights' on its back; 'I don't like the way you're having to squeeze around this table to get to the kitchen – who changed the layout?'). The restaurant manager emerges from the back to greet them, all smiles and hand-shakes, and a bag of samosas is presented to Sameer, who takes it, peeking inside at the crisp golden skin.

'The restaurant is so busy,' Sameer comments as they leave, wondering if his mother will notice if there is one less samosa in the bag.

'*Alhumdulilah*,' his father replies. 'We have been very lucky. Lucky enough, in fact, to be in a position to open another restaurant. We've found an opportunity to acquire a site not far from Spinney Hills.' Sameer looks at his father quizzically – his family had previously considered and rejected the idea of opening a restaurant in that area. 'Now, I know what you're thinking,' his father continues. 'But this is different. The site is a deconsecrated church. It was up for auction and we bought it at a significant discount. The interior needs some work, but it's a beautiful building, with stained-glass windows and high ceilings. It has the capacity to seat up to four hundred. We're going to invest heavily in renovating it, and as well as being a full-service restaurant the idea is to be able to use it for private events and weddings. There's big money in the wedding industry, you know?'

As his father chatters away happily, a knot tightens in Sameer's stomach. He does not say anything as they turn onto Stoughton Drive, the road they moved to after they left Belgrave. His father drives past their old house – a property they like to fondly refer to as their 'starter home', despite the fact that it is a three bedroom detached house and much grander than some of the homes his friends from Leicester still live in today. When Sameer was fourteen years old, the family had left behind the starter life and upgraded to a larger property further down the road. His whole life mapped out in one short drive.

Sameer's father swings the car in front of their gates, which open slowly to a spacious paved front drive, thoughtfully framed by neat arrangements of grass, lavender bushes and small evergreen trees. The sight of the house delivers such comfort that Sameer almost lets out a sigh of relief.

His mother is waiting at the front door, ever the picture of understated elegance in a simple blue salwar kameez and a row of gold bangles. '*Beta*,' she says, embracing Sameer tightly. *Son.* 'What's taken you so long to come home?' She jabs Sameer with her index finger and he quickly hands her the bouquet of roses.

'Zara!' he yells. 'I'm starving, come down!'

'*Salaam bhi na kay?*' The disapproving voice of Mhota Papa, his father's eldest surviving brother, appears from behind him. *He doesn't even say hello?* Mhota Papa hobbles towards Sameer and hits him gently with his walking stick. Sameer bends down to embrace his uncle's small form.

'*Salaam*, Mhota Papa,' Sameer says apologetically. 'I didn't see you there.'

'*Mehne koi joi nee*,' Mhota Papa mutters in response, but returns Sameer's embrace. *Nobody notices me.*

'Sameer *bhai*!' Zara bounds down the stairs and flings her arms around her brother's torso. There is an eight-year age gap between them; Sameer's parents had struggled to have another child after he was born and, after years of trying, eventually managed to conceive with I V F. Sameer can remember that a lot of drama surrounded Zara's birth, but he is hazy on the details. He is sure that Zara had been born a twin, but her twin had not survived. His family do not speak of it, and he would never ask. He is not even sure if Zara knows.

'How's revision going?' he asks, as the family head through into the kitchen and breakfast room. Zara is in her final year of sixth form, studying for the A levels she needs to meet her offer from Edinburgh University. There had been an awkward period last year when Zara had been condemned by their mother for applying to go as far away as Scotland, berated by their father for failing to apply to Cambridge (as Sameer had done), and reviled by both of them for selecting anthropology of all things as a degree. But now that it had been done, and they had realised that (although it was a waste of their hard-earned money) because she was a girl it didn't really matter what she studied anyway, the family narrative around her revision focused on the simple goal of achieving good grades – rather than getting into university.

'It's OK,' Zara replies, as the men take their seats at the table. She retrieves drinks from the fridge and begins to fill their glasses. 'Anyway, I don't want to talk about it. I'm taking this weekend off to spend time with you.'

'But your exams are in three weeks?' Sameer takes a sip of Pepsi. His mother sets a casserole dish down on the table and steam rises from a layer of browned cheese.

Zara brings a bowl full of salad and a plate of garlic bread to the table. 'Don't make me change my mind, *bhai*,' she warns. 'It's just a day. One day isn't going to hurt.'

Sameer gives her a wry smile. He doesn't ever remember thinking that when he was studying for exams. He remembers the opposite.

Dad, can I go and watch the game? Jeremiah's got tickets through his brother. Please, Dad, Premiership clubs never come to Leicester. It's just one day! It was the summer of Year 8 and Leicester City were playing Liverpool at home for a pre-season friendly. It was also the summer that Sameer had been told that he needed to get into Leicester's best grammar school, a school that prided itself on not being limited to a catchment area, but instead asked prospective pupils to write personal statements and sit a three-hour entrance exam. Up until that point, Sameer had been going to the local comprehensive school in the Belgrave catchment area. It was not a bad school, but his parents wanted to move him out for his GCSEs and A levels. Sameer did not want to leave Jeremiah and his other friends. But his parents had insisted that Sameer sit the entrance exams for St Thomas High. The Patels' son was there, after all. *Look,* his mother had explained patiently to her young son, *if you're with stupid people, it brings you down to their level. If you're with smart people, it brings you up to theirs.*

The day that Sameer had asked his father if he could go to watch the football match, there were still two weeks until the exam and Sameer had not spent a single day of his summer holiday outside his bedroom. *It's just one summer,* he remembers his father saying. *Everything we've done, every sacrifice we've made, we made for you, son. Now you're getting an opportunity we never had. Get into this school and you're set for the future: GCSEs, A levels and then Oxford or Cambridge. And you'll pave the way for Zara too – because if you've been to this school, she can go to this school. Think about it this way: do you really want to throw away your whole future, and your sister's future, just to go to one football match today?* Sameer did not want to do that, and so he did not go to see the match. Instead, he continued to study, passed the entrance exam – and then his GCSEs and A levels – with flying colours, gained admission to Cambridge and secured a job at one of the top law firms in the world.

'So, tell us about your deal then,' Sameer's father says, as his mother begins to serve up. 'You've been so busy.'

'There's a lot to tell.' Sameer takes a deep breath; a mouthful of pasta bake has settled in his stomach solidly.

'Well, you'll have to tell all the best parts again tonight,' his mother warns. 'Yasmeen Foi and Haroon Fua will be here for dinner.'

Yasmeen Foi is Sameer's auntie, his father's older sister who lives across the road with her husband, Haroon Fua, both of whom work in the family business. Their daughters, Shabnam and Samah, are both married. Shabnam is six years older than Sameer and had married when she was young, into a well-known family from the local mosque. She has a little boy. Sameer had always remembered her as aloof, not wanting to play, and just wanting to do girly things like paint her nails and call her friends. Samah, on the other hand, is only a year younger than Sameer, and the two of them had done everything together growing up. They particularly enjoyed the fact that both of their names could be shortened to Sam, and in the earlier years of their childhood, when their small selves retained that androgynous look of bowl cuts and dungarees, they used to pretend to be one another. Whenever Sameer spoke about his family, he always referred to his sisters, as he saw Samah as one of them. There had been a considerable amount of controversy a couple of years ago when Samah had brought home a white man, wanting to marry him. But once he had converted to Islam, the family relented, and the couple married and moved to Leeds, where Samah's husband was based. Sameer had not seen her since the wedding.

'How's Samah?' he asks, helping himself to salad.

'Hard to know when she's all the way in Leeds,' his mother sniffs.

'You can ask her yourself if you come home next weekend,' his father says. 'Her and John are coming to visit.'

'Well, she's coming to visit Shabnam, actually,' Zara says, reaching across Sameer for garlic bread. 'Shabnam's pregnant – I hope this one isn't going to be as fat as little Ayaan though.' Sameer stifles a giggle.

'He's only four years old, leave him alone,' his mother tuts. 'You can't be fat at four.'

'Yes you can.' Zara stares at her mother, shaking her head in disbelief. 'But I suppose that's what happens when you move in with your in-laws, they fatten up your kids like Christmas turkeys.' She sighs. 'I'll never move in with in-laws, I'm going to stay here forever.' Sameer's parents look at each other and smile. He can almost hear his father's thoughts: *That's my girl!*

'But you know that's what happens when girls get married, sis,' Sameer teases. 'You won't be a part of this family any more – you'll be a part of that family. My wife, on the other hand. She'll join this family.'

Zara rolls her eyes, but sees an opportunity. 'Speaking of which. When are you getting married, Sameer? I so want a little niece or nephew.'

'*Hah,*' Mhota Papa's ears perk up and he stops chewing for a moment. *Yes.* He sticks a finger in his ear, pushing in his hearing aid. His voice shakes, but holds. '*Shadi kyareh karwanoh? Shadi karvou ta tarou dharam che. Shadi karva ma dhiel nahi karai!*' *When will you get married? You know marriage is part of your deen. You shouldn't delay it!*

'I know, Mhota Papa,' Sameer says kindly. 'But there's no rush. In your day it was different. Things have changed.'

'*Kayanj nathi badalyoon shadi bara maa,*' Mhota Papa mutters in response. *Nothing has changed when it comes to the matter of marriage.* Mhota Papa returns to masticating slowly, the skin under his neck wobbling like a wattle. Pity pulls at Sameer's heartstrings. Mhota Papa's wife is dead, his children have abandoned him – one lives in America, there are two who live in Leicester but did not want to live with him after Mhoti Maa died. Too wrapped up in their own lives. But at least he has Sameer's father, and is in reasonably good health for eighty-four.

'Now, Sameer,' his mother says, eager to give her tuppence worth to the marriage conversation, 'I've told you before and I'll tell you countless times again. When you find a nice

Muslim girl that you like, you marry her, you understand? None of this dating-shating.'

Sameer rolls his eyes. 'Mum. Again. That was your generation. You can't expect us to get married to people we don't know.'

'I'm not saying you have to have an *arranged* marriage,' his mother snaps in response, flicking her spoon in Sameer's direction. A piece of pasta lands near his plate and he pinches it off the table and puts it in his mouth. 'I'm just saying that nothing has changed about *haraam* and *halal*. Love comes –'

'*After* marriage,' Zara quips, finishing her mother's sentence and bursting into laughter.

Sameer does not join in and looks at his father imploringly to save him from this conversation.

'So let me tell you what we're planning next,' his father obliges. Their plates are nearly empty and Sameer's mother rises to scoop the last of the pasta bake onto Sameer's plate. He protests and she ignores him. 'Our next big job – we're building an extension to the house.'

Sameer looks out through the doors of the conservatory into the large, expansive garden. He squints; the sun is blinding and he cannot see the end of the garden from where he is. 'An extension? But why? What for?' The house already has five bedrooms and three bathrooms. Sameer finishes the last of the pasta and his mother immediately takes his plate and begins to clear the table. Zara gets up to help.

'We need more space,' his father says. Mhota Papa rises and hobbles off towards his bedroom. 'Since the girls left home, Yasmeen and Haroon have had to live in that large house all by themselves. We were thinking that it would make more sense for them to move in here. And, well, your mother's right – you're getting to that age now where we need to think about what we're going to do when you marry. You'll need your own space.' Sameer is about to say something, but his father continues. 'And when Zara marries too – I'm talking in the future, but I want our house to be a place where there is room for all of us to live comfortably.'

Sameer fidgets in his chair. He wonders whether he should tell his family about Singapore now, give them time to digest the news before his aunt and uncle arrive. He opens his mouth, closes it and opens it again. His father gets up before Sameer has plucked up the courage to tell him. He is smiling at Sameer, bathed in the afternoon light. 'Come into the garden with me, Sameer,' he says. 'It's a beautiful day.'

Sameer obeys and heads through the conservatory into the garden. The air is crisp, but the cloudless sky removes the need for a jacket. He tilts his face up towards the sunlight and closes his eyes, letting the sun warm his face.

The garden is vast, ending with a hedge that poorly hides a full-size tennis court that Sameer has not used for a long time. There has been some attempt near the conservatory, where the ground is paved, to add colour – a white trellis intertwined with ivy leads to a swing, but flowers do not bloom here yet. His father steps down onto the grass, hands clasped behind his back, balding head shining in the afternoon sun. Standing behind him, watching his small figure potter forward, Sameer is suddenly overwhelmed with a sense of affection. This is quickly followed by a wave of guilt.

They start to walk towards the end of the garden slowly. 'Ramesh tells me that Rahool is coming home,' his father says eventually, voice soft. Sameer presses his lips together, hard, as if the action might stop his father from speaking any further. 'You know, Sameer, I can still remember the day you were born. A Friday – an auspicious day, of course – at three minutes past two in the morning. You cried and cried, and then they let me hold you and you stopped crying. That was even before your mother got to hold you.' His father pauses. Sameer watches a magpie bounce around on the grass in front of them. One for sorrow, he thinks.

'You still remember, hey?' he eventually offers, because he does not know what else to say.

'It is quite something, having your first child. You never forget that moment. And then, before you know it, they have grown up.' And completely disappointed you, Sameer thinks. 'We have worked very hard, Sameer, to give you this life you have,' his father says. 'We made so many sacrifices that you wouldn't understand. We've built an empire from nothing.'

'I know, Dad. And I'm grateful.'

'There comes a point, son, at which it is only right that you should start to give back.'

Sameer swallows. 'But isn't this what you wanted for me, Dad?'

'I am proud of you, son.'

A warm sensation courses through Sameer, ending in a stupid smile. 'Thanks, Dad,' he says. They reach the hedge towards the end of the garden and stand there for a moment, looking out on to the tennis court. A breeze makes the net dividing the two halves of the court ripple and Sameer shivers.

'But that was only ever a temporary arrangement. You were always going to come back, weren't you?' But it is not really a question. His father sighs deeply. 'We are not getting any younger. We need your help.'

'Dad,' Sameer begins, taking a deep breath, 'the thing is –'

'Son,' his father interrupts, 'it is the right time. You have been in London for five years now, and away from home for eight. Isn't that enough? Rahool is coming home, he thinks it is the right time.'

Sameer stops walking. Several responses run through his mind: *Well, I'm sorry Rahool isn't your son and you are stuck with me; You don't understand – it was pointless for Rahool to stay in London, he has nothing there; I've just been offered an incredible opportunity to launch a new office in Singapore – and they've offered it to me, Dad, because they think I'm actually pretty good.* He says none of these things. His father has carried on walking and has nearly reached the house. Sameer kicks a dandelion in frustration. He cannot bring himself to tell his parents this weekend. Not the weekend that they have found out that Rahool is coming home.

At dinner that evening, the house is filled with the fragrance of spices. Sameer's mother has made a feast: guar curry – juicy beans in spicy tomato sauce; fluffy pilau, with lamb so tender it slides apart when touched; rich chicken curry. There are samosas, *khichdi* and *kadhi* for those who want it, hot *rotli*, *kachumber*. Yasmeen Foi and Haroon Fua are so happy to see Sameer; they pull him into hugs and shower him with kisses. Yasmeen Foi hands him a bag and whispers, 'I was just shopping and saw these and thought of you. It's just something small.' Zara looks on enviously.

There are seven of them, and they use the dining room to seat everybody. The ladies dish out the food while the men talk. Sameer's father and Haroon Fua discuss the plans to extend the house. Sameer listens, half interested. His mind wanders to a life under this roof, days spent managing the business with his father and Fua, visiting the restaurants, opening new ones. Not having to answer to clients and partners at any hour of the day. Being able to create and control something. Overseeing other people working for him. Idyllic. Then he thinks of the fact that there had been a time, before he was born, when Yasmeen Foi and Haroon Fua had lived in London, where Haroon Fua had worked as a management consultant and Yasmeen Foi an accountant. Then, when

Yasmeen Foi became pregnant with Shabnam, they had given up their jobs and moved to Leicester to help Sameer's father with the growing business. Haroon Fua was the partner his father had always wanted, his father's brothers all being too old or dead or far away. As a young child, Sameer had always admired their relationship, viewing it through the rose-tinted glasses that come with the innocence of childhood. But as he had got older, he had started to notice things – and hear things from Samah – that made him uncomfortable. Haroon Fua was not a shareholder, or even a director of the company. He was an employee. He didn't have the power to take the business in any direction, he just did what Sameer's father told him to do. His salary filtered through Sameer's father's watchful eyes. There had been that argument about the car Haroon Fua had wanted to buy. Then there had been the really awful time when Yasmeen Foi had come to the house in tears with a young Shabnam and Samah, sobbing that she would leave him if he couldn't put the family first. Sameer had only been about ten years old at the time, but he still remembers the bitty black streaks making trails down Yasmeen Foi's face.

He wonders what it would be like, not earning an independent salary. Needing to draw on the family account and ask his father for permission every time he wants to spend money. Being completely dependent on his parents, just like he was when he was a teenager. No scope for disagreement. A painful memory rises like a bubble to the front of his mind. *No, of course we had nothing to do with that. Don't be upset, just forget her, Sameer. You've got us, haven't you? We know what's best for you. We'll always be here for you.* He thinks of the freedom he will have in Singapore.

As if he has sensed Sameer's thoughts, Mhota Papa suddenly wails, '*Mane mari dikri Amira bahooj yaad ave che.*' I miss my Amira – his daughter in America. '*Hoon mari jaysh to paun enei kayi dukh nahi thai.' I could die any time and it's as if she doesn't care.*

Yasmeen Foi's eyes narrow as she grinds a piece of *rotli* between her teeth. 'Such a selfish, thoughtless girl –' she begins.

Sameer's mother cuts her off. 'Mhota Papa,' she says gently, touching his arm. *'Khuda na kare.' God forbid.* 'Of course she cares. All of your children care.'

Yasmeen Foi glances at Sameer's father; they know that their brother is about to start crying. 'Bhai,' Yasmeen Foi says loudly, 'do you remember when it rained in Uganda? How it used to come down in sheets and sheets?'

'And these huge puddles would form in the villages and the street and there would be crocodiles in them?' Sameer's father adds.

'I used to go out in that rain and my mother would scream at me,' Haroon Fua joins in, catching on.

'It really wasn't safe!' Sameer's mother laughs.

Mhota Papa's eyes light up; they always do when talk turns to Uganda. Mhota Papa starts to speak, and Sameer zones out. Making sure his father can't see, he rolls his eyes at Zara. She rolls hers back and they begin to talk in low voices about new music they've been listening to as the adults continue to reminisce about the old days.

After dinner, Zara disappears to help Mhota Papa to bed. Sameer's mother makes tea for everyone and then announces loudly that she is going to pray (despite this, no one else joins her). Sameer flicks the TV on, volume low. The adults are talking about someone he doesn't know. He hears snippets of the conversation – unbelievable the way she just walked in there like she owned the place; every time, it's like this with her, people don't change, you know; it always comes down to money in the end! – but he is uninterested in listening to the family gossip, which focuses on a different person every week.

He suddenly feels uncomfortably restless; he needs to get out of the house. He retrieves his phone from his pocket, opens WhatsApp and scrolls to a group titled 'Leicester League 2k2'. There are at least fifteen numbers in the group, mainly friends from secondary school, before he went to St Thomas High. Over the years, people have left and joined, but the group has continued to exist and Sameer has not been ex-communicated yet. He's had the group on mute for several months; there are hundreds of unread messages. Sameer ignores them all and types.

Sameer (22.30): *Lads, footie tomorrow?*

He waits a moment, flicking through the channels on the TV. *Harry is typing.* Harry (22.32): *Sam, mate, where the fuck u been?*

Roy (22.32): *Can you not read any more?* Roy has replied to a message above, sent earlier that day, organising a kickabout at 11.30 in Victoria Park.

Sameer (22.33): *Been busy. But I'm back this weekend. See you tomo.*

Jaspreet (22.34): *We're honoured, mate.*

Sameer grins.

Sameer (22:34): *You should be.*

His mother enters the living room, having returned from her prayers. 'Oh, Mum – I'll be out tomorrow morning,' he says.

'Who with?' she asks, frowning.

'Friends, Mum,' he groans.

'Which friends?' she snaps back. 'Rahool?'

'No, the boys from Belgrave – you know, the group with Jeremiah.'

His mother is still frowning. 'Well, I want to know when you're going and when you'll be back. I don't want you spending too long with those boys. You came back to see us, not them.'

'OK, OK,' Sameer says, suppressing the urge to roll his eyes. Why does it have to be so difficult?

That night, he struggles to fall asleep. His bed is king-sized, and the sheets are fresh and smell like soap, like home. He tosses and turns and eventually fitful sleep comes, in which he dreams that he forgets to tell his family about Singapore and only remembers when he is on the plane there, but the plane crashes mid-flight, and he dies.

Eight people show up to Victoria Park the following morning – just enough for a game. Sameer is tired and does not play well – his team ends up losing, which annoys him: having been absent for so long, he'd wanted to impress. After the game, Roy, Jaspreet and Harry ask Sameer if he wants to grab some food. Sameer shakes his head – his mother will be making lunch – but then he thinks: Fuck it.

Over burgers and fries, the boys catch up. Roy is still living at home with his mother on an estate in St Matthews, but is saving steadily and the plan is to move them both out as soon as he's got enough. Roy left school at sixteen and became a plumber, so he has nearly ten years' worth of savings. Sameer almost feels guilty as Roy speaks: Sameer's yearly salary is probably more than Roy will save in a lifetime. Jaspreet is also living at home, in Melton, but only because it is easy – he's a dentist and is doing very well. Harry, who works as an estate agent, is the only one who has moved out of his parents' house – he's bought a flat with his girlfriend.

Sameer does not tell them about Singapore. He needs to tell his family first. He makes a mental note to tell Jeremiah and Rahool – especially Rahool – to keep it to themselves for now.

'So did you hear about Batts?' Harry asks. Sameer shakes his head. Johnny Batt was one of the original members of their group, who lived on the same estate as Roy. 'He's in prison.'

'What?' Sameer racks his brain, trying to remember the last time he saw Johnny. He draws a blank.

'He started hanging out with the lads from North Road – know what I mean? We took him off the WhatsApp group when we realised what he was doing. We're not really about that . . .' Harry tails off and Sameer nods; Harry does not need to say any more.

There is silence for a moment. Sameer sucks up some Diet Coke from his straw.

'He was desperate, you know?' Roy says. 'He didn't finish school, he didn't have any GCSEs. Dad not around, his mum not much either. He used to spend a lot of time at my house – my mum would make food for him and that.'

'I think he felt a bit shit when we all went off and started making money,' Harry says. 'But it's like he didn't realise that we had to work for it, and we weren't exactly making big bucks straight away. I mean, both Roy and me, we didn't do A levels, we didn't go uni, but we tried to do something with our lives. Now we're not doing too bad.'

'Obviously we're nothing compared to you two,' Roy adds. 'A lawyer and a dentist.'

'Yeah, but you forget – Asian parents,' Jaspreet says and the boys laugh. They talk for a while longer and Sameer feels the satisfaction of knowing why his friends are his friends; knowing that they can go for months without speaking and nothing has changed. At 4 p.m., he stands, grabbing each of their hands and promising not to leave it so long next time.

When he gets home, his mother is in the living room, just finishing the late-afternoon prayer, on her knees, scarf wrapped loosely around her face, where her hair stubbornly escapes from its ends. He watches her for a moment as she turns her head to greet the angels on her shoulders – right first, then left. She looks younger somehow – the lines in her face have fallen away. His mother, the only one in the family who observed the five daily prayers, who had tried and failed to get her children to copy her, who muttered that if their father had prayed, then she is sure that her children would have prayed too. His mother, for whom prayer delivered comfort and peace, not rigidity and obligation. She notices him and calls him over and he sits cross-legged next to her while she whispers *duas* into her hands and blows them over his face. 'Where have you been?' she asks.

Sameer ignores the question. 'Mum, I brought these.' He hands her the jeans he is holding: a peace offering.

'OK, *beta*,' she says, taking them from him and leaning on his shoulder to get to her feet. 'I'd better go and put them in the wash so that they're dry by the time you leave.'

His parents ask after his old crew over dinner. Sameer tells them about Johnny Batts. His mother purses her lips and tuts. 'Now, this is exactly why I don't like you hanging out with those boys.'

Sameer's father hushes her and says, 'That is unfortunate and sad – a waste of a young man's life. He must have felt very alone to turn to something like that.'

'Exactly.' Sameer is sometimes surprised by the depth of his father's insight; it confuses him. 'That's exactly what I said.'

'You know, when we first came to Leicester in the early seventies,' his father says, 'and we all lived on top of each other in these tiny flats in Belgrave, the government decided that there were too many of us in the local schools and we needed to be moved to different ones.'

'They had quotas for us,' his mother says in a single breath. Sameer's face burns at the use of the word quota. 'Once the local school had reached its quota of immigrants, we had to go to another school.'

'They put us on these buses, and we were sent from Belgrave to schools in what were essentially white areas.'

'We were so young. I was seven years old when my family moved from Kenya to Leicester; your father came from Uganda a few years later. How old were you, Rizwan – twelve?'

His father nods. Sameer and Zara exchange glances.

'How could they get away with that?' Zara asks. 'It seems so racist?'

'Well, they said it was to force us to integrate, force us to learn English,' his father shrugs and takes a sip of water. 'Even though my English was actually better than my Gujarati.'

'It didn't work,' Sameer's mother adds. She glances at the clock hanging on the kitchen wall and begins to collect the dishes from the table; Sameer will have to leave soon. 'It just made things worse. The white kids would call us "the Paki bus kids". Of course, most of us were not Pakistani – we were East African Indians, from Kenya, Tanzania and, of course, Uganda. There were Afro-Caribbean immigrants at that time as well. But they would call the black kids Pakis too.'

'We'd arrive at school as a group,' Sameer's father says, 'and we would have to leave early as a group. The bus monitor would come into the classroom and say in front of everyone: immigrants please. Every kid that wasn't white stood up.'

'That's crazy,' Sameer says. 'You could never imagine something like that happening now.' Zara nods in agreement.

'Well, I never, ever wanted you kids to feel that way,' his father says. 'That is why we worked so hard as a family, to improve our circumstances and make the best possible life for you both.'

'Yes,' Sameer's mother calls from the kitchen. 'It's only because of your father's sacrifices that you are where you are today. You mustn't forget that, *beta*.'

His father reminds them how hard he worked to get them into St Thomas High, although the way his father tells the story it's as if Sameer played no role in sitting the entrance

49

exams. He listens patiently while his father recounts the numerous sacrifices that he has made for his children.

Sameer does not tell his father that he and Rahool made up two of only four brown kids in the entire school, and that he has not stayed in touch with anyone other than Rahool from St Thomas. He does not tell his father that he felt more at home at the comprehensive near Belgrave, with his Asian and black friends, than he ever did at St Thomas, with the posh white boys. He does not tell his father that he is grateful though, because at least St Thomas prepared him well for Cambridge, where he also struggled to meet other people like him. He does not tell his father that he had tried to join the Indian society, but they were all from India, and were nothing like him. He does not tell his father that he had tried to meet other Muslims by attending the Islamic society, but the boys there expected him to agree with them that it was *haraam* to look a woman in the eye. He does not tell his father that, in the end, he did what he knew best and joined the football society. He does not tell his father that the boys in the football society spiked his Coke with vodka for a laugh, and before he knew it, he was drunk for the first time in his life.

4

To my first love, my beloved

15th August 1947

I must tell you what has happened to our daughter, Farah.

I write to you today from my study on the second floor of our house. Shabnam has gone out shopping with her friends, the children are at school, the ayah tends to the babies. The door is locked and I will not be disturbed. You did not know this study; it had not been built when we first moved here. But you loved scenery, and you would have loved the view from the window – from the highest point of the house, the land is net-worked beneath us. You loved the sprawling, fierce landscapes of Uganda. Remember how we used to sit on the shores of Lake Victoria at sunset, careful not to get too close to the water, and watch as the pinks and the golds and the reds infused with the blue, cloud-streaked sky, the way tea diffuses through water? 'Can you feel Allah's presence?' you would say, leaning your head on my shoulder.

It has been nearly three years since you left me, but time has not abated the intensity of this loss. When I think of you, you feel so close; my shoulder, still warmed from the place where your head rested; the sunset, still blinding me beneath my eyelids. I have traced your footsteps as they left this house a thousand times over. I have prostrated, asking Allah: Why her? But God sends us trials to test our faith. The worst trial that a man can endure, I suffered with you. Now, I must exercise strength to deal with Farah. Now, I must exercise patience.

But first, let me tell you of a momentous occasion: India has today gained independence. I have followed reports on the departure of the British, who sold our ancestral land for blood. There is no creation in the absence of blood, is there? The mother cannot give birth without pain. This wrenching of India from Britain, and of Pakistan from India, has cost thousands of lives. But I suspect that the worst is yet to come. Jinnah now has his Pakistan, and Muslims living in the new India must leave for it at once. It seems somewhat ironic that Jinnah himself is a convert's son, a man of Lohana descent, his own grandfather a Hindu to Khoja-Ismaili convert. Why should a change in religion prompt the creation of a new country? He cannot change that he is of India. We all are.

I must admit that hearing reports of the barbarism that has engulfed India is almost shameful. Indians have lived in peace for centuries – must they fall apart now that the British are to depart? It frightens me to think what will happen to Uganda if it is ever to gain independence.

I am sorry to say that I have not been able to bring myself to ask after your family in India. I have seen your father in the mosque, greeted him quickly and moved on; I have passed the shadows of your siblings. An intense sorrow hangs like a dark cloud over them, and I am enveloped into it when I am near. You understand, don't you? I cannot bear to be around them. But I can promise you that I have prayed for the safety of your family. I hope that it is enough.

Perhaps if I'd had relatives in India, I would have found the courage to speak to your family; perhaps we could have shared mutual concerns for the welfare of our loved ones. But I was born here, I have never been to India, and I did not travel with you on the occasions you went back. Dadi, Dada and Ma are all buried here. You are buried here. And I will be buried here, next to you, one day *inshallah*.

But although my family no longer has a physical connection to India, we have preserved our Indian culture and our values – Muslim values – the values of our parents and their parents, the values of our ancestors. In leaving India, we have clung to those values more tightly than ever before, guided by a powerful instinct not to forget where our ancestors came from and what we left behind. Papa instilled this in me; Dadi and Dada made sure that I knew who I was. It gives me great pain to say it, but I have failed to instil these same values in Farah. I have failed in my duty as a Muslim, my duty to you, my duty to my ancestors.

Shabnam tells me of her fondness for Uganda; that it reminds her of home, but a better version – here, there are no caste or class divides: there are only Indians. Just as you were, she is friends with the Sheiks, the Lakanis, the Narulas and the Sodhas. She has mingled into their circles and assimilated into their structures in a way, she says, that was not possible in India. She too has left behind a family in India and since news of the violence reached Uganda, she has waited anxiously to hear from them, hoping that they will one day be able to join us. But, she tells me, 'I will never go back to India. Our life here is so much better. This is our home now – and we can bring India here.' And that we have done. Our small minority of Hindus, Muslims and Sikhs has created for itself a little India, an integrated India. Shabnam delights in the fact that together we all celebrate each festival – be it Diwali, Vaisakhi, Ashura, Khushali or Eid – without distinction.

But in the midst of all of this, Dadi and Dada did not let us forget who we are, as Muslims, or the ways in which we do things. Papa chose you and me for each other, my dear, based on those same values that they saw in your family. There is a structure to be maintained in our small community; it shuns and accepts in equal measure. We have never been seen to touch alcohol, we observe daily prayer. We stay away from things *haraam*; we provide the biggest donations to the mosque. I suppose it is to be expected that I should be tested in such ways; indeed, when Allah loves a people, he afflicts them with trials.

India's independence has coincided with the holy month of Ramadan, and Eid is only a few days away. This will be my third Eid without you. Ramadan has always been a time of comfort for me, both spiritually and socially. But since you passed away, I have been unable to devote myself fully to Ramadan. When my stomach growls, or my feet become numb from standing in prayer, your absence plays on my mind like a cruel joke. This year has been even worse. I have been almost completely disengaged, worrying about Farah.

Yesterday, we hosted an *iftar* at our home for some sixty people. I have not hosted guests for *iftar* since you passed away. But this year, Shabnam said to me that enough time has passed, and that we must fulfil our duty to feed our community during Ramadan. Enough time will never pass, I thought, but I relented. Two days were spent preparing the food; Shabnam insisted that the ladies of our house must make it themselves. Tasneem and Farah were recruited to the kitchen, and platters and platters of food were prepared. Shabnam has learned slowly, from Tasneem – who learned from you, my dear – to fuse our traditional Indian recipes with Ugandan foodstuffs: she can now make peanut and sweetcorn curry, lemon chilli *mogo*, corn *rotli*. Her food will never compare to yours, of course, but she is improving.

The guests came in hordes – you will remember Ashkar, who now runs the largest foreign-owned bank in Uganda; our friend Sakib, the owner of the sugar plantation near Jinja – he has come home for Ramadan; the Singhs, in the retail management industry, now running the new shopping mall that has just opened in Kampala. As we spoke, I felt a growing sense of accomplishment. Despite constituting such a small percentage of this country's population, we are part of a very special club. Together, we have boosted Uganda's economy and inflated its revenues. There is opportunity everywhere here and the native population does not understand how to use it: we, on the other hand, have capitalised on it.

After dinner, we cleared space for the Muslims to pray together. I stood at the front, leading my community in front of God. My dear, we need these communities to give us our sense of belonging. And what is happening with Farah threatens that.

If you were here, I know that you would be able to reason with her. You were always very close to her – and she is the spitting image of you: wide-set eyes, fair skin that flushes easily, brown hair the colour of a chestnut. Perhaps because of her resemblance to you, she has always held a special place in my heart – my little girl, always excelling at school, praying her namaz on time, dutifully helping Shabnam in the kitchen. Perhaps that is why she can break my heart in a way that none of my others could. Farah will soon be eighteen years old – of marriageable age – and whilst I encourage her to study and I have no objection to her attending university, I also believe that it is right that she marries before she does. She cannot be living away from home in university dorms, able to mix freely with men. That is not right. That is not our way.

Papa, Shabnam and I spent some time canvassing the appropriate family for Farah. When we found one, Papa reached out to his contacts to verify their history and lineage. They came to our house one evening whilst Samir and Tasneem took Farah to the pictures. We got along very well; you would have liked them. They are from the same province of Kutch as my own family. The boy is called Noor.

After they left, Farah came home and I sat down with her to tell her about the boy. She has known for a long time that this day was coming. We have given her every freedom she has wanted, I have put her through school, allowed her to go out with her friends, bought her anything she desired. Now it is time for her to settle down.

How do I tell you what happened next?

She began to cry; she took my hands and knelt at my feet. 'Papa,' she said, 'I can't marry him. I'm in love with someone else.'

I felt my heart stop, Amira. 'Who?' I demanded. She shook her head, pressing her lips together tightly. I grabbed her by the shoulders and spat 'Who' into her face until she whispered the name, and I let go of her shoulders and stumbled backwards. I must have clasped my chest because she leapt up in concern, asking if I was all right. I did not respond. I did not ask her questions. I did not want to know the details. 'Papa,' she said, still crying, 'he will convert to Islam. We have talked about it, and he is willing to convert.' I looked at her wide eyes, and I slapped her hard across the face. My Farah, who I have never laid a finger on. She held a hand to her cheek, sobbing silently. I told her to get away from me, to get out of my sight.

We gave her life. I have fed her, clothed her, sheltered her, given her an education. And all I have ever asked in return is for her to show *akhlaq*, respect towards me, towards our cultures, our values, our traditions.

How was I to break this news to Shabnam, to Papa? The shame – the embarrassment – that my daughter – my Farah – could even contemplate such a thing. Those in the house knew that something was wrong. I told Shabnam that Farah was not to go out, not even to school, not to leave her room. Shabnam begged me to tell her what had happened, but I could not bring myself to do it for several days. In the end, though, there is only so long that you can wait to return to a family who has offered a proposal. I called Shabnam, Papa, Samir and Tasneem together and, unable to look them in the eye, told them. There was a long silence, heavy with the weight of shock and disappointment. Our sweet Farah, with a Hindu boy. Of all things – a Hindu.

You remember when the Usmans' daughter ran away with a Sikh boy? What shame she brought upon their family. The grandfather died of shock on the spot, and the wretched girl did not even attend the funeral. We stared at the Usmans with pity, we whispered behind their backs about how they had failed to bring their daughter up properly. The Usmans retreated – and rightly so – to the fringes of our community and then their business encountered financial difficulties and they became bankrupt. It was as if that daughter had been a curse. We might have tried to help the Usmans, but we did not want to risk becoming associated with their misfortune. They returned to India.

I have thought and thought upon it – what had I done wrong with Farah? Had she been spending too much time going to the pictures with her friends, watching Bollywood films, romanticising about the meaning of *pyar*? After several hours of discussion, Tasneem said that we should call Farah to the family meeting. It hurt to see her enter the room with her head hung low, eyes raw and body drooped, entirely dejected. But I did not let her see even a shred of my sympathy: I wanted her to feel pity for me. 'You have brought shame upon this family,' Papa said angrily, shaking his head. 'We will never hear you speak of this again, do you understand?' Farah did not say anything, and I stared at the wall behind her. Finally, Tasneem said gently: 'You only need to meet him once. Meet the boy, and if you do not like him, we will call it off.'

I wish you were here, Amira. Now, I feel like I need you more than ever.

5

It is May and the late buds of spring are in bloom. The air is charged with a nervous kind of excitement, seasons on the brink of change, unsure whether they are coming or going, whether it is summer or spring. Ramadan will be upon them soon. Although Sameer is not particularly practising, fasting is a must in the holy month. He has fasted during Ramadan every year since he was a teenager; even living alone in London and when at work he observes the month of Ramadan, refraining from eating, drinking and other worldly pleasures between the hours of dawn and dusk.

Rahool has returned to Leicester. Sameer has not been home since his last visit; he has vowed to himself that he will not return until he is ready to tell his family about Singapore. In the meantime, his life in London continues, but it's not quite the same as before: on weekends, he is alone; Rahool no longer around, Jeremiah always busy in the studio. And ever since their night out, something has changed between Sameer and Ryan; the air between them stretched to the uncomfortable point of breaking. Now that Sameer has seen the ugly inside of Ryan, he cannot unsee it, and he can't help but feel that every time there is mention of Singapore, Ryan looks at him in a funny way. Ryan continues to joke with him, invites him on nights out with his friends, asks him to join the others in the pub after work. But Sameer declines each time, reluctant to be around Ryan when he is drinking.

One balmy Saturday morning, Sameer sits alone in his bedroom, scrolling through the contacts on his phone, and wondering whether he really has any friends. No Jeremiah, no Rahool, no Ryan. Although most of his friends from Cambridge came to London after university, he did not stay close to them; there was a WhatsApp group, like the Leicester one, once active with hourly messages, that has now dwindled to the occasional message every few months. There is probably a more active, smaller group, but Sameer is not a part of it.

As he scrolls down his list of contacts – an impressive list, carefully collected over the years like an assortment of useless souvenirs – his finger stops at the name Hannah. They haven't spoken in several weeks; she didn't respond to the last one he sent her. It is a bright, clear day and it would be nice to leave the flat and perhaps have brunch; very soon it will be Ramadan and brunch will no longer be a possibility. He considers it for a moment, and then calls her. It rings out for a few seconds before she picks up. 'Hello?' Her voice is cautious; weary.

'Hi.' He suddenly doesn't know what to say.

'Sam?' Hannah says, voice faint on the other end of the line. 'Are you still there?'

'Yes, sorry,' he responds quickly. 'Yes. I just wondered if you wanted to do something today – have brunch, maybe go for a walk? It's a nice day.'

There is a brief silence. Then Hannah says: 'Look, Sam, we kind of need to talk about all of this.'

'All of what?'

'All of this thing – you and me,' she sounds exasperated. 'But now's not the right time – I'm busy.' He hears a voice in the background; Hannah covers the microphone and sends a muffled response. There is a pause, while Sameer waits, staring at the wall. He feels nothing. A longer pause and then – 'I've managed to step outside for a minute,' Hannah's voice is finally clear. 'But you know what I'm talking about – I'm not really up for carrying on like we do. Why are you even calling me on a Saturday morning? Because everyone else is busy?'

Sameer considers this. He doesn't see the point in lying and so he says nothing.

She sighs. 'Look, what I'm saying is if you want to do this properly, I would be up for trying that out. But I'm kind of done with being your booty call.'

He nods.

'Sam?'

'Sorry,' he says. He thinks for a moment and then says carefully: 'You're a great girl, Hannah. But I'm just not looking to settle down right now. I like that we can have fun –'

'You know what – actually, I've got to go. Goodbye, Sam.' She doesn't wait for a response and ends the call immediately.

Sameer knows with a certain sense of detachment that he will not see her again. This does not bother him. He lies back on his bed and stares at the ceiling. After a moment, he unlocks his phone, opens his contacts and deletes her number. Although there is nothing much for him to do – the deal has been quiet for a few weeks now and there is no telling when it will spring back to life – he'll go into the office and review documents that have been sitting on his desk for some time. The office will be empty, but he doesn't mind.

On Monday morning, Sameer stops by the office of the deal partner, Mark Lewis, to discuss next steps. Sameer does the majority of his work for Mark and he loves it. There is an instinctive affinity between them; a familiarity, a sense of acceptance: it has always been comfortable and easy. There have been trips to New York and Hong Kong in each other's company, clinking glasses of champagne while lounging back into the cushions of their business-class seats; long nights thrashing out documents, bouncing thoughts and proposals between themselves; multiple conversations about the deals, the clients, and their lives. Mark has always seemed to have a genuine interest in Sameer's development, giving him the best parts of the deal to work on, ensuring that when he involves someone else, he consults Sameer first to make sure no aspect of the work that he is interested in doing will be devolved away. Sameer is certain that Mark has been instrumental in securing his place in the Singapore office.

They speak briefly on the client's comments on the latest round of documents; Sameer raises a query which they discuss critically; Mark approves Sameer's suggestion. As Sameer is leaving, Mark says, 'Actually – Sam, hang on a second.'

He stops in the doorway.

'Shut the door for a minute, will you?' Mark is looking shifty now, fidgeting. 'Well. I just wanted to let you know before it's announced. I'm leaving the firm.'

Sameer exhales; he didn't realise he'd been holding his breath. He gives Mark a sad smile. There has been no announcement yet of the partners who will be going to Singapore and Sameer had distantly hoped that it would be Mark, although he knew deep down that it was unlikely, as Mark had not mentioned it. Mark tells him that he is moving to another firm – a firm known for being one of the highest-paying in the City. Sameer tries to shake off the feeling that he has been abandoned, recognising that it is childish; he is leaving for Singapore after all, and why should Mark not move to a firm where he can earn double what he is currently on? He wonders distantly whether Mark would have asked him to join him if he was not going to Singapore.

'I kind of hoped you would be coming to Singapore with me,' he says, half-heartedly trying to force his smile to prolong itself.

'Really?' Mark says, surprised. 'I thought you knew that

wouldn't be my sort of thing – thought you knew that you and I were cutting ties when you accepted it,' he laughs, and Sameer shifts uncomfortably on the spot where he is standing. 'Anyway, the partnership is still working out who's going to Singapore – there are a number of potential candidates in the pool.'

Sameer nods.

'Next week is my last week. I'm taking most of my clients with me, but the ones who want to stay with the firm will be handed over to other partners. You'll obviously still be on those deals.'

Again, a wave of betrayal – if Mark is leaving in a week, then the firm and the clients would have known for weeks, possibly months – followed by self-reprimand: Sameer, as a junior associate, had no right to know anyway. He congratulates Mark on the new job. Mark says that they will of course keep in touch, and that these are new beginnings for both of them. 'We'll have to have a drink to celebrate,' he says as Sameer is leaving the room.

'Sure,' Sameer replies, without looking back. As he walks back to his office, a fleeting thought crosses his mind: he wonders whether his decision to go to Singapore has caused some kind of monumental cosmic shift, some kind of displacement and unsettlement of the elements of his life that have held together, suspended so well and in balance for so long, his neatly placed pockets of people: Jeremiah, Rahool, Mark. All leaving, changing, metamorphosing into different things, spreading away from him onto different paths, like the multiple veins of a river delta, prompted by his decision to leave for Singapore. He immediately shakes the thought; it's self-absorbed and unfair.

Mark's departure is announced formally the following day. Farewell drinks are hosted on the office floor on Thursday, followed by drinks at a pub round the corner. It is the day before Ramadan starts, but Sameer cannot miss Mark's leaving drinks, and so he attends, chatting to a group of his colleagues, some of whose names he cannot remember. As the evening draws on, Ryan joins this group several times and then staggers away; he scoops himself back up and returns, only to stumble out again. Whispering his hot breath into Sameer's ear, Ryan asks whether he would like some cocaine; Sameer politely but firmly declines. 'I don't know how you do it, mate,' Ryan retorts, staggering off to the toilets. Slightly repulsed by this experience, Sameer goes to the bar to get another drink.

'Sam,' Mark grabs him as he walks past. Mark is standing with a couple of partners who Sameer recognises but has not worked with before. 'This is one of my best, I'm going to miss him,' he says to the other partners, drawing Sameer into their circle.

'Mark just cannot stop singing your praises, Sam!' one of the partners, Chris Richmond, is smiling at Sameer. At six foot five, Chris is large to the point of intimidation. He spits slightly when he speaks, dangerously waving about one of his huge hands on which he sports a signet ring on his little finger. 'I'm very glad about that,' he continues, 'as we're going to be working together quite closely over the next few months – I'm taking over the deal you've been working on with Mark.'

'Great – I look forward to it.'

'So what are you drinking?' Chris asks, leaning forward to get a closer look at the dregs left in Sameer's glass. 'Vodka Coke? On me.'

'Just a Coke thanks,' Sameer replies. 'I'm not drinking tonight.'

There is immediately a collective outcry; a shared sense of

outrage that growls from the bellies of those around him who are drinking: this is an insult.

'You can't not drink at my leaving drinks, Sam,' Mark whines, pushing forward his own tall pint, offering it to Sameer. A small collection of drinks already purchased for him wait patiently on the table. Mark will be bought drinks all night; there is no reason for him to hoard one. Besides, there is no selfishness when it comes to trying to engage others into drinking; Mark would gladly give Sameer the lot if he would drink them.

'Sorry – no thank you.'

'But why?' Chris roars.

'Ramadan starts tomorrow. You know,' Sameer says, voice light, 'the month when Muslims fast from sunrise to sunset. I can't really be hung-over for that.'

'Right,' says Chris. 'Well, I didn't know you were a Muslim.'

Sameer shrugs: what can he really say to this?

'Aren't Muslims not supposed to drink at all, not just not in the month of Ramadan?' Mark laughs. 'I've definitely seen you drinking.'

Again, Sameer shrugs. These conversations make him clam up with awkwardness; he wants to extricate himself from this group as quickly as possible. Before he has the chance to try, Chris asks: 'So why do you do that then – fast? What's the purpose of it?'

'Um. I've always done it. Since I was a teenager.'

'Yeah, but what's the idea behind it?' Chris asks, staring at Sameer. 'You starve yourself, but what does that achieve?'

Sameer racks his brains, but nothing enlightening materialises. He can see the other partners are getting bored; Mark's eyes have started to wander, scanning the room for someone else to talk to. 'Well,' he says quickly, 'I suppose one drink wouldn't hurt . . .'

•

Sameer's first fast of Ramadan is a struggle. He ended up having more drinks than he should have, he ended up missing the pre-sunrise meal *suhoor*. There is a WhatsApp message from Zara on his phone in the morning: *Ramadan Kareem, big bro! May Allah guide you and bless you this month and make the fasts easy for you to bear.* He feels a pang of guilt.

At work, he struggles to concentrate; his vision weaves in and out of focus. Chris asks him to amend a straightforward document, and he makes small, stupid mistakes. 'This is disappointing,' Chris says, reviewing the hard copy in his room. Heat rises to Sameer's face. He mutters a response, not wanting Chris to be exposed to the smell of his breath, which reeks an unpleasant odour from the fasting.

Back in his office, Sameer kicks his desk in frustration: it takes five minutes to make a good first impression, but five months to fix a bad one. Ryan asks him if everything is OK. It gives Sameer small pleasure to remind Ryan of his failures; he has tried to do this more and more since he was offered the role in Singapore. Outwardly, Ryan is sympathetic; inwardly, Sameer thinks, he is probably delighted.

The deal starts to ramp up and Chris becomes increasingly difficult to work with. He calls Sameer at all times of the day – and if he doesn't pick up, Chris phones his mobile repeatedly until he does. Although Sameer knows more about this deal than anyone else now working on it, he is taken off the negotiations and the key deal documents; he is allocated the most junior workstreams and more senior people are introduced to pick up where Sameer left off. When he tries to delegate some of the low-level work to a trainee and Chris finds out, Chris admonishes him over email – *I asked you to do this, Sam. Not the trainee. There was a reason I asked you to do it. Can you think why?* – copied to the whole team, a stain of embarrassment. There is always a snide remark to be made, something small and subtle to put him down – when he makes a positive contribution, 'That's one of the most obvious points, come on, dig deeper – we need to add value'; when he sends out a draft document with a small typographical error, 'It's just fucking embarrassing, you know. Embarrassing'; when he proposes a solution to a problem, 'Are you sure about that, Sam? What is it that you haven't fully thought through? Go on, think.'

There is some strange insensitivity in Chris's approach: for two weeks in a row, Sameer is still in the office when *iftar* approaches and he has to break his fast at his desk with a sandwich. Chris does not seem to care that Sameer is trying to observe Ramadan while working. He organises a lunch with the client for those working on the deal, despite the fact that he knows that Sameer is fasting and will not attend. In fact, he telephones Sameer and asks him to make the booking: 'I would normally ask my PA to do it, but I really fancy Lebanese food so I think you'll know where's best to go.' Sameer stares at the phone blankly. He doesn't even like Lebanese food.

For the first time in his life, Sameer starts to doubt his own abilities, and even briefly wonders if he should stop fasting to see if matters are corrected.

The counter-effect of working with Chris is that it seems to vastly improve his friendship with Ryan, who eagerly seeks details of the latest disaster, which Sameer offers generously. 'It'll all be fine once Ramadan is over,' Ryan says sympathetically, but his eyes gleam hungrily. 'You're fasting right now, so you have to be considered, you know, handicapped.'

A couple of weeks into Ramadan, Sameer arranges to see Ryan at the weekend for a late dinner. Jeremiah is never free any more and this has had the unexpected effect of making Sameer feel like he is shrinking. He dreads long weekends of nothing stretching ahead of him and dreads weekdays having to deal with Chris; yet he still cannot bring himself to go back to Leicester. In response to Sameer's proposal for dinner, Ryan sends him a brown thumbs up. Sitting cross-legged on his sofa in front of the TV, Sameer stares at the small brown thumb and wonders – is he being mocked?

Sameer (18.23): *Why is your thumb brown? lol*

Ryan (18.24): *Inclusivity, mate! I don't see colour* – and he sends another brown thumb.

Sameer might have laughed at this before – he remembers a time when Mark had said exactly the same thing when Sameer had pointed out at a work Christmas party that the person Mark had referred to as Jaya, the Sri Lankan Tamil new junior associate, was in fact Prudence, a black secretary. But now Ryan's comment gives rise to a flicker of irritation. He thinks about saying something, but then – given Ryan is his only friend right now – decides against it. They have a perfectly pleasant conversation over dinner, and he leaves feeling happy that he has managed to socialise.

The days drag on, and as Ramadan draws to a close, the thought of returning to Leicester – and delivering news of Singapore – plays on Sameer's mind. The Eid celebration that follows Ramadan is always glorious: after a long month of fasting, Eid-ul-Fitr has a festivity about it that doesn't compare to other holidays (it's our Christmas, Sameer would patiently explain to his colleagues); everyone's moods are lifted by the fact they can eat again, there is a new sense of empathy for the hungry and charity is distributed widely. Sameer half wonders self-destructively whether he can avoid going home for Eid by saying that he is working, but then he imagines himself alone in his flat in London on Eid day and he is overwhelmed by a moment of self-pity to the point that he nearly books a train ticket right there and then.

•

On the night of the twenty-seventh fast, Sameer is sitting in front of the TV, eating a bowl of cereal, when his phone rings. It's his father. 'Son?' Instinct pricks Sameer's ears to attention: he immediately knows that something is wrong. 'I have . . . I have some very bad news.'

His body becomes aware before his mind that something has happened, or is about to happen, that might change the course of his life irreversibly. The room begins to spin, blood rushes from his head to his feet. He suddenly realises that it is stupid that he has been avoiding going home.

'It's the Patels – their son Rahool.'

Sameer exhales deeply, with the guilty relief that follows the knowledge that it is not his family, but his heart feels like it is beating in his throat: what has happened to his friend?

'He was attacked, Sameer . . . He's been beaten very badly.'

Sameer opens his mouth to say something, but nothing comes out. He can't remember the last time he spoke to Rahool. He had felt – perhaps somewhat childishly – that an understanding, a sort of pact – the two of them, going it alone – had been broken when Rahool had cut the cord with London and retreated into the fold of his family business. They hadn't spoken in weeks. 'Is he OK?' he asks at last. There is a long pause. 'Dad?'

'His brain is swollen, son. He's in a coma.'

This news comes with the unthinking understanding that he must give up these silly games and go to Leicester at once. He immediately calls Jeremiah and they decide that they will travel back to Leicester together in the morning. Sameer's deal has started to ramp up again, but without hesitation he emails Chris: *Family emergency. Need to go home for a couple of days.* It's nearly the weekend; he will only be out for two days.

The boys meet at the train station in the morning. It is the first time that Sameer has seen Jeremiah in weeks and it's a relief to see his familiar face, although he somehow seems taller now, broader – his shoulders are bigger, like he's been going to the gym. On the journey, the conversation is at first devoted to Rahool, but the topic is quickly exhausted with the limited knowledge they have. As they fall back into comfortable chatter, Sameer feels strangely happy to be with Jeremiah despite the horrible circumstances that have brought them together. Jeremiah boasts about his work in the studio; Sameer tells him about Ramadan, about Chris. Jeremiah's expression is suddenly serious. 'It sounds like something you might want to escalate, mate.'

Sameer looks at him, surprised.

'It's not OK to behave like that. Someone should be told.'

'Yeah,' Sameer replies, a note of uncertainty in his voice. 'I think you're probably right.' He won't act on it of course. Jeremiah's response – the condemnation of Chris's behaviour – is enough.

On arrival into Leicester, the boys order an Uber to the hospital; it is not far from the station and they do not speak during the short journey. Sameer looks out of the window as the car winds through a part of the town centre. The familiar streets glare back at him; now that they have witnessed what has happened to Rahool, they appear menacing, unfriendly.

The hospital is not a place that Sameer is particularly familiar with; he's been blessed in his twenty-six years with good health and, generally speaking, so have his immediate family. Jeremiah lags behind with obvious apprehension, so Sameer takes the lead through multiple sets of doors and down long, starched corridors, his nose tickled by the mawkish smell of bleach mixed with something else he cannot quite place.

Rahool is in the intensive care unit, behind a locked set of doors with a buzzer. While they wait to be let in, Sameer dispenses gel from a mounted box on the wall outside the unit and rubs his hands together until the cold sensation of the alcohol evaporating has left him.

When the nurse eventually comes, she is with Rahool's father. There is a heavy tiredness to his body; never a slim figure, his large belly sags; soft, puffy pockets of liquid collect in bags under his eyes; even his long earlobes hang heavier than usual. Sameer embraces him, and he hangs on to Sameer tightly, eyes closed, hopeful. In the midst of this embrace a fleeting thought crosses Sameer's mind that if Rahool – the only child of the Patels – had not come back to Leicester, he might have been OK.

'I really appreciate you both dropping everything to come,' Mr Patel says as they enter the unit. 'It means a lot to us.'

'Of course,' Sameer responds immediately. 'Rahool is one of our best friends.'

The boys follow Rahool's father past rows of curtains, mostly drawn, but some open; nurses fussing, hunching over bodies obscured from Sameer's view. Some families, perhaps friends, wait nervously next to bedsides. The pervasive and unpleasant smell of what must be hospital food lingers everywhere. Sameer keeps his eyes cast downwards. He does not want to intrude on the privacy of these people and wishes that they would shut all the curtains. Past a few more beds – one empty – and then – Rahool. Mr Patel pulls back the curtain and Sameer and Jeremiah step inside.

Rahool is connected to a cacophony of wires and devices; they spawn out of him like angry growths, beeping and buzzing and draining and replenishing. Behind all the tubes, Sameer can barely see his friend. He steps forward, peering over the edge of the bed, and he doesn't recognise the face that lies blankly on the hospital bed. Blackened, swollen, sunken, bruised. Bandages around the head, crusted blood around the mouth – why has no one wiped that up? – the tube entering Rahool's mouth reveals several gaps where teeth used to be. Sameer's eyes swell immediately with tears and he backs away, stumbling into a machine beside the bed. A nurse pops her head around the curtain at the sound; she smiles kindly and tells Sameer that everything is going to be OK. He glances at Jeremiah, who looks equally floored.

'Can he hear us?' Sameer eventually asks Rahool's father.

'We don't know. We haven't left his side,' he adds in a small voice. 'We're staying in the hospital accommodation – it's just round the corner. Preeti stayed with him all night, she didn't let herself fall asleep. But he's never been responsive.'

They spend an hour or so with Rahool; at one point Rahool's father leaves and Sameer and Jeremiah start to talk to Rahool about the everyday, ordinary things. Jeremiah whispers: 'Who did this to you, mate?' and Sameer and Jeremiah look at each other as the machines bleep in response. Sameer is desperate to know more. Rahool never got into any kind of trouble; it makes no sense that his quiet, unassuming friend would be the subject of an attack. It's not the right time to ask Rahool's father. But they must find out. When Rahool's father returns, they thank him for letting them visit and tell him that they will be back tomorrow. On their way out – again, heads down in the intensive care unit, rub hands with alcohol on exit – Jeremiah asks Sameer if they can meet Roy for a quick drink before going home.

'Does Roy know what happened?' Sameer asks. He realises that he hasn't looked at the WhatsApp group since he was last home; as soon as he returned to London, it was muted once more. Outside the hospital, the crisp, odourless air delivers an immediate sense of relief.

'Probably,' Jeremiah replies, looking at this phone. 'Come on – we can walk there.'

They meet Roy in an American diner close to the hospital. The boys clasp hands, embrace briefly, and are seated in a red booth. Sameer can smell a frying beef patty and his stomach growls. 'Sorry, bit insensitive,' Jeremiah says, remembering that Sameer is not eating. 'Do you want to go somewhere else?'

'Of course not – it's fine,' Sameer lies.

'Well, we're only getting drinks anyway.'

They chat idly – mainly Jeremiah gushing about his new job – while they wait for their orders to be taken. The waitress stares at them expressionlessly when, after ordering two drinks between three people, they then also don't order any food, but she brings the drinks without saying anything. Sameer lets Jeremiah ramble on for a few minutes more and then cuts him off. 'What do you know about what happened to Rahool?' he says, watching as Roy decants a can of Coke into a tall glass. 'I've scoured the Internet a hundred times – there's no information out there.'

'That's because the media don't care enough to report it when it's an Asian kid,' Roy says.

'What do you mean?'

'Well, look at the guy. He's never been in any trouble, he's got no beef with anyone around these parts.' There's a short pause, where Sameer exchanges a confused glance with Jeremiah. 'It was obviously racially motivated,' Roy spells it out, slowly. 'I mean, everyone knows who did it – this gang of white youths, they've been arrested.'

Sameer struggles to process this; he did not think that these sorts of attacks still took place. 'What do you mean?' he repeats.

'I mean a bunch of Nazi motherfuckers.' Roy takes the empty can of Coke and flattens it with his fist.

•

Back home, Sameer can't stop himself from seeing Rahool's bloated, battered face. His family understand: they have visited Rahool themselves several times. His mother searches for signs of unease, seeking to comfort him and unfurrow his brows; his father is gentle and does not once mention business; Zara is obviously desperately curious, but recognises that he doesn't want to talk about it and so she doesn't bring it up. They have not told Mhota Papa what has happened and Sameer is keenly aware of just how old Mhota Papa is, and just how frail. Life suddenly seems so fragile.

That evening, as he lies on his bed, staring up at the ceiling, he wonders whether he should pray. He knows that it is a cliché to reach out to God in times of need, but he is fasting after all, and so there is some consideration for any prayer offered. He stands up, swigging from a large bottle of water at his bedside, and runs down the carpeted stairs, footsteps padding into the night. The clock in the downstairs hallway reads 2.40 a.m. In a small cupboard under the stairs, he finds a prayer mat stuffed into the darkness, heavy with dust. He sneezes and takes the mat up to his bedroom. There is a ritualistic washing of the head, arms and feet, and then he kneels down on the mat, puts his forehead to the floor and prays.

Sameer stays in Leicester for two more days, until Eid. Both days, he visits Rahool several times, sometimes with Jeremiah, once with his father, always with Rahool's parents. It is very difficult to look at Rahool's mother, and uncomfortable to be around her; she trembles and shudders and comes to tears easily. In the few days that Sameer is there, there is no improvement in Rahool's condition.

Eid day arrives with new clothes, food and family gatherings. The usual ritual unfolds: in the early morning Sameer's mother makes honeyed *seviyan kheer*, flaked with almonds and pistachios, oozing with condensed milk; they gulp it down and go to the mosque for Eid prayers. This is followed by at least an hour of greeting and hugging every person in the vicinity, waiting while Mhota Papa engages in a long discussion about the arrival of mango season. 'I have never had mangoes as delicious as those from Uganda,' Mhota Papa wags a finger at his counterpart, who is talking about Indian mangoes. After mosque, there is a call from Samah: she will not come from Leeds like she promised she would, John apparently being unwell; and for the rest of the day Yasmeen Foi is in a precarious mood. While Mhota Papa naps, the family go for a walk around Victoria Park and Sameer buys them all ice cream from a van on the corner. It is not a warm day and the ice cream makes their skin rise with goosebumps, but they smile with numb limbs, just happy to be eating in daylight. Normally – even in Leicester – they would be stared at; but not today, on Eid day, when the whole park teems with women in brightly coloured salwars and saris, catching the light in a million different ways. In the evening, Shabnam comes to the house with her husband and little boy. She holds her stomach gingerly – a bump is just beginning to show – and she tells them all with a martyred expression that she could not fast this year, now that she is carrying a baby. Zara mutters in Sameer's ear that it is a shame that Ayaan did not fast as he waddles past them into the front room.

Sameer cannot enjoy any of it. The news about the arrests has now broken cover and Sameer has spent most of the day on his phone. He has unmuted the WhatsApp group and the boys share information. 'Sameer, please, get off your phone,' his mother eventually says at dinner, exasperated. 'Come on, *beta*, it's Eid. I just want you to try to relax a bit and enjoy today. We've only got you for a few more hours.' But the day draws to a close quicker than his mother would have desired, and before they know it, Sameer is at the station, waving goodbye to his family – all of whom (save Mhota Papa, who is asleep) insisted on dropping him off. Their colourful Eid garb sparkles and shines at him as the train pulls away.

On the journey back to London, Sameer realises that he has not checked his work emails for several days. A mild sense of panic is quickly resolved by opening his inbox – there are hundreds of deal-related emails and he skims past them quickly, looking for anything directed at him. One email reads: *Our new Singapore partners*. Heart pounding, Sameer opens the email. Right at the top of the list: *Chris Richmond*. He immediately locks his phone and closes his eyes. Leans back against the seat and exhales deeply. He's exhausted. Then his eyes jerk open: he's broken his vow to tell his family about Singapore.

6

To my first love, my beloved,

3rd June 1953

I miss you, my *jaan*. I see you in the reflection of every surface, I hear your voice in the silence between moments. I close my eyes and I can feel my head resting on your breast, your small heart beating, your hands – always smelling faintly of garlic – gently caressing my forehead. I have not stopped needing you. I don't believe I ever will.

Shabnam and I do not speak about things. Instead, she shuts herself in the bedroom and cries. It makes me despise her; the little hiccups escaping in sobs from her plump lips, soft body shuddering with each release. She is no small woman, and her doughy folds roll like the hills of Kampala across our sheets. Not like you – I could lift you, firm and steady, with one arm. We could talk for hours. I often think that Shabnam could not be more the opposite of you. She has settled into this life with ever-expanding hips and bosom and a comfortable ease that eludes me. This life of ayahs and *boyis*, *ascari* and dogs, of more money than she ever could have imagined, of shopping for things that can be stored carefully in our multiple display cabinets, a life in which her clothes have their own bedroom. It is a million miles away from her life in India, a place of which she no longer speaks.

You would be surprised to see all the help we have now – even with Farah and Noor gone to Mbarara, we still need it. Things were so different when it was you and me, when we did not live in this house, and when we did not move in these circles. We have the ayah, looking after the children, and – you will not like to hear this – we also have a cook. There are now two drivers – it seemed necessary for Samir and Tasneem to have their own, and given our slowly growing collection of cars. An *ascari* stands at the gate, whilst the dogs snap at his feet. Can you believe it – dogs! Two large German shepherds, barely restrained by their long leashes, saliva dripping from snouts wet like damp sponges, barking madly whenever a stranger passes. You did not like dogs. Papa says that they chase away angels and gives them the widest berth whenever he passes.

Despite our abundance of servants, I miss Abdullah. He has not worked in the house for some time now. But you would be pleased to hear that this is because he now works as the manager of our retail business, from an office in Old Kampala six days a week. Of course some members of the community were surprised when we did this. But I did not care. You always used to say that Abdullah had a sharp mind and that he deserved to do more with it. I never found the courage to listen to your words back then. Ironic, isn't it, that it was because of you that Abdullah could not reach his full potential. But now that you are gone, I have put your words into action, and he has not disappointed. I've tripled his salary from what it used to be. He still comes to the house every Sunday to join the family for lunch, and afterwards he will make us cardamom chai, just like he used to, and we will sit in the drawing room and talk. Why is it that I feel closest to you when I am with him?

As it turns out, my darling, wealth takes you to many places. I only wish you were here to see it. I sent Shahzeb to England to the London School of Economics to study law. He is enamoured of London, but he comes home at the end of every term, and when he returns, smelling of rain and earth and concrete, the children clamour around him, climbing on top of him and searching through his pockets for English treats. Every time without fail, his suitcases open, spilling with gifts for all – slightly damp copies of the local London newspaper, slabs of vanilla fudge, key rings from which hang miniature red telephone boxes and red double-decker buses. Shabnam, who has a particular affection for all things British, will be gifted an additional, special treat: perhaps a lavender-scented handkerchief, or a tin packed with English Breakfast tea.

It is whilst attending university in London that Shahzeb has become an excellent squash player. You know it is a sport that I have always had a deep fondness for; the first sport I played as a child when I was finally introduced to the British education system, after leaving behind the Gujarati school in which I had spent my primary years.

But squash was never ours to keep; it is a sport that belongs to the British, brought here to be sampled by the select few who can afford a British education. And it continues to tease those who go to Britain for higher education, like my son, only to find upon his return that there are no public squash courts in Kampala. So when Shahzeb came home at the end of each term, we began to sneak into our old secondary school at the weekends to use the squash courts. It became a routine, father-and-son bonding over the thrill of the game amplified by the risk of being caught. And we were caught eventually – by one of the schoolteachers, Mr John Clapham, a fine specimen of a Brit, perhaps only a year or two older than Shahzeb, tall, with blue eyes and a barely there tuft of fine blond hair. He watched us play a full game before he alerted us to his presence. We stood ready to be chided – but instead he challenged Shahzeb to a game! I stared at this lovely white man and wondered whether he was mocking us. But no: he rolled up his sleeves, removed his tie and jacket, took my racquet and they began to play. I watched as Mr Clapham's white shirt became completely transparent and sweat began to run into his eyes. The games were close, but Shahzeb won, four to one. Mr Clapham insisted that he was handicapped by his attire, but he shook Shahzeb's hand very sincerely and invited us to join him in the Kampala Sports Club. Shahzeb and I looked at each other nervously. You remember the Kampala Sports Club? For Europeans Only.

What you would have thought of all this, I do not know. You always had a certain wariness of the British. But back then, my dear, we were not friends with any British people. I think you would like Mr Clapham. He is a good man.

So we told Mr Clapham that should he wish to apply for us to be permitted to play squash at the club, we would have no objection. Mr Clapham made an application – that Shahzeb and I, as upstanding members of the Asian community, Shahzeb being an excellent squash player studying at the London School of Economics and myself being none other than Hasan Saeed of Saeed & Sons, should be permitted solely to use the squash facilities and to play games against any members of the club. And lo and behold, his application was granted.

The Europeans regarded us at first with suspicion. I do not know why it is the case, whether it is a rule of the club, but the Europeans there dress exclusively in white – white tennis skirts and white polo shirts, white visors and white sports shoes. On the trim green grass, sprawled over loungers, flipping through magazines, reclining at the bar, the Europeans in their whites, sipping through straws on fluorescent cocktails, stared at us as we passed. But we walked with Mr Clapham straight to the squash courts, and after the third or fourth time, they stopped staring. A few of them came to observe us playing and I believe that they were entertained.

Before our friendship with Mr Clapham, I did not often spend time with our British counterparts. Oh, we used to laugh as we passed their empty, shiny stores! How those stores survive

I don't know, stores of hats and bags and ready-made dresses, seemingly bereft of any custom, yet somehow chugging along. Somehow managing to make a success out of doing nothing; leaving their mark everywhere like an overexcited, untrained puppy: Elizabeth Avenue, Windsor Crescent; Lakes Victoria, Edward, Albert, George. I have dared to hope that we Indians will be able to leave our mark on this country too. I have dreamt of Saeed & Sons being a household name across the whole length of Uganda; I have dreamt of being a someone whom people will remember the way that I remember you.

You see, the thing is that no matter how much you try, my darling, you cannot avoid the British. And we have a lot to thank them for – if it was not for them, we may not have made it to Uganda at all. Would Papa have followed his uncle here had it not been for the British? We were simple peasant farmers before Uganda – and now we are millionaires. It is through the British that we have become resilient. When the British have attempted to restrain us, we have risen above their restrictions to find a way to succeed, like pests of which they cannot seem to rid themselves. Had it not been for the British laws restricting the sale of cotton to Indian ginneries, we would not have been forced to find new ways to make profits – which we did, by leveraging our networks, our community. We should be thankful to the British. They are a part of us now. They have crept upon us, unwittingly seeped through our skin and into our bones, and settled comfortably inside each of us like veins.

Yesterday, it was the coronation of our Queen. The royal family may not have meant much to you, but had you been here, even you would have felt dizzy with exhilaration. The streets were alive with processions of marching bands, members of the British army and their African soldiers; schoolchildren dutifully waving the British flag. There was a sense of jubilant excitement in the air; the coming together of all of Her Majesty's subjects to celebrate the crowning of Queen Elizabeth *II*; a palpable sense of pride.

The build-up to the coronation had gone on for several days. There were talks of parties and festivals and cross-country motor rallies to celebrate the new Queen. The children have come home from school singing God Save the Queen and carrying purple tins of coronation memorabilia; Shabnam pounced upon each of these tins as they crossed the threshold and refused to allow the children to eat even one Cadbury's chocolate. Shahzeb had finished the final term of his second year of university but stayed for a few days in London so that he could watch the coronation procession live from the streets. Shabnam could barely contain her jealously when she realised that Shahzeb was to be bestowed with such an opportunity. But the coronation was to be televised for the first time in history: a reel of film would be brought to the Kampala Sports Club by a visiting officer the following day, and an event would be held at the club to watch it. After an afternoon game of squash (in which I beat Mr Clapham four games to three), Mr Clapham told me that Shabnam and I were invited.

Shabnam was giddy with excitement. She spent the whole day preparing herself for the event: squeezing herself into a halter-neck dress that Shahzeb had brought for her from England, covering her shoulders with a pastel-pink cardigan; powdering her face to give her a ghost-like appearance, disturbed only by a bright slash of red on her lips. On her feet, a pair of Mary Jane heels – again, a gift from Shahzeb – but they are a size too small and her flesh oozed out around the shoe. Her hair was piled atop her head and framed by a white cloth headband. It was almost comical, and mildly confusing, to see her dressed like an Englishwoman.

We left for the sports club at seven o'clock. The overwhelmingly strong smell of orange blossom, sprayed generously across Shabnam's neck and wrists and in her hair, tickled my nose as she climbed into the car. She had forced me to wear a suit – I insisted it was too formal, but she would not take no for an answer. I took the Mercedes and we drove the twenty-minute journey in silence.

When we arrived at the club, the door was locked. But the noise of cheering and laughter could be faintly heard in the background. There is no doorbell – only a small keypad at the side of the building, but I did not have the access code. Shabnam began to scratch her wrist erratically. 'I've been bitten,' she whispered. I felt very foolish and said that Mr Clapham would be there soon. He had invited us for seven thirty. I banged on the door quite forcefully. Shabnam flinched, looking around sheepishly, and asked me in a low tone what I was doing. I stopped.

Perhaps fifteen minutes or so passed while we waited, saying nothing to each other. Though I did not look at her, I could sense Shabnam's weight shifting from pinched foot to pinched foot and I began to resent her presence. At quarter to eight, I started to bang on the door once again. Shabnam opened her mouth to say something – but then a light, the sound of foot-steps, a clicking sound, and the door swung open. Relief, at last. It was a friend of Mr Clapham's with whom Shahzeb and I had occasionally played squash. He leaned against the door frame, beer bottle in hand. His shirt was unbuttoned enough to see the beginnings of chest hair. I said his name loudly, cheerfully, and Shabnam's face lit up.

'I just popped out to go to the loo and I heard some dreadful banging,' the friend said to me. 'Now, what are you doing here, old chap? And might that be your lovely wife?'

Shabnam blushed and smiled. 'We've come to watch the coronation,' she declared.

The friend looked at me sideways.

'Mr Clapham – John – invited us,' I clarified quickly, taking a step forward. The friend did not move from the doorway.

'Ah,' he said carefully. 'Now, that's slightly awkward, as I'm not sure he cleared that one with the rest of the club.'

'What do you mean?' My voice came out strangely small. 'I think there has been a misunderstanding. Please, would you mind fetching John?'

The friend looked straight back at me, unmoved, although his tone was apologetic. 'I don't think that's going to do any of us any good,' he said slowly. 'You understand, don't you?' He wrinkled his nose, and I suddenly became conscious of the sour smell of fried onions seeping through Shabnam's perfume.

Before another word could be said, I grabbed Shabnam's wrist and yanked her back towards the car. She stumbled behind me, her fat little legs struggling to keep up. 'You're hurting me, Hasan.' A hiccup. The sobbing began in the car on the way home, amongst muffled half-sentences: the shame, treating us like dogs, I thought he was your friend. I did not say a word in response. At home, the children asked us why were we back so early, surely it could not have finished already – it was a three-hour ceremony – what had happened? Shabnam stormed straight past them to bed and I locked myself in the study to write to you.

It was a mistake – a foolish, stupid mistake – to think that we might be permitted to join the club, even if only for one night, even if only to celebrate the Queen's coronation. I do not know what I will say to Mr Clapham when I see him next. But I cannot blame him; he cannot be expected to make a stand for a people of whom he is not a part. It is not his duty. I thank Allah for the community that I do belong to, the community that we have built here, our little India. I don't think that I will be returning to play squash at the sports club again.

7

Everything is different now that Ramadan is over and Sameer is no longer fasting.

He has a beautiful and deep sense of gratitude for the access he has to water he can drink and food he can eat. As he does every year after Ramadan, he starts to buy sandwiches and bottles of water when he sees a person begging on the street. After a few weeks, the feeling will wear off; it will not be so immediate, and he will pass the homeless without looking at them once again. But for now, he sees them and he tries to help in his own small way.

At work, he is focused, faster, accurate: rejuvenated. There are no stupid mistakes, no proofing errors; the answer to a problem comes quickly and easily to his mind. Chris is noticeably less critical but stops short of any praise. For the first time in his life Sameer understands the feeling of being disliked for no obvious reason. The better he does, the more he feels Chris's disdain intensify. It makes no sense. 'He just doesn't like me,' he says to Ryan, swivelling his chair to face him.

'That much is obvious,' Ryan nods with a strange, wide-eyed expression that makes Sameer immediately feel wary. 'You know he's invited a bunch of us to his house for a barbecue?'

Sameer shakes his head.

'Yeah, I saw your name wasn't on the email. Bit awkward seeing as I don't even work with him and I've been invited. Don't know what you've done, mate!' Ryan starts to laugh.

Sameer forces a smile. He doesn't want to go, but it's

strange to have been excluded from the invitation, especially as they are going to be in Singapore together.

Chris brings up the barbecue after a team meeting on the deal, reminding them to bring swimwear, as he wants his pool to be used, please. Sameer stares determinedly at his notebook, not meeting Chris's eyes. So everyone on the team except him is going?

'Oh, Sam –' Chris says, forcing Sameer to look up. 'I didn't send you the original invite – just because it's a barbecue, you know – and I wasn't sure whether that was your kind of thing, what with the Ramadan and everything?'

'Ramadan ended a couple of weeks ago,' Sameer responds evenly.

'Right, well – still. There'll be a lot of booze there and you lot don't drink, do you? You're obviously still very welcome to come if you don't mind being around all of that.'

Sameer wishes that Chris would have had this conversation with him privately. He doesn't know what to say in front of his colleagues. There is a long and uncomfortable pause. Finally, he says: 'I'm good, thanks.'

On the train that weekend – the third weekend in a row that they have been back to Leicester together since they found out about Rahool – Sameer tells Jeremiah about the barbecue. Jeremiah says that Chris sounds like a racist. Sameer reflects on this statement for a moment: he went to a selective school, to Cambridge University, obtained a well-paying job, and was selected from thirty-odd candidates for Singapore. There is nothing about his skin colour that has set him back. 'Why do you say that, J?' he asks. 'What if he just doesn't like me? People don't always get along.'

'It's not that, man,' Jeremiah shakes his head, one foot tapping to a beat Sameer cannot hear. Jeremiah has an annoying habit of always listening to music, even when he is talking to other people. One ear is covered by his wireless Bose head-phones; the other ear is free for Sameer, where the headphone has been pushed back to rest on Jeremiah's head. 'It's the fact that he is singling you out because of who you are. Like this whole Ramadan and not drinking thing. It's all bollocks. First off, you do drink. And second, even if you didn't – why assume you wouldn't want to attend just because of that? He's taking the choice away from you.'

He snaps the headphones back onto both of his ears and looks out of the window. For a moment, Sameer stares at his friend and wonders what it would be like to be him: to be black. To have that ageless cocoa skin, those wide nostrils and that large sensual mouth. To have that naturally muscular build, and the springy island of hair that never fails to bounce back. To be effortlessly cool. What has Jeremiah experienced that bypassed Sameer because of the randomness of their pigmenta-tion; the randomness of who they were born to? He thinks back to his childhood with Jeremiah, starting to feel uncom-fortably warm at the possibility of his own naivety, scanning his mind for memories of times that Jeremiah was treated dif-ferently. He can't think of any, and wonders whether he has missed something, whether he should ask Jeremiah if he saw things differently to how Sameer had seen them, but some-thing holds him back. His friend looks up and smiles at him, tapping his fingers rhythmically on his knee. Things seem to be going very well for Jeremiah. He's finally where he wanted to be after years of trying to make music in his tiny E3 bedroom. With this thought, Sameer reassures himself: surely the type of industry that Jeremiah has broken into is *easier* if you are black. He can't imagine trying to do the same thing himself.

If anything, he is sometimes envious of Jeremiah; at the same time, he is drawn to him because of the very qualities that cause that envy. Jeremiah works hard but doesn't possess the self-indulgence to be perturbed by things that would bother Sameer. A chance to work with one of the studio's most promising new artists had come up, but Jeremiah had no trouble saying no: he wouldn't be able to work for the next few weekends because he'd be visiting a friend in hospital. The opportunity will come round again, he told Sameer. Sameer didn't want to think about what would happen when his deal approached signing. He wished he could shrug things off as easily as Jeremiah and that his decisions – London or Singapore, Leicester or London, lawyer or businessman – did not have to feel like sacrifices.

'So, have you told your parents about Singapore yet?' Jeremiah asks as the train pulls into Leicester.

'Um. Not yet.'

'Aren't you leaving in three months?'

Sameer shrugs as they collect their bags and get off the train. As the departure date has drawn closer, Human Resources have begun to send him more and more information. *You will fly Singapore Airlines, business class. You get two 30kg suitcases and up to three 60kg trunks will be shipped separately – better start packing now! This is the serviced apartment that will be provided for up to the first four months while you settle in and find your feet – it comes with a cleaner, who will take the bins out, make your bed and press your clothes.* A large blue pool smiled up at Sameer from the attachment to the email. *Best of all, the serviced apartments are only a 15-minute walk from the office! When you are looking for somewhere to rent, please do endeavour to find somewhere just as close – remember, this will be a completely new office and so we will expect you to be fully committed to spending whatever time is necessary to build it from the ground up.*

Those going to Singapore have been announced firm-wide: three partners and six associates. Although he recognises some of the names, Sameer doesn't know any of them well, except for Chris. They will all be introduced to each other at the first Singapore team meeting over lunch next week. Sameer tries to imagine what Singapore will be like – he's never been before, but he imagines warm, cloying air and the metallic smell of money. Weekend trips to Bangkok and Bali. He'll make new friends and it will be a blast. But then he thinks about working closely every day with Chris.

'None of it feels real yet,' he says to Jeremiah as they leave the station. Sameer's father will be waiting for them on the side street; he also wanted to visit Rahool.

'I guess you've been pretty distracted by what's going on with Rahool.'

'Mmm. Anyway – obviously – do not mention it to my dad.'

'Course not, mate – it's your problem,' Jeremiah says, flashing a smile as they turn the corner onto the side street.

For the first two weekends that they go back to Leicester, there is no improvement in Rahool's condition. The swelling has gone down and Rahool's face is no longer so contorted, but the bruising remains, patches of deepening darkness spread across his face in a distinctive pattern: eyes, cheeks, lower lip. Most of the time, Rahool's parents are there. Sameer and Jeremiah talk about work and the weather and the news. A steady pile of magazines and books grows on the bedside table – for Rahool to read when he wakes up, because he will be bored. When Rahool's parents are not there, the boys talk about the attack. They promise him that whoever did this will be brought to justice.

This weekend is no different. After visiting hours are over, and at his mother's suggestion, Sameer invites Jeremiah to his house for dinner. Jeremiah – always keen to eat Sameer's mother's cooking – eagerly accepts. Jeremiah has not been to Sameer's house for some time, but he does not forget the custom as he enters the door, removing his shoes and greeting each of Sameer's parents, as well as Mhota Papa, who grunts in response.

Sameer's mother smiles, giving Jeremiah's shoulder a squeeze. 'It's good to see you, *beta*,' she says. 'It has been far too long – now busy with all your music thing, eh?'

'It's good to see you too, thank you for having me. You know what it's like, London,' Jeremiah smiles apologetically as he shrugs off his jacket. 'Very busy.'

'Well, you are always welcome. It makes me very happy to know Sameer is still friends with such an old friend, just like Rahool.'

The boys retreat to Sameer's bedroom, where they spend hours scouring the Internet for information about Rahool's attackers. Sameer opens his laptop at the desk in his room; Jeremiah lies on the bed, using Sameer's iPad. The attackers have been anonymised in press reports but Roy has given them a list of possible names and they search against each: Google, social media. Jeremiah asks Sameer if they can get access to these boys' criminal records, and access to the police files on Rahool's case. 'You're a lawyer, man, you should be able to work it out right?' Sameer shakes his head, reminding Jeremiah that he's a corporate lawyer. 'Useless then,' Jeremiah quips, and his headphones go back on. Sameer frowns, momentarily frustrated. He doesn't know the first thing about the criminal justice system. When Jeremiah is not looking, he googles *access to criminal records* but the search returns nothing useful.

There comes the uncomfortable realisation that the tabloids offer much more content for those hungry for information – and whether or not it is true, Sameer wants to know what they say. He clicks through to the online articles and reads – *Boy battered in 'Paki-bashing' gang-related attack*; *Violence erupts between gangs after postcode war attack on Muslim*. The stories are wildly inaccurate: Rahool is not Pakistani, nor Muslim, nor was he in a gang. Sameer scrolls through the articles in disbelief, wanting to close the screen, yet drawn to the words; half disgusted, half curious. The article signs off and the comments section begins. 'Jeremiah,' he says slowly, 'look at these.'

> *That is what happens when imigants come to this country and try to steal our jobs!!!* (5,000 likes)
>
> *Poor boy but what did he expect going to that area at that time of night?* (100 likes)
>
> *Payback time for Moslems. Don't dish it if you can't take it that's all I can say* (10,000 likes)
>
> *Is it me but are all the kids that get killed brown or black?? Doesn't exactly look like a coincidence . . .* (3,000 likes)

Sameer stares at the words on the screen. The pixels stare back unashamedly. He struggles to believe that 10,000 people agree that the attack on Rahool was some kind of justified retribution against Muslims.

'Yeah, close it, I've seen enough,' Jeremiah says, dismissing the screen and returning to the iPad. 'Have you never read the comments section of the *Daily Mail* before?'

'Um, no?' Sameer responds, unable to tear his eyes away from the screen, continually scrolling to release more vitriol.

'It's always like that. That's really what people think.' Jeremiah looks up from the iPad. 'Don't you know that most tabloid readers think that your religion is barbaric? That fasting is oppressive and dangerous and stupid – for what possible reason would your God require you not to even drink water for a whole day?'

Sameer tucks a knee up to his chest and swivels the chair to face Jeremiah. 'My God?'

'Our God,' Jeremiah concedes, smiling. '"By the Ahava Canal I proclaimed a fast so that I might humble myself before God." Ezra – I forget the verse. But the pastor mentioned it during Ramadan, trying to encourage us to fast as well. I was like thanks, but I think I'll leave the fasting to your lot!'

Sameer grins, impressed: he could not quote from the Quran the way that Jeremiah quotes from the Bible with such ease. Then again, the Bible is in English. He envies Jeremiah's relationship with his faith; it conveys a comfortable sense of belonging. From Jeremiah's neck, a cross hangs on a long chain, resting against his heart; he doesn't often speak of Christianity, but he gives thanks for any success to God, and he still goes to church on Sundays with his mother when he is back in Leicester. Sameer pictures stained-glass windows throwing coloured sunlight onto wooden pews and the majestic chorus of gospel, and wonders whether he might go with Jeremiah tomorrow.

That evening, after dinner and once Jeremiah has left, Sameer tells his parents that he wants to go to the mosque. Light flickers across his mother's face; his father looks confused. 'Of course you should go, *beta*,' his mother says. 'Your father can take you.'

'I can't – my knees,' his father says, gesturing towards his excuses.

So Sameer goes alone: something he's never done before. He can count the number of times that he has been to the mosque in the past five years on one hand – once a year at Eid. He recognises a few of the faces from the community; his face reddens when, surprised to see him, they ask him where his father is. At last, the melody of the *adhan* interrupts the chatter and the men stand to pray, shoulder to shoulder, rising and falling in harmonious unison. Something about the collegiality of it all reminds Sameer of his childhood. He tries to concentrate when the imam recites the words of the prayer, but they are words that he does not understand, and his mind wanders constantly to the image of Rahool, which makes him feel, annoyingly, like he is praying to Rahool.

After the prayer is over, Sameer remains kneeling, eyes closed, palms cupped, head bowed. He thinks: Please let Rahool be OK. There is then the odd sensation that if Rahool is not, it will somehow be Sameer's fault, juxtaposed with a discordant, uncomfortable feeling that prayers do not work anyway if everything is preordained. He opens his eyes and stares at the calligraphy engraved in the walls of the mosque, able to read the words, but not understanding what they mean. Still, the beauty of the writing feels somewhere close to peace.

Back at work on Monday and Sameer has not shaved. Ryan asks him what's up with the new look. 'You look tired, man,' he says as he takes a bite of toast covered in jam. He jabs at the keyboard and Sameer watches as the keys become slightly sticky.

'Nah, I just couldn't be bothered. I think I'm going to grow a beard.'

'What?' Ryan raises an eyebrow sceptically. 'Why would you do that?'

Sameer shrugs. 'Shaving is effort.'

'So is keeping a beard – trust me,' Ryan responds, turning back to his computer screen.

Chris's reaction to Sameer's stubble is what he expected – in a strange way, perhaps what he wanted by letting it grow out. They meet at the Singapore group lunch, which is in a meeting room in the office (the firm not willing to incur the costs of taking the group out); Chris is the only partner there, the others too busy to attend. Deb from human resources opens the meeting with a brief presentation about life in Singapore;

the group are then asked to help themselves to the buffet while they 'get to know each other' over lunch. They stand in an awkward circle, chatting and eating. 'What's with the stubble, Sam?' Chris asks, stuffing two cocktail sausages into his mouth.

'I'm growing a beard.'

'Not sure how that will go down,' Chris retorts immediately. 'Not going to be appropriate in front of clients really, is it?'

'A lot of our clients have beards. It's in fashion now.'

'Yeah, but you're not growing it for fashion, are you?'

'I don't know what that's supposed to mean,' Sameer says calmly. 'What other reason would I be growing it for?'

The room is suddenly silent. Deb clears her throat, making her presence known. Chris does not say anything and then one of the other associates says: 'I don't think Singaporeans are well known for facial hair, to be fair. You'd probably emasculate them!'

Chris laughs, and some of the other associates start to laugh, and the tension is diffused. Sameer does not laugh. He wants to walk over to Chris, grab him by the neck and smash his face into the hotplate of mini sausages. Arrogant prick. Instead, he smiles and forces himself to strike up conversation with one of the associates standing next to him.

The deal is approaching signing. Weekdays spill undistinguished into weekends and regular 3 a.m. finishes give Sameer's days a dazed, dreamlike veneer. Time passes with unnerving speed.

The first weekend that Sameer does not go home Rahool improves. Sameer wonders fleetingly whether he is cursed or whether his prayers have worked; both are equally frightening. As he sits in the office in front of a computer screen, WhatsApp messages flash up repeatedly from Jeremiah with details. Ryan is not here this weekend and Sameer closes the door of the office and phones. Jeremiah tells him the details – signs of consciousness, movement in his eyes and his fingers. The doctors say that he had a bleed on the brain and that he has some permanent form of brain damage. He will be moved out of the intensive care unit and into a specialist ward for people with brain injuries. He will need to learn how to walk and talk properly again. Jeremiah tells him that it will be slow and take time. That Rahool will never be the same again.

After the call, Sameer sits there, stunned. He can see that he has a missed call from Chris on his mobile, but he doesn't return it. He wants to process what he has just learned from Jeremiah; he wants to absorb every detail. Will Rahool ever go on a night out with them again? Will he be able to kick a football around a kitchen, or around a park? Will he even be able to work in the family business to which he so dutifully returned, or will it be his parents who end up looking after him for the rest of his life? Rahool's parents – the Patels, who Sameer had always thought of as an extension of his own family, whose house he had spent countless afternoons playing in as a child; the Patels, his family's first friends in England, with whom they shared Africa as the place they called home. A pain so strong that it makes his vision swim surfaces from these thoughts – but his mobile rings, breaking the silence in the room. It's Chris again. He forces himself to stop thinking, takes a deep breath and answers the phone.

As the police investigation picks up pace, information about the attack filters through – the tabloids had not been so far off the mark; it was in fact gang-related. A retaliation by a white gang of youths on (as Roy puts it) the first Paki they saw after a white boy who was walking home from school had been beaten up by a group of Asian lads. The white boy had escaped with minor injuries, but a video of the incident had gone viral.

And so it was payback time. It is said that the attack was completely random. Rahool could have been anyone – any Paki.

Rahool's attackers appear in Leicester Crown Court charged with GBH. They plead not guilty and a trial, scheduled to last for three days, is set for the following week. Sitting in his office, Sameer stares at the wall until his eyes water. He doesn't understand how the charge is not attempted murder.

Chris says that he is sorry, but it won't be possible for Sameer to take the week off and go to the trial. Sameer tries to protest, but Chris is immovable, and to press the point would be to lose all self-respect. Inside, Sameer burns with the shame of being that friend who didn't attend; it rises through him like stomach acid and makes him afraid to open his mouth for fear of what might come out if he has to speak to Chris. All of his family and friends will be there. He will be the only one who doesn't go. If he had ever thought before that he hated Chris, he was wrong: now he knows what it really means to hate someone. The anger breeds defiance: fuck Chris – he could go anyway, no one could stop him. But doubt draws him back; if he does that, just simply fails to show up to work, then the team and the deal will suffer. He settles instead for resenting the situation that this job is putting him in.

The trial is reported to him through Jeremiah: as the defendants came to give evidence, they changed their plea to guilty. Reduced sentencing to take account of the guilty plea: five years, with eligibility for parole after two and a half.

This news is delivered through a WhatsApp message while Sameer is on a call with a team based in New York. He immediately wishes he had not been looking at his messages during the call – but he couldn't resist checking for updates. Sameer asks his colleagues if they can reconvene in ten minutes as something urgent has come up. Avoiding Ryan's enquiring gaze, Sameer goes to the toilets, where he locks himself in a cubicle and reads the messages over and over until a searing pain makes its way up his leg and he realises he has kicked the door of the toilet cubicle so hard that it's opened and the lock is broken. He's never felt this urge before, to do something – to protest, to demonstrate – anything to scream out at the injustice of it all. Rahool will be disabled for the rest of his life, while these thugs will be free within two and a half years? There is something so wrong with this that his brain cannot compute.

The deal signs the weekend after the trial, at 3 a.m. on a Saturday morning. In their sleep-deprived, dazed states, the opposing teams congratulate each other. The partner on the other side shakes Sameer's hand with vigour and says loudly: 'We've been very impressed with you, Sam.' He looks over at Chris and winks. 'Now, watch out that we don't poach him from you!' he gives a hearty laugh, which Chris does not return.

Sameer sleeps until four o'clock in the afternoon. He hasn't been to Leicester for two weekends in a row and thinks about getting on the very next train, but his mind and body are so exhausted that he allows himself the rest of the weekend alone in London. At a loss for what to do, he leaves his flat and hops on the first bus that comes by, smiling to himself as he realises that it is going – of all places – to Leicester Square.

In the centre of London, he wanders aimlessly, bumping into and dodging tourists. The square is alive, writhing with forms that scream and jump; small hands holding balloons and bags from the M&M store; strong accents with backpacks on their chests, hands protectively placed over the zip. Sameer stares at these people. There is no one like him here – no real Londoners. Real Londoners do not go to Leicester Square at the weekends.

Outside the Odeon, a boy sits on a folding chair, guitar in

hand, plugged up to an amp. He is singing a song that Sameer recognises, but cannot name. A small crowd gathers around him and Sameer finds himself drawn into the circle. The boy croons into a microphone; long brown hair flops towards green eyes, the lips that pucker up to the microphone are soft and plump. He is good-looking, and the crowd consists mainly of teenage girls. Sameer closes his eyes for a moment, trying to place the song. The crowd gets larger and Sameer is jostled. His eyes snap open as he remembers: it's U2. 'I Still Haven't Found What I'm Looking For.' Zara's favourite old-time band, she would play their music all around the house when she was in secondary school. He wishes that she were here; perhaps he will send her a video of the musician. His hand goes to his pocket to retrieve his phone. His pocket is empty.

Immediately, Sameer steps back and out of the crowd, feeling an instant sense of rising panic. He pats down his pockets frantically, searching, searching. Wallet, gone. Phone, gone. He knows exactly where they were: in the front right-hand pocket of his jeans. He searches every pocket anyway. He wants to kick himself. He has been in London for five and a half years and has never had anything stolen from him. Why now, why today? And when did London suddenly decide to switch loyalties and make him a tourist in his own city?

Everyone is a suspect. He looks up, scouring the crowds as though he might be able to identify the pickpocket if he just spends long enough looking. It is no use of course. Common sense takes over: he goes into the first EE store that he sees and has the SIM card blocked; he calls the bank from the store to block all of his cards.

How will he get back to Clerkenwell? Become one of those people he never gives change to – *please, sir – I just need another 50p to make the bus fare home?* Well, he thinks to himself, that is the beauty of living so centrally – it's a forty-minute walk. It is

97

only when Sameer is halfway home that he remembers that his house key was in his wallet. He thinks about stopping a stranger and asking to use their phone, but then he realises that he doesn't know even his parents' phone numbers off by heart.

Outside his front door, Sameer sits cross-legged on the floor, helpless. He doesn't know what to do. An image of Rahool's face appears in his mind with startling clarity and there is suddenly a huge lump in Sameer's throat. He has not cried since he was a small child, but now something deep and painful in the cavity of his chest erupts through his body, shaking him to his fingertips, leaving his body heaving with sobs.

8

To my first love, my beloved

12th October 1959

It seems, my dear, that the anti-colonial movement has begun in earnest. We have lost Abdullah to anonymous threats of violence.

It is hard to believe that it was only last month that he sat here with us on a Sunday evening and took the children to catch *nsenene* in front of the house. The memory of you comes so strongly to me at the end of every rainy season; back when we were only children ourselves, running out into the velvety blackness of those earthy, damp nights to catch grasshoppers. The *nsenene*, arriving in their hordes, a clumsy mass of clicking and flapping, swarming the street lights with heady desire. I thought of you as I watched Abdullah from the front porch. The children shrieked, uncontained, jumping up to try to scoop a handful from the clusters gathered around the lamplights. Abdullah gave a corner of a white sheet to each of the children, and the creatures flocked towards it and were quickly bundled away. And in the same way that he taught us, he showed the children how to strip the wings, remove the feet and the heads, and roast the insects on a charcoal stove. My heart ached to the point that I had to look away. I have not eaten *nsenene* since you passed away. I have no desire to eat them without you.

The children miss him now. 'Papa,' they ask me, 'why doesn't Abdullah Uncle come any more?' The adults will look at each other, faces rigid to hide the discomfort that we can see in each other's eyes. 'Papa, where is the ayah? Where is Mzee?' It is not just Abdullah who we have lost. Gone are the ayahs, gone are our drivers. Only our cook remains, and he cannot leave the house for fear of being seen. Tasneem goes to the grocery store instead, but brings back the wrong things and is admonished. 'How can I make corn curry without *besan*?' he snapped at her, when she brought back corn and peanuts, but no gram flour. Since we employed a cook, it seems that she has forgotten every-thing. I saw you standing in the kitchen, instructing Tasneem as to salt, turmeric, chilli powder. The days when we did not have a cook and you used to teach her your mother's recipes. Me, standing in the doorway, watching you in this very kitchen, a kitchen that is at a loss in your absence. You looked up at me and smiled; there was a streak of some brown powder across your cheek. I wanted to come over to you at that moment, scoop you up and kiss the powder away, but I resisted the urge to embarrass you in front of our new daughter-in-law. I miss feeling that way, Amira. I miss you.

Shabnam is ten weeks pregnant and has severe morning sick-ness. I do not of course condone the pagan practices of the Africans, with their glowing white pastes, their herbs, crushed between palms to release strange smells that make you feel simultaneously nauseous and euphoric; worst of all, the frantic, indecipherable chanting. But in times past, these remedies have helped Shabnam with morning sickness, and Allah knows they have caused less harm than any Western medicine she could take. The cook promised us that he could bring things to cure her, if only he could leave the house. Shabnam implored me to allow it, but I refused. It is too risky; we cannot lose the cook too. Without him, we will have no help at all. Now, I have told her, she will have to make do with our own prayers and duas.

I do not think that any of us, comfortably minding our own business in our small community, expected that the boycott would have such a profound effect. I never imagined a time when we would not have our help, or that we would not have Abdullah. Losing you should have taught me that nothing in life is reliable, that I should never expect things not to change; that there is only one thing that is certain for all of us: death. But we live, and our foolish selves become used to how we live; we become trapped in the illusion of this life and begin to believe that we are secure.

Thankfully, the ginnery has escaped the worst effects of the boycott, which seems not to have spread as far as the Kamuli district. But whispers travel between the lips of our communities, burning with the heat of shame and helplessness: others have not been so lucky – almost all of the men from whom the Waljis bought cotton are now refusing to sell to them.

The *dukas* have not fared as well as the ginnery. The stores in Kampala, Luwero and even Mbale are suffering – such a large proportion of our customer base is African. With Abdullah gone, I have left the ginnery in Samir's hands and turned my attention to the stores. Sales have more than halved. It has been a long time since I have been on the shop floor, but I needed to go in to see what was happening for myself.

As many things do, working in the shop brought back the memory of you so vividly; the early years of our marriage when Papa had me running the shop. So much has changed, yet everything is the same: there are still rows and rows of stacked shelves, the musty smell of stored goods and dust. I saw you in a green sari, coming to the duka at lunchtime, holding a three-year-old toddling Samir in one hand, a tiffin box in the other. My little *duka*, how big it has now become! My beautiful Amira, how meaningless such change feels without you.

The Africans do not trust us. Even those who still dare to venture into the shop despite the boycott accuse us of cheating them, of modifying the scales so that the amounts are recorded incorrectly, of short-changing them and hoping they won't notice. 'Ey, muhindi,' one large black woman wagged her finger at me, leaning over the counter so that her enormous bosom, squeezed into an ill-fitting black polo shirt, rested on the countertop. 'You give me two cents less than you owe me in change! Don't think I don't notice – that is how you make your money, ey?' I had to spend ten minutes showing her why the change I had given her was correct, explaining basic principles of addition and subtraction that any child would know. There was no apology for wasting my time or for wrongly levelling accusations: she left only with eyes full of mistrust, a damp band of sweat on the countertop where her bosom had rested. The Africans were not so wary of us all those years ago when I used to work in the shop, were they? Or have I just forgotten?

Muazzam Kaka, sitting hunched on a small stool beside me, observed the entire interaction with mild interest. I asked him whether this was a regular occurrence and he nodded before reaching for his walking stick and wandering off into the aisles. I watched as he rearranged items on the shelves, slowly but steadily. Muazzam Kaka is in his early seventies now and is developing a cataract in one of his eyes. The younger boys come to the store after school to help him, but during school hours, he runs the shop alone. Perhaps he does make mistakes when counting change. Perhaps it is time he retired.

On Wednesday, an African boy pulled up a stool just outside the shop at the front door. '*Paacha awee geya,*' Muazzam Kaka muttered, shaking his head. I asked him what he meant – who had returned? – but Muazzam Kaka simply pursed his lips and tottered into the storeroom, out of sight. I went to the front of the store with a broom in my hand. The boy could not have been more than thirteen or fourteen. 'What are you doing here?' I asked him in Swahili. The boy stared at me brazenly. 'I have right to be here, *bwana*,' he replied in broken English. 'Outside your shop is not your land.' I thought about striking him with the broomstick, calling the police, forcing him to move – but instead I did nothing and went back inside the shop. That day, his presence deterred any African from entering the store. He had in his small hands a notepad and a pen, and he loudly warned any *karia* who neared the store that he knew who they were, he was recording their attempts to trade with us, and that they should enter at their own peril.

I do not know what the Africans expect will come of this behaviour. That they will force us out of business? That we will stop trading? We will never stop. Trade is in our blood. It is the blood of my ancestors, and it will be in the blood of my off-spring. If the Africans think otherwise, then more fool them. The *karias* do not understand the value of hard work. It is not a part of their culture in the way it is a part of ours. Why do you think the British brought us to Uganda, instead of trying to mobilise the native workforce? I am not saying there are not exceptions – Abdullah is obviously one such exception. But doesn't the exception prove the rule?

When all this began back in February, Abdullah tried to warn me that something sinister was brewing. 'The colonial powers are waning,' he told me. 'The people want an allied nationalist party for Uganda.' The Africans were holding rallies for thou-sands of people in the centre of Kampala. Previously diametrically opposed political parties had united to defeat a mutual enemy – the non-African – and in the sphere of com-merce in particular: the Asian. I dismissed it as a response to populist sentiment. Abdullah's words made me uncomfort-able, but I did not believe that it would lead to anything other than more rallies.

'Hasan,' Abdullah said quietly, 'not everyone in Uganda lives like you – or even me. Allah has blessed us.'

'I know that,' I snapped back, conscious not to sound ungrateful.

'Don't you know that the Ugandan legislature is powerless in the face of the British government? That the British have a veto over everything?' he said, staring into his cup of chai as if he might drown in it. I shrugged in response – what did it matter when life was so good? 'Did you know that Asians were represented on that legislature for more than twenty years before the first Ugandan was nominated to sit on Uganda's own legislative board?' I could feel my face reddening; Abdullah was embarrassing me. He has no right to try to elicit from me a response to the actions of the British; it is not my place to cast judgement.

'When things are working, why change them?' I said shortly.

'Things are not working for everyone, Hasan,' he responded.

I promptly changed the subject.

Then, the very next week, the boycott was declared by the leader of the newly formed nationalist movement: all trade was to be put into the hands of Africans. No African was to enter a non-African shop. We did not go into Kampala that day, but we heard that the Africans chanted *eddembe*, freedom, as they marched through the streets.

The effect of the boycott was visible immediately. Although we still had Abdullah at this point, one of our ayahs resigned, closely followed by one of the drivers. Abdullah reported decreasing sales from the *dukas*. Shabnam began to complain that she felt nervous going into Kampala; I told her not to travel alone, and to take one of our boys with her if she was to go anywhere. It was a tense few weeks, but we carried on, business as usual. And it was not long before the colonial governor acted to ban public rallies and the nationalist movement; by May, its members had been arrested. 'Nobody supports the boycott,' Abdullah reassured me. 'Not the King, not the

Uganda National Congress.' I sampled these words with bitterness. The Uganda National Congress. The political party that Shahzeb had tried to join on his return from London. The party that had rejected his application because he was not African. 'Let us focus now on independence. My son has joined the military,' Abdullah added. 'They are recruiting in anticipation of it.' I nodded and gave him a smile, but I must tell you, my dear, the idea of independence makes me quite uncomfortable.

Despite the ban, the boycott and the rallies continued. The colonial police responded to the rallies with brutal – and in some instances, fatal – force: they will stop at nothing in their attempts to protect our rights. I begged Abdullah not to attend such events, even for information. I may have lost him as an employee, but I cannot lose him the way I lost you. It would be wrong for his soul to join yours before mine does.

In the end, we managed to keep Abdullah until the first week of September.

It was a Sunday evening. We had only said goodbye to Abdullah an hour earlier, and I was having a cigar in the lounge with Samir when the dogs began to bark. Our *ascari* has gone: there was no one to open the gates – and so I stepped out into the static air to see who it could be at that time of night. To my surprise, I saw Abdullah. As I walked towards the gates from the house, I could tell that he was distressed; he was wringing his hands, brow deeply furrowed. We did not say anything to each other until we entered the house. I offered him a cigar but he shook his head. 'Hasan,' he began, but then words failed him; he sighed deeply, reached into his pocket and pulled out a piece of paper. 'Just read it.'

I retrieved my glasses from my shirt pocket and unfolded the paper. An anonymous letter, typewritten, no return address. *To a traitor and* abaliga. *You must resign from your position as*

employee of Saeed & Sons, an Asian-owned business, immedi-
ately. We will not warn you again. If we see you in the company
of Saeed & Sons again, you and your family will be sentenced to
death. Signed, Son of Muzinge.

I passed the letter to Samir to read.

'They know where I live,' Abdullah finally said. 'This letter was posted to my home address.'

I thought of Abdullah's house, a tenement block in Old Kampala, of his wife, their children. It suddenly struck me that I have never visited his home. 'Who is Muzinge?' I asked.

'We do not know,' Abdullah replied. 'Nobody knows. But in the Luganda tongue, it means peacock.'

'The king of the birds,' I said, half remembering an old Ugandan folk tale that Abdullah used to tell me when I was a young boy, the story of a child whose family kept a peacock trapped inside a small cage. The child was warned not to touch the peacock but, feeling pity for the creature, one night she released it and watched as it spread its cramped wings and flew away into the night. But what the girl did not realise is that her family had sold the peacock's eggs for a living and without the peacock they had no livelihood. The girl and her family slowly died of hunger as they spent the remainder of their short lives searching the land for the missing bird.

'And *abaliga*, why have they called you that?' Samir asked. Abdullah told us that *abaliga* is a term used for a cripple. One with crippled feet – the foot that carries you awry, leads you to the door of unfaithfulness. He reached into his pocket again and uncurled his fist; crumpled in the centre of his hand, a leaflet which read: *Every person should act as a detective on his friend.* 'I found this in the centre of Kampala last week. They are watching me.'

Abdullah did not want to go the police or to the King's chiefs. He said that there was no point; there is no way of identifying Muzinge, and if Muzinge were to find out that he had tried, the threats in the letter might well be carried out. He must protect his family.

And so the boycott has taken my Abdullah from me, the Abdullah who has been by my side since I was a small boy. Yet another person in my life whom I have loved who has abandoned me. And it is not just the store: to be on the safe side, Abdullah does not visit the house any more either. Will he get another job? How will he feed his family? He said that he had savings, and that everything would be all right. This boycott will not last forever, he promised. I pressed a bundle of notes into his hands the last night we saw him. He tried to refuse, but I insisted. 'If the boycott will not last forever, then this is just your advance salary,' I said. He accepted the money. He has promised that he will return to me, and I have to believe him because he is the only person in my life who has ever promised me such a thing.

It seems that somewhere along the path to independence, the Africans behind the boycott gave up on the existing institutions and the protectorate government, and sought to take matters into their own hands. Shahzeb tells us that it is important for us also to involve ourselves in the pre-independence dialogue, that we should be proactive in seeking to secure our rights, but that we should do it by engaging as Ugandans – not as Asians. I shrunk away from this talk as he spoke to us animatedly over dinner. We do not want to cause any trouble, I reminded him. There is nothing wrong with relying on the institutions that already exist to protect our rights. We have been protected in Uganda under British rule, and we will continue to be protected afterwards. Shahzeb shook his head and rolled his eyes, turning his attention to his siblings. I wanted to slap him for such rude behaviour, but I did nothing. He is young and naive; he does not understand yet what there is to fear from change. Since he returned from university, he has been so vocal about politics and what he calls the 'focus of Asian participation in the African political space'. I have tried to keep him busy in the business, but every spare moment that he has, he seems to be plotting.

The truth, Amira, is that I am scared. I could only admit this to you, but I fear what independence will bring. I fear that our Indian associations and Muslim councils, who have always looked towards the protectorate officials for protection, have chosen unwisely. Perhaps it was always the African elites with whom we should have been engaging. Shahzeb says that we have been wrong to seek independent protection and that we must lose that mentality if we are ever to be truly Ugandan.

As independence approaches, will anyone remember us during this scramble for rights? We are not natives and we are not Europeans. India has disowned us; Nehru calls us 'guests' of Africa. We are not guests. We are Africans of Asian origin.

9

It's quiet in Leicester. Sameer has not noticed this before, only ever coming back for one night over a weekend packed with things to do and people to see, only ever coming back when there was never enough time. But now that he will be home for several weeks and the pace is slower, he notices how quiet it is at night. No blaring sirens, no screaming, no laughter. Just silence. So silent it feels oppressive; the only way he can fall asleep is by listening to music.

He has six weeks off work. Then, a few weeks back in the office to tie up any loose ends. And then: Singapore. In these six weeks, he will tell his family that he is moving. He cannot leave it any longer. At work, they asked him why he needed so much time off. He said: because I haven't taken any leave in almost a year, because my leave will refresh when I get to Singapore and because there are a number of administrative matters I need to sort out before going to Singapore. He thought: because the partner I work with despises me, because one of my best friends nearly died in a racially motivated attack, because I feel like everything is falling apart, and because if you don't let me take six weeks, I will leave this office right now and never come back. They let him take six weeks.

Naturally, his family are delighted. He's told them the time off is accumulated holiday he's been forced to take; his father thinks it is a sign that he is seriously considering joining the family business. Sameer does not bother trying to dissuade him from such thoughts. 'We'll get you involved from Monday,' his father had said excitedly when he picked him up from the station. 'We get six whole weeks with you, eh? It's like a six-week interview for us to impress you enough to make you want to leave London. Wish us luck!' Sameer is not sure why he did not just tell his father there and then that there was no question of that happening because, actually, he had accepted a role in Singapore for two years and after his six week holiday, he would be leaving the very next month.

Now that he's back in Leicester, he will finally get to see Rahool conscious. It'll be the first time that Sameer will visit Rahool without Jeremiah. The idea makes him strangely nervous.

Rahool has been moved out of the intensive care unit and is on a general hospital ward. He's awake and sitting up in the hospital bed when Sameer arrives. Rahool's father had warned Sameer that he should not expect very much; that Rahool cannot control movement well, he cannot walk yet, that he has apraxia and finds it difficult to coordinate his mouth to form speech. He didn't tell Sameer how he should behave, and so he acts normally. Seeing his friend awake and conscious brings such relief that Sameer instinctively gravitates towards the hospital bed to give him a hug. Rahool's face immediately contorts with terror; an arm lashes out, uncontrolled, and hits Sameer in the chest. Rahool looks imploringly at his father and says: 'Donuthim, whoz-ee.'

Alarmed, Mr Patel apologises to Sameer, who immediately retreats, heat searing the length of his body to the point that he can feel his underarms dampen. There's no need to apologise, he tells Rahool's father, understanding that Rahool does not recognise him. 'It's me, Sameer,' he says gently, not daring to move any closer.

Rahool looks panicked. His face does not register the slightest recognition.

Sameer begins to back out towards the door. 'I think maybe the best thing would be for me to leave.'

Rahool's father steps out with him. 'I had no idea – I'm so sorry,' he says.

Sameer shakes his head, hoping the sweat on his brow is not visible. 'I'm sorry I upset him by going in for the hug. I just didn't imagine that he might not recognise me.'

'Mmm.' Rahool's father glances anxiously towards the door that is closed behind them. 'They did tell us that there would most likely be memory loss, but they didn't tell us that he might not remember people . . .'

'Did he recognise Jeremiah?'

'Oh yes, Jeremiah has been very good with him. He's been a real help. Good kid.'

Sameer swallows: he is small and insignificant.

'Um, I'm not sure if it's a good idea for you to go back in today,' Rahool's father says delicately, 'I think Rahool just needs a bit of time, you know?'

Sameer nods vigorously. 'Yes, completely agree. Of course.'

Rahool's father exhales. He looks at his watch. 'I'd quite like to stay and talk to my boy for a bit.'

'Of course – I'll ask someone to pick me up.'

Sameer's hands search for his new phone. He wishes he had brought his sister's car. He calls his parents: neither of them pick up. He calls Zara: it goes straight to voicemail. Uber? Closest one is ten minutes away. He keys his address into Google Maps: an hour's walk. This is perfect: he needs to clear his head; he wants the time to think. But part-way home, it starts to rain, lightly at first and then intensely. He doesn't have an umbrella or even a jacket with him. He thinks about the expensive new phone he has just bought: it's probably going to get destroyed.

When he finally arrives home, Sameer is soaked through.

He stands under the shelter of the front door and rings the bell repeatedly. He needs a house key. His mother opens the door, an apron tied around her waist. *'Arey, beta, hou thayoo?'* she exclaims. *What happened?* 'Why are you so wet?'

Sameer does not respond and walks into the house, kicking off his shoes at the doorway. His socks are wet and he leaves footprints on the floor as he goes into the kitchen, closely followed by his mother, who yanks his ear with a floury hand. *'Badmaaz,* speak to me!' she says.

'Ow, Mum,' he rubs his ear as he retrieves his phone from his pocket; miraculously it is still working. He rips off a sheet of kitchen roll to dry it. 'I had to walk back – Mr Patel couldn't drop me off. Tried to call you, no one picked up.'

'Then you should have got a taxi,' his mother retorts. 'You'll catch a cold like this. We didn't pick up the phone because we're entertaining – Mr Shah has come to stay.'

'Who?' Sameer stares blankly at his mother.

'Uff-oh,' she responds, annoyed that he hasn't recognised the name. Sameer feels a flicker of irritation: there are a million and one names for all of the extended members of his family, for aunties and uncles who are not in fact related to him at all and who he's never met; he can't be expected to know them all. 'You know,' his mother presses, 'your father's old family friend from Uganda. The one who went back. Clean up please, and go and greet him.'

Mr Shah is sitting in an armchair in the living room with a cup of tea when Sameer goes in. He sets down the tea and stands up to shake Sameer's hand: a strong grip, black hairs covering the backs of his hands, gold rings squeezed into the gaps between fat, stubby fingers. A rose-gold Rolex Daytona is wrapped around his wrist – very nice. His jet-black hair, slicked back, is barely receding for a man his age. A large stomach protrudes from his short, stout frame, which is decorated by a garish purple jacket. Clean-shaven and smelling like musk, his eyes grin at Sameer as they shake hands. 'You must be the lawyer, eh? Good to meet you, *beta*.'

Later that afternoon, when Mr Shah has retired upstairs and Sameer is standing in the kitchen, munching on a carrot while his mother and Zara prepare dinner, he asks his mother about Mr Shah.

'He runs sugar factories,' she says, pushing him out of the way to access the cupboard where the rice is kept.

'He's rich,' Zara supplies flatly, as she chops a cucumber.

'Obviously,' Sameer turns to his mother, jumping out of the way to avoid being hit as she slams the cupboard door shut. 'But how do we know him? And how come he's so rich?'

'So many questions, eh?' his mother opens the kitchen tap over the bowl of rice and begins to wash it. 'His father knew your dada – they all knew each other back then, it was a very close-knit community.' She drains the water from the rice and not a single grain escapes into the sink.

'And the money?' Sameer ventures, stealing another carrot from the dish in front of Zara, who protests and pretends to threaten him with the chopping knife.

'They were very successful there,' his mother shrugs. 'He went back to Uganda when they invited us back and I guess he made it all over again.'

'Why is he staying with us then, if he's so rich?'

Zara laughs at Sameer's question and responds in a thick Indian accent: '*Arey, bacha*, don't you know anything about our people? Why spend the money on a hotel when you can stay with your relatives for free?'

'But he's not a relative.'

His mother shoves him with her hip. 'Then go and ask him yourself!' she exclaims. 'Or ask your father,' she adds, suddenly concerned that such a direct manner of questioning might be perceived as rude. 'Go on,' another shove. 'The kitchen is no place for a man!'

Yasmeen Foi and Haroon Fua join them for dinner in the evening. 'So, law, huh?' Mr Shah says, looking at Sameer. Mr Shah eats like a true Indian, shovelling rice with his fingers into his mouth. Sameer watches as a small piece of rice flies out of Mr Shah's mouth and onto Zara's plate. She does not seem to have noticed. 'Good foundations, solid start, yes,' Mr Shah says. 'But not forever. You'll never be anybody if you work for somebody. You need to run your own business, be your own boss, eh? We Asians were born to be entrepreneurs, it runs in our blood. You can't waste your natural gifts, son. You've won the great lottery of life, being born one of us,' and he laughs heartily at this last comment.

Sameer's father makes approving noises before chiming in: 'I've been telling him this for years, Sohail.'

'The boy is young, give him time.'

Sameer despises it when he is discussed as if he is not present, as if those discussing him know what's best for him, as if they are his puppet masters. He reaches for his glass of water so that his hands have something to do.

'Now, I hear you've had some bad news recently, something happened to your friend?' Mr Shah's eyes flicker towards Sameer, who doesn't say anything. 'Terrible, terrible. This can be such a terrible country. That's part of the reason I went back, you know? Mind you, we've had some tough times of our own in Uganda.' Mr Shah shakes his head. 'They don't like to see us succeed, that's the problem. Nowhere is really safe for us these days. Not even India. But then that's no home to any of us, is it?'

After dinner, Mr Shah asks Sameer's mother if she minds if he has a cigar. 'Of course not,' she says, her voice unnaturally high. She opens the window near to where Mr Shah is sitting. Mr Shah retrieves a box of cigars from his briefcase and offers them around to the men. Sameer has never had a cigar before, but he takes one. 'Now, don't draw the smoke into your lungs,' Mr Shah says, reading Sameer's mind. Zara watches them as they light up. Sameer places the fat stub between his lips, drawing the smoke into his mouth and letting it sit there, gently burning. The taste is not unpleasant. Soon the room is filled with a soft aroma of burning grass that no number of open windows can dispel. Sameer asks Mr Shah about Uganda. What's it like? 'Oh, my son, it's the most beautiful country you will ever see. You know, like you've seen in the films? Jungle green. Smells and looks exquisite. Money grows on trees there. So rich, so prosperous. It's not a place you can forget easily . . . It's a paradise, *beta*. You must understand – it's our home. That's why I just knew after we were expelled that one day I would go back.'

Haroon Fua's eyes gleam as Mr Shah speaks. 'I often wonder whether we should have done that,' he says. Haroon Fua's family were also migrants from Uganda to Leicester, although they hadn't known Sameer's family before they came to England.

'But we are happy here now,' Sameer's father interjects. 'Happy and successful.'

'Not as successful as me!' Mr Shah's laughter booms before he starts to cough. Zara immediately springs to her feet and brings him a glass of water. 'Thank you, my dear,' Mr Shah says between splutters. He begins to sip slowly and the coughing subsides. Immediately, he takes another drag of the cigar.

After only a few puffs, Sameer no longer wants to smoke and he smashes the cigar butt onto the small silver plate his mother has brought in (incidentally for placing over chai to keep it hot – not for use as an ashtray).

'What kind of animals do you see in Uganda, Uncle?' Zara asks Mr Shah politely.

'Well, everything you would expect to see in the jungle. Of course there's nowhere near as many as there used to be back when we first lived there. Do you remember how we used to watch hippos bathing in the Nile, Yasmeen?' Mr Shah chuckles. 'Your father doesn't remember any of this, of course – he was too young when we left. You want to hear stories about old Uganda, ask Mhota Papa while he's still alive.'

Not likely, Sameer thinks. Mhota Papa can barely hear and rambles the same boring stories they have heard a million times before. He wants to know more about what the country is like now – and how Mr Shah found success after returning there. They talk as the evening draws on, Sameer supplying a steady stream of questions, and one by one, Yasmeen Foi and Haroon Fua leave, Sameer's family retire to bed, until just Mr Shah and Sameer remain. He hears about the old sugar factories that Mr Shah found in ruins on his return; the money, time and effort spent to rejuvenate them. 'It wasn't easy in the beginning, you know. My grandfather and father had built up such a successful enterprise. We came back to Uganda as the next generation – my brothers and sisters, my cousins. We didn't know how to work together without him and we all wanted different things. We fought bitterly.' Mr Shah drags deep on his cigar, while he stares into the distance. Then, his eyes snap up and he smiles. 'My younger brother and I manage the business now,' he says cheerily. Despite his burning curiosity, Sameer resists the urge to ask what happened to the rest of Mr Shah's family.

At 2 a.m., Mr Shah rises with tired eyes. He glances at Sameer's barely smoked cigar and asks him to pass it over. 'Shouldn't waste,' he says, cramming the stick back into the box.

•

The working week has begun, and Sameer sits with his father in the office, going over the plans for the new restaurant and wedding venue. The family also has a small side business – a petrol station just on the outskirts of Oadby, which had been purchased about five years ago in an auction sale. A nice little side earner, Sameer's father likes to call it. The petrol station is really all about the shop. Given its slightly out-of-town location, there was enough space on the forecourt to build a shop with a small hot-food counter, coffee machine, clothes rack, magazines, general groceries. It runs twenty-four hours a day and has three full-time employees. Sameer has not been to the garage for some time, but his father takes him to check in on it that week. The forecourt somehow seems smaller than he remembers; dingier. Sameer is struck by how unsophisticated everything is: the food counter stocked with food made by one of the community aunties; the awkward rack of clothes, purchased off the back of a van at a significant discount to what they are sold for in the shop.

Sameer looks at the land around the forecourt: there is a lot of empty, unused space. He closes his eyes, imagining a Costa Coffee, a real supermarket.

'Dad, have you ever thought about putting some well-known names in the forecourt?' he asks as they drive back that evening. 'Instead of having the coffee machine, why don't we have a Costa cafe? Having a real barista would make such a difference – people will pay good money for proper coffee. We could renovate the whole shop, use the forecourt space a bit better?'

'Mmm. I looked into all that a few years ago when we first bought the place. But it runs all right as it is – it'll cost a lot to make the kind of changes you're suggesting. It's really not our priority right now.'

'Fair enough.' They drive along in a comfortable silence for a while, Sameer's mind whirring. Then he says: 'It might not take as much time as you think, you know. And even if it did, it might be worth it. I think you'd make a lot more money in the long term.'

'Mmm.'

'I could have a look into it for you?' Sameer suggests. 'In fact, I'd love to – a little project for me over the next few days.'

'I don't think there's any need for that,' his father shakes his head. 'We've got a lot of other things going on that I'm going to need your help with.'

Sameer suppresses a smile. His father has no real idea of the kind of hours Sameer is used to working. He will make enquiries, model the costings and projected profit, and propose it formally. Come to think of it, Sameer realises that he doesn't know who in the family to propose it to. Who are the directors? The shareholders? He doesn't even know how much money the business is making.

'Dad, can I look at the company accounts?'

'Why?'

'So I can get a better understanding of the business.'

His father thinks about this for a moment before saying, 'You know, I still don't know exactly what you earn.' Sameer does not respond to this. 'Really, it's all one pot. You should be sharing your income with us to help this business, which is your business, to grow. That's the way our types of families work. All of this and everything it's earned will come to you eventually.'

'What do you mean, sharing?'

'Put that money into our account, so we have one joint family account. You don't need a separate account. I'm sure the Patels' son is doing it.'

Sameer imagines asking for permission to spend anything

out of the account; imagines his father sitting down on a Sunday afternoon trawling through his weekend expenditure: *What?! The boy spent £120 on dinner! What is this Hakkasan?*; the boozy brunches, the cost of Yeezys . . .

'You should be on the family credit card,' his father adds.

'The family what?'

'We're all on it,' his father says as they pull into the drive. 'You should be too.'

Sameer is surprised to learn of this, and slightly hurt that he has not been asked before. Then again, he doesn't want to spend his family's money. He doesn't want one big joint account with the family.

Zara gets her A-level results on Thursday. She missed out on the one A she needed to get into Edinburgh: she will go to her back up, Leicester. The family are thrilled – Zara can live at home; exactly what they have always wanted for their daughter. Sameer had searched Zara's face as she announced the results in the morning, but her expression was inscrutable, the news delivered matter-of-fact. Afterwards, he had tried to catch her alone, but for the rest of the day she had been absent, out with her friends.

In the evening, they go out for a meal to celebrate: Yasmeen Foi and Haroon Fua, Shabnam and her husband and their son Ayaan, even Mhota Papa and Mr Shah. The only people missing are Samah and John. They go to the best curry house in town and the usual chaos ensues: they order, change their minds and reorder; Ayaan begins to cry uncontrollably after being reprimanded for spreading mango chutney on the walls. The waiter looks perplexed as he attempts to comprehend what's going on.

At the end of the meal, Sameer's father proposes a toast: *To my daughter staying home, and to my son coming home. We couldn't be prouder of both of you.* Sameer groans at this remark, but his discomfort is drowned out by the sound of applause and clinking glasses. Now is definitely not the time to tell them about Singapore. When the bill arrives, Sameer sneaks a look – as he suspected, the waiter has got it wrong, the total is less than it should be. He doesn't say anything: his parents will scrutinise the bill, as they always do when it comes to paying for things. They will only say something if they have been overcharged.

Zara, Sameer and Mr Shah stay up after everyone has gone to bed. Mr Shah, sitting comfortably in an armchair in the front room like a fat, lazy cat, pulls a small bottle of amber liquid from the inside of his jacket pocket. With one hand, he takes a swig; with the other, he pulls out his cigars. 'You won't say anything, will you?' he says, winking at them.

'Please may I have a cigar?' Zara says boldly. Sameer thinks about asking for a sip of the whisky, but doesn't want to in front of his sister, even though he could really do with it today. Mr Shah nods at Zara, his chin somehow retreating deeper into the folds of skin under it, and gives her what Sameer recognises to be his own half-finished cigar.

'Don't smoke too much, sis,' he says feebly, wondering again whether she is as happy to stay in Leicester as the family are. He wants to ask her, but not in front of Mr Shah. Instead, he says: 'Tell us more about your business in Uganda, Mr Shah.'

Mr Shah leans back into the chair so that he almost becomes a part of it, and smiles lazily as the effect of the whisky begins to travel through his bloodstream. He tells them of red earth sprouting sweet, turgid sugar cane, the crunchy juiciness of eating it raw – no, they have never tried it – of how easy it is to run the planation and the factory in a country where there are so few people exploiting opportunities, markets are not saturated like they are here and there are limited labour laws; he tells them that it is like living in the past with knowledge of the future.

'We could have gone back,' Sameer posits, eyes shining.

'You know, your grandfather wanted to,' Mr Shah says, tapping his cigar into a small plate. 'He was very attached to Uganda. It was all he had ever known. And trust me,' he adds sombrely, 'to go from there to here, with all the grey and cold . . . well, it felt like you were going from paradise to hell. So when we had the opportunity to go back, your grandfather wanted to take it with open arms.'

'Why didn't we go?' Zara asks.

'Well . . .' Mr Shah pauses uncomfortably. 'As I understand it, the rest of your family were very opposed.'

'But why?' Sameer presses.

Mr Shah sighs deeply and pinches the bridge of his nose with his forefinger and thumb. 'Look, *beta*,' he says after a while, 'to be turfed out of the country in which you were born, the only country you've ever known, like you're no one, like you're nothing . . . it's a betrayal. God willing, you kids will never know what it's like to experience that. But for people like your father and your aunties and uncles, what was done to them at such a young age, it was very painful. After that, they grew up in this country and it became home for them. Why would they choose to return?'

Sameer nods, trying to imagine what it would have felt like for Yasmeen Foi, Haroon Fua, for his father. But then he thinks of the dreary concrete of London and the grey interior of his office building and all he can see is the jungle-green dollar signs of Uganda.

There is not a moment in the following week where Sameer stops: the regular 2 a.m. finishes continue; it turns out he can't rid himself of the drive to work, it lives in him. Mornings are spent visiting the hospital (where Rahool still views him with suspicion); the afternoons are spent at the new Kampala Nights site with his father. In every spare moment, Sameer looks into the cost of renovating the petrol station to establish new retail units. He talks to builders about converting the forecourt space and researches the Costa franchise, drawing up a table comparing costs with projected growth. In the evenings, he talks to Mr Shah late into the night, telling him of his plans. Mr Shah spurs him on, agreeing that it's all a very good idea: 'Now you're thinking like your father's son! Think big and go for it. With your heritage, you can't fail.'

Sameer wishes that Mr Shah would stay longer, but, by Friday, it is time for him to leave. They swap phone numbers and, gripping Sameer's hands in his podgy own, Mr Shah says: 'You *must* come and visit me in Uganda.'

'I will,' Sameer replies, and he really means it.

10

To my first love, my beloved

15th December 1967

You were not a believer in karma, my darling, were you? That
what goes around comes around, that you reap what you sow.
You would have said that what is given to us in this life is a trial
for the next. Yet life has a way of being ironic to the point of
design sometimes, doesn't it?

Ever since we were forced to sell the ginnery to the cooperatives, we turned our attention to the retail stores. And here
is Irony Number One: the ginnery in the hands of the cor-
ruptible African has resulted in such crippling inefficiency that
the government has had to intervene to establish an investigation into the cooperatives' workings. Their mistake was to
assume that they could just take us out and replace us with the
African. I must admit, I found this rather comical, with the
sort of nonchalance that comes with no longer caring what
happens: let them suffer for what they have done. In the meantime, whilst we focus on the retail business, I present to you
Irony Number Two: the government, in attempting to control
the price of foodstuffs, has ended up selling those foodstuffs
almost exclusively to Asians! It is us who ended up with a
monopoly on the goods, and us who can inflate retail prices as
we wish.

Whilst this is all mildly amusing, I do concede the government one victory in their attempts to trouble me, a win perhaps
that matters above all else: my legal status in this country.

I went with Shahzeb and Abdullah's son Ibrahim to the Immigration Office to try to negotiate with them. My son, Shahzeb Saeed, with a first-class honours degree in law from the London School of Economics and Political Science. Abdullah's son, Ibrahim Atek Adyang Okide, member of the 106th Battalion, reporting directly to the brigadier of the Fourth Division – recently promoted in the current state of emergency. Brain and brawn. Intellect and power.

Abdullah did not come with us – by offering us Ibrahim, there was no more that he could do. Abdullah, my oldest friend, as close as a brother, my substitute mother; the son of a servant, a servant himself. And look at him now. The most senior Saeed & Sons employee (and the most well paid!). Dare I say, he is as good as you were at managing the business. Indeed, you would have made a fine team together.

It may not surprise you to hear that Abdullah told me that he had thought about starting his own business; that he had an idea whilst the boycott was ongoing. I smiled when he relayed this. I did not want to tell him how we had struggled during the six long months that he had been gone; that not only had the business suffered as a result of the boycott, but that the store had also suffered; that Nazir's son, whom I had employed as a replacement, was no comparison to him. If Abdullah wanted to leave us for pastures new, I would not stand in his way. When he asked me how the business had fared in his absence, I simply said, 'You know, the boycott was not good for any of us.'

You were always so supportive of him, that – to tell you the truth – it grated on me at times. Telling me that you felt uncomfortable that Abdullah was sleeping in the boys' quarters and you wanted him to have a room in the house. The fight we had, when I told you that if it mattered to you so much, you could swap places with Abdullah and he and I could sleep together in the master bedroom, and you could take his place outside. It all seems so senseless now, thinking back to those early years. Abdullah has not lived with us for such a long time now, and for even longer he has not used the boys' quarters. To imagine him there now is utterly peculiar. We become used to the existing state of affairs so quickly, don't we, my dear, that we forget that there was a time when things were so very different.

For a while now, Shahzeb has been expressing his growing unease with our status in Uganda. This coincided with his marriage; perhaps a new sense of responsibility for our welfare, for the welfare of his wife and children. He says that we cannot ignore the warning signs to which our East African neighbours alert us, where an unsettling pattern of Asian flight has begun to occur. Business and land nationalised overnight in Tanzania. Mandatory work permits in Kenya for which Asians must show, as a condition of such permit, that there is no Kenyan citizen who could do the work they do. Tens of thousands of Asians have fled – back to India or Pakistan, some to Britain.

The intention is not to put us out of business, the government says, but to make trade more balanced; to achieve integration. But, my darling Amira, if Saeed & Sons is not the prime example of integration, then what is? Abdullah is the manager of our retail stores. He is paid a salary that I would pay any one of my sons for doing the job. No, he is not a shareholder or a director of the business, but that's because it is a family company.

Abdullah does not know how lucky he is, to belong without effort. We were divided in the house when independence came. Shabnam wanted – of course – to remain British. How beauteous it was at that time to have the luxury of choosing – we had everything we could have wanted, and we had a choice of who we wanted to be! To tell you the truth, prior to independence, I had never given much thought to the matter.

My Indian ancestors had sailed, unhindered, across land and sea to arrive in Africa many decades ago. There was nothing to stop them from aligning themselves with this country – to the contrary, everything about this country appealed to them, it begged them to come. Who knew then that the creation of passports would allow one to question the very existence of oneself?

Shahzeb helped me to prepare the papers. I was to apply for Ugandan citizenship, and Shabnam would remain British – once I obtained my citizenship, she would be my dependent, as would our young children. It is far better to have a British passport, Shabnam warned me. 'What else do you need a passport for other than to travel? It will be easier to travel on a British passport than a Ugandan one. The world respects the British.' But she was wrong in thinking that the only function of a passport is to facilitate travel. It is much more than that; it is a mark of identity: for the first time in its history, we would be able to identify ourselves as citizens of Uganda. An independent Uganda, birthed from the departure of the British with very little blood. An allegiance of a kingdom and political party, a democratic election: each concept, new to Uganda – but anything to get the British out.

I thought of you, my darling, and my dear papa, when I made my application to become Ugandan. As I swore before a magistrate that I would no longer be British upon receipt of my new nationality, I smiled, recalling your disaffection with the British. As I renounced my British citizenship before the British High Commission, I thought fondly to myself that Papa would have taken Ugandan citizenship if he were still alive. But I would be lying if I did not admit that it felt rather peculiar to let go of Britain. After everything, as I signed the renunciation papers, I thought: if only we could have both. It seemed so solemn to have formally to say goodbye.

But then that was it: I had relinquished Britain, and she had relinquished me. I was free to be who I chose. I took the Certificate of Registration to the Immigration Office, manned by dozy *karia* clerks with vacant expressions, and finally: I became Ugandan.

Shortly after I obtained my new passport, Samir, Shahzeb and I travelled to Tanzania and Kenya. With each marriage, our family grows; we now have family in various locations across the East African subcontinent and for some time we have been discussing expanding Saeed & Sons into these countries. A Saeed & Sons superstore, for all your household needs and more. One superstore per country, run by the members of our extended family. The boys had retained their British citizenship, even Shahzeb – which surprised me – but he seems to have become somewhat disillusioned with Ugandan politics in recent years. I travelled proudly, however, as a Ugandan citizen.

So you can imagine what a shock it was to receive a letter from the Ugandan Immigration Office just last week, advising me that my passport was no longer valid.

The letter said that I had not renounced my British citizenship 'within the mandatory time limits prescribed by the law'. I spent several hours frantically searching my office for documents I had received more than four years ago – and finally, after scrambling, removing drawers, papers everywhere, I found it: a letter dated 6th September 1963, curling at the edges, from the Immigration Office, enclosing my Certificate of Registration. I gave it to Shahzeb to inspect. 'The letter says you needed to have renounced your citizenship within three months. When did you renounce your citizenship, Papa?' It had been sometime in November, I recalled. It was at the end of the rainy season and the *nsenene* were out . . . 'OK, Papa. So you did it within three months of the date of the letter. That should have been enough. We'll visit the Immigration Office, we'll explain everything to them.'

It was Shahzeb's idea to bring Abdullah's son – Shahzeb said that he was sufficiently high ranking in the military to warrant it: 'Trust me, Papa, the power of this government lies in the army.' Ibrahim towers above both myself and Shahzeb. I liked the idea of his physical presence on our side, lending us more weight in the negotiations.

So off we went, the three of us, to the Immigration Office, and produced the letter to the clerk behind the counter. Lazy eyes scanned it. 'We need to speak to your seniors, sir,' Shazheb said calmly. 'Something is wrong, because my father did make his renunciation within three months of this letter.'

The clerk jabbed at the papers with one finger and spoke slowly, as if he was talking to idiots. 'Certificate of Registration dated April. Three months after April is July. You did not do it in time. You must now apply for non-resident permit, please, I will give you the papers,' and he began to turn his back.

'But he did not receive the Certificate of Registration until September, so it would have been impossible for him to renounce his British citizenship by July!' Shahzeb pointed at the covering letter which had enclosed the certificate.

The clerk shrugged. 'That is not my problem.'

'It is your problem,' Abdullah's son spoke up, banging his fist on the desk. 'There is obviously a problem in your system if this man did not receive the Certificate of Registration until after the deadline had passed.'

The clerk, credit to him, stopped in his tracks. 'And who are you?' he asked Ibrahim suspiciously.

'I am an officer of the Ugandan Army under the command of Brigadier David Musawanje, 106th Battalion, Fourth Division,' Ibrahim stuck out his chest. 'And I am friends with some very powerful people. This is an injustice. You would not want my friends to know of this injustice, would you –' he squinted at the badge on the clerk's shirt – 'Adeka Bako Ogwetyang? I know who you are.'

The clerk looked at us blankly for a moment and then said: 'I'll get my boss.'

We waited. Eventually, the man at the top of the pyramid emerged from the cavern in which he had been hiding, visibly annoyed to have been disturbed. 'Give me all of your papers,' he said, and Shahzeb handed over my documentation. The man disappeared with the documents into the dark. We waited again. I started to sweat in the damp little room. After waiting for an hour, Ibrahim went back to the clerk and spoke to him in a language I did not recognise. The clerk nodded and went behind the desk; he reappeared with my papers and handed them to Ibrahim. 'You must write to the President,' he said.

There was nothing more to be done. Shahzeb drove us home. In the car, he began to talk about what we should do next: that we should write to the President, but at the same time, we must start the process to re-register me as British immediately – 'Otherwise, Papa, you will belong to neither country.' I said nothing in response and simply stared out of the window at the red and green land rolling by.

11

At the end of his second week off work, Sameer sits down with his parents and presents his idea. It is Sunday afternoon, and they are sitting at the dining table after breakfast. Zara has taken Mhota Papa for a walk around the garden and Sameer can see them toddling along through the glass door panes in the kitchen. 'I've been thinking about a growth strategy for the petrol station,' he says, barely able to keep the excitement out of his voice. He is extremely pleased with his resourcefulness, almost enamoured with his own productivity in the space of a few short days. 'I know it's not your primary focus right now,' he adds. 'But I've had a few ideas I think are worth exploring.'

He pulls out copies of a digital sketch from a folder on the table and hands them to his parents, who look slightly perplexed. 'This is the garage with the forecourt reimagined. This is where the Costa franchise would go –' he points to the building in the left-hand corner – 'and over here we would have our shop – you'll see I suggest we get rid of hot-food counter and expand our retail stock range. These two buildings, redeveloped, would be available for rent to third-party retailers. The space is much better used, isn't it?'

Sameer waits for his parents to respond, but they just continue to look at him. He clears his throat. 'What I'm suggesting,' he says gently, 'is that we redevelop the garage. We focus on premium items, like proper coffee. We have a couple of retail units in the forecourt space and let them out to popular brands to increase customer traffic. I looked at the company's accounts, Dad. Petrol is such a small part of how the garage makes money – it's all about the retail sales.'

Again, silence.

'Look,' Sameer pulls copies of an Excel spreadsheet out of the folder and slides them across the table. 'I've modelled it. This spreadsheet sets out everything – assumed costs, capital requirements and our projected returns over a five-year investment horizon.' He pauses. Their reaction has deflated his ego slightly; he wishes they would speak. 'That's it,' he says. 'That's everything I wanted to show you.'

At last, his father says: 'This is all very interesting, and well done for the research and effort you have put in, son. We are really impressed with your enthusiasm for the family business, it makes me proud.'

'Thanks, Dad.'

'But,' his father continues, 'you know that the petrol station was – well, we didn't buy it because we wanted to go into the garage business. We bought it because it was a low-cost investment and would make a small, steady return for us without much management. This, what you're suggesting, would be a major distraction at a time when we have a significant acquisition for Kampala Nights. What we know and what we do is the restaurant business, *beta*, we're not petrol station managers and we don't want to be.'

'OK, yes – I understand, you haven't done this before and that's fair enough. But don't close your mind to it.' Sameer tries to stop himself from sighing audibly. 'I've spent days researching this, Dad, and there's real opportunity here, there's money to be made. And it's a platform for growth, we'll be able to scale it – if we opened a couple more with the same model, what's now a small side investment could become a large operating business in its own right.'

'Sameer . . .' his father's eyes look tired. He hates it when his father uses his name like this to start a sentence. 'Restaurants are where the money is. We've been doing this for a long time now, and look at how successful we are. Opening a few shops in a petrol station isn't going to make much money in comparison.'

His father has scooped up the papers and pushed them back across the table towards him. Sameer looks at his mother, who has said nothing but nodded repeatedly at his father's remarks. Sameer allows a flicker of irritation to pass his face openly. 'Dad,' he says, gritting his teeth, which makes his tone sound angrier than he intended it to, 'you're not listening to me. You've just closed your mind to it because you've already decided you don't want to do it. But it's not just shops, it's rental income as well. And the most important thing is that once we have a model that works we can just keep doing it, replicating it around the city, around the county.' He sighs with frustration. 'Why do you never listen to me? Is it not possible for you to contemplate that for once I might actually know something that you don't?'

'Sameer, don't take that tone with me,' his father is angry now, arms folded across his chest. 'You think you know everything there is to know about business? You've never run a business in your life. You just read laws all day. How are you so arrogant to think you know better than us?'

Sameer groans inwardly. He should have known better than to think that he could raise this; he wishes he had not – the lecture that he had become so adept at avoiding will begin: Sameer does not understand, and he will not understand, because he did not come from nothing like they did; he has had everything given to him on a plate; he does not realise how lucky he is.

'Are you listening to me?' his father snaps.

Sameer jumps to attention. 'Yes,' he barks.

'What did I just say?'

Sameer stares. His mother's eyes have not left his face. 'Mum. Dad. I have to tell you something.' He looks down at his fingers, which are interlocked in his lap. He takes a deep breath. 'My firm, they've offered me a job in Singapore. I've accepted it.'

'*Ay-Allah!*' his mother gasps.

'Singapore?' Sameer's father looks completely crestfallen, his voice small and shrunken. 'But, I thought . . . ?'

A rush of regret courses through Sameer. He should not have blurted it out like this; he should have reconsidered at the end of his six-week period of leave; he might still change his mind? 'It's an amazing opportunity,' he says automatically. 'I'll probably get made partner there,' he adds, thinking: no chance if Chris has any say in it. 'Anyway, I have to go. To see Rahool.' He stands up awkwardly. He should not leave it like this. He should talk to them, tell them what it is that has led to his choices, ask them for their advice. It is entirely unnecessary, but he adds: 'You know, Rahool, my friend who came back to Leicester to work in his family business and was nearly beaten to death.' His mother lets out a little cry, but instead of looking at her, Sameer turns and walks out of the room.

He texts Zara: *Borrowing your car.* He needs the freedom of not being tied to anyone else's timetable today. No time to tell Zara about Singapore, and his family will do this in their own way before he gets back. Probably paint him in the worst possible light. Traitor. Deserter. *Just like Amira who ran off to Um-rica and never came back.*

Jeremiah is home for the weekend and they have arranged to visit Rahool together. Blasting music from the speakers to drown out his thoughts, Sameer drives to the block of flats where Jeremiah's mother lives and sends Jeremiah a WhatsApp: *Outside.*

Jeremiah's biceps bulge under the short sleeves of his T-shirt as he enters the car; the fabric ends to reveal dark skin that is as solid as a rock. He smells good. 'What's all this?' Sameer says, wrinkling his nose as they pull out of the parking space and head towards the hospital. 'You look built.'

'Thanks, man, been gym a couple of times.'

Sameer snorts. He knows that with Jeremiah, a couple of times really does mean twice. He thinks about how many gym sessions it would take him to get even half the muscle that materialises on Jeremiah after just two sessions.

'I meant to tell you actually,' Jeremiah suddenly sounds shy. 'I've met someone.'

'You what?' Sameer begins to smile, mood lightened for the first time that day.

'I'll tell you all about it after. Dinner tonight?'

Sameer thinks about going home to face his family. 'Perfect.'

When they arrive at the hospital, Mr Patel is there. Jeremiah gives him a hug and Sameer stares. He has never seen Jeremiah hug Rahool's parents before.

Rahool is sleeping and the three of them sit around his bed, speaking in low whispers. Rahool's father tells them that he will be discharged tomorrow; that the doctors say he has made great progress; that he can walk, but he is still relearning how to write. Without thinking, Sameer asks how long until Rahool is back to normal, and then immediately remembers the prognosis was that some of the damage is permanent. Mr Patel exhales deeply; Sameer kicks himself. It's awkward now, but there is no point trying to make excuses for why he had to deliver this painful reminder. He had only forgotten momentarily in the hope that Rahool would remember him again.

As if on cue, Rahool's eyes flicker open. Sameer instinctively scrapes his chair back, conscious not to frighten him. 'J'miah,' Rahool says, looking at Jeremiah. A little drool dribbles onto Rahool's chin and his father wipes it away.

Sameer keeps his distance while Jeremiah and Mr Patel talk; Rahool throws Sameer the occasional suspicious glance, aware that this man has come to visit him several times, but still unable to recollect who he is. They stay for another fifteen minutes while Rahool is awake; he tires easily and gets irritable. Just before they leave, Rahool has a light-bulb moment: 'J'miah,' he exclaims, 'wefell in the r'ver!' Rahool begins to chuckle softly, pleased with himself for having remembered this and even more pleased that the memory was a funny one.

Jeremiah grins nervously. 'We're heading off now, Rahool,' he says slowly and loudly, but Rahool's giggles have already turned into snores. 'What was he talking about?' Jeremiah mutters as they leave the room.

'He was remembering rowing along the Soar,' Mr Patel says quietly. 'But that wasn't with you – it was with Sameer.'

In the first week of sixth form, Sameer had joined the school rowing club and pleaded with Rahool to join too. Preparation for if I get into Cambridge, he had said. The first session was in the gym, on a rowing machine. Rahool had fought with the machine, grunting and puffing, going red in the face. They had laughed about it afterwards when he'd complained that his arms were in agony; Sameer had said: You don't use your arms, mate, you weren't doing it properly. The next morning, 6 a.m., their first ever outing on the river, and Rahool's arms had completely seized up and he couldn't keep hold of the oars. He had called out to Sameer – help me! – and Sameer had let go of his oars and the boat had capsized. They had laughed about it for days.

Rahool had remembered this, but in that memory Sameer

was Jeremiah. Did that make any sense at all? Sameer imagines himself fading out of Rahool's memories altogether, dissolving into little pixels that blow away with the wind, and the strong, sturdy figure of Jeremiah appearing in his place.

As they leave the hospital, Sameer texts his mother: *Won't be home for dinner.* There is a message from Zara – *Singapore?* (crying face emoticon) – which he ignores.

Jeremiah tells him about the girl, Angela, who he met at a party. She's doing a PhD in philosophical science and she's intelligent and beautiful and kind. Sameer is happy for him. He looks at the Instagram profile proffered keenly by Jeremiah – she's half-Portuguese: olive skin, olive eyes, glossy brown hair. Most importantly she is Fun, according to the multiple, filtered shots of #girlsnightsout, #lbd, #wasted, #doesmybumlookbiginthis? He imagines for a moment their bodies intertwined, olive skin on black.

Dinner turns to drinks: Sameer has a half pint of beer, followed by three Coke Zeros. Jeremiah, who is not driving, has four pints. He hasn't stopped talking about Angela and Sameer is struggling to stay focused. 'I'm taking you home now,' he says at 10 p.m. 'I've got to get back.'

'OK, OK.'

As they walk towards the car, Jeremiah says: 'I think I love her, man.'

Sameer laughs. Jeremiah has known this girl for three weeks and been on four dates in that time, and he reminds him of this. 'No, man,' Jeremiah insists, as they get inside the car. 'When you know, you know.'

'Right. So did you tell her you love her then?'

'God no, she'd freak out.'

Sameer shakes his head and smiles. That was Jeremiah for you: fell in love so easily, and had his heart broken even easier. He was always hooking up with the wrong kind of girl: girls who wanted, as Jeremiah put it, the Black Guy Experience.

When Sameer creeps back into the house, he is relieved to discover that his parents have gone to bed. Zara is sitting in front of the television alone, eating popcorn and watching reruns of *Family Guy*. 'Yeah, I've been waiting for you,' she says accusatorily as he enters the room. But she stretches out the bag of popcorn and he accepts a handful. 'What's all this Singapore business? How did you not tell me?'

'I'm sorry,' he says as he collapses onto the sofa next to her, eyes locked on the TV. 'I really wasn't sure about it. I didn't want to tell anyone until I was.'

'So now you are?'

Sameer shrugs in response.

On the television screen, Stewie is beating Brian to a pulp and demanding money and they laugh, breaking the silence. Zara shakes the bag towards Sameer and he takes another handful. 'How long will you be gone for?'

'It's only two years,' he admits. 'But I'll stay for longer if I like it. Maybe move there permanently. I don't know yet.'

'Wow. That will be strange. Mum and Dad are really upset, you know.'

'I know.'

'They genuinely thought you were going to come home and join the business.'

'I don't know where they got that idea from,' Sameer says, exasperated. 'I've never wanted to. I've always wanted to make it on my own.'

'It's not always about what you want,' Zara says, turning her head away from the television screen and looking her brother in the eye. 'It's about what you owe them. You're the only son of a desi family, what did you expect?'

Sameer stares back at her. 'I'm sorry about your grades,' he says finally.

'It's all right. I'm happy being at home in Leicester.'

'Don't you want to try living out?'

'Maybe. But I'm also like, what's the point? They're just going to marry me off to someone from the mosque as soon as I finish uni anyway, I know it.'

'Doesn't that bother you?'

Zara considers this for a moment before saying, 'As long as he's nice and I like him then, no, not really.'

'OK . . .' Sameer cannot understand this, cannot understand how she could be happy with no freedom – not even the freedom to choose her own husband – but he doesn't want to create issues for Zara where she doesn't seem to see any. 'Well, in that case, don't you want to go and try to live a bit before you get married?'

Zara laughs. '*Dilwale Dulhania* style?' she asks. 'I'm all right. If I'm going to meet the love of my life at uni, I can still do that while living at home.'

Well, he supposes, this is the right response for a good Muslim girl. Zara has accepted her fate without protest; more so, she seems content with it. If making peace in this way is weakness, then why is there something so admirable in that beatific smile of hers? 'They're lucky to have you as a daughter,' he says, sensing that this response is somewhat inadequate.

Zara offers him the last of the popcorn. 'They're also lucky to have you as a son,' she says.

The following day, Sameer tags along with his father obediently: to the office, to the new restaurant site with Haroon Fua, to Yasmeen Foi's house. His auntie and uncle don't appear to notice that Sameer and his father are barely speaking – in fact his father positively tries not to speak to him at all – and there is no mention of Singapore.

Later that evening (after an awkward dinner where there had been almost complete silence at the table), lying on his bed, Sameer's fingers drift to his email inbox, wondering what he has been missing. To his surprise, there is an email from the managing partner, just ten minutes earlier, copying Chris: *Pls give me a call as soon as you can. J.*

Sameer studies the message quizzically. James will probably still be in the office, he thinks, dialling the landline number. His heart begins to pound as the phone rings out. What on earth could this be about? James picks up on the third ring. 'James Butcher speaking.'

'Hi, James, it's Sam. You asked me to call you?'

'Oh, hi, Sam.' The tone of James's voice changes instantly; Sameer does not recognise it. 'Can you give me a second? I think Chris is still around – would be good to have him in the room for this call.'

'Actually, I'd prefer if –' Sameer begins, but he is speaking to hold music. His fingers start to sweat; the phone becomes slippery and he nearly drops it. The partners click back on.

'So this is quite an unusual situation,' James says delicately. 'We just wanted to bring it up with you discreetly.'

'What is it?'

'Well. We had a phone call from your father yesterday,' James says. 'He left a voicemail at reception. It was eventually routed to me.'

Sameer immediately feels a sudden and violent desire to throw up.

Chris interrupts James's gentle tone and says brusquely: 'He said that you've decided to pack it all in, that you don't want to go to Singapore any more, that you're resigning from the firm.'

The nausea has passed and Sameer stares at the wall in front of him, nodding, mute.

'Well? Is it true? Fucking strange way to hand in your notice if you ask me.'

Sameer can detect a hint of glee behind the sharp tone: Chris is either delighted at the news or taking the piss – probably both. He wishes he was physically in front of him right now. 'No, it's not true,' he whispers into the phone.

'I didn't think so,' James says reassuringly. 'But I think you might need to have a conversation with your parents . . .'

'God, yes, sorry, I'm so embarrassed,' he gabbles. 'I think they were just a bit upset at hearing the news – I'll sort it out, don't worry. Sorry again.' He hangs up the phone. For a moment, he sits there calmly as he tries to process what has just happened, and then, quite suddenly, his blood begins to boil. He storms down the stairs and into the front room, where his parents are sitting with cups of tea. Zara is lying on her stomach on the floor, reading a book. Sameer slams the door behind him so hard it rattles. His father looks up, unconcerned. 'How dare you,' Sameer begins, voice so low it is barely audible. 'How dare you?!' he screams.

His father has clocked what has happened and multiple expressions flit across his face – irritation: *it did not work*; sadness: *it did not work*; anger: *how dare his son speak to him in this way?*

'Do not take that tone with your father,' Sameer's mother says. 'What is wrong with you?'

Clenching every muscle he possibly can, Sameer stops himself from screaming or shouting or doing something worse. He closes his eyes and counts to five very slowly in his head. Then he says, controlled: 'You called my boss and told him I was resigning. You had no right to do that.'

Sameer glances at Zara and registers shock. His mother looks unperturbed: naturally, they were both in on it.

'You want to talk about rights, son?' his father's face is red with anger. 'You have no right to abandon us to go to Singapore.'

'Zara, get out,' Sameer says. Zara immediately leaps to her feet.

'Zara, stay,' his father commands. 'It's about time you saw your brother for what he truly is – selfish.' Zara, torn between the wishes of her father and her brother, gives in to her father and sits down again, crossed-legged, on the floor.

This interaction, Zara's presence, diffuses Sameer's anger quite abruptly, and he is exhausted. He has no desire to fight with his parents. He feels numb. There was a time when he would have talked to Rahool, asked him why his family behave like this, whether it's an Asian thing, being fucked up. And then he loathes himself momentarily for wishing he was from somewhere else. His father is speaking, face hot, eyes angry, gesticulating. His mother stands behind him, nodding seriously. The unit. Unbreakable. He does not listen to what his father is saying. His mind drifts to that wretched memory.

He is seventeen years old and giddy with the excitement of first love. His insides squirm; he flushes easily when he thinks about her lips; his every thought is of her. Her name is Raha and she has joined his sixth form from a different school. The first day that he met her marked the beginning of the rest of his life, as she walked into his maths class with not a care in the world, effortlessly beautiful, skirt pulled high to reveal long brown legs: girls were supposed to wear tights, but he didn't know then, as she would later tell him, that they didn't make tights in their colour. His parents can tell that something has happened to him. He is distracted, constantly on his phone, he no longer wants to study at home, preferring instead to go to the 'library' (hot, fumbled, groping in the back seat of his car).

He can't be without her; they will coordinate their university applications – bound to get into at least one together, that's where they'll both go. She tells him that she doesn't want to apply to Cambridge. He doesn't want to risk even one of their choices not being the same: it's not worth it.

When his parents discover that he has changed his mind about applying to Cambridge, they are horrified. They ask him why. In the end, he tells them about Raha: he has to, because one day she will be his wife anyway. Now we understand, they say. Now we understand why you have been acting so strangely. They tell him that what he is planning to do is not right. This is his future; she is a distraction. He dares venture that he's in love and that he intends to marry her one day. They tell him that if she really loved him she would never want him to give up Cambridge for her and that she would still be there at the end of his degree, waiting for him. OK, he says, finally relenting. He would still apply to Cambridge. Would they release him now?

Later that day, a text message from Raha: It's over, Sameer. I don't want to see you again.

This is the moment that he will look back on as defining him: he cannot see, he cannot breathe. Why would she do this to him? He calls her multiple times; she does not pick up the phone. He sends her countless text messages. She replies to the first one. I'm sorry, it says. She doesn't reply to the rest.

But it doesn't make sense. They had talked about what came next; the plans they had made were for a future together. At school, she walks straight past him as if he doesn't exist, as if he was a shadow that simply disappeared when the sun went in. He struggles to understand how someone could be so cruel. Why does it hurt so much? He stops eating and he cannot concentrate at school. His parents are worried.

He receives a letter from Cambridge: they want to interview him. But by the time of the interview, he has not improved. He has lost a stone. His mother blows prayers over his head as he leaves on the morning of his interview; makes him drink Zamzam water for luck. Cambridge is more beautiful than he imagined, but that only makes him think of her. The interview passes in a blur. Dad picks him up, asking him question after question. I can't remember anything, he says. I'm having a complete blank. He warns his parents that he has bombed the interview, but the weeks pass and he receives a letter from the college he applied to: they want to offer him a place, all he needs is three As. He is stunned and elated. His family are ecstatic. They host a party at the house, all of the extended family come. He suddenly has a new lease of life, a new energy. Something to work towards. Something to live for. He dedicates himself to revision, gets the grades and is off to Cambridge for his first year of university.

In the summer after his first year, he bumps into Raha in Leicester town centre. She is wearing a white crop top and her shoulders are exposed. Still completely beautiful. She smiles warmly at him. They have both grown up a bit. She does not make him weak at the knees any more. He wants to reach out and hug her, but physical touch seems inappropriate for some reason, and so he says: Where did you end up?

Leicester actually, she replies, not quite meeting his eyes. I know you went to Cambridge, of course, she adds. You were in the local paper.

Yeah, he shrugs, acting casual. It's all right. Not all that.

They chat aimlessly for a few more minutes – about the weather – and then she says: Well, I'd better be going.

He nods, but he cannot resist: Raha – can I just ask you . . . why? After everything we had planned, why did you break it off with me so abruptly like that?

The air between them turns cold. She frowns, staring at him, deciding whether to give him what he's asked for because it's clear that he still doesn't know. But he's man enough to take it now. Your parents called me, she says. They told me I was going to ruin your life, that I was not the right girl for you and that if I cared about you *even a little, I would break up with you for your own good. They were your parents, she adds, eyes imploring him to understand. And I was young and stupid, so I just did what they said.*

His balance is unsteady. He's so angry he may not be breathing. The depth of this betrayal is beyond comprehension and all he can say is: They . . . they had no right to do that.

She smiles and takes his hand and he immediately begins to feel warm. I really did love you, Sameer, she says gently. She tiptoes to kiss his cheek. She smells like peaches. But we're both happy now, aren't we? You're at Cambridge, you're going to do brilliantly, I know it. I'm in a new relationship, and I'm happy.

He watches her go. Much later, he learns that she moved to Canada and married a man her family had chosen for her. He never sees her again.

12

To my first love, my beloved

2nd February 1971

Last night I dreamt about the bodies. Lifeless, bloody shapes, strewn along the road, dragged hastily into ditches. I am not one to shy away from death: I have seen it many times before. But not in such numbers, or with such carelessness.

The coup came from nowhere, it seemed. That is not to say that things have been easy – far from it, in recent years. But these were difficulties of the Asian, not difficulties of the African. I did not know that dissatisfaction fractured the government from within; I did not know what problems Amin believed he would be resolving for the Africans by taking control of this country.

You remember our old friend, Manish Mehta, who ran a small *duka* and a boutique hotel in Mburo? Lakeside Lodge, not more than ten rooms, but with such focus on detail, each room with its own personal touch. We stayed there for our fifth wedding anniversary, in the Coral Room. I close my eyes and I can picture it now: gauze curtain flapping in front of open shutters, where the walls were painted salmon pink and the door handles were shaped like shells, where the four-poster bed with white and orange linen was a steamy enclosure contained within the draped mosquito net, where your skin turned the same coral colour as I rose above you . . . I have been back to Mburo a few times since, but I never stayed in the Mehtas' hotel again.

The last time I saw Manish, he asked me for money. You would not have recognised him. He had lost so much weight! His belly was concave, cheeks hollow, and his eyes darted and flickered about the place, swivelling black beads.

Now I knew that business had been difficult lately for the Mehtas. They had been struggling to comply with the new trade licensing laws – the kind of money those laws demand businesses to show in liquid capital is no small ask for a modest business like his. I had offered to loan him the money at the time the laws came into force, but he had refused, saying he would sell the *duka* before he took money from me. But when he showed up at our door, I did not connect his appearance to his trade – I thought he was coming to tell me that he was gravely ill.

'Mrs Mehta and the children are not with you?' I said, peering behind him. 'Well, I do hope they are well. What brings you to Kampala, *bhai*?' We sat in the drawing room. He refused my offer of tea.

'Hasan *bhai*, I'm going to get straight to the point. I need money,' he said. Sweat collected at his temples in spite of the soft whirring of the fans. 'Not a lot,' he added. 'Just enough to keep us going while we wait to get out of this godforsaken country.'

I looked at him, puzzled.

'I sold the *duka* and used the money to get the licence,' he explained. 'But very quickly we found that we were not making enough money with the hotel alone. So I raised rates . . . and we lost custom. Eventually I had to use the money supporting the licence to put food on the table and, well . . . the licence was revoked. So that's it.' He hung his head, 'I have no choice now. We have to leave.'

'Manish, I told you. I can loan you the money you need for the licence.'

'No, *bhai*. The time for that has passed. Perhaps I should have accepted your offer when you first made it . . .' he ran a hand through what was left of his hair and gave me a small, sad smile. 'I never thought I would say this, but I am ready to leave. This is not my home any more.'

'Where, then, is your home?'

'We will go to Great Britain,' he said. The Mehtas had not taken Ugandan citizenship when they had the opportunity, and had instead retained their British citizenship. This was the reason the licensing laws had applied to them, as non-citizens, in the first place. 'But you know what the British have done to the system now?' Manish continued. 'It is not enough these days to have a British passport to enter the country. You must have been born in England, or have parents or grandparents born in England, to get into the country.' He shook his head in sad disbelief. 'And if you were not, then you must wait your turn in a long queue for an entry voucher. We have been lucky. An old school friend of mine works at the British High Commission and he's given me a personal assurance that we will have our entry vouchers within two weeks. But, *bhai*, we're living on nothing right now. You know I would not ask you if I was not desperate, but I need to feed my family.'

I opened my wallet and pressed a large wad of notes into his hands: enough to keep him going while his family waited for the entry vouchers, and more.

'Thank you, *bhai*. I cannot thank you enough.' He rose to leave and then hesitated. 'Hasan, can you not see what is happening? Have you not read his Common Man's Charter?'

I shrugged uncomfortably. 'It is a party manifesto. It is rhetoric, he will not do anything.'

'*Arey*, *bhai*, he has already started doing things. With the greatest respect, you are being naive. The licensing rules. The nationalisation pronouncement. The requirement for non-citizens to carry work permits. This is just the beginning.'

I did not say anything, but I could taste unease in my mouth.

'At the very least, do you have money in Britain? You can open a bank account in England easily.' Manish's voice took on a lower tone. 'Undervalue your export, overvalue your import – leave the difference abroad. Most people are doing this, you know.'

'We are not most people,' I stated, looking him straight in the eyes.

'I did not mean to offend you,' he said quickly, and he lowered his head deferentially. 'But I am telling you, as your dear friend, that you must try to get your things in order so that you can leave at the shortest notice.'

Those were the last words he said to me before he left. That was nearly a year ago.

I cannot deny that things have changed, my love, compared to thirty years ago when we were starting out. In the days with you, we benefitted from the tax system, the price-setting, the competitive market. All these wonderful incentives kept coming to our family just after we were married, because I had you, my lucky charm. Now, not only have these advantages been stripped from us, but the new government has sought positively to disadvantage us. These trade licensing rules, for example. They only apply to 'non-citizens' – meaning, of course, Asians! Worry not, the government says, the idea is not to disadvantage the Asian, but merely to require the Asian to share with the African.

But tell me, my darling, how can we share our blood, which holds the key to our success? You give an African ten shillings today and he will spend eleven shillings tomorrow. That is just their nature.

Not all Africans are the same, of course. Abdullah is a fine example of an African who thinks like an Asian. Still, we did not make him a shareholder in the business when the licensing rules came about. You see, there was some uncertainty as to whether the new rules applied to Saeed & Sons – whether, in the light of the letters I had received from the Immigration Office, I was still a 'citizen' of Uganda. (On that matter, our plans for expanding into our neighbouring countries have ground to a halt: I have not travelled on my Ugandan passport since.)

You would have asked me why we did not make Abdullah a shareholder at that point. This would have resolved the matter: with Abdullah as a 50 per cent owner, the licensing rules simply would not apply to our business. You always reserved such empathy for Abdullah, harbouring what you believed to be injustices on his behalf, though I do not recall him ever asking you to. But I am not writing to argue with you. I agree with you, my dear. Abdullah is a great asset to Saeed & Sons. No, it was not because I believed that he was lacking in any aspect that I did not make him a shareholder. The reason I did not make him a shareholder, my dear, is because Saeed & Sons is a family-owned company. Papa founded this company in the year 1910 and since then it has always been kept within the family. That chain of history is our legacy.

In any event, we did not need Abdullah to stand in as our citizen owner. We were luckier than the Mehtas. The officials enforcing the licensing scheme were happy to pocket some extra cash in exchange for applying a more liberal interpretation of the rules.

Nevertheless, Shahzeb continued to express discomfort with my citizenship status. Shortly after the Mehtas left Uganda, he asked me to apply for the British quota voucher scheme. 'Why would I do that, son?' I asked him. 'I have no intention of leaving Uganda.'

'Just in case, Papa. You know how the rules work. Ma can't apply. Only you can.'

I laughed. 'Beta, I renounced my British citizenship years ago. I have no grounds to apply for such a voucher.'

'This is what I mean, Papa. We need to fix this mess once and for all: work out how to get your British citizenship back.'

Something about the way he talked unsettled me. 'Everything I have and know is here,' I said. 'Our entire family empire has been built here. We have succeeded here and we will continue to succeed.'

'Papa,' Shahzeb said softly, 'will your love for your empire continue to blind you? Can't you see what is happening to us? Obote is a man obsessed. He does not see our success independently of their failure. He sees their success as dependent on our failure.'

I had nothing to say in response to this. Just a few days later, Shahzeb told me that both he and Samir had, behind my back, applied for the voucher scheme. 'We are not trying to leave the country,' he said. 'It is just a precautionary measure.'

'And then what happens when you get the voucher, eh? You're just going to leave your mother and me here, leave me to run the business alone?'

'Papa,' Shahzeb said gently, coming closer and trying to take my hand. I batted him away, turning so that he would not see the hurt in my eyes. 'Papa, we've been told that it is a five-year wait.'

This, I must say, caught me by surprise. The Mehtas had obtained their vouchers so quickly only a few months earlier – how had things changed so drastically in the space of such a short period? I looked at my son then, suddenly feeling sorry for him. 'Well, that is the British for you,' I said.

Now, nearly a year has passed and Shahzeb and Samir are still in the queue for a voucher. I am still a non-Ugandan, non-British, non-Indian nobody. And Amin has staged a coup.

It has been exactly one week since the coup. We were at the airport when it happened, dropping off Zakir, who was to return to the UK for university after the winter holiday. The flight was at one in the morning. We arrived just before 11 p.m., just myself, Zakir and Samir; I had told Shabnam not to come because it was so late. The airport is wonderfully quiet at that time – midweek, late night – there must have been about ten other people in sight. Almost peaceful, really. The three of us were having chai at a small table in the waiting lounge, when suddenly, at midnight: a piercing, rapid firing noise – gunshots! 'Get down!' Samir grabbed his brother with one hand and me with the other and shoved us under the table. I looked around: the other passengers were also on the floor. Within seconds, a troupe of Africans in military gear, slinging assault rifles from their shoulders, marched in.

'Get up!' the front officer barked. Nobody moved. 'There will be no flights until further notice!'

The majority of the soldiers left the room; two stayed at the door.

'What the hell is going on?' Samir muttered. One of the other passengers rose from the floor and sat back down in his seat; the soldiers did not react and eventually the rest of us resumed our seats.

'What does until further notice mean?' Zakir whispered. 'The flight is delayed, or the flight is cancelled?'

'I don't know, *beta*.' I scanned the faces of the other passengers for clues – we were all passengers for the same flight, but nobody seemed to know what was going on. Time passed slowly – 1 a.m., then 2 a.m., then 3 a.m. At 3.30, one of the soldiers made an announcement: 'There will be no flights today! Take your things and leave.'

Nervous glances were exchanged. Samir took Zakir's trunk and we made our way out of the airport and back to the car.

Army tanks had materialised in the car park and they sat staunchly, guns poised and waiting; soldiers stood to attention, some smoking, some snapping at us to move along quickly. We reached the car: the driver was sleeping on the back seat. I rapped sharply on the window. How he could sleep with the noise going on around him I will never know. By this point, the sky was tinged with the faintest thread of light, a pink-and-orange hue against a starless night. The road began to illuminate as we drove homeward.

What can I tell you next, Amira? We came across a body five minutes into the journey, on the road. I did not realise what it was at first – perhaps a deer? But the shape was too long, too slim. The driver swerved to the other side of the road as we approached and it became clear: it was a man. In military uniform, twisted awkwardly. 'Should we stop?' Samir breathed.

'There is nothing we can do for him,' I replied.

It was not the last body we saw.

It was nearly six in the morning when we reached home. The roads were crawling with soldiers. The whole house was awake and seated in the drawing room on our arrival; Shabnam ran into my arms and burst into tears. 'We were so worried! We've just been hearing gunshots and explosions. I think they set off a bomb somewhere in the middle of the night.'

'Obote was not in the country, he went for the Commonwealth conference,' Samir remarked. 'There must have been some kind of coup by the army.'

'Abdullah's son is in the army,' I said. 'Ibrahim.' Silence. 'I will go to the office to see Abdullah today.'

'No, please,' Shabnam said. 'The roads are full of tanks, you can still hear the soldiers firing shots. None of us should go anywhere today.'

'Shabnam,' I began sternly, but – seeing the look on her face – I tailed off. '*OK. I won't go. It's OK.*'

Nothing aired on television. Radio Uganda blared out the processional, clanging sounds of horns and trumpets, nothing else. At around 7.30 a.m., we heard a news bulletin from the *BBC*: fighting, troop movements, gunfire in Kampala city.

We ate lunch in terse silence. Cups of chai circulated, largely left untouched. Finally, in the late afternoon, the music playing on Radio Uganda stopped and a heavily accented man's voice began to speak in stumbling English: 'The army has taken power from Obote and handed it over to a fellow soldier, General Idi Amin Dada. Obote's government is corrupt. He has failed to hold elections in eight years. His policies benefit only the rich, big men, who have fleets of cars and buses and even aeroplanes, while the rest of Uganda suffers high taxes and prices and becomes poorer. Obote has favoured the Langi, his own tribe, who have the most senior roles in army and government.'

It went on like this for a few minutes, and we all listened attentively. Was it really the end of Obote's regime? I began to feel a nervous sense of excitement.

That evening, Amin Dada himself graced our ears with a personal broadcast.

'Fellow countrymen and well-wishers of Uganda. I address you today at a very important hour in the history of our nation. A short while ago, members of the armed forces placed this country in my hands. I am not a politician, but a professional soldier. I am therefore a man of few words and I shall, as a result, be brief. Throughout my professional life I have emphasised that the military must support a civilian government that has the support of the people, and I have not changed from that position.

'Matters now prevailing in Uganda forced me to accept the task that has been given to me by the men of the Uganda armed forces. I will, however, accept this task on the understanding that mine will be a thoroughly caretaking administration, pending an early return to civilian rule. Free and fair general elections will soon be held in the country, given a stable security situation. Everybody will be free to participate in these elections. For that reason, political exiles are free to return to this country and political prisoners held on unspecified and unfounded charges will be released forthwith.'

There is jubilation in Kampala. The streets have been filled with people cheering, waving green branches in front of army vehicles, drinking and dancing with men in military uniform. But after 7 p.m. there is a strict curfew and soldiers patrol the streets.

There is a change in the breeze, my dear; the air is different somehow, perhaps sweeter. A new era has been ushered in with the dawn and now all we can do is wait to see what it will bring. I pray to Allah it is for the best for my family and me.

PART II

13

The lights have been dimmed, but Sameer cannot sleep. He looks out of the window; small ice crystals are collecting behind the plastic, patterns against the bluest sky. He raises a fingertip to the window, pressing the place where the snow-flake shapes are beyond his reach; a sticky impression of him is left on the windowpane.

He has not slept in over twenty-four hours: since boarding the flight, through the short stopover in Dubai, and on to his final destination, Entebbe. His AirPods remain in his pocket, the remote control for the miniature television screen has not been touched. His mind races continuously: *It's about time you saw your brother for what he truly is – selfish*; *We were doing what is best for the family, you've never thought about that, have you, always doing what's best for you*; *You have no right to go to Singapore.* The awkward week that followed, during which he spent most of his time out of the house, hanging out with the boys or visiting a friend who no longer recognised him; his surprise that he had felt hurt when his mother did not ask where he was going or when he would be coming back. When he was in the house, there was no conversation at mealtimes, and neither of his parents would look him in the eye.

He had waited until the morning of the flight to tell them that he'd been in contact with Mr Shah, and that he was going to visit him in Uganda. His father had looked at him properly for the first time in a week. 'Why are you going there?' he'd asked, shaking his head disbelievingly. Sameer had shrugged and said nothing. He did not really know why he was going.

He just knew that he needed to get away from Leicester and London. Uganda seemed as good a place as any. 'You won't find whatever it is you're looking for there,' were the last words his father said to him before he left for Heathrow.

A loud, two-toned beep jerks Sameer from these thoughts as the flight attendant announces through the intercom: 'Ladies and gentlemen, we are now beginning our descent into Entebbe. Please make sure your seat backs and tray tables are in the upright position. Thank you.'

From the window, he can see squares of different shades of green, neatly organised like a patchwork quilt, rising into hills, scattered with red and white buildings. He was not expecting to find that it almost looks like the English countryside – this is not how he pictured Africa; he had imagined a dry, arid landscape, dusty and barren. As the plane draws closer to the ground, passing over a gleaming body of barely rippling water that stretches beyond view, a nervous pang passes through him and he wonders for a moment what he is doing: why has he travelled here to meet someone he barely knows? Then the plane doors are opened and warm air hits him. He inhales deeply.

Mr Shah is waiting in arrivals, waving, a huge smile spread across his face. Standing slightly behind him is a tall, wiry black man, hopping from foot to foot.

'Sameer, *beta*,' Mr Shah pulls Sameer into a hug that smells like cigars and cologne. 'Hope you had a good flight. Long, isn't it, from London? Nothing direct. Did you sleep? You must be tired.'

The man standing behind Mr Shah exclaims: 'You are welcome!' and takes the handle of Sameer's bag. There is a short tug of war – Mr Shah says: 'Let him take the bags, this is Paul, our driver. He's been with our family for years' – and Sameer lets go reluctantly.

Paul nods, revealing beautifully white teeth. 'I am happy you have come to my country,' he says, and his smile is filled with such joy that Sameer's face can't help but respond.

'We both are,' Mr Shah says, patting Sameer on the back. 'Come on then, to Kampala.'

Outside, the sky is a bright and brilliant blue, with not a cloud in sight. The ground underfoot is concrete, but not grey like English concrete. It is concrete the colour of warm orange dust. Against the blue sky and the red land the grass is a sharp, bright green. It is a trinity of colours that Sameer will see again and again. A Pepsi advert looms overhead on a blue sign: WELCOME TO THE PEARL OF AFRICA.

There is no abeyance of colour as they walk towards where the car is parked; among the greenery of the trees spring red and yellow flowers. A huge flock of birds suddenly swoops over their heads, blotting the sun momentarily. Sameer stares as one of the birds breaks off, landing on the side mirror of the car in front of him. It's beautiful, with a black head melting into grey and white wings. 'What are these birds?' he asks as they stop in front of a silver Mercedes S-Class. Paul flips out the keys and remotely unlocks the car, hurriedly moving around to open Sameer's door for him before placing his bag in the boot.

'Ah, you're a bird lover?' Mr Shah says, climbing into the car, and before Sameer has the chance to respond – 'Well, you've come to the right place. We have over a thousand species here in Uganda. Those you just saw are nothing special, common migrant birds from Europe and Asia. White-winged terns. Actually, they brought bird flu here a few years back, so we were trying to exterminate them for a while. Couldn't work out how to stop them from coming back, though – you can't exactly stop birds from flying, can you? They don't recognise borders – they go where they will . . .' Sameer shivers: the

AC has been enthusiastically cranked up by Paul; it feels sub-zero. 'In a way, I suppose, we are all birds of Uganda,' Mr Shah chuckles. 'Anyway, just wait until you see what else we have to offer. You'll be blown away. I'm going to take you to the safari parks, the gorilla reserves – there's so much to see, two weeks hardly feels like enough time! Well, I might not take you myself, personally –' he adds quickly, as his phone starts to ring – 'but you've got to see it all. Will you excuse me?'

Mr Shah speaks rapidly, and only partly in English – Sameer tries to follow the conversation but quickly gets lost. His hand moves instinctively for his phone; he wishes they had waited a bit longer at the airport – perhaps he could have got a Ugandan SIM card. Instead he stares out of the window, drinking in the landscape rolling by: rust-red earth barely holding back jungle foliage, trailing vines and leaves the size of a dog, red-roofed housing developments sprouting between trees on either side of the highway. There are birds everywhere: swooping between the leaves of the jungle and in front of the cars on the road; watching them disinterestedly from the grassy mounds; silhouetted resplendently atop tall, branchless trees. Black hadada ibis with iridescent green wings; small, fluttering, yellow-bellied weavers; marabou storks with hooked beaks and wrinkled, wobbling necks.

As they cruise down the dual carriageway (which is better than Sameer thought it would be: he had, for some reason, imagined potholed dirt tracks rather than maintained roads), Sameer does not tire of the scenery or the wildlife. It feels like barely a moment has passed before Mr Shah's call has ended and he says: 'Sorry, business . . .'

'Speaking of business,' Sameer says, tearing his eyes away from the window. 'I'd really like to see what you do. Is there any opportunity for me to shadow you?'

'Of course, *beta* – nice that someone takes an interest. Settle in, enjoy your first weekend in Uganda, and I'll bring you along on Monday if you like.'

'That would be great – thank you.'

'It's a family business; my brother and I, we run it together. My nephew's involved as well, we try to keep the management in the family, know what I mean? I've got two daughters, no sons I'm afraid. My eldest is married, she moved to Kenya, that's where her husband is from, very wealthy family, almost as wealthy as us, ha ha. No kids yet, but it's still early days, they've only been married for a couple of years. Nice ceremony, we had it here at the Kampala Serena, then we all went to Nairobi for the *walima*. My youngest is at university – in London actually, at the SOAS, did I mention this to you when I was in England? Bright girl but studying history of art of all things,' he winces. 'Doesn't give me high hopes that she'll want to come back to the business when she's done, but let's see. Anyway, she's home for the summer, you'll meet her . . .' he tails off, not noticing that Sameer has not said a word during this monologue. 'Anyway, enough chat about business! You just wait until we get home – Rehana has had a feast prepared for you, everything Ugandan. If you think you've had mogo before, you're wrong, you can't get cassava in England like the cassava you can get here,' and then hurriedly, 'though I must say I enjoyed your mother's cooking very much when I came, of course. You like fruit? You won't find juicier fruit anywhere else in the world, the pineapple, the papaya and of course the bananas . . .'

Sameer lets Mr Shah carry on like this, nodding and smiling at appropriate intervals. As they enter Kampala, the traffic begins to thicken. The road is still good, but the foliage has disappeared, replaced by precarious-looking buildings, stacked atop one another and flanked by giant painted signs screaming the sale of various wares: fridges, tyres, batteries, sports betting. They pass a bank that looks like it was built in the 1920s and is in serious need of an update; the words 'FIRST BANK' have been painted on in letters that are fading so that the sign looks, from a distance, like it reads 'R ANK'. Corrugated tin walls obscure some of Sameer's view; the tin has been painted blue and advertises bottles that look suspiciously like Coke, Fanta and Sprite but are branded 'Riham'. As they approach a roundabout, what seem to be thousands of motorcycles and pedal bikes appear from nowhere and flood the roads. Some passengers are wearing helmets, most are not; some of the bikes have as many as five people stacked on the seats.

Eventually, the mania gives way to wider roads, the traffic dies away and the green foliage returns. Neatly trimmed hedges border Sameer's left, interrupted only by towering steel gates. A large, grassy parkland borders his right. It is a completely different world from the frenzy of the town. 'Welcome to Kololo,' Mr Shah says.

On a quiet road lined with acacia and banana trees, the car stops in front of a wrought-iron gate, its gunmetal-grey bars intertwined with gold leaves. The gates open – 'We have a twenty-four-hour security system, manned in the day by our security guards, and at night by camera' – into a wide driveway, with stone cherubs playing in a fountain centrepiece. Paul stops the car near the front patio and opens each of their doors.

The Shahs' house is palatial. In the entrance hall alone, huge patterned carpets rest on white marble floors; glitzy chandeliers hang from high ceilings; crystal bowls of potpourri sit on mahogany tables. A huge silver mirror hangs on the wall, spanning nearly the length of the room and exaggerating its proportions. The faint smell of food makes Sameer's stomach grumble.

A plump lady comes bursting through a door and into the hall, dressed in an embroidered turquoise salwar kameez that emphasises the greenness of her eyes. There is gold on her wrists and neck and ears; make-up sits in the creases of her face; she brings with her the scent of something floral and soft. She gives Mr Shah a quick kiss on the cheek and envelops Sameer in a hug. 'I've heard so much about you, *beta*,' she says, eyes following Mr Shah, who disappears through a door leading off the hall. 'How lovely to have the Saeed's son staying with us.'

'Well, I'm very grateful to you for letting me stay,' Sameer replies politely, extricating himself from her embrace. 'My mum and dad send their *salaams*.' There is a brief silence in which he feels slightly awkward. 'You have a beautiful house,' he adds.

'Thank you, *beta*,' Mrs Shah smiles, gesturing around the room. 'The carpets are Persian – we have a collection throughout the house. This one is from Shiraz. We bought that mirror in Goa, actually. And those little tables. Lovely trip we had there a few years back, it's a nice holiday destination. Have you been?'

He shakes his head.

'Well, you must if you get the chance. Anyway, Paul will show you to your room. I'll go and check on dinner. You must be hungry, *hai na*?'

He had not noticed that Paul was behind them, but there he is, standing in the shadows, carrying Sameer's bag in one hand. 'Follow me,' Paul says, leading the way down the hall. A hideous and violent abstract painting of reds and browns hangs portentously over the stairwell. Trying not to look at it, Sameer follows Paul up a spiral staircase, where he is shown to a room that is bigger than his parents' bedroom back in Leicester.

'Anything you need, you just ask me,' Paul says, standing in the doorway. 'I show you swimming pool now?'

They leave the house from the front door and walk round to a large beautifully landscaped garden, where Nandi flame trees sport bright red flowers, guava fruit hangs from swollen branches, and small purple buds sit shyly among the green leaves of jacaranda that are almost beginning to blossom. It looks like a domesticated, vividly colourful jungle – Sameer half expects a leopard to appear slinking lazily from between the bushes. Past a patioed area with tables and chairs, a small rose garden, and they turn a corner to find a pool in the shape of a teardrop. Sameer can see a tennis court in the distance.

'Nice?' Paul grins. Sameer nods, slightly dumbfounded: this house is like something from a movie.

'Hello! You are most welcome,' a young Ugandan lady carrying a platter of drinks in glass bottles appears from nowhere, smiling as she extends the tray. There is a wide variety of soft drinks and Sameer selects a Coke Zero, surprised to see all of the brands he knows. Before he can thank her, she has disappeared. Paul takes the bottle from Sameer's hands and flicks the lid open with a bottle opener before handing it back to him. Seamless. 'OK, please,' he says, 'we go to the dining room now.'

He follows Paul back into the house to the dining room. A long mahogany table stretches out, large enough to seat more than a dozen people. Paul pulls out one of the chairs for him to sit down. 'You will eat here,' he says as he slips out the door. 'And don't forget – anything you need, you ask me.'

'Thanks so much,' Sameer calls after him, feeling a little overwhelmed. He waits, looking around. A Monet-style painting of water lilies (the first art he has seen that he can bear to look at) hangs above a fireplace at the end of the room. His hosts have disappeared. Just as he is thinking he might take a shower or – curiosity tugging at him – try to explore the rest of the house, the door opens.

'Hello, you must be Sameer.' A young woman is standing in the doorway. 'My dad told me you were coming.' Long brown hair streaked with blonde reaches the small of her back. She's wearing a sleeveless kurta that exposes the softness of her arms; an orange Hermès bangle adorns one wrist and a gold-and-white Omega watch the other.

'Hi,' he says. 'You're at SOAS, right? I'm sorry, I don't know your –'

'Aliyah,' she says, an amused expression on her face. 'Typical of my father to tell you where I'm studying but not tell you my name.' She rolls her eyes and he notices that they are green, just like her mother's. 'Well, look, dinner won't be ready for –' glancing at her watch – 'another thirty minutes probably. You don't have to just sit here and wait.'

'Thanks, I think I might take a shower,' he says at the same time that she starts to say: 'I'd be happy to show you –'

She breaks off, smiling. 'Of course,' she says. 'Someone will call you for dinner.'

He is about to ask her what she was going to say, but tiredness overwhelms him. He retraces his steps to the bedroom, strips and jumps in the shower. The hot water beats down on his back, massaging his body, relaxing his muscles. What a way to live, he thinks, as he stands under the showerhead. The feeling is so good that he does not want to get out.

Sameer is woken by a knock on the door. Mildly disorientated, he rubs his eyes and takes in his surroundings, then scrambles to his feet, wrapping a towel around his waist. 'One sec,' he calls, as he hops towards the door and opens it a crack.

The same lady who brought him drinks gives him a smile. 'Dinner is served, Mr Saeed.'

'Thank you,' he replies, wondering how long he has been asleep. 'What's your name?' he adds, but she has disappeared once again.

Mrs Shah and Aliyah are seated when Sameer comes down – there is no sign of Mr Shah. A row of chafing dishes heated by candles have been laid out along the table.

'Please,' Mrs Shah says, beckoning him to sit opposite her. 'We don't normally eat here, it's for dinner parties, guests, you know? But it's your first day here and you are our guest, of course. *Hai*, the house seems so empty since Asiya moved to Kenya and Aliyah went to university. If only we had had a son, then his wife could have moved here! Aliyah, I hope your future husband moves into this house, otherwise we'll have no use for it at all.'

Aliyah reaches for her glass of water.

'Where is the rest of the family?' Sameer asks politely. 'Uncle mentioned working with his brother and nephew?' He can't help but think that if it were his family living in such a big house, they would all live together, brothers, sisters, cousins and all.

'Sajid lives closer to the sugar plantation, though his son, Raheem, lives not far from here on the border of Kololo – they have a wonderful little place, you should see it. The rest of us are spread out – I have some family living in Jinja, some up near Kidepo. Anyway, we should eat,' Mrs Shah looks over her shoulder, nodding at the housemaid, who hurries forward and removes the lids from each of the dishes. Steam rises in swirls: it is a feast fit for a small country. 'We won't wait for Sohail. He's always late.'

'Really, Auntie, you shouldn't have gone to such effort,' Sameer says, staring at the exorbitant amount of food. It smells incredible.

'It's no bother,' she says, standing to survey her handiwork.

'Now, you must try everything, *beta*. We've got curried cabbage, fried *emputta* – that's freshwater perch from Lake Victoria, you like fish, don't you? – mutton pilau, chicken curry. Oh, I also asked the cook to make some traditional Ugandan dishes for you – *luwombo*, right here, it's a sort of beef soup, quite delicious. And chapattis and *matoke* are here. You know *matoke*? The Ugandan banana, it's more savoury than sweet. You can eat it with the groundnut sauce.' She loads his plate so high that he begins to sweat just looking at it.

Just before they start eating, Mr Shah enters. 'Sorry, sorry, business call,' he says, taking a seat next to Sameer. 'Please don't wait for me to start.'

Sameer puts a spoonful of *luwombo* into his mouth. 'This is really delicious,' he says to Mrs Shah, wondering – given Mrs Shah's mention of a cook – whether she had actually made any of the food herself.

'So, Sameer, do you have any plans for what you want to do while you're here?' Aliyah asks.

'I haven't thought about it too much,' he says. 'I guess I'd like to see the house where my family used to live. And the stores they used to own.' He had not had any plan to do so when he organised this trip, but now he is here, it seems silly not to.

'Well, we can certainly help you with that,' Mr Shah says, as he puts a parcel of chapatti and chicken in his mouth; this does not deter him from continuing. 'Your father used to live up on Nakasero Hill. It's not too far from here.'

After dinner, the house servants come in and clear away the dishes. Sameer marvels at the fact that no one has to leave the table: both Mr Shah and Aliyah are looking at their phones; Mrs Shah is instructing one of the housemaids. Sameer wonders if Mr and Mrs Shah even know what their kitchen looks like.

They retire to the drawing room, where Mr Shah lights up a cigar. Mrs Shah turns the T.V. to a black-and-white Bollywood film.

'Do you want to come out and see some of Uganda?' Aliyah asks in a low voice, as if to say: I know spending the evening here is going to be so boring. The only thing Sameer really wants to do is sleep. He looks towards Mr and Mrs Shah.

'Yes, go, please, you young things,' Mr Shah says, with a wave of his hand.

'Thanks, Papa,' Aliyah says, blowing a kiss in Mr Shah's direction. She turns to Sameer. 'Just let me run upstairs and grab my bag. Paul will take us.'

Paul drops them off at a nondescript building that's only a five-minute walk from the house.

'It's a private members' club,' Aliyah explains as they enter the building. She flashes a card and a smile at the security guards (both wearing AK-47s slung over their shoulders, Sameer notices); they surrender the contents of their pockets to an X-ray machine, pass under a metal detector, and the guards promptly call a lift near the door.

The lift opens into a softly lit rooftop bar, where house music is quietly playing. They take a table among potted olive trees and lights strung along wooden trellises. The bar hosts a mixture of people, black, white, South Asian and even South East Asian – but they all have one thing in common as far as Sameer can tell: everyone is wealthy.

'This place has just been taken over by new management, they've given it a new look, rustic chic – that's what's in now,' Aliyah says as they sit down. She picks up the bar menu, looking at her phone. 'Some of my friends may join us a little later, that OK?'

'Of course.'

'I think I'm just going to get a Bellini,' Aliyah says, glancing at the drinks menu.

'I'll have a Coke.'

'Oh, right – OK, in that case, so will I,' Aliyah says quickly.

'No – it's completely fine if you want to drink. I'm just knackered.'

The drinks arrive; Aliyah opens a tab. Sameer feels relaxed and sleepy. The night air is warm and his jacket hangs redundantly behind him. This is what Singapore will be like, he thinks. Rustic chic. They talk about London; he asks her what she wants to do in the future, whether she will join her father's business or do something completely different. 'Oh, I don't know,' she says, ordering another Bellini. 'It's too early to tell. I think I want to start my own business, you know. Collecting art.'

He has no idea how this is a business. 'Sounds cool,' he supplies lamely.

'Rani!' Aliyah squeals suddenly, leaping up to embrace a girl who has just walked in. Introductions are made, a few more of Aliyah's friends arrive, all girls, all South Asian. Sameer is relieved he does not have to lead the conversation: he sits back, nodding every now and again and nearly dozing off as the girls chatter around him about who they went to school with and what the other people in the bar are wearing.

For the first time in weeks, Sameer sleeps properly. He wakes up late, around midday, feeling slightly embarrassed. No one came to wake him up. He unlocks his phone. A single WhatsApp from his mother stares sadly from the screen: *Have you arrived safely?*

Downstairs, the house is large and empty. He wanders through the rooms, marvelling at the decor (tribal masks that remind him of Kampala Nights' interior, what looks suspiciously like a pair of rhinoceros horns, cowhide rugs and leopard-skin hangings) and wondering how much everything must have cost.

'Hello, good morning!'

A cheery voice makes Sameer jump and he tears his eyes away from the leopard spots to look behind him. The Shahs' housemaid is smiling at him. 'Morning,' he says.

'No one is home, they wanted to let you sleep. Would you like some breakfast?'

Sameer nods and thanks her, and this time he gets her name – Ama.

He sits at a breakfast bar in the enormous kitchen, asking her questions while she makes him a plate of scrambled eggs and toast (he had suggested that he could do it himself if she showed him where the food was, but she had just laughed). He doesn't want to eat alone, and so the questions keep flowing, while Ama stands and answers patiently, politely: 'Do the Shahs have many people working here?'

'There is myself, I am doing the cleaning and looking after the house. Paul is the driver. And the cook, Jonathon, he comes in the afternoons.'

'So do you live here?'

'Me? I do not, I live with my family in Kampala. Paul lives here, he is from the village, he goes home when he takes holiday. Please, you need anything, you just ask me or Paul,' and Ama gives Sameer such a genuine smile that he immediately gets the sense that nothing would be too much trouble for these people.

'Thank you,' he says, feeling slightly uncomfortable, but smiling back at her all the same. 'I'd like to walk to Nakasero now if that works with the Shahs' schedule. Do you know what time they'll be back?'

Ama shakes her head. 'We do not advise walking, it is very far,' she says. 'Better to ask Paul to take you later. He has taken

Mrs Shah to the shopping centre, but I can find out what time he can come back, maybe they won't be so long.'

Sameer checks Google Maps – his family's old house is a thirty-five-minute walk away, no highway crossings or main roads. 'It's fine,' he says. 'I can walk, don't worry.'

Ama wrings her hands with a worried smile. 'OK, please. I will tell them where you go. If you come back late, you call us – you should not walk at night.'

'Got it. Thank you again for breakfast.'

The afternoon is mild but humid and very quickly he starts to sweat as the walk is determinedly uphill. Google Maps takes him through the suburbs, past grand-looking barbed-fence houses with signs denoting ambassadorial residences, up streets where the pavement is a dirt track or disappears into no pavement at all (he walks cautiously on the roads), past a vast bright green golf course.

And then, there it is: number 44. Sameer stands outside the steel gates, staring, suddenly apprehensive. He imagines his father leaving the gates to walk to school, the grandparents he never knew standing in the exact same spot as he is standing in now. Who lives in this house? Who has replaced the foot-steps of his grandparents?

If he doesn't enter now, he never will. He forces himself to push the pedestrian gate, which opens to a paved drive con-taining a few old cars. Beyond the drive is a large red-roofed two-storey house fronted by white pillars supporting a shady veranda that is overwhelmed by bright pink bougainvillea. It is grand and old-fashioned; in sepia, Sameer can see a young version of his father skipping down from the porch and onto the drive.

A man steps out of a kiosk with a baton. Dogs in a pen nearby begin to bark. 'Hello, how are you. What is your name?' the guard asks. 'Who are you here to see?'

'I'm not here to see anyone in particular,' Sameer says hesitantly. 'My name is Sameer Saeed. My father used to live here.'

'Please wait here.' The guard points to a chair on the veranda and disappears round the back of the house.

Sameer sits under the shade of the bougainvillea, admiring the way it sprawls, untamed, over the white stucco front; waiting, waiting, until – the front door swings open. A man is standing in the doorway, leaning on a walking stick and surveying him through large glasses. 'You are a Saeed?' the man asks.

Sameer stands. He can see children have lined up behind the man, hiding; one of them lets out a squeal as he catches her eye and she ducks out of sight. 'Yes,' he says, extending his right hand. The man shakes it. 'My father is Rizwan Saeed. My grandfather was Hasan Saeed, he used to live here I think?'

'Yes,' the man says, 'yes, he did. Please, come in.'

The house does not compare to the Shahs' in terms of grandeur; the large entrance hall, flooded with daylight from open windows protected by mosquito netting, is bare save for a shoe cabinet on which stands a small vase packed with pink flowers. In the drawing room, where Sameer is invited to take a seat on one of two rather miserable looking sofas, there is no more than a couple of brightly patterned floor cushions, a drawing cabinet, a coffee table. Did the room look so . . . well, bare, when his father lived here?

'So, Sameer,' says the man, settling opposite him on the sofa. 'You finally came.'

'Were you expecting me?'

'We weren't quite sure what to expect, you know, after everything . . .'

Sameer wants to ask the man what he means, but they are interrupted by a woman entering the room, holding a glass of a pink liquid. She offers it to him, unsmiling. He looks at her, dressed head to toe in black with a sheer black scarf draped over her head, and is immediately struck by her beauty. Her cheekbones are high and shining, her eyes large and wide, her lips two-toned, one dark brown, the other deep pink. There is a small black mark somewhere above her lip, deeper than the darkness of her skin, a beauty spot. He blinks. 'Thank you,' he says quickly. 'What is it?'

'Tamarind juice,' she replies shortly, not looking at him and taking a seat next to the man with the walking stick. Her voice rings like bells chiming; this manner of speaking – softly, sweetly – is distinctly Ugandan.

'This is my daughter, Maryam. She is a doctor,' the man says proudly. 'My name is Musa. My grandfather knew your grandfather.'

'Forgive me,' Sameer says, taking a sip of the juice and marvelling at the taste. It is unlike anything he has ever tasted before: woody and earthy but sweet, disconcerting. He steals a glance at Maryam, who is staring resolutely into the distance. 'But I actually know very little about my grandfather – how are you connected to him? I would love to find out more about him.'

Maryam turns to her father and begins to speak rapidly in a language that Sameer does not understand. She is gesticulating; despite the low volume of her voice, and the melodic nature of its sound, the tone is aggrieved. He wonders whether this is the limit of Ugandan anger, still so gentle. Although concerned to know what has caused her distress, he's also pleased for the outburst: it gives him full permission to stare at her openly, undisturbed. He never knew that he was capable of thinking of black women as being this beautiful – perhaps because he's never been with one before, although he remembers suddenly, almost victoriously, that he had kissed a mixed-race girl in a club once. And, just as suddenly, he feels ashamed at these thoughts and his face burns.

Her father responds to her sharply and she folds her arms across her chest.

'Sorry, what were you asking me?' Musa says, turning to Sameer, half grimacing and offering no further explanation. 'Oh yes, how did our grandfathers know each other,' he pauses, throwing a glance at Sameer, eyes narrowed. 'You don't know who we are?'

Sameer shakes his head. Should he?

'I see,' Musa nods. He almost sounds relieved. 'Well, when your grandfather left Uganda, he gave this house to my grandfather. My family – my parents, my daughter, my brothers and sisters, their families – we all live here together, as many of us as can fit. Just like your family used to, all of them under this one roof. We have a lot to thank your grandfather for.'

Sameer is watching Maryam, who has something of a look of distaste on her face. She has not looked at him once.

'So our grandparents were good friends,' Sameer concludes: they must have been for his grandfather to have left them the house. 'My grandfather used to run a store in Kampala. Do you know anything about that?'

Musa smiles sheepishly. 'Well, actually, your grandfather also left my grandfather the store. So we run the store now. It is still called Saeed & Sons, believe it or not.'

Although Sameer's father rarely talks about it, Sameer is aware of the history, the forced expulsion, the fact that they were not allowed to take anything with them. But he had never really given much thought to their belongings, their businesses – all the things that they had to leave behind – and what had become of them. By the time he was old enough to be conscious of it, his family were already very comfortable and he had never known anything else. There had never been any need to investigate the history before. 'I'd like to visit, if that's OK?'

There is a short pause before Musa says: 'Of course. You are welcome to have a look around any time, son.'

'Right,' Maryam speaks up. For the first time since she came in to the room, she looks him straight in the eye. He looks straight back and feels a frisson of energy, like something has snapped, or welded. Her chin is tilted slightly upwards so she can look down at him along the bridge of her nose; her long, slender neck – in spite of the attempt of the scarf draped over her head – exposed, pulsating. She is indignant and exquisite. 'Let's get to the point,' she says shortly, although her voice is still soft. 'Are you here to take it back? Is that what you want? This house? The store?'

'What?' he stares for a moment, confused. 'No. You've got it all wrong. That's not why I'm here. Not at all.' She is still studying him distrustfully and he can't tear his eyes away from hers. They have been looking at each other for so long now that it almost seems rude to have excluded Musa from their gaze. 'I wouldn't have any power to do that anyway,' Sameer adds. 'All these things, they belong to you.'

Musa exhales deeply and Sameer breaks the spell, looking away from Maryam to her father. 'You are a good man,' Musa says, 'just like your grandfather.'

'We don't know that yet,' Sameer hears Maryam mutter, but her father does not seem to notice.

They speak for a little longer (Maryam says nothing, although the animosity seems to have left her); Musa tells him that he was very young when Sameer's grandfather left Uganda, but that his father knew him well. Sameer is eager to find out as much as he can, surprising himself at his thirst for more knowledge of his family's history.

'Maryam can take you to the store,' Musa says, attempting

to rise. Maryam rushes to his aid, giving him the walking stick. 'My father is working there today.'

'*Taata*, I am very busy,' she begins in a low tone as she helps him up. 'You know I have lots to do –'

But her father shushes her and insists – 'He is our guest. Do you need a place to stay, Sameer?' Musa asks as he shuffles towards the door. No questions are asked about how long he might be staying for. Sameer notices the expression on Maryam's face freeze.

'Thank you, Uncle, that's very kind,' he says, 'but I have somewhere to stay – not far from here.'

'Well, you are welcome in this house any time. Please treat it as your own.'

'*Taata!*' Maryam protests, but her father has already hobbled out of the room. She throws Sameer a doubtful look, lips pursed. He experiences a strange thrill that they have been left alone together; he tries to smile as warmly as he can, but he ends up baring his teeth and she looks at him like he is deranged.

'Look –' he begins, but she interrupts him.

'Come on,' she says begrudgingly, drawing her scarf closer to her, tighter around her neck, 'I'll take you to the store.'

As she walks out of the room and he follows, he can't help but stare; Maryam's buttocks struggle to be hidden by the fall of her dress. He shakes his head to clear his mind of these thoughts.

It smells like cinnamon inside her blue Toyota Corolla. 'Thanks very much for taking me,' he says, and she nods curtly. He wants to make conversation but he doesn't know what to say, and she says nothing, so they drive out of the Nakasero suburb and onto Kampala Road in silence. They are quickly stalled by traffic; outside, it is wild and noisy. The traffic is gridlocked, and the vehicles chug out black fumes. People piled atop each other on motorbikes, some carrying babies, others carrying furniture, move between the four-wheeled vehicles, teetering dangerously. He sees livestock among people in an open-backed truck, cages of chickens squawking, deformed street beggars, people walking between the cars selling water, groundnuts, candies, anything. Still, the jungle green appears through the cracks of the pavement – wherever it can, it tries; among the chaos, there is a persistent struggle for life.

A small girl with a runny nose in torn, dirty clothing knocks on the window as they wait in the traffic. Sameer instinctively reaches for his wallet, taking out some notes. Maryam watches him out of the corner of her eye.

'I wouldn't do that if I were you,' she says eventually. 'If you open the window, they might take your whole wallet.'

'Oh.' He immediately puts his wallet back into his pocket.

'She'll be OK. Look, she's already wandered off.'

She is right – the little girl has gone. 'Thanks for the heads-up,' he says, happy to have a dialogue going. 'Look. I'm sorry to burst in on your family like this – I really didn't mean to impose. And I'm sorry to inconvenience you like this.'

She does not say anything and so he carries on talking, telling her that his ancestors were brought here from India by the British, that his father and his grandfather were born here, that they ended up in Britain through no choice of their own. She doesn't say much but eventually offers, 'We have all been affected by British colonialism.'

The store is not far from Nakasero market, on a street lined with shops at the bottom of large two- or three-storey buildings – these shops sell everything from mobile phones to hardware, bathroom sinks and tubs to appliances. He marvels at the number of shops with Asian names – Zara's Boutique, Alam & Sons, Anika's Jewellery – but, squinting from behind the glass, they mostly seem to be manned by Ugandans.

She parks the car in front of his grandfather's old shop. It is strange to see his name on the storefront, in red letters against a yellow background: SAEED & SONS – and in small, italicised lettering underneath: *For your everyday needs and more!* The wording has faded rather sadly and he wonders if it has been updated at all since his family left.

Inside, any vestige of the store's Indian history is gone; it now sells brightly patterned *gomesi* and African foodstuffs. The shelves are stuffed with clothing, containers, detergent, soaps. There are so many things haphazardly organised that Sameer is slightly taken aback. A boy working on the shop floor greets Maryam with enthusiasm and openly stares at Sameer with curiosity. Maryam asks the boy a question and he points towards the checkout desk. An old man sits in a chair behind the till, his tight black curls peppered with grey, face gently lined.

'Jjajja,' Maryam says loudly, pushing Sameer forward slightly. 'This is the Saeed grandson.'

The man gets to his feet, taller and sturdier than Sameer expected, and a huge smile spreads across his face. He is missing two of his teeth, which for some reason makes Sameer's heart swell. 'Hasan Saeed?' the man asks. Sameer nods.

The man's wrinkled eyes instantly fill with tears. 'I can tell, you know. You look like him. He was darker than you, but you have the same way about you,' he says. 'What's your name, son?'

'Sameer,' he responds and then adds, 'I've come to find out more about my family and their history.'

'Wonderful. We are so happy to have you. My name is Ibrahim. My father and your grandfather were close, very close. Saeed & Sons was the number-one general goods store back in those days, before all these large supermarkets came, you know? And your grandfather, he didn't just have a store in

Kampala. There were at least another two or three in other parts of Uganda. In Mbarara, I remember, there was a store being run by his daughter, and there was one in Jinja too.'

'I didn't know,' Sameer replies, wondering if he will be able to visit these places, wondering who runs them now.

'My father was the general manager of the Saeed & Sons stores,' Ibrahim continues, 'and everyone knew them – my father and your grandfather – the two of them, the perfect example of a black–Asian working partnership. That is what they were, partners,' he says proudly, pausing for a moment. 'But then we lost them both and we lost the stores for nearly ten years. It is just this one now, the first Saeed & Sons store, this is all that remains.'

'How long you going to be talking for? Can a woman get some things round here, or should I go somewhere else, eh?' A woman holding a few items in her hands speaks up from behind Sameer.

Ibrahim laughs and apologises profusely. 'Eh, sorry, Mama,' he says cajolingly. 'I didn't see you there. This is my son, he has come to Uganda for the first time.'

Sameer nods and the lady is appeased. 'You are most welcome,' she says sweetly. 'How do you like Uganda?'

'It's only my first day,' he admits. 'But so far, it's beautiful.' He glances at Maryam, unthinkingly, and receives a rush of pleasure at the sight of a small smile.

'Listen,' says Ibrahim, 'you will have to come to our house for dinner. There is much to be said, and we must talk. You are welcome any time.'

Sameer is bursting with questions: there is so much he wants to know now, but instead he politely thanks Ibrahim and promises that he will visit.

Outside the store, he leans against the door of Maryam's car, staring for a minute at the shopfront. 'The sign could do with an update,' he says absently. 'There are a few things that could be updated, to be honest.' He closes his eyes briefly and tries to imagine what it would have been like fifty years ago when his grandfather ran it. Had Sameer's father, much like himself, spent his childhood toddling past customers, waving hello while his mother called him to return to the back room where she sat tallying stock after the most recent delivery? As his father had got older and started going to school, had he dedicated his weekends to helping out, just as Sameer had? Was this chain of history simply a part of his genetic make-up; inevitable and unstoppable, something that couldn't be helped even if it was resisted? His father's family had arrived in England from Uganda, his father had gone on to obtain a degree and yet – afterwards, he came home to the sari shop run by his brothers. Sameer wonders: had his father ever had a craving for something beyond the four walls of Saeed & Sons; had he ever wanted more?

Something small suddenly hits Sameer on the side of the head. He looks to see what has fallen: it appears to be a receipt that has been rolled into a ball. 'Eh, *muhindi*!' someone shouts. He looks up, but the street around him contains no answers, only the occasional passer-by, and as they saunter past, they all seem to be smirking.

'Let's get in the car,' Maryam says.

Sameer obliges. 'What just happened?' he asks. Maryam has locked the doors but hasn't turned on the ignition.

'*Muhindi* means Indian person,' she says hesitantly.

'You know whoever said that actually threw something at my head?'

There is a pause, while Maryam plays with the sleeves of her dress. 'Look, don't take it to heart,' she finally says, avoiding his gaze and looking out of the car window. 'It was just some stupid boys who should be in school.'

'But why would they throw something at me?'

'Boredom?' she suggests. 'Frustration?'

He shrugs and there is a brief silence.

Her face contorts, as if she is suppressing something, and then, unable to contain whatever is troubling her any longer, she bursts out: 'They're probably not in school because their parents can't afford to send them. And they're not in work – and their parents are not in work – because it's difficult to compete with the Asians. And by that I don't just mean South Asians like you,' she adds. 'I mean the Chinese as well.'

'I don't understand,' Sameer says slowly.

'It's complicated,' Maryam says dismissively. 'Can I drop you somewhere?'

He twists his body to face her. 'If it's complicated, then explain it to me,' he offers, adding: 'Please – I want to understand.'

She fidgets, still looking ahead. 'How can I explain . . .' there is confusion in her voice, as if he has defied her expectations; that she did not expect the stranger sitting next to her to ask. 'Well,' she begins cautiously, 'the South Asians who used to live here, like your family, they were running huge businesses – manufacturing, steel, cotton. Businesses your average Ugandan would never have been able to run, because they don't have the capital.'

Sameer nods, encouraging her to go on.

'But now, well, now we have the Chinese migrating here – a lot of them, and many of them illegally. And they're not doing what you guys did – they're doing what the local Ugandan would do, small-scale stuff, you know, selling clothes in the market. But they're getting the same products – from China – a lot cheaper than we can get them. So, we're getting pushed out.' This rushes out of her quickly, almost ashamedly, as if she begrudges the hopelessness of her people to resist the ever-evolving attacks of the migrant.

'OK,' Sameer says. He understands what she is saying, but he cannot reconcile the warm, friendly attitude of the Ugandans he has met so far with the callous receipt throwing at his head just because he is Asian. 'But . . . I'm not Chinese?' he says eventually.

'I'm just guessing,' she mutters, now decidedly embarrassed about her convoluted and exaggerated explanation for the behaviour of these children. 'I'm probably assuming a lot. They're just dumb kids.' She pauses, looks down at her hands. 'I heard what you said about what you would improve. You know this business is everything to my family. It might not be as grand as you would have it, but it's not doing badly.'

'So you feel the same way, huh? Would you like to throw a receipt at my head? I think I've actually still got it,' he says, digging into his pocket.

She cannot help herself, a giggle escapes her lips and he is delighted to see a shadow of dimples. He wants to make her laugh more, but he has run out of funny things to say. 'Look,' he says gently, 'I have absolutely no intention of taking this business away from your family. I never knew my grandfather. All I'm trying to do is understand my history.' She looks at him, head tilted slightly, and he feels a tremor of nerves. He wants to say something momentous, to impress her. 'If you don't understand where you've come from, you'll never really understand who you are or where you're going, don't you think?' This sounded better in his head, but it will do for now.

'OK,' she says.

'And anyway,' he adds, 'I'm moving to Singapore. I've accepted a job offer there. I start in a couple of months.'

'Oh,' she says. 'Congratulations. Singapore – what will that be like?'

'No idea, I've never been before.'

There is a comfortable silence, in which they both watch

the passers-by. 'Would you like to see some more of Kampala?' she says suddenly, turning to face him. 'I could show you around, only if you want to of course.' A true peace offering.

'Yes, please – I'd love that.'

Maryam takes her phone from her pocket, looking at the time. 'I have a few hours before I need to go to work. Are you hungry?'

She is more talkative now as they wander through the streets, reeling off discrete bits of information – as the road slopes up and down: 'Kampala was originally built on seven hills, but it's expanded to cover more than twenty, people just keep arriving, and we don't have much education in the way of birth control . . . '; as they pass huge baskets of still yellow and black insects: 'those are fried white ants, and those are roasted grasshoppers – don't worry, I'm not going to suggest we eat them this time, ha ha.' She tells him that to see the real Kampala, they will have to do a street-food tour – and she promises she will also eat everything she makes him eat. They start with a 'Rolex', bought from a stall close to the store.

'This is now probably the most famous of our Ugandan street food,' she says, as she peels back the paper wrapping. 'But it would never have existed if it wasn't for you guys.'

Sameer laughs: it is a chapatti filled with eggs, tomatoes and onions. 'But why Rolex?' he asks. He cannot see any relation to the watch.

'Roll, eggs . . . isn't it obvious?' she says, laughing as she takes a huge bite.

She takes him down dusty, winding backstreets where he has to dodge ditches filled with putrid green water, past stalls with squatting women selling colourful stones, tailors wielding traditional printed fabrics. The smells are an assault on his nose: the fragrance of citrus and peanuts is punctuated at random with the aggressive stench of sewage – and something worse. His shoes are no longer white – he tried, at first, to avoid the dust, but this distracted him from what he was seeing, and so he embraced it. It is chaotic and discordant, yet somehow comforting – he is reminded of London. She asks him if he wants a *muchomo* – meat skewer – warning him that his stomach might not take it well, and he says yes; from a street stall, she orders two and roasted maize. They walk further into Kampala, through alleyways and backstreets, where skinny children shriek '*Muzungu, muzungu!*' and point at him, running away laughing.

'What does that mean?' he asks.

'*Muzungu* is white person.'

'I thought I was a *muhindi*?'

Maryam laughs. 'You are a foreigner, that's all you need to know,' she says, dodging a football rolling towards them from a group of young boys kicking up red dust nearby. 'Now, a very serious question: do you have a sweet tooth?'

She takes him to a stall where a man is deep-frying what looks like small pasties. She orders two and hands one to him. '*Mandazi*,' she says. He takes a bite – it is like a doughnut, but lighter, fluffy, and not too sweet. He orders another two and she laughs.

'I guess you like it then . . .' she says. Sameer nods enthusiastically, mouth full. The sun is streaming between the buildings, illuminating her from behind. He realises that he is watching her lick the sugar off her fingers and looks away quickly. She checks her phone: their time is up. 'It's good to try the street food, that way you get to see a bit of Kampala too, but I'll take you to a real restaurant next time.' He finds himself smiling at this.

He declines her offer of a lift home. She tells him to download the Safe Boda app to get around the city and laughs when he offers to walk her back to her car. 'I think I'll be OK – it's you I'm worried about, *muzungu*!' she calls in that melodious voice, waving, and disappears into the crowd.

Sameer stares at the spot where she had stood just moments ago, trying to hold on to the memory of the places she had taken him, the new experiences she had shown him. People are staring openly at him now – were they before, when Maryam was there? – he can't remember. He suddenly feels very alone. The city is different without her next to him, directing him around and whispering history into his ear. He knows he will get lost if he tries to take the backstreets like she did; surreptitiously, he retrieves his phone to direct himself to the nearest main road, and finds himself climbing a hill that leads to the Uganda National Mosque. According to Google, you get the best views of the city from its minaret. Perhaps he will make it in time to pray *asr*, the late-afternoon prayer, in congregation.

14

To my first love, my beloved

10th July 1972

We rejoiced in the beginning.

The streets of Kampala were wild with music and dancing as Amin announced that he had secured the return of the *Kakaba*. My dear, I do believe these people initially thought that the *Kakaba* would return alive! I have never taken much heed of the local politics of the African, but everyone knew that the return of the King (even if it was only his body) meant a lot to the Baganda, and we were swept up in the excitement that gripped the city. Kampala was sick with *Kakaba* fever; for some days it was crushed with the weight of an additional hundred thousand from all over the country; the excitement infected us all. 'Long live Amin Dada,' we cheered. They said that the queue to see the King's body stretched over five miles.

But it was not to last. My sons and daughters, my wife, my employees, my community: they look to me to provide guidance in times of trouble. But what happens when the one person, the only person, to whom you turn for counsel is no longer here? Are you watching over me? Whilst your body rests in the darkness of your grave, has your soul floated free of its sweet enclosure – and I do pray that your soul rests in sweetness – to watch over me?

Within weeks of the coup, Amin's promise of fair and free elections was 'postponed' – by five years, he said. If we thought at first that he would be good for us, for this country, we were wrong. He is not a politician. He is a military man.

I shall confess, I did not truly understand the meaning of that term until one late-summer evening, when Farah arrived at our house, the baby wrapped in her arms and her elder daughter Leila clinging to her legs. Farah was trembling uncontrollably; she had the look of a person about to go mad. The ayah took the baby from her and Shabnam sat her down with a mug of chai.

'Where is Noor?' I asked, as I opened my arms for my grand-daughter to come to me. Leila sucked her thumb and dug herself further into her mother's legs. Farah's mouth opened and then closed. She tried again; nothing came out. I called for Tasneem. If Farah was having marriage difficulties, then she should talk to the ladies first. I stood to leave.

'Papa,' Farah croaked, halting me in my footsteps.

'What's the matter, *beta*?'

Her lip quivered momentously, like a moth fluttering dangerously close to a flame, before she burst into tears. Leila began to cry too, in earnest.

'Your cousin has a doll's house – do you remember it?' Tasneem said to Leila, leading her out of the room.

It took Shabnam and me twenty or so minutes to calm Farah down and coax the story out. 'We were just sitting at home, doing nothing, you know, relaxing. Suraj was managing the store; it's the first weekend since the baby was born that Noor and I have had together. The next thing we knew, there was a bang, coming from the kitchen, and gruff voices – we could tell they were *karias* by their voices. It was so horrible, Papa. Noor told me to stay put and that he would go to investigate – but he had nothing, no weapon, no way of defending himself. I just knew it was going to be awful, I could just sense it, I'd been feeling uneasy all morning. I'd broken my favourite dish that

morning, as if Allah had been trying to warn me, you know.'
She paused, wiping her eyes; Shabnam passed her a tissue and
she blew heavily into it. 'Before Noor even had the chance to
get up they stormed into the drawing room – carrying axes and
machetes. Have you ever seen a machete up close?' She shud-
dered, wrapping her arms around herself. 'It's such a cruel
instrument, the way it glints. Anyway, there were three of them
and they were wearing military uniform – Amin's men! The
baby starts screaming, Leila starts crying, Noor stands in front
of us all bravely and asks the men what they want, why they are
in our house. The way these men are standing, swaying, from
the smell, the look in their eyes, Papa . . . they were completely
drunk! I'm thinking to myself, we're about to die.'

'*Ay, Allah,*' Shabnam breathed.

'It's *OK*, I'm here, na?' Farah stood up quite suddenly, looking out of the window hopefully, and then sat back down.
'Where is he . . . ?' My palms were throbbing. I hadn't realised
it, but as our daughter's story had unravelled, I had begun to
clench and unclench my fists rapidly. My face was hot with
anger. Believe me when I say that I have never felt such fury as
I did in that moment: how dare these people do this to my family? How dare they?

'What happened then?' I pressed Farah. 'How did you get
away?'

'They wanted money, didn't they? They wanted our things,'
she reached her hand up instinctively to her neck, which was
bare. 'They ripped my gold from my neck and my ears. Noor
told them we didn't have any money in the house, that we kept
it all at the bank, but they wouldn't leave. The leader of the
group kept shouting at Noor: we know what you cunning
wahindi are like, you think you can fool us? We control this
country now – not you.' Farah recalled, tears rolling down her
cheeks.

I wanted to find these people, to hunt them down and rip their tongues from their throats.

'Noor begged them to let me go. You've taken what you want from her, and these are just children, he said. Let them go and I will go to the bank with you if you want, give you all the money we have. They said they weren't willing to go anywhere with him, but they would release me and the children. I cried, protested to Noor, but he firmly pushed me out of the room. I walked out of the house with nothing but my baby and my daughter. My hands were shaking as I put the children in the car, Papa,' she said, looking down at her hands as if she could not believe her own eyes, 'I couldn't stop thinking about what they might be doing to Noor in the house. I drove like a mad-man to the police station, but the police were useless. You know what they said to me when I told them our house was being robbed?' she looked at us, red eyes wide. 'They said: are you sure, madam? I screamed in frustration and begged them to come with me. But they wouldn't come. I went to the store, told Suraj what was going on and asked him to come back to the house with me. He is a good man, Papa, may God bless his soul. He told me to wait at the store with the children and he went alone to the house with – can you believe it? – just a base-ball bat. The next hour was the most excruciating wait of my life.'

Farah stopped talking. Shabnam and I looked at each other and then back at her, dreading what she was about to say next. I could hear Shabnam reciting the *Quls* under her breath. Farah stood up and went to the window. '*Alhumdulilah, alhumdulilah,*' she mumbled, pressing her hands to the windowpane and sink-ing to her knees. 'He's here. It's Noor.'

It turned out that Noor did in fact keep cash in the house – 20,000 shillings under the mattress in the bedroom. He handed the intruders the money and they promptly departed; by which time Suraj had arrived and Noor was clearing away the broken glass in the kitchen where the intruders had smashed their way in.

It is not safe for Farah and her family to stay in Mbarara any more. They have lived with us since then, their house abandoned, the Mbarara branch of Saeed & Sons closed until further notice.

After that, I gathered up all the cash we had in the house and deposited it in the bank. The same went for Shabnam's jewellery – to the bank's safe. I wanted nothing in the house. I knew that it was only a matter of time before they would come, and our *ascari* and security dogs would not be enough to scare them away. If they wanted anything of value in this house, they would have to take what they could carry: our furniture, the television, the ornament cabinet.

So, it is business as normal. Except it cannot really be business as normal. We went to Mbarara a few times after Farah and Noor arrived, to collect their things. There are checkpoints every few miles, and the army will stop you and harass you, taking everything they can except the clothes on your back. I have stopped travelling for trade.

I am sorry to say it, but it seems the notion that Africans are *kondos* – a word you hated so much for it meaning loathing and public executions – is proving to be true. They are bestowed with a single, initial opportunity – a first chance to taste power – and they completely abuse it. Gone from the military ranks are the educated, like Abdullah's son, Ibrahim, replaced by the stupid, drunken brutes of Amin.

Ibrahim has been missing for three months now and Abdullah is distraught. Our Sunday catch-ups have become infrequent; Abdullah continues to manage the retail stores, but I see him perhaps only once a month. Since Ibrahim disappeared, Abdullah has aged in a way in which I did not know it was possible for Africans to age. 'I can feel it in my heart,' he says, shaking his head.

'We must be patient,' I tell him. 'We need to keep praying, keep making *dua.*' But, in truth, the words sound hollow even to me.

The way we are being treated by the military is nothing short of awful, but the way they have treated themselves has been worse: carving themselves up into pre- and post-Amin men. There are stories, shared in hushed voices and passed on at the mosque, whispered hurriedly over tea, murmured only to those strong enough to take it. Stories too terrible to repeat.

Clearly, Amin is a madman. His bloated, wet face blots out our television screens, his eyes hungry. His official title, we are told by the newspapers, is His Excellency President for Life, Field Marshal Al Hadji Doctor Idi Amin, VC, DSO, MC, Lord of All the Beasts of the Earth and Fishes of the Sea, and Conqueror of the British Empire in Africa in General and Uganda in Particular. Is that not ludicrous? A man who proclaims himself to be a Muslim, and yet calls himself Lord of All the Beasts of the Earth. To be in his favour is to be in a precarious position indeed: for one moment you are loved, and the next, utterly loathed! In the beginning, he loved the Jews, who supported his coup, taking his first ever diplomatic visit to Israel. And then, when they refused to fund his crazy ideas, he promptly broke off diplomatic ties and demanded that the Jews leave Uganda. In the end, it's always about money, isn't it?

It was around the time that Farah came to us that Amin announced Asian citizenship status would be reviewed. In retrospect, it was naive of me to believe that this was the opportune moment to straighten matters with respect to my somewhat fragile citizenship. A headcount of Asians followed, and we were all given green cards, which we have to carry with us at all times.

Then, at the end of last year, the government held a two-day conference of Asian leaders in trade to which we were invited, and I finally saw clearly what worth we Asians are considered to have in this country. The Asian leaders gave a presentation setting out our hopes for a new Uganda under Amin, a future in which the Asians and Africans of Uganda worked together and in peace; showing the Defence Minister in attendance just how critical Asians are to every aspect of life in Uganda – education, trade (of course), finance, among other things.

On the second day of the conference, Amin himself appeared. I had seen him many times in grainy black-and-white footage, but never before in real life. He is an enormous man – both in stature and weight; such that his clothes appeared to be bursting at the seams, giving the impression of a man seeking to escape the structure his attire imposed. He spoke carefully and his words were measured, taking great pauses to allow us to digest what he was saying, referring back several times to his notes.

For so long I have closed my eyes to the difficulties we have been facing; for so long I have tried to believe that the actions of the government were well intentioned. But it was at this conference that I realised that the truth is that Amin despises us. He accused us of being corrupt, of keeping all of our money to ourselves, of being shrewd and cunning, of being disloyal to Uganda. Blow after blow he landed. That we have used Uganda's money to obtain degrees and then refused to share our knowledge with the country; that we are guilty of 'economic crimes'.

Is that how Abdullah sees us? Is that what he thought of us when Papa first employed him, when Abdullah was just a child? When he had nothing and was a nobody; when no one would have cared whether he lived or died; when he had no name, no faith; when he used to sleep on the floor of our small kitchen above the *duka*, curled up like a dog; when he ate our leftovers for his supper?

It is not fair for Amin to accuse us of such an array of crimes. We have done so much good. Look at how we brought Abdullah out of the bush and into the success he now enjoys; out of the darkness of ignorance and into the light of Allah. I have treated him well – and I have been forgiving. For Amin to suggest that we have sucked Uganda dry, like hungry parasites, is to do us the greatest disservice. This country needs the Asian. It would not survive without us.

What, then, of Amin's announcement at the conference that he was cancelling all pending applications by Asians for Ugandan citizenship? What will become of us? What will become of me? The leaders of the conference tried to appease him by offering a significant number of shillings but it made no difference at all.

What, my dear, in all this, is Amin's key grievance? What, according to Amin, lies at the core of our willingness to commit economic crimes, our inability to give back to the country in which we and our forefathers were born? It is that apparently only six of our girls have married Africans. And so I stand corrected: in the end, it's always about money or sex. Amin revealed these statistics towards the end of the conference with all the rancour of a disillusioned fanatic; he read out a letter, alleged to have been authored by an Asian woman married to a native Ugandan, claiming that the couple had been reviled by the Asian community and shunned.

What is one to say to that? Of course, it is not right.

We are not meant to intermarry. Look at how our community has flourished by keeping to its own; how we have preserved what we brought from India generations ago. Why would we dilute what Allah has blessed us with naturally? Just think of those confused, *chotara* children, not knowing if they are black or if they are brown.

15

Sameer wakes up to the remnants of a pleasant dream. He swings his legs out of bed, opens the blinds, and then – seeing the soft hazy rays of the morning sun – opens the window, savouring the warmth on his body. He is energised today; he is lightweight, untethered. Today, he is good. Then his mind drifts to home and to Rahool. He picks up his phone, scrolling to Jeremiah. Last WhatsApp:

Sameer (02.00): *I'm going to Uganda for a couple of weeks.*

No response.

Sameer (08.30): *Hey, mate, how's R doing? I'm in Uganda now btw.*

Downstairs, breakfast is served in the kitchen on an island loaded with an assortment of cereals, oven-hot croissants and toast. Mr and Mrs Shah both get up from their bar stools to greet him; he returns the greeting, motioning for them to stay seated. There is no sign of Aliyah.

'Now just tell Ama how you like your eggs and she'll whip them straight up,' Mrs Shah hands him a plate. Ama, who Sameer had not noticed was standing quietly behind him, steps forward and takes the plate from his hands with a blindingly white grin.

'Scrambled, I guess,' he says, feeling strangely guilty. 'Please.'

Mr Shah pushes a glass of thick orange liquid towards Sameer. 'Drink this,' he says, toast still in his mouth. 'Papaya, it's delicious.'

He takes a sip of the juice, which is creamy and a little musky, barely sweet. 'Mmm,' he says, unsure whether he likes it. 'Thank you.'

'Good, right?' Mr Shah takes a swig from his own glass of papaya juice. 'So what's the plan for today? Do you play golf, son? I'm meeting some friends at the club if you want to join?'

'That'll be so boring,' Mrs Shah protests. 'Do you like art?' – and without waiting for Sameer to respond – 'Well, you might have noticed I do.' Sameer nearly chokes on a piece of croissant in his rush to agree. 'Why don't you come with me to the opening of a new art gallery in the Industrial Area? That's where they're opening things these days.'

They both look at him expectantly. Ama scurries over and puts a plate full of fluffy, orange-yellow eggs in front of him. He stares from the eggs to Mrs Shah to Mr Shah.

'Are they bothering you?' Aliyah's sleepy figure, wrapped in a long silk dressing gown, appears in the doorway. There are streaks of mascara under her eyes. She wanders into the kitchen and picks up a piece of toast.

'And what time did you get home last night?' Mr Shah says in a voice that Sameer assumes is meant to convey sternness, but Mr Shah is smiling.

'Oh, Papa, please,' Aliyah plonks herself down next to Sameer. He can smell stale alcohol. Mr Shah does not ask again; he has pulled out a pair of reading glasses and is studying a newspaper called *New Vision*. It crosses Sameer's mind with a detached sort of awareness that he has never known Zara to be home after 10 p.m.; that he has never heard Zara speak to his parents in this way. 'I'm going out on the lake with a few of my friends today,' Aliyah says, leaning towards him conspiratorially. 'Do you want to come?'

Sameer glances at Mr and Mrs Shah before saying yes. They do not seem to mind; to the contrary, they seem pleased. He wonders if he is imagining it, but Mrs Shah's smile seems strangely satisfied.

The trip with Aliyah and her friends, departing on a large speedboat from a sprawling hotel and spa resort just off the shores of Lake Victoria, is a surreal blur of overstated luxury: this is how the Rich Kids of Uganda live. Slinging about their manicured laughter in their glinting pristine white trainers, Ray-Ban sunglasses and luxury watches. Barbecued lobster and wagyu (surf 'n' turf!), with an endless supply of Budweiser and – for those who want to go 'local' – Nile Special. Drake blaring from the speaker system as they dance along to 'God's Plan'. Is this what Singapore will be like? Sameer wonders. Her friends – a mix of girls and guys, mostly South Asian and white – ask him first what his parents do, and when he mentions he lives in London, they nod, murmuring sounds of Tramp and Scott's – places Sameer has never visited. A year ago, he might have feigned recognition, drank until he felt comfortable enough to make himself the centre of attention; he would have wanted Aliyah's friends to remember him afterwards. He probably would have done something silly, like try to kiss her, or even stupid: there might have been an injury, something to laugh about later. Now, for some reason, this holds no appeal, and he is subdued. He watches them with mild interest from a distance, trying to imagine this scene in Singapore's marinas, trying to put himself in their shoes.

On Monday, Mr Shah takes Sameer to the sugar factory. It's nearly a two-hour journey, with Mr Shah driving – 'I leave Paul at home for Rehana's benefit really' – past rich greenery on either side of the road, intermittently replaced by rows of ramshackle shops and the ambling silhouettes of locals.

'The closest town to the factory is Jinja,' Mr Shah says, 'where we used to live. We had a lovely house overlooking the Nile . . . but you know how it is, things change. We export less sugar than we used to, and we lost some of our farmers to neighbouring factories,' he pauses for a moment. Then, in a brighter tone, he says: 'The key to continued growth, son, is diversification. That's how we've succeeded. My focus is now more on tourism, real estate and our other business ventures. I only go to the sugar factory once or twice a week.'

Eventually structure and dirt drop away and the land on either side of the road becomes reams of swaying green reeds. Mr Shah overtakes a large yellow open container truck bursting with what looks like wild grass; three men sit atop the heaps, chewing and spitting, watching as the silver Mercedes glides past.

'That was sugar cane,' Mr Shah says. 'They're probably on their way to our factory. And those –' he points to each side of the road in turn '– are sugar-cane plantations. You've never had raw sugar cane, have you? You must try it – it's delicious.'

The car climbs a hill leading to a road lined with casuarina trees and yellow bell bean bushes. A faint rumbling sound becomes louder as they draw closer to a large metal gate on which the words SHAH'S SUGAR are painted in blue. The gate is manned by security kiosks, but it swings open without Mr Shah having to stop.

Behind the gate, the factory is made up of a number of enormous structures, roofed and walled by corrugated-iron sheets. A strong, sweet smell permeates, despite the windows of the car being up. Mr Shah drives past a queue of trucks loaded with sugar cane waiting to enter one of the factory buildings. 'That's the beginning of the refining process – the cane yard,' he says. 'We produce about 100,000 tonnes of sugar a year. That's a fifth of Uganda's total yearly production, you know? We've got almost three thousand farmers growing sugar cane for us. This factory employs five thousand people. Can you believe that? We try to reinvest back into Uganda, you know, create as many jobs as we can.'

Across the red dirt they drive, past more buildings and machines, trucks and workers in shiny plastic helmets, and through to a white one-storey building at the west end of the factory site, which stands slightly out of place next to the bare factory structures. Inside the air-conditioned interior is Mr Shah's office, with mahogany floors and panelled walls, ornate mirrors and some questionable art. An old computer sits on a large desk beside an enormous potted blue orchid in full bloom; rows of filing cabinets and stacked paper stand behind the desk.

'Here we are,' Mr Shah says. 'My brother's office is next door – he's not in yet, but you'll get the chance to meet him later.'

'It's a lovely office,' Sameer says politely, his eyes resting on a particularly grotesque painting of a bald eagle tearing into a small furry animal framed just above Mr Shah's desk.

'It's not bad, huh? Now listen, I'd love to take you around myself, but there's a few things I need to sort out this morning. So I'm going to call someone in to give you a tour of the factory.' He reaches for his phone and within minutes a smiling, softly spoken young man has arrived to collect Sameer.

The man ushers him into an open-top buggy and takes him across the factory grounds, from the feeder machines and mill turbines, where everything is rust-coloured and groans, to treatment and reduction rooms, where enormous silver machines remind Sameer of an old sci-fi film. In the warehouse, where bags of sugar piled as high as the ceiling sit waiting to be collected, the man offers Sameer a hunk of raw sugar cane. 'We use the fibre to create electricity,' he says cheerily. 'Nothing is wasted.'

Sameer bites into the turgid stalk; juice explodes and dribbles down his chin, leaving behind strands of the fibrous inside. *Nothing is wasted.* He wipes the sticky liquid from his mouth with the back of his hand, pondering these words, marvelling at the ingenuity, the resourcefulness, and thinking to himself: no wonder Asians were so successful here. They saw money in absolutely everything.

Mr Shah takes him for a late lunch at a restaurant overlooking the Nile in the nearby town.

'I love this place,' Mr Shah says, tucking into a club sandwich. 'Great for birdwatching. See that blue kingfisher?' Sameer nods eagerly. He delights at the sight of a pair of green turacos with red tuft mohawks – 'They mate for life,' says Mr Shah solemnly – and – 'You're in for a treat, it's our national bird!' – a pair of grey crested cranes, perfectly regal, their bodies a plume of grey and maroon, their heads decorated by a golden crown.

'So, what do you want to do for the rest of the day?' Mr Shah asks.

'We're not going back?'

'Nope. We're done for the day.'

Sameer looks at his watch; it is only 2.30 p.m.

'I'm at a certain position in my life now, son,' Mr Shah explains as a waiter arrives to clear their table. 'In the sugar business, I leave most of the management to my brother. He oversees the day-to-day operations of the factory. But we've established methods and practices that are followed by our employees, and we've hired general managers that we trust. There comes a point when your systems are at maximum efficiency, everything is working the way it should be, and your role is really just supervisory.'

'That sounds great,' Sameer says, blinking rapidly in the sunlight. His heart is beating with a strange intensity.

Back at the house, Mr Shah suggests a game of tennis

before dinner. Sameer obliges; he is rusty though, and he cannot seem to beat Mr Shah (although the games were very close): he possessed the stamina of youth, but Mr Shah's technique was superior. In the end, Mr Shah seems so pleased to have beaten a man several decades his junior that Sameer is glad he didn't win and feels almost guilty for trying.

Ama brings them cocktails as they sit on loungers in the sun; Mr Shah in his damp tennis whites, Sameer in his shorts and trainers. Sameer closes his eyes and imagines for a moment being Mr Shah: wealthy, limitless possibilities, his family happy, relaxed and uninhibited. What a life.

When Sameer goes upstairs to change, he sees that Jeremiah has finally replied to his messages.

Jeremiah (17.47): *Rahool is getting better, u should text him u know.*

Jeremiah (17.50): *Also, how is Uganda? You going back to your fam's old house?*

Sameer suddenly remembers Ibrahim's invite: *You will have to come to our house for dinner. There is much to be said, and we must talk.* But they had not arranged a day, or a time. Could he just show up as he had done before? He takes a quick shower, throws on some clothes and bounds down the stairs into the drawing room, where Mr and Mrs Shah are talking.

'Come, join us, my dear,' Mrs Shah says, beckoning him towards them. The light catches her chest as she gesticulates; a fat piece of jewellery glints in the crack of her bosom.

'Actually, I was going to pop out – if you don't mind?'

'Oh. Well, of course not. For dinner?' Sameer has no idea if he will be invited into Maryam's house for dinner, but he nods. 'Well, I do feel bad that we haven't taken you out yet,' Mrs Shah smooths down the kurta she is wearing. 'But we will of course take you somewhere before you leave – there are a few nice places around here. Where are you going? Can Paul drop you anywhere?'

Sameer gratefully accepts this offer, asking Paul to stop round the corner from the house, where he climbs out of the car and approaches the drive on foot. The sky is a still shade of lilac as dusk approaches, the air calm and close. As he walks towards the house, he hears whispers on the air. Beads of sweat begin to form on his forehead. The dogs are starting to bark; they have sensed that he is near. He feels like a stalker: but that is stupid, he was invited. Finally, he enters through the pedestrian gate, nearly bumping into the security guard, who stares at him with suspicion. The dogs are going wild, jumping and snapping as they try to escape the restraint of their leashes.

'Hello, it's Saeed,' Sameer says to the guard. 'Remember, I came here a few days ago?'

The guard does not show any sign of recollection. 'Wait here,' he says, leaving Sameer in the company of the dogs.

Sameer stands by the kiosk, looking up at the house. The sight of the erupting bougainvillea causes goosebumps to appear on his bare arms. He starts, thinking he has seen Maryam's face briefly in the window, but then it disappears. Minutes pass; he begins to wonder whether he should have come at all.

Then, the front door opens and Maryam steps outside, closing it gently behind her. He walks unsurely towards her.

'Hello,' she says. A gentle breeze causes the scarf draped loosely over her head and shoulders to ripple, and she pulls it closer around her.

'I just thought I'd come by – Uncle invited me when I was in the shop –'

'I know,' Maryam interrupts, smiling, and Sameer swallows. He'd forgotten how beautiful she was. 'We've been waiting for you.'

They stare at each other for a moment; then the door opens behind her and Ibrahim is standing there.

'Sameer,' he says, beaming. 'I felt that you would come today. You will join us for dinner, yes? You are very welcome, please, come inside.'

Dinner at Maryam's house is a very different experience to the Shahs'. There are eight adults and five children living in the house; in contrast to the Shahs', it is brimming, chaotic, crowded; hands grab him and pull him into embraces from all directions, some stroke his hair, others his arms, their voices sweetly saying: 'You are welcome' as the children scream and run between his feet. Never before has he experienced such warmth radiating from the company of strangers: it is flattering and mildly discomfiting.

He is seated next to Maryam at a long table in the dining room, and Musa begins the introductions. 'We have already met of course. I am Musa, Maryam's father. Maryam is my only daughter, her mother died during childbirth,' he sucks his teeth at this and then mutters: '*Inna lillahi wa inna ileyhi rajioon*' – Sameer glances at Maryam; she is staring at the table.

Ibrahim speaks next – 'I am one of nine children – that may seem like a lot to you! Musa is my son, this here is Imran, son of my brother who has now passed, may he rest in peace.'

Imran's eyes light up at the sound of his name. 'You are very welcome,' he insists. 'I would be most pleased to show you Uganda, we have much to offer. You are from England? You will tell your friends to come, yes? You are very welcome.'

'OK, *Taata*,' a lady sitting next to Imran laughs. 'My father is a tour operator, that's all he means by it. I'm Abidah, and this is my husband Dauda. We are very happy to welcome you.'

The husband nods and gives Sameer a brief smile. Another one of Imran's daughters, sitting opposite, introduces herself as Zaynab, pointing to the man next to her as Abdul, her husband. Sameer nods, trying to connect their faces to their names. His head is spinning; the children are not sitting at the table and he is glad he has not been told their names; they scamper up and down the hall, gathering in the doorway cautiously, curiously, eyes glistening, teeth shining, staring at Sameer and then – when he catches their eyes – bursting into fits of giggles. They are batted away by the adults, who tell the eldest of them – who himself cannot be more than ten years old – to take charge. 'Many of us to remember, I understand,' Ibrahim says, having sensed Sameer's confusion. 'Well, you are lucky that the others are still in boarding school – otherwise there'd be another five of us here!' He looks at his watch. 'Come, it is time for *isha*. Let us pray and then we will eat. Maryam, help me to lay out the mats in the sitting room.'

Before he knows it, Sameer has been bundled out of the dining room and into a large front room, where reed mats have been spread at an angle in the direction of Makkah. He hasn't seen this room before, perhaps the largest of the house – and also minimalist in furniture and decor – but he admires the large windows and high ceilings, the embroidered wall hanging containing a passage from the Quran. He doesn't have *wudhu*, but no one has asked him and Musa has already begun to recite the *iqama*, signalling that they are about to start, so he joins the men's line, sweating slightly and wishing he could have at least washed his hands. The children of the house have become solemn; scarves have been pulled from nowhere and draped around the women. He is suddenly thankful that he's not wearing shorts, but then conscious of how low his trousers sit on his hips, he wonders if the women standing behind him will be exposed to his butt crack as he prostrates. Hunger pangs across his stomach and he fervently prays for it not to expose him. Squashed between the shoulders of the men, following Ibrahim's lead, Sameer tries to find some peace in spite of the intensity and speed of the entire affair. Growing up, he had never prayed in congregation at home with his family. Congregational prayer was reserved for the mosque; otherwise – save in the case of his mother – prayer was rarely observed. How strange it must have been for Maryam to grow up in a family like this, a family welded together by this ritualistic and regular practice.

After the prayer is over, they return to the table and dinner is served by the ladies of the house in an assortment of colourful plastic dishes. Lids are raised to steaming foods accompanied by explanations from Maryam: pointing to a stodgy white carb – '*posho*, it's compacted maize'; yellow mash in banana leaves – '*matoke*, you know that one, right?'; a purple-red sauce smelling richly of peanuts – 'chicken stew in groundnut sauce'. Sameer's plate is loaded with generous helpings of everything.

'So, Sameer,' Ibrahim says, once everyone has been served, 'you must have many questions, no? How I knew your grandfather? Shall I start there?'

The table listens attentively; Ibrahim is the only one present who has any real memory of Sameer's grandfather. 'My father's name was Abdullah,' he says, motioning for Sameer to start eating. 'He came to Kampala from Gulu as a young boy looking for work and was employed by your family to look after your grandfather, who was without mother or siblings. Your grandfather's family had a small shop on Market Street where they lived and worked. They did not know then how big the store was going to become!' Ibrahim pauses to take a mouthful of food; Sameer notices that he uses his fingers to eat the *posho*, in the same way that Asians do when eating rice and curry. 'My father had two wives. He married his first wife when he was very young. They had six children together, but only one is still living, my half-sister. My mother was my father's second wife, he married her when he was much older and they went on to have nine children together. I am the eldest of them.'

Sameer wonders where the rest of Ibrahim's extensive family are; those who don't live under this roof. He tries to remember which of the people at the table were Ibrahim's siblings, which were his children and which were nieces and nephews, but his mind draws a blank.

'Your grandfather's business grew to be very successful and my father started helping out. He proved himself quite quickly, and by the time I was ready for secondary school he was the general manager of your family's retail business. It was quite rare at that time to see an Asian and Ugandan working together so closely and so successfully. They were a model for the wider community.'

Sameer glances around the table half sheepishly; the faces of Ibrahim's family are glowing with a pride that reflects back onto him. He blushes, simultaneously pleased and embarrassed to be associated by birth with this man. Why had his parents never told him this before?

'Then, well, you know what happened of course, the Asians were told they had to leave. Ninety days to pack up their belongings and go. Those were very difficult days, under Amin. By that time, Sameer, I was in the army and certain of us were not looked upon very favourably. I had to disappear.'

They talk late into the evening without moving from the table; Sameer hears stories about his grandfather's plans to expand Saeed & Sons into the rest of East Africa, the success of their cotton ginning business; he learns about the gradual stripping of his grandfather's rights to citizenship, the revocation of his passport, the restrictions imposed by Uganda's post-colonial government on Asian trade. Various members of the family join the conversation, asking Ibrahim their own questions or reliving distant memories from their childhood. Bellies full, conversation unending, dishes are left empty, neglected on the table; no one wants to leave to clear them away. The children run in and a small and particularly bold one, braided hair adorned with beads that clack against each other as she moves, clambers onto Sameer's lap, throws her arms around his neck and begins to attempt to braid his hair to the sound of raucous laughter from the adults. Clutched in her hand is a small pink bead, presumably removed from her own hair as a token of friendship. 'Ruqaya hasn't quite developed an understanding of personal space,' Maryam says, smiling and pulling the child (who is clinging so fiercely to Sameer's hair that she nearly pulls it out) from his lap. There is something so natural, almost maternal, in this gesture, Maryam removing the small child from him, that when his eyes meet Maryam's a strange ache comes to his consciousness, as if they had lived a past life together. The moment passes almost immediately.

Eventually, Ibrahim rises. 'I do not have the stamina I used to,' he says, resting a hand on Sameer's shoulder. 'But please know that you are welcome here any time. It has been a pleasure, really it has.'

Sameer does not want the evening to be over, but he doesn't know how to extend it. Hours have passed in the space of minutes. He turns to face the various members of Maryam's family, wanting to express thanks for their hospitality but suddenly at a loss for words.

'Oh, before you go,' Ibrahim interrupts these thoughts. 'I have something for you. Don't go anywhere.' He disappears before Sameer can say a word.

The rest of the family say their goodbyes with *salaams* and hugs and kisses, Imran pressing a business card into his hand

('Wild Uganda Tours – take a walk on the wild side!'), Ruqaya insisting he take one of her beads. Maryam waits with him outside on the porch for Ibrahim to return.

'This was fun,' she says spontaneously. 'I'm glad you came.'

Sameer catches her eyes briefly before she looks away. He cannot make out her irises.

'I didn't realise how close our families were,' she adds, tucking her scarf around her ear like it is a piece of hair.

'Me neither,' he admits, and this time when she looks up he notices that he can see the reflection of the moon doubled in her eyes.

'I've got a free day on Wednesday,' she says. 'Would you like to see more of Kampala?'

'Yes,' he says, 'I'd like that very much.'

They stand there for a moment, smiling at each other in the dim light. Then the front door swings open. Ibrahim is holding a package of paper wrapped in twine. 'These are yours,' he says quietly, handing the package to Sameer. 'I have never opened it.'

'What is it?' Sameer asks, staring at the yellowing bundle.

'Your grandfather left them here,' says Ibrahim. A strange look flickers across his face – regret, perhaps, or sorrow. There is a moment when Sameer thinks Ibrahim might say something more but instead he gives a small smile and says: 'Come now, Maryam. Goodnight, Sameer. Come again soon, won't you?'

Before Sameer has the chance to ask more, before he even has the chance to say goodbye, they have slipped inside and closed the door, leaving him standing, bewildered, in the glow of the porch light. The Uber driver is waiting for him, but for a minute he does not move; the light switches off automatically and he stands in the darkness until he can make out the softly pointed shapes of the bougainvillea petals, their vivid colours neutralised by the moonlight.

16

To my first love, my beloved

2nd November 1972

I write to you from Entebbe airport. For the first time in my life, I am truly alone.

I had always thought after I lost you that I knew what it meant to be alone. But now that I have been separated from my children, my grandchildren, from Shabnam, now that I have been stripped so callously of everything that I possessed, the very basis upon which I believed I existed . . . I understand that, really, before, I was not alone. To be alone, truly, is not to know oneself. To wake at the darkest, deepest hour of the night and to have the sickening panic of not knowing who you are.

I am consumed with shame for what has been done to us. How would you have comprehended this? You came from India, aged seven, to a new country for a new life, leaving behind another home. Gujarati, your mother tongue; India, forever your mother home. Myself, I was born here; I never knew India. Papa came here in youth, at a time when you had the freedom to choose who you wished to be. He chose to become Ugandan; he came to shed himself of India. And as a result, my dear, I have no other home.

Amin said that it began with divine command – that Allah came to him in a dream and told him to expel us from Uganda; to seize our money, our property, our businesses, because we were sabotaging the economy. I was driving home from the office with Shahzeb when we heard Amin's voice barking through the radio, delivering these fanatic proclamations – and more, now: that we should have ninety days to put our affairs in order and get out of his country; that we were Britain's responsibility.

Perhaps my biggest mistake was that in the beginning I did not take him seriously. I was quietly cautious – as one must be with all political statements – but I did not believe that we would truly be forced to leave. The evening of the day that Amin made the announcement, I called a few of our close friends over to the house and we talked late into the night. I'm telling you, my dear, not one of us believed that it would actually happen.

'There'll be a reason for the announcement,' Sakib rationalised. 'Some kind of dispute he would have had with the British, it'll be resolved soon enough. You know what he's like, he changes his mind quicker than the rains come and go!'

'Yes, this will all blow over by tomorrow,' said Roshan. 'We just need to get the Madhvanis' daughter to agree to be his eighth wife!'

But matters were not resolved by the following day. Instead, the radio brought news that India had declared that it would not take Asians with British passports: again, India parroted, we were Britain's responsibility. A panic descended upon Shahzeb, who began frantically to rifle through the papers in my office, pleading with me to visit the British High Commission to determine, once and for all, my citizenship status. I watched from the doorway, feeling nothing.

But, before I knew it, I was standing in the centre of Kampala, watching as Mercedes after Mercedes departed the city forever. It was 9th of August, and Amin Dada had signed a decree cancelling all entry permits and residency certificates for non-citizens. The only official document I had from the Ugandan government – a flimsy piece of translucent paper, stamped to mark its authority – was now invalid.

At last, it dawned on me that this was no joke; no stunt designed to elicit some favour of which we were unaware, no: this was our reality. That truly I might have to leave Uganda was a reality.

So, how to stay?

Option 1: Amin had said that professionals – including lawyers – were exempt from the decree. Perhaps if Shahzeb could enter into legal practice, he could remain, and Shabnam and I could stay as his dependants.

'Papa,' Shazheb said gently, 'Britain has agreed to take those of us with British passports. It has abandoned the quota system. I don't have to stay . . . and I don't want to. I'm sorry, Papa. Nadiya and I will go to Britain.'

This hurt deeply – more deeply than Shahzeb could have imagined – but, it being necessary in such moments to maintain one's self-respect, I tried not to show it. I may have asked him once or twice to reconsider, but in the end, it mattered not – merely a few weeks passed and Amin had changed his mind. There was to be no exemption after all: All Asians Must Go.

Option 2: Amin had said that Asian Ugandan citizens would be allowed to stay if they could show valid citizenship documentation by 10th September. I scrambled for my passport – of course I had been told it was invalid, but it had never been taken away from me – perhaps in all the madness I would slip through the net? We could obtain proof of our identity by acquiring a special red card, the *kipande*. A number of our Ismaili friends had obtained it using their Ugandan passports.

Shahzeb and I went to the Immigration Office to wait in a queue a mile long – it took an entire day to reach the front! My dear, that long wait under the sweltering Ugandan sun felt like my sure descent to hell. I watched as the man in front of me, a man I knew from the community, was presented with the *kipande*. As he left, he turned to me and curled his lips, looking quite mad, one of the lenses of his glasses cracked right in the centre, branching off into a thousand tiny fissures. He had crossed the great chasm that divided us to become one of Them.

The clerk scanned my papers and nodded, tight-lipped. I barely dared to look at Shahzeb.

'Saeed & Sons?' the clerk eventually asked. I nodded, afraid to break my silence. He held up the papers to the light – my passport, my entry permit – and with a sudden and startling ferocity, ripped them to shreds right in front of my eyes.

Shahzeb banged a fist on the table: 'How can you do that?' he screamed.

'Your papers were not valid,' the clerk responded automatically. '*NEXT!*'

When such calamity befalls a person, life takes on a sheen of surrealism; as if you are living another's life for a short while, observing indifferently. Everything grinds to a halt, because nothing matters in any event: not your livelihood, not your mortgage, not school for the children. None of it is yours any more.

Now, a change in focus: not how to stay, but how to leave?

Option 1: appeal to the British High Commission, as Shahzeb had always wanted me to. 'I know a man with a Ugandan passport who managed to get a British passport,' he told me. 'Explain your situation, I have no doubt that they will be sympathetic.'

For, my dear, every member of my household – save for myself, of course – had elected at the time of independence to remain British. If each member of my family was to be ensured safe passage to Britain, surely we would not be separated; surely there was a way for me to go with them?

And so we queued once again, this time to enter the British Embassy, this queue tripled in size from the last. It took us two full days to reach the building front. Kampala ground to a halt whilst its Asian population waited like cattle; rows upon rows of white knuckles holding on to our precious identity papers for dear life, the sun beating down on us with a new, cruel intensity. Shabnam packed tiffin boxes and we sat on reed mats and waited, swatting away flies and street sellers, sweat dripping into our eyes whilst the soldiers sat watching the entire spectacle in the shade of acacia trees. A man from the British press came to observe us with a camera and an enormous microphone, stalking up and down the queue gaily, looking for someone who would talk to him. I turned my face away from the camera's roving gaze, deeply embarrassed. Waiting two days in a queue is no easy feat, let me tell you. Dignity is lost in queues of such length; we pissed behind trees already stinking of stale urine, unable to wait in yet another line for the toilet. My poor boy Shahzeb slept in that queue overnight.

The closer we got, the worse it felt to be so close – until, finally, we arrived at the front – and after a quick flick through the papers, the officer behind the counter confirmed that Shabnam and the rest of the family were sanctioned to travel to Britain. Enthused, I presented my situation: please, officer, please allow me to enter. Do not separate me from my family. Recognise that I have no citizenship not through any fault of my own but for reasons I cannot explain.

But the officer was unmoved and he politely but firmly declined my appeal. I sensed no animosity, only sincerity: these were the rules and he was sorry, but he was obliged to follow them. I gave him a small and understanding smile, resigned to my fate.

Shahzeb took a harder line, declaring that he was a lawyer. 'What you are doing, sir – turning your back on my father like this – is illegal according to the laws of the nations.'

'I am sorry,' the officer said, 'but he renounced his British citizenship. He freely chose to do that and I'm afraid that's on his head. There is simply nothing we can do in such circumstances.'

Option 2: well, my dear Amira, it seems that there were no more options left for me.

If you do not have Ugandan citizenship, and you do not have British citizenship, then you have no citizenship at all, and you are a 'stateless' person, as I found myself to be. To become stateless is to be expelled not only from Uganda, but from anywhere on Earth. I imagined myself as Armstrong, floating in outer space, untethered.

There was not an evening at home when Shabnam did not cry herself to sleep. Over the years I have grown used to her presence, her smell, her touch. 'I will be lost without you,' she whispered when I brought back her passport, which had been carefully inscribed with the names of our young children. 'Where will we go?'

I paused. The Ugandan Argus had been placing advertisements from local organisations in England. The latest: Do not come to Leicester, Leicester is full. They have too many Asians already. But Leicester rang a bell, faintly. Yes – it was where the Mehtas had ended up after they had left Uganda in 1970! 'You will go to Leicester,' I told her. 'The Mehtas are there, there is an Asian community there. Go to Leicester and I will come and find you.'

But even after they got their passports, their right lawfully to enter Great Britain, they did not go. Shabnam shuffled close to me at night. 'They are not taking us, there are no planes yet,' she murmured. 'Maybe we will go somewhere else, not to Britain. Maybe we will stay together.'

'Maybe,' I replied, squeezing her shoulder and turning round so that she could not see my expression. Still, Amira, I had this fluttering, instinctual feeling that, somehow, in some way, I would stay. Maybe it is because your body is laid to rest here.

But the very next day, Amin declared that those of us who stayed beyond the deadline would be rounded up and sent to internment camps. This time, Shabnam choked on her tears as her fists pounded softly on my chest: 'Enough, Hasan,' she wept. 'Please. You must leave.' And this time, I accepted her instruction: even if she did not love me, at the very least, she needed me.

Tail between my legs, I went into Kampala to the United Nations' office. Here, the queue was only a couple of hours' wait; here, I saw my brown brothers and sisters leaving with expressions of relief. There were no soldiers watching, no press reporting. White faces smiled at me kindly. I exchanged a few completed forms for a plane ticket, and that was it, no questions asked.

So, there it was: we were all to leave Uganda, seemingly forevermore.

It had been some months since I had last seen Abdullah. The store is on temporary lockdown. Things have become difficult for people like him, who have sons in the military. Ibrahim has still not been found. But after I secured my passage out of Uganda, he came to the house to see us for one last time.

We all gathered in the drawing room.

'I will go to Belgium and they will go to England,' I told him as dispassionately as I could manage.

'But I have no doubt you will return, my friend,' Abdullah took my hands, which were trembling considerably. Aged by the tumult of the past few years, he seemed wiser than ever before.

Shahzeb's eldest daughter – your namesake – only six years of age but perceptive enough to understand the significance of what was happening, said quite solemnly: 'No goodbyes, Uncle.'

'No goodbyes,' Abdullah whispered back.

The silence in the room then was so heavy. I turned to look at the papers I had collected. Everything was ready: the stock transfer forms, the title deeds. 'We're giving everything to you, Abdullah,' I said.

He raised his hands in protest. 'What good will it be to me? I cannot even manage the store. They are coming for me.'

'This will all die down,' I replied firmly. 'It's not you he wants to destroy, it's us. And anyway, this is only a temporary measure.' My voice began to shake. 'We can't take these things with us. To abandon them would only mean they would fall into the hands of someone else. I entrust them to you, for now, for safekeeping. Until I return.'

I could not help it now; my eyes filled with tears. Abdullah said nothing. He came towards me, a man perhaps only ten years my senior, who as a child had raised me like a father, who over the years had grown close to me like a brother. The closest friend I have ever had, the only friend who knows me perhaps even better than you, my love. We embraced.

'I don't know what to say,' he said eventually. 'I am sorry for everything.'

I did not protest this apology; I allowed him to have it. He took the papers and left us for the last time; he walked through the doors of our house on Nakasero Hill and he did not look back.

It was only a short while later that it transpired that what we had done, in transferring our assets to Abdullah, was in fact a criminal offence. Amin had announced a new law requiring all Asians to declare the totality of their assets, and any attempt to transfer them would result in imprisonment. What can I tell you, my dear, of what has been said of Amin's prison . . . it is enough for you to know that they call it the 'one-way' prison. But our assets had been transferred before the law was promulgated; surely we were safe? No, Shahzeb warned us, the law would take no account of when such assets were transferred: any transfer, at any time, was illegal!

Every day, Amira, the announcement of a new law or regulation. As we began to prepare for our departure, we were suddenly told that each family was only to take a maximum of a thousand shillings out of the country. The Shahs purchased a round-the-world ticket immediately – 'We'll get a refund when we get to England. Or we'll just go round the world!' they told us gleefully. But the Shahs had cash in foreign accounts. We had nothing: all of our money, by my doing, was here in Uganda. Shabnam wept dearly at this news: 'We will be separated and I will be penniless! How will I live?' Of all the vagaries of Amin's regime, this surely must be the worst. What would we do if we could not take our money with us? How would any of us live? 'We will go and buy as many round-the-world tickets as we can,' I promised her. But although we went to the travel agent the very next day, we found ourselves too late: the government had learned of this little trick, and now we were only permitted to buy tickets to one destination. Worse still, any ticket purchased had to be officially endorsed by the Bank of Uganda.

Hindsight, my love, is clarity. Now that I look back, I think of all the things that we should have done, but the realisations came too late. Is this to be a constant pattern in my life: not knowing the truth until it is too late? We could have cashed our money abroad, we could have sent it to the Mehtas. We could have saved some of our cars by driving them into Kenya before she closed her borders. But I was not quick enough, I did not react in time. I failed myself and my family by believing for too long that Amin's policies were nothing more than a fantasy.

Shabnam and the rest of the family were due to depart for Britain just days after we had their tickets endorsed by the Bank. It is difficult to fit your entire life into a single piece of luggage; all the more so when you know that luggage will be ripped open at the airport and cleaned of anything of value. The stupid, expensive ornaments that we had bought would sit in the beautiful Spanish oak cabinet, gathering dust. Then there was the gold, extracted from the safe and lined up in rows on the bed, gold that Shabnam had been gifted when we married; gold that she had acquired to gift to our daughters and granddaughters upon their marriages. I saw her struggle to choose what to leave behind, putting things in and out of her suitcase multiple times.

I accompanied them to the airport. We went in a convoy of three cars; I took the lead in the blue Mercedes. There were checkpoints every few miles, manned by soldiers with blood-shot eyes, their long rifles dangling. Twice they forced us to get out of the car. 'Where are you going? What time is your flight?' Once they opened the suitcases and picked through them, carelessly throwing into the dirt what precious little had been so carefully packed. The other time they took the women aside and patted them down; I could see the shame radiating from Shabnam's body. It took all of my willpower not to lunge at them. They found nothing of course: the women knew better than to wear jewellery.

But it began again at the airport, which was a chaotic mess of confusion: every suitcase opened, every individual searched. 'Where is your tax clearance?' one of the army officers snapped at me. 'I am not travelling today,' I explained to him. 'I am just here to drop off my family, that is all.'

How to explain what it was like to say goodbye? As I watched each of them clutching the small cases containing all their remaining worldly possessions – my wife, my children and their spouses, my grandchildren, three generations of Saeeds – they had never looked so dear to me. Shabnam looked especially beautiful in an old rosebud-pink cotton sari. My throat constricted. I could not speak. I said nothing to any of them, no last words. I just raised my hand as I watched them walk away from me. Why is it that I have such an inability to talk at times when it matters most?

The house felt so immensely vast without them, it frightened me. I could hear the ghost of Shabnam's bangles jingling as I walked through the corridors. The cook stayed – '*Bwana*, we will stay until you leave, who will feed you otherwise?' – perhaps this was kindness, but I thought I could detect a hint of glee underlying his voice. Maybe I am being paranoid. I told him the house belongs to Abdullah, but he didn't seem to hear me.

The commercial district of Kampala is like a ghost town manned by the military. Our store is closed, the stock cleaned out after the announcement that we could not take money, but before the announcement that we could not take goods. All Asian stores have the lights off, shutters down. The scent of the wind here has changed; my city has undergone a profound change in character. The Africans stare at the few of us who remain with open contempt. The soldiers spit and taunt. With our numbers dwindled, the *karias'* resentment has emerged to show its ugly face like a pack of angry wolves descending upon a stray.

The official deadline to leave is 8th November. I will be on the second-to-last plane leaving the country. Getting to Entebbe was a different experience in the United Nations bus: we went straight through the checkpoints without question. Still, they tried to search me at the airport, their grubby hands feeling inside the band of my trousers, baton between my legs. But there was nothing to find. I have taken nothing with me but these letters. I will read them in this new country, and I will remember home.

Amin Dada. Daddy Amin. A man who calls himself a Muslim. A man who has been far from a father to us, let alone a brother. Amin has denied us our home in the belief that it should belong to the African, that the African should take precedence. But a man is not distinguished by his colour in the eyes of Allah. He is distinguished by his intentions and his deeds; he is distinguished by his *taqwa*.

I made sure, my darling, to visit your graveside yesterday. You rest in the best spot in the Kololo cemetery, not crowded with other graves. I did not go there to say goodbye. I went there to tell you that I will return, and I will find Abdullah.

It is a funny thought, but for some reason it has just struck me that I never asked him what his name was before he took the name Abdullah.

17

'So when are you coming home, *beta*?'

Sameer sighs, staring out of the window of the guest bedroom and onto the illuminated garden below. 'I told you, Mum,' he says patiently, 'it's a two-week trip. I've only been here a few days!'

'Are you eating properly? Are the Shahs looking after you? I hope you're not doing anything dangerous, it's not a very safe country, you know. Oh, my heart hurts when you are away from me like this, *beta*, I can hardly bear it.'

'Mum. I'm fine.'

'I don't know how I'll cope if you go to Singapore,' his mother says darkly. The line crackles; he half hopes that it will cut out. 'Well, at least it's a safe country, *hai na*, unlike Uganda. But you know, your father and I are getting old. We're not going to be around forever.'

'Mum, please –'

'Anyway, speaking of your father, I've just heard the door. I better go. I love you, *beta*.'

'Love you too, Mum,' Sameer responds automatically.

His father did not say a word to him in the week before he left for Uganda and they hadn't spoken since. *He just needs more time*, his mother had said fretfully on the call. Sameer is perfectly fine with that; in fact, he prefers it this way, not speaking. This way is stress-free. He had spent the day at Mr Shah's office in downtown Kampala discussing the potential acquisition of a run-down hotel in Tank Hill and thoroughly enjoyed it, the experience made all the better by Mr Shah's compliments over dinner: 'This boy is full of bright ideas. We could really use someone like you in our team. In fact –' Mr Shah had paused as he served himself another spoonful of biryani – 'if you ever think about moving here, we'd be very happy to have you.'

Sameer reddened as he smiled. 'That's so kind – thank you. But I'm actually moving to Singapore . . .'

'Don't then,' Aliyah shrugged. 'It's simple enough. Stay here and work for my dad instead. Sounds delightful . . .'

They had all laughed. But for the rest of the evening, Mr Shah's words had given him a warm glow.

After dinner, he had excused himself to speak to his mother and gone upstairs. Now that the call is over, he sits crossed-legged on the bed, wondering what to do.

The package of papers Ibrahim handed him the day before sits untouched on the bedside table. Sameer looks at the bundle; it looks back. He reaches over and puts the pile on his lap. Heavy. He gingerly unties the twine wrapping. A musty smell rises; the yellowing paper curls, recoiling at being touched, at being exposed. He peels off the first paper and unfolds it gently. Rows and rows of small, faint cursive.

To my first love, my beloved. It is my wedding night tonight.

Heat springs to his face and he snaps the paper shut, hearing Ibrahim's voice: *Your grandfather left them here.* Are these his grandfather's love letters? He puts the letter back on top of the pile and reties the twine. The package goes back on the bedside table – and then, on second thoughts, inside the drawer.

There is a thunderstorm overnight and Wednesday is brought in with the damp, heavy smell of rain on earth, reminding Sameer almost of England; but no – rain in London smells like wet concrete; here, the scent is raw, visceral. It is the first time since arriving that he has seen clouds in the sky. For some reason, this is exhilarating, the mercy of rain. Or perhaps he is excited by the fact that he is seeing Maryam today. After breakfast, encouraged by the brief respite from the humidity afforded by the rain, he walks to her house, avoiding small rivulets along the street and hoping he is not too early – they did not arrange a time to meet. The security guard nods at him this time, seating him on the porch. Beads of water from the bougainvillea petals hit his face as he waits.

Within moments she appears, dressed in a patterned red skirt and orange blouse, hair hidden by a matching head tie. Something about her astounds him each time he sees her – something he forgets when he's not with her and that he's reminded of when he is, something amorphous, like the existence of beauty or happiness. Today she looks regal, and he wonders what she thinks of him, suddenly conscious of the creases in his shirt.

'Hello,' he stands, meeting more drops of petal water that roll down his cheeks like tears; he brushes them away.

'Hello,' she says, half smiling. 'Let's go – there's no one home,' she adds. 'Kids are at school, adults at work.'

'Ah,' he says, remembering that she works shifts. 'It must be annoying to have such an irregular schedule?'

'I like it,' she shrugs. 'It's nice to be alone sometimes. The house can feel so full, I don't really get much privacy.'

They climb inside her car and close the doors; she smells of talcum powder and strawberries.

'So is there anywhere you want to go in particular?' she asks as they pull out of the driveway. 'I don't know what you've seen already?'

'Not much,' he admits.

The cloud is clearing and sunlight has begun to filter through. 'Let's go to the Baha'i Temple,' she suggests. 'It's beautiful.'

As they drive out of Nakasero and into central Kampala, he can see paving on side roads dissolving into red dirt. In the veins of these dirt tracks there are clusters of ramshackle corrugated-tin structures; clothing strung up and drying in full view; plastic bags clogging ditches; men sitting on fraying sacks, staring; small, barefoot children in ripped vests with runny noses: this is the Africa that he has seen on the television. It is a stone's throw from the salubrious suburbs of Nakasero, but might as well be a different world; in the skyline he can see the gleaming metal towers of the central business district where Mr Shah's main office is located.

'There's so much wealth in Kampala,' he says, looking away. 'Why so many slums?'

'Only some people are wealthy,' Maryam corrects him. 'A small proportion. People like you,' she adds, with a smile. 'The Asians living in Kampala. The Europeans. Some of the Chinese.'

'There are rich Ugandans too,' he offers. He has seen them among Aliyah's friends.

'Sure. But not many. Whereas a very large percentage of the non-native population is wealthy.'

He nods. The Baha'i Temple is located on the other side of Kampala and the traffic has become heavier since they entered the centre. Maryam cranks up the A/C as the car inches along. 'Well, I'm glad your family is doing well,' he says conciliatorily, and then immediately regrets it, wondering if she will find this statement patronising.

'Sort of.' She is tapping her finger on the steering wheel to a song that plays faintly on the radio in the background. Her fingers are long and slim; he finds himself wondering if they are cold or warm. 'We've done OK, because we always had the house. And the store,' she adds, expressionless. 'So, yes, I suppose I should thank you for that.'

223

'Your grandfather ran that store, not mine,' he says quickly. 'So you can thank him, not me.'

Maryam suddenly bangs a fist on the windscreen, where a shirtless man has started to wash it down with a small pail of soapy brown water as they stand in the traffic. '*Genda eri!*' she shouts, although the windows are wound up and the man probably cannot hear her. 'Sorry. What were we . . . ? Oh yes, the house. I'm thankful.'

He says nothing, sensing that there is more. She engages the gearstick and drives forward as the traffic throbs on.

'My mother was from a slum in Kisenyi, it's not far from Nakasero. She was lucky to meet my father,' she says matter-of-factly. 'Her family still live there, while I get to live in a beautiful house in Nakasero.' One of her hands rests on the gearstick; Sameer has an urge to cover it with his own, but he does not move. 'Our neighbours in Nakasero are not like us. They're like you,' she says, but he can hear in her voice that she does not mean any offence by it. 'It's a strange feeling to live among strangers, among neighbours who aren't like you and don't understand you . . .'

She throws him a glance from the corner of her eye; he catches it and nods almost imperceptibly, thinking back to England, how he felt among his colleagues and even among his family, and his eyes respond with an understanding that obviates the need for him to say anything.

She smiles and turns up the radio. 'I love this song,' she says, as a light, jovial beat plays from the speakers, a rhythm that makes him think of sunsets and swaying hips. 'Do you have Bobby Wine in England?'

He shakes his head. He wonders if grime has reached Uganda, but she looks so content nodding along to the music that he does not interrupt her and nods along to it himself.

•

The Baha'i Temple, located at the top of a hill among jaca-randa trees and rose bushes, is an oasis amid the chaos of Kampala; there is no one around save for a man standing at the entrance of the building, who waves them through with a big smile and a leaflet about the Baha'i faith. The green mosaic dome reminds Sameer of a mosque; light filters in through green and amber patterns like the stained-glass windows of a cathedral. As they circuit the small interior in respectful silence, there is such stillness that he imagines time has stopped.

They exit to a cloudless, brilliant blue sky and begin to walk across the extensive grounds. He likes how this feels, to be alongside her, their shoulders bumping occasionally.

'Do you come here often?' he asks.

'I think this is the second time I've ever been,' she says, laughing. 'I suppose I don't really spend a lot of time being a tourist in my own city.'

'I know what you mean.' They pause to admire the view of Kampala spread out below them between the Nandi flame trees. 'Hey,' he says impulsively, 'you should come to London sometime so I can show you around.'

She smiles. 'I should,' she says.

'Do you get much holiday?'

'I can't remember the last time I took one,' she admits.

'Me neither. Aside from this, of course,' he adds. 'I mean, it's the first holiday I've taken for a very long time.'

'Well, I'm glad you took it,' she says lightly, but there is something about the ease with which she says it that gives him a strange sense of déjà vu.

'Me too,' he says, beaming.

'It's so rare for all of us to be off at the same time, you know?' she shakes her head. 'People are always working weekends, taking business trips. It's a holiday if we just get one day together as a family. I guess sometimes – on public holidays – we might go to the village to visit our relatives.'

'When are you next going to the village?'

'Oh, I don't know,' says Maryam, absently fingering the leaves of a waist-high shrub. 'I haven't been for a long time. I won't go if it means one of my patients will be left without a doctor,' she explains, 'and that's what it usually means, so . . .'

'Ah,' he says. He had not taken much holiday since he had started working not because there were not enough people to cover him; to the contrary, his team was large. It was because of a belief that he was needed, that he was indispensable to the team, that if he left for a week or two, everything would fall apart. He wants to tell her what had led him to take this holiday, how he felt that his life had started unravelling, but his woes suddenly seem so meaningless. 'Holiday is important though,' he says, as if he knows what this means, 'or you'll burn out.'

'Well,' she says, pausing as a pair of white egrets totter in the grass in front of them; they stop walking for a moment and watch. 'I burned out a long time ago,' she continues as the birds fly away.

She takes him to a local Ugandan restaurant close to Nakasero for lunch. He orders goat *luwombo*, she orders fried fish. As they eat, she tells him about the hospital where she works. He watches the way her eyes crinkle, the way she presses her lips together between sentences, the flutters of her hands. She tells him that her job is often frustrating – that there are not enough doctors and no consultants on the wards; that doctors earn a quarter of what a civil servant or an accountant earns, so why would anyone bother; that patients in need of urgent care end up waiting hours or even days to be seen. 'I think if I hadn't gone to Canada and seen how things could be, maybe it wouldn't affect me so much,' she says, separating a piece of fish from the bone with her hands.

'You lived abroad?'

'Yup. In my fourth year of studying medicine, on an exchange programme for six months. How long are you going to Singapore for?'

'It's supposed to be two years, but it will be longer,' he says. 'Forever, maybe.' This seems so final, so inescapable, that he suddenly wishes he had not said it. 'So what was it in Canada you saw?' he asks, wanting to draw the conversation back to her and away from him.

She closes her eyes briefly. 'Just, you know – doctors, equipment – they had everything you needed. But it wasn't really that. It was the fact that there was the type of structure in place that allowed the hospital to be a reliable institution. Look, Mulago doesn't have the equipment, but even if we did, there would be no one who could maintain it, know what I mean?'

'Mmm. Have you ever thought about just working at a private hospital?'

'Ugh,' she sighs, stabbing the fish with her fork. 'It just feels so wrong, prioritising those who can pay over those who can't. Let me put it this way. We don't have enough doctors. We don't have enough equipment. The government is not paying us enough – or at all sometimes. If we do get equipment, maybe the hospital will sell it to the private hospitals and make a little profit, because those patients will pay for it. But it means our patients, who have no money, suffer.' Maryam pauses, moving food around her plate with her fork. 'I hate myself for doing it, but yes, sometimes, when I really need money, I'll pick up a shift at the private hospital.'

'I'm sure everyone does it.'

'Does that make it right?' she asks. 'Most of my friends from university just left, you know. Didn't bother trying to work here. They just went. To Kenya, South Africa, England if they could.'

'Have you ever thought of doing the same?'

'No,' she says slowly. 'My father is unwell, I have to stay to care for him.'

There is a pause. Sameer wonders what condition Musa suffers from that has crippled his body, that makes him look older than his own father, Ibrahim, but he does not ask.

Then Maryam says abruptly: 'My mother died in Mulago.' She lets out a hollow laugh. 'Over something so preventable. You know, it took me years to find out how she died, because they don't keep proper records of anything here.'

Without thinking, Sameer reaches out and squeezes her hand: human instinct has overwhelmed him, that need to communicate empathy by physical touch at the first sign of distress. It is the first time he has ever touched her, and her eyes register surprise, but she does not immediately pull away. After a few moments, she moves her hand from under his and clasps both of her hands together on the table in front of her, as if in prayer. Then she says, looking at her small fists: 'She bled to death. After she gave birth, the doctors and midwives left. They just left her there.' Maryam finally looks up from her hands and at Sameer. 'I've never told anyone that before,' she says quietly.

Sameer does not know what to say to this; some invisible boundary has been crossed and he is unsure whether she wanted to cross it at all. After a moment, he just says: 'That's really awful. It must have been so hard for you to learn that.'

'It's crazy,' she says, 'you know, to think that just one quick injection of oxytocin might have saved her life. But I guess we'll never know.'

The last stop on Maryam's tour is Nakasero market, which is an explosion of colour, smells and sound. Someone calls after him as he passes each stall: 'Am-rica?', 'Welcome, *muzungu*!', even 'Man-U forever!' He nearly trips over the carefully stacked piles of bizarre-looking fruit and vegetables: baby aubergines the size of grapes, large misshapen jackfruit, lemons green and tomatoes yellow. A street seller breaks a single baby banana from a smiling bunch of a dozen for Sameer to try; it is both sweet and slightly tangy, leaving an aftertaste that makes his mouth water. He asks the seller if he can have the whole bunch of bananas. 'Three thousand,' the seller bares yellowed teeth at Sameer, who retrieves his wallet, working out that this is less than a pound. So cheap!

'*Nedda, tonziba!*' Maryam has appeared and starts arguing with the street seller. She hands the seller a 2,000-shilling note in exchange for two bunches of bananas. '*Muzungu*, never take the first price!' she says, eyes teasing. 'Good luck eating them all,' she adds, laughing as she gives him the bunches.

As they delve deeper and deeper into the marketplace, Sameer struggles to keep up with Maryam, who glides through the chaos as if she is floating. He is intrigued, wanting to stop and sample more; but sweating, trying to keep a hand on his phone and wallet at all times because – as Maryam has warned him – he will certainly be pickpocketed if he does not. He will not allow that to happen again.

She says something to him, but he cannot hear her over the din of the street sellers. He points at his ears, hoping that she will slow down, but she laughs and slips deeper into the crowd. She disappears and reappears like a bobbing ghost, and he starts to feel desperate: he will never catch up with her here.

Eventually, they have looped around back to her car and Sameer's head is spinning. She offers to drive him back to Kololo. 'I couldn't keep up with you,' he admits as they climb inside.

'Don't worry – you just need to get used to it. You should go back. Still got your phone and wallet?'

Sameer pats his trouser leg – panic – and then the other one: they are there. 'Yes,' he breathes.

There is a brief silence while they drive along, and then Maryam says: 'We all grew up hearing *Jjajja 's* stories about the Saeeds – your grandfather is considered something of a hero in our household,' and her eyes light with warmth; this is the first time that Sameer has seen her be genuinely complimentary of his family, instead of fearful or reserved. 'Those papers *Jjajja* gave you, he always talked about keeping them for your family – it was the last connection he had to your grandfather.' She glances at him almost apprehensively. 'We never opened them. We always wondered what they were. But *Jjajja* was very clear about that – we weren't to touch them.'

Sameer can sense her burning curiosity, her seizure of this moment of opportunity. He smiles, amused by her interest. 'They're letters,' he says.

'Of course,' she breathes, 'that makes –'

'Love letters.'

'Oh,' she says, barely able to keep the intrigue from her voice.

'I haven't read them,' he adds, laughing. They are already in Kololo, and he gives her the Shahs' address, feeling dismay at the speed with which the day has passed. She parks outside the gate and switches off the engine.

'Thank you,' he says, turning to face her. 'Thanks for showing me around.'

'No problem,' she says, meeting his eyes. 'It's felt like a holiday,' she adds, grinning.

He is conscious of how close they are in the front seats of her car and his ears suddenly feel uncomfortably hot. 'Well, I hope you get the chance to take a real holiday soon.'

She doesn't say anything to this and the brief silence makes him feel awkward.

'Well, thanks again,' he says, breaking eye contact and opening the car door; he is starting to sweat. As he steps out, he pauses. 'Hey, Maryam?'

'Yeah?' she leans across the gearbox, engine on and car purring, ready to go.

'Are you on WhatsApp?' he asks, and her face breaks into a smile.

After dinner that evening, Aliyah asks Sameer if he wants to go to out. Every part of him wants to decline but Mr and Mrs Shah encourage them with waving hands and eager smiles and Sameer feels like he cannot say no. Aliyah runs upstairs to change and reappears in a short, skintight green dress, hair loose and flowing down her back. There is a shimmer on her cheeks and her eyelids. She is undeniably beautiful, and when she offers Sameer an arm to link, he takes it.

Paul drops them off nearby, in an upmarket district called Bugolobi. 'It's a cocktail bar really, but they have a DJ,' Aliyah says blithely, leaning towards him in the back of the car.

The bar is large and sexy, illuminated in soft purple and aired by open floor-to-ceiling windows which carry in the warm evening breeze. Most of the people there look like expats or tourists; he turns to Aliyah and asks: 'Where are your friends?'

'Oh, it's just you and me tonight,' she replies, nudging him towards a stool at the bar. For some reason, this statement makes him sweat.

'Let me get you a drink,' he says.

Aliyah shakes her head. 'I'm ordering for you,' she says, beckoning the barman and asking for a drink he has never heard of.

Two matching cocktails arrive within minutes, served with a smile. 'It's made with *waragi*,' Aliyah explains, taking a sip. 'Uganda's local spirit. Try it – go on.'

Sameer obliges. 'Not bad,' he says.

Three cocktails later and Sameer has relaxed. They talk freely – Sameer doesn't know exactly what about, but it's fine, they're having a great night. The DJ turns the music up, it's afrobeats, and Aliyah stands unsteadily and grabs his wrist. 'Let's dance?' she asks. Sameer is not sure – no one else is dancing, won't it look weird? But he follows her lead closer to the booth, where the DJ grins at the pair of them, nodding encouragingly. Aliyah lifts her arms and places them around his neck, pushing her body against his. Her hair smells like summer; he places his hands on her waist. Her body responds and this should feel good, so why does he feel annoyed at himself?

He wakes at eleven the next morning with a headache. He rolls over, rubbing his eyes, and pulls his phone off the charger. There is a WhatsApp from Jeremiah:

Jeremiah (01.00): *Yo, did you message Rahool?*

And then a screenshot of messages between him and Rahool:

Rahool (20.38): *Doing ok, having weird dreams though.*

Rahool (20.38): *Btw*

Rahool (20.39): *What happened to Sameer?*

Jeremiah (20.48): *Yoooooo dawg, you remember Sameer?!!!*

Sameer blinks, rereading the messages twice, three times. He opens his WhatsApps with Rahool: last seen five minutes ago. Their last conversation was so banal, nearly three months ago. Tentatively, he begins to type.

Sameer (11.15): *Hey, man, it's your old pal Sameer. How you doing?*

He locks his phone and throws it on the bed. Then he picks it up again and searches for Maryam in his contacts.

Sameer (11.17): *Hey, it's Sameer. I had fun yesterday. Hope you booked some holiday!*

It sits there, a little green message, the first message between them, and it looks stupid. He wishes he had said something else. He wonders whether he should add: *Would love to see you again*, but no, that sounds creepy.

Downstairs, none of the Shahs are around. Ama is sweeping the kitchen.

'Good morning, Sameer!' she sings, abruptly stopping sweeping when she sees him standing in the kitchen. 'Can I make you breakfast?'

He nods. 'Please,' he adds. 'Where is everyone?'

'Mr Shah is at work, Mrs Shah, I don't know,' Ama says. There is no mention of Aliyah and Sameer does not ask. After a quick breakfast, he makes his way to Nakasero market on foot.

It is the same burst of colours and sound that disorientated his senses on his first visit, but this time he's not trying to keep up with anyone. He takes his time, wandering through the stalls slowly, one hand always in his pocket on his phone and wallet. He stops to buy passion fruit and guava and ends up with an assortment of other fruit and vegetables that appear in abundance – lemons, beetroot, ginger, bananas – always making sure to offer half the price they first give him.

Back at the Shahs', and with Ama's help, he throws the fruit he has bought in the blender. She brings a strange-looking brown nut from a cupboard, cracks the shell open and tells him to add the fleshy pod inside to the mix. 'What is it?' he says cautiously.

'Tamarind,' Ama says. Sameer can't help himself; he smiles as he remembers the first time he tried its juice at Maryam's house. 'Lots of healing properties,' Ama adds, winking.

Sameer tries to breathe discreetly into his hand: is it that obvious he is hung-over? He throws the pod into the blender and switches it on. The resulting mix is rich, zesty and slightly sweet. Within minutes his headache starts to clear.

Two days pass and Sameer has not heard back from Maryam.

He has divided his time between Mr Shah's office, where he has effectively been working part-time, and wandering the streets of Kampala, where the fruit-stall sellers of Nakasero no longer try to fleece him. With Ama's help, he has been making his own fruit juices in their blender: adding a dash of turmeric to a mango and pineapple blend, a pinch of cinnamon to a mix of passion fruit and orange, crushed cardamom to watermelon and apple. The resulting concoctions are mostly delicious and an idea begins to take shape in his mind. There is something so simple about it: no app, no tech, just squeezing juice, blending traditional South Asian spices with local Ugandan fruits. The beverage version of Kampala Nights. He is drawn to its simplicity, its traditionalism.

The message to Maryam sits there staunchly in his Whats-Apps, ignored. He thinks of messaging her again, but he doesn't want to scare her away. He thinks of showing up at the hospital where she works, but this seems stalkerish. He wonders if he injures himself badly enough, he might find his way to the hospital. Then he remembers that she works in obstetrics and gynaecology. His first week in Uganda is coming to an end, and although he doesn't understand why, it is bothering him that he might not see her again.

With this thought, Sameer's phone buzzes. Maryam's name flashes up on the screen and he nearly drops the jug of juice he is holding.

Maryam (17.05): *So sorry for the delay – we had an emergency and I've been at the hospital for two days straight, just got home. Imran is asking if you want to go to Murchison Falls, or anywhere else – he really wants to take you! So I've been thinking. If you want to go, I might try to take a couple of days off . . .*

It is a long message and he reads it several times and smiles. No wonder she hadn't replied: she had been at work for two days in a row. Had she remembered in this time their conversation about holidays? Had she been thinking about him, sleeves rolled up to her elbows, translucent gloves on, as she delivered a new life into this world? He wonders whether he should wait to respond, then decides: he doesn't care.

Sameer (17.08): *No worries, sounds tough! Would love to – ready to see some more of Uganda!*

Too many exclamation marks, but never mind.

When Sameer arrives in Nakasero at 6.30 a.m. on the day of the trip, Imran is dressed in full safari gear, looking so much the picture of an eager tour guide that Sameer almost laughs. He offers Sameer a generous discount for the trip, which Sameer refuses – he will pay the full *muzungu* price, and petrol – and Imran immediately accepts with a beaming smile. Maryam is holding Ruqaya's hand – 'She's coming with us' – and Ruqaya nods her head furiously, beaded braids clapping in response. They climb inside a jeep, Sameer and Ruqaya in the back and Maryam and Imran in the front. He wonders briefly whether Maryam would be sitting next to him if Ruqaya were not there.

Ruqaya talks non-stop. In a small plastic backpack she has a colouring book and pencils, a rag doll and a box full of beads. She shows him each of these things seriously and carefully, twisting her tiny body to get comfortable on the seat (he wants to mention seat belts, but no one is wearing one). In the front of the car, Imran speaks over his shoulder, asking Sameer questions about life in England, the royal family, the weather. He is so delighted with Sameer's responses that Sameer has to quell the urge to laugh, imagining Imran frolicking about Buckingham Palace in the rain. 'I didn't know you were such an Anglophile,' he says. 'You should come to visit me in England.'

'If only getting a visa were that easy,' Imran replies sadly.

Sameer frowns: it can't be that hard, he thinks; and he continues to speak of snow that turns quickly to sludge and Christmas lights, Sunday roasts and fish and chips on the blustery Brighton coast, until he almost misses home for a moment. Ruqaya listens attentively to the conversation at first, but quickly grows bored and tries out her colouring pencils on his arm. 'Your skin is the colour of paper,' she giggles, pressing down so hard that Sameer winces.

They drive down the rolling roads of green hills interrupted by flashes of small mud homes; dirty, round-bellied toddlers chatting to one another quite seriously on the street; people pumping at wells into plastic containers; men herding cows with long, curved white horns; and the precarious gait of cyclists with bundled long grass the size and width of men strapped to their backs.

It takes over four hours to reach the town where they stop for lunch and (having made only bathroom breaks up to that point, or 'short haul' stops as Imran had put them, warning Ruqaya that there were to be no 'long haul' breaks in the ditches along the side of the road) Sameer is glad to stretch his legs. He sits next to Maryam as they eat at a small restaurant with outdoor tables, laughing and talking in the late-morning sun. She is the most relaxed he has ever seen her, and when she throws a cheeky glance in his direction before stealing a chip from his plate, he is almost stunned by the intimacy of this seemingly innocent act. (There had been a moment of indecision when, after Sameer ordered a burger and fries, Maryam and Imran had ordered local food. He had wanted to change his order; but then, deciding it was better to resign himself to the fact he was undoubtedly a *muzungu*, he left it, supposing it was better to look like a *muzungu* than a sheep.)

Lunch is followed by prayer in the town's local mosque. Sameer had noticed, when passing the little villages of tin roofs and mud huts, almost all had a beautiful, well-maintained brick building, a mosque crowned with a crescent moon and star; Muslims were less than 15 per cent of Uganda's population; how had they infiltrated to such an extent? As he takes his place next to Imran, he tries to imagine what it would be like to try to incorporate daily prayers into his life back home. Prayer was rhythmic to these people; a part of their life, like breathing, or sleeping. Unobtrusive and unavoidable.

Their journey continues to the park entrance, where hundreds of baboons appear from the depths of bush on either side of the wide red road, scattered in small groups, watching the jeep. 'You need to be wary of the baboons,' Maryam warns. 'They're very intelligent and all they want is food. They'll do anything they can to get it.'

Ruqaya gasps, craning her head to get a better view from the window.

At the entrance to the park, a khaki-clad ranger exchanges jokes with Imran, laughing heartily as his long rifle smacks against his leg. Money changes hands while Sameer looks through the window at a baboon that has approached the car, wondering at the exposed red buttocks which look raw to the point of infected. The baboon stares at him, its small, lined eyes so human-like; Sameer pulls a face, half expecting the creature to copy him; it continues to stare, deadpan, and then scampers away.

Through the park they roll, past long grass savannah, acacia and palm trees, waterbuck and warthogs, and now the road is bumpier and they jolt and jerk, while Imran points out the midnight-blue starlings and yellow-bellied weavers, stopping to allow them to look through his binoculars, flicking through a pocket-sized book to tell them the names of birds that he has forgotten.

The jeep eventually reaches the banks of the Victoria Nile, where it meets several other jeeps and a few vans. Imran seems to know all the other drivers and they chatter away, while Maryam holds Ruqaya's shoulders to stop her from running down into the water, where Sameer can see the ears of hippos so still just beneath the calm reflective surface. The ferry that finally arrives to take them across the river is not a boat but a flat metal rectangle that Sameer is amazed can even float; the vehicles board and their passengers stand between the cars as the ferry breaks the water, Sameer gripping Ruqaya's hand quite tightly in his own, Maryam on his other side, their shoulders brushing.

Across the river, the diversity of wildlife increases: Sameer yelps more than Ruqaya as he sees elephants, cape buffalo and giraffes. The roof of the jeep has been raised and Imran stops the car to allow them to stand and watch the animals stalk gloriously beside them. Maryam is quiet, and Sameer wonders if she is amazed; when he asks her how many times she's been to Murchison before, she reveals that it is her first time. 'We have ten national parks,' Imran explains. 'In my line of work, I have been lucky enough to visit all of them, *alhumdulilah*. My family, on the other hand, they have no time for our country! My grandson, you did not meet him yet, but when he is back for the school holiday, I take him with me if the tourists don't mind so he can learn about his country. It's good you came,' he adds, 'Maryam had no excuse not to visit.'

There is just enough time to drive up to see the waterfall before the sun sets. At the top of the hill, where the Nile suddenly plunges into thundering white foam, orange marbled rock of the cliff side juts unrestricted by barriers or railings; get too close and one small slip would send you crashing to a certain watery death. Imran holds Ruqaya a safe distance from the edge and shouts to Sameer to go and 'take a shower'; he follows other *muzungus* down some crudely cut stairs and (finally) past a suspect-looking railing, through to a small opening in the cliff where the spray of the falls is so heavy he can barely open his eyes. It soaks him through.

'Shit,' he hears Maryam mutter next to him; it is the first time he has heard her swear. 'My shirt!' She is wearing white and it has gone see-through. Sameer tries not to stare at the outline of her bra (black? lace?) and shouts, over the din of the falls, 'I can't see anything anyway!' but she has already disappeared.

Back at the car, Maryam has thrown a shawl around her shoulders. She throws Sameer an embarrassed grin and he can't help it, he starts to laugh. A moment passes, and then she starts to laugh too, until they are both laughing uncontrollably. Ruqaya stares at them as if they are crazy. 'What's so funny?' Imran asks as they get back inside the jeep.

'Nothing, *Taata*, nothing,' Maryam says, gasping for breath.

The lodge where they are staying is located in the park on the banks of the White Nile; Sameer did not know the Nile had so many names, but apparently Victoria and Albert come before the merger of the White and Blue. After they have checked in (Sameer and Imran sharing one room and Maryam and Ruqaya sharing another), he stands at the restaurant balcony overlooking the river.

The sun has started to fall rapidly from the sky, leaving behind a blazing trail of colours that, against the tree-scattered horizon, moves him to silence. When Maryam walks past, he reaches out to touch her shoulder and she stops and turns. Her skin glows, illuminated by the fading light. 'Isn't it beautiful?' he whispers, nodding towards the sunset.

'Don't you get sunsets like this at home?'

'I've never seen anything like this before.'

She laughs. 'I'm going to the room – see you at dinner.'

'Stand with me for a few minutes?'

She shakes her head. 'It's *maghrib*,' she says. 'I'm going to pray.'

'Oh. Right.'

And then he is watching the back of her as she walks away from him, feeling slightly guilty that he hasn't rushed to pray, but also having no intention of leaving the balcony. As he stands there, he thinks about the way she moves – with such steady grace – it's not so much a physical thing, but it's in the way that she carries herself. He admires her sense of self, her sense of sureness, almost to the point of envy.

There is a boat cruise the next day – a real boat this time, complete with top deck, toilet, tour guide and bar. The four of them take a seat on a bench on the lower deck, Ruqaya squashed (much to her disappointment) between Imran and Maryam, Sameer on Maryam's right. He relishes the sensation of their thighs touching; if she is conscious of it, she does not move away; if she is not, then he wonders why it is that he can feel the heat of her body searing through her dress and into him. As the boat hums along, the tour guide points out the red-throated bee-eaters nesting fastidiously in the cliff edges, the black kite swooping above their heads, the deathly still crocodiles waiting patiently for the semi-naked black silhouettes paddling in long wooden boats to shore up on the banks of the river.

'Sameer, would you like to go to the top deck?'

This offer from Maryam is welcomed; they leave Ruqaya in Imran's company and take the stairs into dazzling sunlight.

They stand at the front of the boat, hands clutching the railing, eyes on the horizon. Cruising down the Nile in peaceful silence, wind in his hair, Maryam by his side, Sameer realises he is happy. There's no tightness in his chest, no need to check emails or worry about what is happening at work. His life in London is already a distant, fading memory, like it might never even have happened.

He reaches into his pocket and takes out a folded piece of paper. 'Will you read it?' he asks, handing it to her. A mixture of emotions – shock, intrigue, excitement – flicker across her face but is quickly suppressed; she pushes the letter back, surprising him.

'I'm sorry,' she says. 'It's not mine to read. But if you want to, you can read it and then tell me what it's about. If it feels too strange, just stop.'

He can't argue with that. 'OK,' he says, unfolding the paper slowly, hands trembling slightly.

When he is done, he folds the letter carefully and puts it back in his pocket. She turns to him and touches him gently on the arm, voice tender: 'Are you OK?'

'I'm fine,' he says, and then – because he likes the sensation of her hand on his arm: 'I think. It's a letter about loss.'

There is a short silence, during which she doesn't remove her hand from his arm.

'My grandfather's first wife,' he says. 'He loved her so much. Their eldest son – my uncle – had just got married. They'd just moved into the house your family lives in now. They were doing really well,' he pauses for a moment to watch a pair of birds with large orange beaks skim the surface of the water in front of them. 'And then she died.'

'That must have been very hard for your grandfather,' Maryam says.

'I think it was.' He wants to tell her more – that he could feel his grandfather's sorrow dripping from the pages, about the longing, the regret – but then he remembers what happened to her mother and that her father never remarried, so he says instead: 'It was the end of the Second World War, and they had no troubles in the world,' he laughs incredulously. 'Can you believe that? No wonder they thought Uganda was a paradise.'

Maryam removes her hand from his arm at last. 'You know the Second World War didn't escape Uganda though,' she says. '*Jjajja*'s brothers fought in the KAR.'

'The KAR?'

'The King's African Rifles. The colonial government's army?' Maryam looks at him and he raises his eyebrows, as if to say: *Of course! King's African Rifles!* 'They rounded up any man they believed could fight, trained them and sent them off to Burma for more than a year.' She looks back to the horizon. 'Not all of *Jjajja*'s brothers came home,' she continues in a toneless voice, 'and those who did were never paid properly for their service . . .'

Sameer swallows. 'My grandfather doesn't mention –'

'Your family weren't affected by the war. It's a good thing,' she says, quickly turning to face him, smiling to show she means it. He smiles back, encouraged. But the moment passes and she turns away. 'The British didn't ship off any of the Asians living in Uganda at that time, you see. They were too important.'

This is just a fact and there is nothing to be said to it, and so he says nothing as they stare out at the horizon together.

18

To my first love, my beloved

28th February 1973

I have been in Belgium for three months now and have not written to Shabnam once. In the beginning, I didn't even know where to write: no one thought to tell me where they were taking my family. It did not occur to them that I might want to know.

There must be five hundred of us here, and most of them are families: sharing rooms, eating together; young siblings fighting with one another only to reconcile; tired fathers with their arms around the shoulders of their weary wives. I have watched them enviously and tried to imagine my own family in Britain, all of them together; the picture almost, but not quite, complete. Has Farah's youngest learned to walk now? Is Leila going to school? Has Tasneem been able to find the right ingredients to make your warm guar curry? Have my sons found jobs? Is Shabnam, my wife Shabnam . . .

I could not bring myself to write to her. I could not put on paper to her what it felt like to be here without all of them, knowing that they were together, knowing that I may never join them. The outcast. The idiot. Were my sons woefully shaking their heads, thinking: if only Papa had decided not to become a Ugandan citizen, like the rest of us? Was Shabnam pursing her lips and tutting, thinking: if only he had listened to me? Were they all thinking: I told you so, Papa, I told you so?

In the end, she wrote to me. She knew where I was, and she found a way to get a letter to me. I sat alone on a bench in front of the coast and read her letter. First, they went to Hobbs Barracks, Surrey; then, they made it to Leicester. There, Shabnam said, they sleep four people per room, can you imagine!

But even after I received her letter, I did not write. She wrote to me again, asking for a reply, asking if her letter had reached me. Still, I did not write. Instead, I sit here and write to you, because I know that this letter is between us alone, that its contents will never be read, that its secrets remain safe. But I have learned something about Shabnam these past few months. She possesses more determination than I had thought. Her letters had mentioned a petition to the British to allow stateless husbands like myself to join their families. Well, my dear, it seems that the petition worked. The British are allowing me to go to their country.

I will not be sorry to leave Belgium; I regret only that Britain will no doubt be as cold. My boys who had been to London for university had warned us, but I did not take heed: it penetrates through your coat and layers, and then your skin, until it reaches your bones. I shiver constantly, skin like a plucked chicken's, teeth chattering.

It is worse near the sea; here, the bitter salt-wind slices through you like a guillotine. The building that we inhabit is a holiday centre, conveniently located on the beach. As if this were a holiday for us, a fun little outing. But there is nothing remotely holiday-like about Belgium's coastline in February. Everything is gloomy; pale sands stretch out bordered by mounds of faded long grass, the colour drained from the scene. Tower block buildings behind you and the choppy brown sea in front. The water is so dull, nothing like the green-blue coast of Mombasa. But I take long walks along the coast, particularly at dusk. Just across that sea are the unyielding white cliffs of Dover.

I have had a lot of time to think here, you see. Time to reflect. 'Allah increases *rizq* for whom He wills, and straitens it from whom He wills, and they rejoice in the life of the world, whereas the life of this world as compared with the hereafter is but a brief passing enjoyment.' Did I do something to displease Him? Or is this all a test, a lesson to show me that our time in this *duniya* is so fleeting, so temporary, that what we have here is insignificant, meaningless?

I think a lot on Abdullah, and I wonder what he is doing now. I wonder if Ibrahim has made his way home, what has happened to Saeed & Sons. I wonder what has happened to all of our shops, the shops of the Asians, Market Street trussed up in all our colour, inviting you to come in and spend your money. We amassed so much wealth in the end. We were the backbone of the whole economy. Uganda, you cut off your nose to spite your face. Without us, it is surely in ruins. How will it cope?

How are you coping? That is what the counsellor asks me. I do not want her pity. I may have nothing to my name, but I demand dignity. I would not wish for anyone what I saw on our way to Belgium, when we stopped in Nairobi airport: one of my fellow passengers, a mother, alone with a small child, waiting for a table at a cafe, and immediately upon its occupants vacating, she began to rummage through their leftovers. I looked at the few notes I had in my possession and I bought her a sandwich and a bottle of water. But I could not look her in the eye, so embarrassed I was.

It is a strange feeling to have nothing.

Lately, I have suffered some kind of guilt-induced torment of images of those emaciated African children – begging at the side of the road, approaching you with only one arm, or one eye, moaning softly: *saidia, bwana, saidia*. I recoiled from those children; pretended not to see them. It would annoy me greatly when you used to stop to give them money or a little food – I had warned you so many times that it was likely a pretence; that they had probably been sent out to work by their good-for-nothing fathers who could not stop going to bed with every woman in the slum. But a niggling doubt remained: for the ones squatting at the side of a stinking gutter, sifting through the brown-green water, black faces pale with the crust of dried mud. God only knows what they were searching for. I always hurried past them quickly, as though if I did not see them, then they would not exist.

It is not fair of me to say we have nothing.

When we disembarked from the plane, we were received by a line of white people. You would have laughed to see them waiting on us like that. Apparently, the coverage of our story has prompted some sympathy: these were volunteers, Christians, charitable organisations. They fussed over us, escorting us to the holiday centre, where everything had been prepared for our arrival. A man, perhaps my age, perhaps older, handed me a tan-coloured coat and said something like: Here you go, you look like you'll be needing this, I hope it fits you well. I took the coat (checked the label: it was made of fine wool!) and had to look away. Kindness is painful.

We are never short of food here either. Downstairs in the canteen, there are fridges full to the brim to take from as we please, and we are fed three meals a day. Those meals are very bland, but I am never really hungry, so I cannot complain. There are so many things here that we can take at no cost, and I have filled my pockets with it all: napkins, plastic cutlery, packets of ketchup. You never know when it will come in useful.

What else is there to do, except wander and eat? The leaders of the centre have all of our names on white clipboards. They survey us over the boards with concerned eyes. I feel like a laboratory rat, and it does not help that I am being psychoanalysed. The counsellors come once a fortnight. Marie, a rotund white lady with a bouffant of blonde hair, has been assigned to my case. She sits down with me and asks questions and listens. I have never said much to her. I find it hard enough to write to my own family; how could I talk to her, a woman who is a world away from understanding? The only person I could ever really talk to was you.

The third time Marie came, she asked me for the third time how I would feel about 'going back to work'. I shrugged my shoulders, pulling on a thread that had just begun to fray on my tan coat (that's the issue with wool – catch it once and it is never the same again).

'I've got some exciting news, Hasan,' she said gaily, folding and unfolding her legs like she was doing some kind of elaborate dance. Her hands started to fidget in her lap, whole body succumbing to the invisible rhythm. 'There's a job opening in Bruges. Six jobs in fact. Isn't that exciting, Hasan?'

She did not mean to be patronising, bless her good Christian heart, but it came across awfully so. I looked at her blankly for a few seconds, not saying anything. Her dance intensified. 'What is the job?' I finally asked.

'Well, I'm very glad you asked, Hasan,' she said. (I wonder if it is part of her training, but she has this terrible habit of saying my name at the end of every sentence. Perhaps she was taught that it would appear more personal, or maybe it is a way for her to remember her patients' names. Either way, how she said it grated on me – Ha-San – the way all white people do.) 'The fact that you asked tells me that you may well be interested. There's no obligation, of course. It's completely up to you whether you wish to take the job or not. Now I want to start by saying that I know it's by no means what you're used to, but you need to remember that it pays a salary, which you need right now. It's a start – it's not a forever job.' She smiled at me encouragingly.

Nothing is a forever job, Marie. Building and managing your own successful business is not a forever job.

The role was at a canning factory. A fish-canning factory, to be more precise. It involved the processing and packing of fish into cans; operating machinery, conveyor belts and the like. I closed my eyes, imagining myself among the stench of raw fish, guts and eyes around me, gloved hands glistening with blood and grime; the sound of the machines chopping, pulsating, sealing at my command. Is this what our ginnery factory workers had felt like each day? I had never imagined what it might feel like to be a worker. Is this what I was destined to do now? I politely declined, and told Marie that they have been kind to me and I was grateful for that, but they should offer the job to someone else.

All of the canning factory jobs went in the end: five to heads of families, one to a stateless man who was in Belgium alone. The stateless man's family, like mine, had been scattered into the air and left to lie where they fell. His trade, like mine, had been entrepreneurship. But, unlike me, he sought to integrate. Every night he sat with a small teach-yourself book and practised Flemish. It is a strange language, and I do not know why he did it – nearly all of those who volunteer at the centre, and every person I have come across, speaks English. But he insisted on learning it. 'Language is the most powerful tool of civilisation,' he told me one evening, struggling with the pronunciation of one of the more knotty Flemish words. 'It all starts with language. Learn the language, and you master a people.'

The rest of us single men, we were restless. We did not want to take offers of jobs not just because we have never worked for someone else, but also because we were convinced that this was a purely temporary arrangement and that we would be leaving soon.

Not too long after we arrived, a dozen of the families were offered new lives in Belgium: to become citizens, to have real homes. I watched with a certain melancholy as they packed up their few belongings and left. How lucky that they were together, that they could just be tossed from one place to another and create a new home. This can be done anywhere it seems; what matters is not where you are, but whom you are with. Then again, to have to settle in this cold and grey country . . . my heart aches for the warm colours of Uganda. Now that I am soon to be reunited with my family, will I be able to call England my home?

Some nights I can almost feel my soul leaving my body with longing. It pushes at my ribcage, pummels my heart, yearning to escape. In my final session with Marie, she watched me clutch my chest and asked me what was wrong. The next thing I knew I was being kept in the local hospital overnight for 'tests'. It is just that my soul is aching, I wanted to tell them. It wants to go home.

19

It is Thursday evening and Sameer only has three full days left in Kampala. Something is bothering him, crawling under his skin, coming to rest lightly on his chest. It is not an unfamiliar feeling. But it had faded while he was in Uganda. Perhaps it is the thought of going home that is giving him anxiety. He stretches out on the Shahs' comfortable guest bed and opens WhatsApp.

Sameer (21.49): *Hey – are you around the rest of the week at all?*

An immediate response:

Maryam (21.49): *Hey!*

Followed by:

Maryam (21.50): *I'm actually working every day, including the weekend, sorry*

Oh. The creature on his chest digs in its heels and settles deeper. He had not imagined that he would not see her again, but now that seems like it might be the case, he feels deflated. He locks his phone, chucking it across the bed, and reaches for the bedside drawer where his grandfather's letters are bundled. The days have passed so quickly in the company of the Shahs that he has barely found the time to be alone. But late at night, he has read three more of the letters, heart beating with exhilaration as his family's history unfurls under the lamplight at his bedside, revealing itself to be multifaceted: a strange sensation of pride is mixed with unease. He had wondered whether he might talk to Maryam about what he'd read; apart from her, he has not told anyone about the letters. Now it seems he will have to process them alone.

There is a knock at the door – 'Come in!' he yells, shoving the letter under his pillow. Aliyah stands in the doorway, skin slightly pink, wet hair hanging down her back.

'Sorry,' she says, 'I just came out of the shower. I'm going out. Do you wanna come?'

He looks at her: hair dripping, sultry green eyes, hip leaning against the door frame, one arm raised over her head to expose the soft curves of her figure. He imagines for a moment fucking her from behind, twisting her long hair around his wrist. But the image, fleeting, disappears as quickly as it comes, replaced by an abrupt feeling of emptiness. 'Thanks,' he says, 'but I'll give this one a miss. Have a good night.'

'Suit yourself.' Aliyah shrugs, flashes him a smile, turns on her heel and closes the door behind her.

He scrambles across the bed to retrieve the letter; his hands find his phone, which is flashing a message.

Maryam (21.55): *When do you leave?*

Sameer (21.55): *Monday*

Maryam (21.55): *Do you want to meet for breakfast before I go to work tomorrow?*

He can't help it; he's grinning like an idiot.

They meet at a rooftop crêperie within the exclusive suburb of Kololo where the Shahs live. For the first time, Sameer notices that people in the restaurant are staring at them openly. He wants to stare back, but he's embarrassed by the fact that his awkwardness shows so clearly in the colour of his face. 'People stare a lot here, huh?' he whispers to Maryam as she takes a seat.

She nods. 'It's strange to see a Ugandan and Asian couple.'

'A couple?' he repeats, raising an eyebrow.

'You know what I mean,' she says quickly (and he is unable to tell whether she is blushing), 'people might – wrongly – assume . . .'

He'd never given it any thought before; even when Samah had married John – the first of his entire extended family to marry outside of their own race – the thought had not crossed his mind. But now, sitting here with Maryam, it strikes him that despite the fact that both sides of his family are East African Asian – his father's Ugandan, his mother's Kenyan, and between them at least a dozen siblings – none of them married black Africans. This was just the way things were and there had never been any reason to be surprised by it.

'People don't stare in London,' he says after a pause, thinking of its familiar streets fondly. He could take her there and she'd be blown away by the mix of colours, the blacks the browns the yellows the peaches the whites.

'Are you sure?' she says sceptically.

This question prompts a thought: would *Maryam* be stared at in London, as a black hijabi? Would they be stared at if they were seen walking down the street together? Is it easy enough for him to say that Londoners don't stare because he's never actually been in a situation that merited stares? Before he has the chance to say anything, the pancakes arrive, stacked high and topped with whipped cream.

Thankful for the distraction, he changes the subject. 'Is this place Ugandan-owned?' he asks Maryam once the waitress has gone. In Mr Shah's office, he has learned that Ugandans do not own the luxury lodges across the country. They are owned by foreign investors; managed by carefully sourced bright young Europeans desperate to get away from their stolid lives in Belgium or England or France and throw themselves into Africa with passion; staffed by a sample of the ever-smiling pool of the polite, docile local population.

'I don't know. But here in Kololo? I doubt it,' she takes a mouthful of pancake.

'Is it Asian-owned?' he ventures. Maryam doesn't know; she

shrugs, and Sameer says, between mouthfuls, 'The pancakes are really good.'

She nods enthusiastically in response. There is a brief silence while they eat, and then Maryam says: 'You know most of the Asians here are not like your family, right?'

'What do you mean?'

'Most of them aren't Asians who came back, you know, after '72. Most of them have come here straight from South Asia for the first time.'

He has seen these people in Nakasero market; the women in plain saris with plaits running down their backs, the men with fat moustaches and scummy flat sandals; he has watched them arguing with the street sellers, heard their fresh accents rolling broken English around their tongues. These South Asians are not like the Shahs, and they are not like Sameer.

'I guess it's not that surprising,' he says slowly, thinking of his father. 'Probably a lot of people who were thrown out didn't exactly feel comfortable about coming back.'

'Mmm.' Maryam digs her fork deeper into the pancake stack. 'I'll tell you what is rare to see though,' she says. 'A Ugandan employed by an Asian at a very senior level. Those positions are usually for their families and fellow Asians.' She pauses for a moment. 'Your grandfather was different. He employed my great-grandfather at the highest level of the company.'

Sameer's smile freezes as he thinks: But he wouldn't make him a shareholder in the company, not even to save his own business.

'Have you read any more of his letters?' she asks.

Sameer nods, unsure of what to say. 'He saw your great-grandfather as a brother,' he eventually supplies.

'Which meant so much back then,' she replies, oozing a

gratitude that he is not sure is entirely deserved. 'So the British had this system, right, which was that the Asians should be the buffer between them and the native. Asians weren't allowed to own agricultural land, so they had to trade. Africans were restricted from trading, so they had to farm. Your grandfather, having my great-grandfather as his business partner, was one of the first to break those boundaries.'

'Oh, I don't know about that,' Sameer says, brushing off this last comment. He finds her admiration, her readiness to believe the best of his grandfather, somewhat distressing. 'Do you want to order anything else?'

'Do you see how the whole problem was started by the British?' she demands, ignoring the question. 'And then our post-independence government tried to force the British structures apart, but their policies didn't discriminate between you. They ended up affecting people who were already integrated, like your grandfather. I'm sorry for that.'

The pancakes are cold now and Sameer sits there, chewing glumly. Maryam does not seem to notice the change in his demeanour and she asks him, glibly, whether there is anything else that he has read that he wants to share. He turns the conversation to his grandfather's grief, the common denominator of all human relationships. 'It really hurts to lose someone you love. I've never known that.' Then he remembers, again, that she lost her mother and his face colours – 'I'm sorry –'

'It's OK,' she is smiling. 'I didn't know her. I think I must love her. But I never knew her.'

There is a short silence and then Sameer finds himself saying: 'I nearly lost my best friend.' She asks him what happened, and he tells her – before he knows it, it has all spilled out: the shock, that Rahool was the last person you would associate with any kind of violence; the pain and confusion as he tried to understand the motive; the horror at seeing his friend like that in hospital; the guilt at not being able to attend the trial; the punishment when Rahool failed to remember who he was. They have been messaging almost every day since he has been in Uganda, but the conversation is stilted, forced – it's just not the same. She listens quietly, nodding and saying the right thing at the right time. When he is done, and her eyes are unblinking, her face attuned to his stress, he feels quietly heartened.

As they get up to leave, she says spontaneously: 'You should come for dinner again before you go. Come tonight, our cook will be there. You'll get real Ugandan food.'

'What did I have last time?'

'Remember that chicken stew? Well, let's just say cooking has never been one of my strengths . . .'

'I thought it was delicious.'

She laughs as they exit the restaurant and begin to walk towards where her car is parked. 'I never cared about learning to cook. All I cared about was becoming a doctor.'

Sameer thinks of Zara, who can cook as well as their mother and puts all her enthusiasm into it. A happy but odd thought crosses his mind – he can't wait for Zara to meet Maryam.

'Either way, it was delicious,' he insists.

'That's because you're not used to Ugandan food.'

'I am,' he protests, 'my mother makes it at home.'

'That's not real Ugandan food – that's Asian fusion.'

'Real Ugandan food *is* Asian fusion – look at your Rolex!'

'Oh, yeah,' she laughs. 'I guess you're right.'

They have arrived at her car. Sameer turns to face her and the morning sun is still low. When she smiles at him, the dimples in her cheeks make him wish suddenly that he was funnier so that he could see her smile more.

'Well, thanks for breakfast,' she says.

'Thanks for meeting me,' he replies. Instinct causes him to lean forward for a hug, but she flinches, drawing back, and he immediately retreats and puts his hands in his pockets. They look at each other for a moment and then she smiles weakly, looking around.

He takes a step back from the car, from her. But then, as she retrieves the keys and gets inside the car, she gives him a wave: 'So I'll see you for dinner at home tonight?'

'Yes,' Sameer replies. 'Definitely!' he adds, but her car has already pulled away.

He watches her car become smaller and smaller until it disappears around a corner. Standing there, blinking in the light as he watches her go, he is very aware that he feels something for her, but he doesn't know yet what it is. He is not even sure if she likes him at all, and this in itself is unsettling.

Shaking these thoughts from his mind, he pulls out his phone and orders an Uber. He's taken to making his own energy juices in the morning and this morning's concoction requires tamarind and ginger. Nakasero market is the natural destination, of course, but he finds himself heading for his grandfather's old shop.

Musa is working and his face lights up when he sees Sameer, hobbling out from behind the till and embracing him. 'You won't find Maryam here,' he says, chuckling.

Sameer immediately blushes, ducking into an aisle so that Musa cannot see his face. 'I didn't come here to find Maryam,' he calls back, affronted. 'I came here to buy something . . .'

'What do you need, son?' Musa appears in front of Sameer and gestures towards the sanitary towels and panty liners in the aisle. 'I assume none of this?' he chuckles again softly.

Sameer smiles sheepishly. 'Can you show me where the

fruit and vegetables are?' he asks, as he follows Musa past the sanitary towels, down an aisle of canned goods and finally to a stand at the side of the store. 'Why don't you have labels for the aisles? It would make it easier for your customers.'

'Who said we want to make it easier for the customers?' Musa says as he watches Sameer root through the stubs of ginger. 'They come to buy one thing, they leave with ten other items . . .'

Sameer laughs at the obvious logic of it, digging into his pocket to retrieve a couple of crumpled notes. Musa shakes his head, and no matter how much Sameer tries, he won't take the money. 'Thank you so much,' Sameer says, eventually giving up. 'Oh, also, um. Maryam said I should come for dinner tonight. I don't know if that's OK . . .'

'Of course,' Musa smiles widely. 'We're expecting you.'

That afternoon – his last afternoon in Mr Shah's office – is quiet. Sameer has just completed a report on the new luxury lodges that have opened in Western Uganda over the past few months, comparing their location and service offering to the Shahs' resorts; Mr Shah is reviewing monthly management accounts. 'Thanks for that,' he says as Sameer's email arrives in his inbox, looking up from the files on his desk. 'Feel free to head on home, *beta*, no need to wait for me. I can't believe it's already your last day here.'

Sameer swivels on his chair, looking around the office, not dissimilar to his own back in London but brighter for some reason, happier; perhaps because of the way the windows let in the yellow light of the sun, perhaps because of the sheer amount of space – with only six employees on the floor, it felt enormous, liberating. A wave of melancholy washes over him now that it is time to say goodbye. 'I've learned so much, thank you,' he says, and he wishes he'd got Mr Shah a gift to show his appreciation, something his mother would have reminded him to do if she were here (although God only knew what you could get a man who had everything).

'We should be thanking *you* – you've been a huge help,' Mr Shah replies. 'Although I'm not sure it's been much of a holiday for you coming to the office with me!'

'Honestly – I've loved it. I didn't know work could be so . . . well, fun,' Sameer says, laughing and simultaneously cringing at himself for saying it.

'Well, son, this is Uganda. It's really easy to make money here – all you need is a little capital and the right idea.'

Sameer swallows. 'I did have this one idea,' he says.

Mr Shah raises an eyebrow. 'I'm intrigued.'

Hesitantly, Sameer begins to explain what he's discovered in the two short weeks he's been in Uganda: an East African Asian fusion, good for mind and body – turmeric and orange immuno-booster, tamarind and watermelon hangover cure, chilli and mango aphrodisiac, mint and lime cleanse and refresh. He's making it up now but the list could go on and on – any tag line you want, as long as it has some broad relation to the ingredients, and he's convinced it would sell. All natural, locally sourced ingredients, no preservatives, no added sugar – and not just delicious, but actually does what it says on the tin: it cured my hangover! When he is finished, he forces himself to look nonchalant, although his palms are sweating.

'Brilliant,' Mr Shah says. 'Absolutely brilliant. I could help you establish links with the retailers where we sell our sugar products – you could rent a commercial kitchen space at quite a low cost – oh, also we know some excellent local packaging manufacturers for the bottles – were you thinking glass or plastic?'

Sameer's heart pounds as his body courses with adrenaline;

he wasn't expecting this response, not at all. 'Uncle,' he says, 'it was just an idea – I'm moving to Singapore, remember?'

'Of course, of course,' Mr Shah bats away this comment with a wave of his hand. 'Pull up an Excel, come on – let's model it.'

Over the course of the next few hours, and with Mr Shah's input, Sameer draws up a spreadsheet to see what it would cost to start producing and selling Saeed & Sons juices in Kampala: renting a kitchen and machinery, purchasing the fruit and packaging, arranging transportation to retail outlets. The spreadsheet spews out the numbers: he could run the business for a year and not make a single shilling of profit, and it would still only cost him half his savings. He stares at the numbers and checks the formulas again, verifying the assumptions with Mr Shah. By the time they are finished it is evening, and Sameer's heart is fluttering with a new kind of excitement: the excitement of possibility, of adventure. He feels renewed, powerful, like he could conquer the world.

Mr Shah drops him off outside Maryam's house (politely declining Sameer's suggestion that he come inside) and Sameer is welcomed at the door by the smiling members of the family. His feet cross the threshold of his father's old house with a new and strange sense of belonging: this is his home, Musa had said, and today he feels like it is. It feels the way he has always imagined home should feel: happy and comfortable, somewhere you can be unashamedly you.

And Maryam was right: the food is even better than the first time he came. Over dinner, Musa tells them the story of how he met Maryam's mother, when he came off a boda boda near Kitange, falling right at her mother's feet – 'I literally fell for her,' he says, laughing – and she went with him to the hospital and stayed until he regained consciousness. Maryam must have heard this story a million times before, but Sameer watches her eager face turned up in Musa's direction.

At one point during the evening, Ibrahim asks him if he has read the papers that his grandfather left in the house. Sameer shakes his head slowly, swallowing a piece of meat. 'I haven't had the chance to yet,' he lies – catching Maryam's eye; she raises an eyebrow. They are not seated next to each other this time; she is diagonally opposite him, but he is glad because it means that he can look at her without it being obvious. 'I've been so busy and everything,' he continues, 'I'll probably read them when I'm back home in England.' Ibrahim nods and says of course, but Sameer can sense disappointment. Did he really want to know what the papers were? In that case, was it really true that in all these years he had never read them?

'Why did you lie?' Maryam asks him later, when they are alone on the porch after everyone has said goodbye.

'I don't know.'

She says nothing, standing in front of the doorway, weight resting on one hip, arms wrapped around her waist as if she were feeling cold. Her expression is unreadable.

'Some of the things he says embarrass me,' he says quietly.

'What do you mean?'

He's read half a dozen of the letters. There is a beauty and pain in those letters which is written into his history and towards which he feels a strange responsibility. This is the seed from which his father's expectations sprang, the bedrock of the traditionalism of his Mhota Papa – who he has tried and failed several times to reconcile with the politically engaged Shahzeb. It fascinates him to dig deeper into the family psyche, to unroot its foundations. But this is not without consequence: there are also things that have been bothering him, sitting at the edge of his mind, awkward and horrible, which he can't seem to shake off. He says: 'I don't know.'

'Your grandfather was a wonderful man,' she says gently. 'He did a wonderful thing –'

'He's not as great as you think,' he blurts out, reddening for speaking ill of his grandfather – it seems wrong, somehow, to criticise him, but at the same time – 'He never saw your great-grandfather as an equal, and refused to make him a shareholder in his business essentially because he was black. He believed himself to be superior to black people. He was a hypocrite, he was selfish, he –'

Maryam moves at last, throwing her hands up and causing him to stop. 'OK,' she says. 'I get it.'

Sameer hangs his head while they stand there in silence. 'I'm sorry.'

'There's nothing to be sorry about,' she says softly. 'Everything your grandfather thought or did was a result of his personal experiences, his own personal circumstances. He was a product of his time,' she shrugs. 'Just like we're a product of ours.'

Sameer frowns. 'It just feels so strange to have your whole family always applauding him,' he says, 'when you didn't really know him.'

Maryam looks at him with an expression he can't decipher; and then, so quickly that he might have imagined it, her eyes say: *Well, I don't really know you.* On this look – which has already disappeared – Sameer suddenly feels queasy as he remembers, with painful intensity, his own thoughts, red and hot, when he had first met her. What would she think of him if she knew? He stares at his feet, almost wanting to cry.

'Well, you can't change the past,' she says at last. 'But it doesn't have to define your future. And anyway, whatever he was like, you're not him, are you?' and these last words are said gently, coaxing him to lift his head without touching him.

He looks up and she is smiling. She is radiant. He exhales, her words causing the demons in his head to scatter and flee. He'll never read another one of those letters again. He'll take them to a flame until they crumble to nothing, he'll erase that part of his family's history. He'll be a better man.

20

It is Sameer's penultimate night in Kampala, and he still can't quite believe that Maryam sits in front of him.

He'd thought their time together had run out; he'd accepted that he wasn't going to see her again. But in the Uber as he drove away from her house for the last time, he'd realised he had nothing to lose from trying, and he'd messaged and asked if she would have dinner with him the following night. She said yes.

He had spent over an hour researching where he might take her for dinner. There were upmarket restaurants in Nakasero and Kololo, but he'd walked past them in the evenings and seen old white men sitting with two or three young and beautiful Ugandan women, which made him uncomfortable. At the same time, he wanted the night to be special, to be memorable. He didn't just want to take her to any old restaurant in downtown Kampala. In the end, he settled on a steakhouse in a complex close to Kabalagala; it wasn't perfect, but it would do.

The restaurant is almost empty, which might have been a bad sign in London, but here Sameer is grateful for the privacy. They sit at a table scattered with tea-light candles and shadowed by a huge leafy plant; exposed, slanted wooden beams form a canopy over their heads. The menu is French and Belgian; he orders steak, she orders fish, and they fall into comfortable chatter like old friends. What made you want to go to Singapore? she asks, and he tells her that it will offer him a straightforward route to partnership. She asks him if that's what he wants – to be a partner. He shrugs – it's the next logical step, it's what everyone in this job works towards, the pay jump is huge. He admits that a part of him is just ready to leave London; that his friends have left, or moved onto newer, more exciting things, and he feels left behind. As if, by staying in his successful job, living in his penthouse apartment, he is somehow stagnating, failing to develop. As he speaks, he feels stupid. He wonders why he feels the need to do something different just because his friends have. But she says that she understands, that sometimes it all seems pointless: the same routine every day, the same frustrations every day, and that it feels like nothing will ever change. He can't remember the last time he talked to anyone – even Jeremiah – like this. Why is she so easy to talk to? Is it because she doesn't come from his world?

'The thing that always grounds me, though, is my faith,' she says. The waiter has already taken away their empty plates and brought the dessert menu with a smile. 'However frustrated I feel. Does it really matter what you achieve, or just that you tried to achieve something? Life is short and so, so temporary, you know?'

He thinks about this for a moment. 'I wasn't brought up in a particularly religious household. I mean, my mum prays, but it's always been more about community and culture than religion,' he says, and then, delicately: 'I've noticed Ugandans pray a lot.'

'It's a part of our culture,' she shrugs, 'to believe that whatever you're doing in any given moment, you're only doing it by the grace of God. So you can interrupt it for prayer. This may sound strange, but it's the one thing we all do. You get Muslims who pray but then go out gambling and drinking.'

This surprises him and he thinks triumphantly: well, at least we're not hypocrites. But he doesn't say this, he just looks at her and then says: 'Why do you wear the hijab? None of the other women in your family wear it.'

'I started wearing a head tie when I was a teenager,' she says slowly. 'My hair is really brittle and it just kept breaking,' she steals a glance at his hair and smiles. 'You probably have more hair than me. And then, well . . . I never took it off.'

'So it's not a religious thing?'

'It didn't start as a religious thing,' she frowns. 'I didn't grow up in a house where it was considered mandatory that women should wear it. But I started wearing it and it's a part of my identity now. I'm happy to be identified as a Muslim because of it. Does that make any sense?'

He nods. The way she speaks makes the world make sense. He thinks of the things in his life that he struggles with; he imagines the twisted labyrinth of these thoughts being straightened and corrected through conversation with her, if only they had more time. But the waiter arrives to take their order; they are already onto their final course.

'A partner at work once asked me why I fasted,' he says after the waiter has gone. 'I didn't know what to say.'

'Why *do* you fast?'

'I don't know. Habit? Because I was raised fasting in Ramadan. Because it's just what I've done my whole life.'

'So much of what we do comes from how we were raised,' she says, tracing her finger along a crack in the table slowly. 'There comes a point when you stop doing things because of your family and you start thinking independently, right?'

Sameer nods uncertainly; independent thought is a betrayal of his family's values.

'And then it becomes a question of why we do any of these things – fast, not drink, pray,' she smiles as her eyes meet his. 'So, Ramadan. God says that we should do it because it is better for us – we don't know it, but He does. So I fast because I am God conscious. I fast out of humility. Whatever I was given in this life came from God.'

265

He is receptive to this idea, the idea that all he has – his health and his wealth and his life – was not of his own making, but was allotted to him by a higher power. But then he thinks of the sickly Ugandan children he has seen squatting at the side of the road, barely clothed, dirt-streaked ribs protruding above their abnormally enlarged bellies; he thinks of Maryam's mother's family living in a slum in Kisenyi. What made God give him this life and give others so little? He wants to challenge her now, to push her to see how far she will go.

'So we just do what God says blindly even if it's dangerous for us?' He thinks of the stupid errors fasting cost him at work, wonders how Maryam can fast in a job like hers where lives might be at risk.

'Of course not,' she replies without missing a beat, signalling that she is ready to be challenged and that she will relish it. Sameer is aroused by the way her lips part as she speaks; it seems wrong that he has found their discussion about God a turn-on, but the idea that it is wrong only makes her seem sexier. 'Allah isn't trying to make us suffer,' she says, and then, as if she has read his mind: 'I won't fast if I'm operating. If you genuinely can't fast, you don't have to. But if you have faith in Allah, you'll believe it when He says that He knows what is best for you.'

If you have faith in Allah. There is much more that could be said, but he is also aware that his knowledge is limited (whereas hers seems vast) and so he settles for: 'You make God sound like an annoying parent.'

'Maybe that's the way to look at it.'

'I guess fasting is humbling. I do always feel so grateful when Ramadan is over.'

They look at each other for a moment and then burst out laughing.

As the evening draws on, time begins to slip through his

fingers like sand. Before he knows it, they are back at her house and he is standing on the porch, saying goodbye to her family and promising to come back to Uganda again soon. One by one, Maryam's family retreat inside the house until only Ibrahim, Maryam and Sameer remain.

Ibrahim has already said his goodbyes, but there is something else, and he takes Sameer's hand in his own, searching for the words. 'I never knew if we had done something to anger your family,' he says. 'They came to take the body back to England, but they never came to this house – their house.'

Sameer looks to Maryam for explanation, but she has wandered a safe distance along the porch: this is between Sameer and Ibrahim alone. 'The body?'

'Your grandfather's,' Ibrahim says.

'I thought my grandfather died in England?' Both of Sameer's paternal grandparents – who had died before he was born – are buried in the Leicester Muslim Cemetery; the family goes to visit their graves several times a year. But now that Sameer comes to think of it, his parents have never mentioned where his grandfather died, or – for that matter – how. Sameer had always assumed that his grandfather had died in Leicester, of something related to old age. He'd never thought to ask and his father had never brought it up.

Ibrahim shakes his head. 'My child, your grandfather died here, in this house, in 1981 when he came from England to visit. On the first night of his trip, he died here in his sleep.'

At this, Sameer knows immediately what his father's thought process would have been: he wouldn't have died if he hadn't gone back to Uganda. No wonder his father had never talked about it.

'I found him in the morning,' Ibrahim says, looking past Sameer and into the distance. 'There was a letter on his bedside table, and a stack of papers – other letters, I'm guessing. I put them all together and I waited for someone to come for them. But no one came until you. I never knew if they were upset with us.'

'There's no reason for them to be,' Sameer says carefully. He leans forward and embraces Ibrahim, feeling the fragility of old age.

'May Allah bless you, Sameer Saeed,' Ibrahim says, gently patting Sameer on the head. He gives him one last look and then hobbles inside, closing the door behind him.

The sound of the porch creaking underfoot makes Sameer turn his head: Maryam has returned to him. 'Are you OK?' she asks.

He nods. He doesn't want to think about his grandfather, or his father, or his family right now. He wants to focus on her. They talk light-heartedly for a few minutes about meeting in the future – he tells her that she should seek him out if she's ever in Singapore and she promises that she will, although they both know that she will not come. He makes a bad joke about seeing each other next at each other's weddings, it being the only reason people travel any more, and she grimaces, telling him that she will never get married.

'Why not?' he asks, unable to stop himself.

She sighs. 'I'm old, Sameer. Past marriageable age.'

'What does that mean?' He had always assumed she was the same age as him.

'I'm thirty-six, very soon to be thirty-seven.'

'OK. So?'

'I wasn't interested in marriage when I was younger. And now I'm older, guys aren't interested any more. So, yeah.'

Sameer opens his mouth to say something – but all the things he is thinking of saying sound stupid even inside his head and he's not sure they are the right thing to say anyway.

Women can be funny about their age. So instead, he says: 'Thank you for everything – for being my friend out here.'

She fidgets with the edge of her sleeve. 'You're welcome,' she says automatically. 'I've enjoyed it.'

It is a strange goodbye; he has that feeling, when you leave the house for the airport, or when you're halfway there, that you have forgotten something. There is an awkward moment where he thinks they might embrace, but she raises a hand and waves, smiling, as she backs away into the house and disappears.

That night, Sameer struggles to sleep. Maryam's words ring in his head: *God conscious*. He cannot stop thinking about the fact that God saved his friend's life. That God brought him to Uganda – to Maryam – just like God brought his grandfather back to his true home to die.

At 3 a.m., he wakes from a half-dream, the memory of it evading him, and wonders if he is in love with her. The thought seems silly, childish even; he barely knows her, he has only spent time with her on a handful of occasions, he has barely touched her, let alone kissed her (can you fall in love with someone you have never even kissed?) – and yet. He leans over the bed, retrieves his iPad from where it is charging and types skyscannner.com into the Safari app. Before he really knows what he is doing, he has bought a single from Entebbe to England in two weeks' time. The ticket was stupidly expensive, but he doesn't care: a weight has been lifted from his shoulders. For a moment, he sits there on the bed, unable to stop grinning. Then, quite quickly, he wonders if he has gone crazy. He will check into a hotel of course; he does not want to be a burden on the Shahs.

He reaches for his phone, surprised to see a notification: WhatsApp, Maryam. He opens the message, heart pounding.

Maryam (01.51): *I enjoyed spending time with you*

Maryam (01.51): *Hope you come back soon*

His eyes, dry from the lack of sleep, stare at the message. She wants to see him again. She actually wants to see him again. This thought rises like a bubble of confidence: he wasn't an idiot for extending his trip, the decision was justified. Now, he knows she likes him; now, he is sure of it.

Sameer (03.08): *I might have extended my trip by a couple of weeks . . . When are you next free?*

There is something new about the morning when Sameer wakes up; it is somehow different from the others. For the first time that he can remember, he feels a strange yearning to learn more about the shadowy edges of the religion that he was born into, which he has half practised, half-heartedly, his whole life.

The national mosque is not really walking distance from the Shahs' house, but the day is bright and clear and Sameer enjoys the hour-long stroll through the suburbs of Kololo, into Nakasero and down towards Old Kampala. On the way, he comes across a small Islamic bookstore and he spends some time rifling through the available material, eventually selecting a rather large but beautifully patterned hardback translation of the Quran.

He arrives at the mosque just as the call to the early-afternoon prayer rings out. The group of men (all locals) gathered together to pray is small, less than ten, but they welcome the Muslim *muzungu* with huge smiles. It is this feeling of being accepted by strangers because they are bound together by their common belief, because they share a secret which makes them part of an exclusive club, that Sameer craves. He lines up with the men and they pray together, shoulders touching.

After the prayer is over, Sameer takes a seat on the carpeted floor, leaning against a wall close to the breezy archway doors. He opens his translation. The introduction explains that he should eschew any preconceptions; that the Quran is unlike any book he has ever read; that he cannot expect to read it in a linear format, front to back, but rather it is more easily accessible by identifying a theme and finding passages relevant to that theme. He flips through the volume and stops at a random page. Surah 30: The Romans. Sameer's eyes are drawn down the page to the words at verse 21:

> And of His Signs is that He created for you mates from your own kind that you may find peace in them and He has put love and mercy between you; surely in this there are Signs for those who reflect.

Why did his fingers land on this of all pages?
He reads on to verse 22:

> And of His Signs is the creation of the heavens and the earth, and the diversity of your languages and your colours; indeed there are Signs in this for those who are wise.

Sameer studies the words, reading them over and over again. He has always been able to recite the flowering Arabic, but until now, he had never bothered to learn what it meant.

That evening, the Shahs take Sameer out to dinner at an expensive restaurant in Kololo. 'I've barely seen you the past few days,' Aliyah complains, pouting at Sameer across the table, 'and now you're already leaving!'

'Actually, about that,' he takes sip of water. 'I'm staying another two weeks.' He catches Mr and Mrs Shah looking at each other across the table and quickly adds: 'I've booked myself into a hotel – you've been so generous, but I've imposed enough.'

'Well, that's wonderful,' Mrs Shah smiles. 'What prompted you to stay?'

'Because you've decided to pack in the legal career and start working with us?' Mr Shah suggests hopefully.

'Because he obviously wasn't ready to say goodbye to me,' Aliyah says, batting her eyelashes flirtatiously at Sameer.

'Um . . .' Sameer laughs nervously and takes another sip of water. 'I just want to travel a bit, you know – see the rest of Uganda.'

'Ooh, where do you want to go?' Aliyah asks, leaning forward, green eyes wide, head resting in her palm.

'Not sure, haven't made a real plan yet,' Sameer says vaguely.

'Well, let me know if you want any help. I could definitely give you some tips.'

'You'd better not be a stranger,' Mr Shah adds. 'I expect to see you stopping by the office and the house.'

'Of course,' Sameer says. The Shahs have been nothing but generous to him and when the bill comes, he insists on paying for it.

It is slightly strange going from the Shahs' house to a hotel; he'd got used to the house and its endless number of rooms, to Ama and Paul, to the sunshine-filled tennis court. He'd got used to going to work in the mornings with Mr Shah. But when he arrives at the hotel the following morning, lounging by the poolside until he is able to check in, he finds that it's also a bit of a relief to be alone.

He's aware that he needs to tell his parents, who are expecting him back tomorrow, that he has decided to stay, but he is not quite ready to do it yet. He will tell them at the last moment, when he has to – as he always does – and his mother will be sad and disappointed – as she always is. His father is not speaking to him anyway, and Zara will not care. He opens WhatsApp and rereads the message he received from Maryam earlier that morning.

Maryam (08.23): *Imran is going to Mbarara tomorrow to pick up some things for the store. I can try to swap one of my shifts if you want to go with him to see Mburo National Park?*

A flutter of excitement moves through him. He immediately flips open his iPad to look for a lodge they could stay in.

Imran and Maryam collect him from the hotel on the day of the trip. Sameer is glad of this, guiltily wanting to avoid seeing Musa and Ibrahim, wondering what they would think of his extended trip, what kind of obligations they might believe he was assuming by deciding to stay. Even the thought of seeing Imran makes him a little nervous. But Imran barely seems to notice that his trip has been extended from its original length, and when he sees Maryam for the first time since he said good-bye, any worry about what her family might think disappears. The sight of her, when he had come so close to never seeing her again, makes him realise that he would have moved mountains just to see her again.

'So what have you learned about Ugandans in the weeks you've been here?' Imran asks Sameer as the journey begins. Imran is driving, Maryam in the passenger seat. Sameer sits patiently in the back, surprised to find himself missing his partner in crime, Ruqaya, and wondering why she had not come.

'What have I learned? Well, you're always smiling. Oh, and you have your own version of English. Sometimes I have no idea what you're saying.'

'Ah. U-glish.'

'It's taken some getting used to. I was so confused the first time I asked for directions. Slope that way, branch here, shall I give you a push?'

The three of them laugh. 'I'm guessing you got lost with those directions,' Imran says.

'But you can't tell anyone that of course,' Maryam says, 'because being lost means something completely different in U-glish.'

'What does it mean?'

'Lost is like, it's been too long since I've seen you,' she says softly, looking over her shoulder momentarily to catch Sameer's eye.

'What you need to realise about Ugandans is that directions are not important anyway,' Imran says. 'No Ugandan is ever on time for anything!'

'Well, that's one thing we have in common,' Sameer says, laughing.

Mburo is perfect, and for a long time he will look back on the trip as the highlight of his time in Uganda. Imran drops them off at the lodge and excuses himself to go into the nearby town of Mbarara; Sameer and Maryam, left alone, check into their respective rooms and take a long, lazy lunch as they look out over the savannah and at the small klipspringers standing on the rocky outcrop around them. Sitting with her over lunch and watching her animated face as she chatters away happily, he knows that she has a hold over him in a way no person has ever had before: he would do anything within his power to make her happy. Proving the point, after lunch, Maryam suggests the horseback safari, and although Sameer has never ridden a horse before, he agrees because she wants to do it (and regrets it later when the horse, which he finds himself completely unable to control, canters across the grass, smashing his balls spectacularly hard against the stiff leather saddle). They are led by a guide across the grassy plains, getting within touching distance of zebras and buffalo; the guide asks if they would like him to take a picture of them together and they laugh in the realisation that neither of them has brought a phone. This is it with her: the rest of world becomes irrelevant.

In the early evening, Imran returns from Mbarara and the three of them have dinner together, watching as the lodge's staff coax the shyest, cutest bushbabies out from the trees for their guests' entertainment. The evening is brought in with a chill; slapping mosquitos from their arms and ankles, they sit close to the fireplace and play two games of Scrabble after dinner. Sameer, as the only Englishman, is slightly embarrassed to lose a game to each of Maryam and Imran – he insists that he had terrible letters and asks for a final game, but Imran, laughing, says that he is going to bed.

'There's no moon tonight,' Maryam says, once Imran is gone. 'Let's step outside to look at the stars.'

He follows her as she walks out from under the lodge's large wooden awning, led by torchlight past the still, black swimming pool and onto the rocks overlooking the lake. Maryam surveys the rocks with the torch and sits down, patting the area next to her for him to sit, and he obeys. 'Lie back,' she whispers, stretching out her own body onto the rock. He copies, making sure that the length of their bodies are touching.

Spread out nakedly above them in the black velvet of the cloudless night, there are stars as Sameer has never seem them before. There are millions – or billions – spraying the sky; these are the stars of the galaxy that he has seen in pictures, twinkling whites streaked along the hazy smudge of the Milky Way. The careful flourish of an artist's hand against a blank canvas. He stares at the blackness and brilliance and depth of it all, and is stunned into silence. Suddenly he feels very small.

'*Subhanallah*,' Maryam breathes next to him. Taking him completely by surprise, she takes a hold of his hand. Her fingers are cold and he rubs the crevices of her joints.

'What does that mean?' he asks, unable to tear his eyes away from the sky. 'By the grace of God?'

'It means God is perfect,' she replies.

Under the canopy of the star-washed night sky, holding Maryam's small hand in his own, Sameer thinks about his relationship with God. He has a long way to go, but Maryam has awakened something inside him, a hunger for knowledge. He did not know before he met her, that beyond a partner in mind and body, he was looking for a partner in spirit; but now that he is lying next to her it seems so obvious that anything else would leave him incomplete. *I think I'm in love with you*, he wants to tell her. He recognises that her body is dilating towards him, that she is opening like a flower. But he does not do anything or say anything. She is thirty-six years old, looking after a sick father and living in Uganda; he is moving to Singapore in a few short weeks to start building his career in earnest. After these weeks are over, they will never see each other again. So, instead, they lie there in comfortable silence, hands still interlinked, until their backs start to hurt, signalling that it is time to go.

The next two weeks pass in a blur. Sameer spends his days looking further into how he might run a business from Kampala, or in the mosque, reading the Quran. He has stopped by Mr Shah's office several times, Mr Shah answering his questions about starting a business, but politely declines offers to have dinner at the house. Instead, he spends his evenings at Maryam's house, talking to Ibrahim and Musa (who barely registered surprise at his appearance), letting Ruqaya and the other children play with his hair. Sometimes, he will meet Maryam for breakfast in the morning before she goes to work; once, he met her outside the hospital straight after a shift and they went for an evening walk. They never speak of his grandfather's letters any more, but he asks her to tell him about Uganda's colonial legacy from the Ugandan perspective, and she tells him that in the Asian expulsion perhaps a dozen Asians were murdered but hundreds of thousands of Ugandans were killed. Her knowledge thrills him and makes him want to learn more, to better himself. He spends hours on his iPad, reading about Uganda's history, and walks through the ring-road-fenced enclaves of Nakasero and Kololo with fresh eyes, seeing for the first time the Asian buffer between this Kampala and the rest of Kampala. He reads about colonial favouritism towards to the Buganda people, and imagines the British evaporating from Kampala on independence, leaving the Asians – facilitators and beneficiaries of British colonial policies – caught between the elite and the masses. Maryam warns him that a tension remains, although its parameters differ; it has morphed to take shape against the newest threat, the Chinese, tolerated as a result of the Ugandan debt burden, unable in this day and age to be expelled by crude policies.

As his trip once again draws to a close, Sameer starts to feel a familiar and horrible sense of desperation. And there it is, like the fleeting passing of any period of happiness in life: his last evening in Kampala. They are back at the same steakhouse, and the only thought running through his mind is that he cannot believe that he never even had the chance to kiss her.

The dinner is over before he knows it, and they walk back to her car in silence, slowly. Maryam rummages for her keys in her handbag for several minutes, muttering that she cannot find them; she eventually retrieves them and unlocks the car. They both stand in front of the car, not moving.

'Sameer –' she begins, at exactly the same time as he begins to say her name, and they laugh awkwardly, too loudly and for too long, as if this might prolong their time.

'You first,' Sameer says when the laughter has died to

nothing and there is only the close night air, thick with the sound of crickets.

'I wasn't going to say anything, really, just, you know, that it's been fun.'

'Oh. Yes – for me too.'

'Well, have an amazing time in Singapore,' she garbles, avoiding his gaze and reaching for the car door, 'make sure to keep in touch –'

'Maryam.'

He puts his hand on her arm and gently removes it from the car door: there is no resistance. He takes hold of both her arms and pulls her towards him; pulls her closer until their foreheads are almost touching.

'The thing is,' he says softly, knowing that he is about to say what is in his heart, 'I'm in love with you.'

She tilts her chin up so that her full lips graze the surface of his. It is barely a kiss but is enough to send his body into overdrive. He can feel her heart pounding through her slender frame.

'You barely know me,' she whispers uncertainly. 'People can seem very nice and you think at a particular time that you get along. Then, well, they turn out to be crazy. Only time can tell.'

He wonders what experience she has been through that has made her say this, and he burns as he imagines her feeling something for someone else, for anyone else. Her eyes search his face, and when he doesn't respond immediately, she tiptoes to kiss him again, harder this time, so he can feel blood rising to his mouth in response. He has never been more certain about anything; instinct tells him that with her by his side, things will always be all right.

'I'll take that risk,' he says when she pulls away. 'Will you?'

PART III

21

Sameer is simultaneously exhilarated and nauseous, as if he is about to go onto a stage to make a speech; loud thumping in his chest, uncontrollable and wild; mouth dry, hands twisting nervously in his lap. He has never felt like this before, not ever – not even with Raha (which now seems so juvenile, so silly – he thinks of his parents' attempts to interfere as harmless, even with fondness: they only did it out of love). There is colour and beauty in everything; a sad story in the news brings a tear to his eyes, a happy story does the same. His mind drifts to Maryam constantly; she is in his days and in his dreams. He pictures the way she looks when she smiles, the dimples which create that impression of mischief and innocence at the same time; the interminable black of her eyes; the fullness of the pink, wet lips that she brushed against his own only twice before he left Uganda. He sees them lying on the grass outside the Baha'i Temple, her head on his stomach, while she tells him about her favourite childhood memory, while he traces the lines on her palms with a finger.

Falling in love has brought him closer to God, where he finds clarity and reassurance. Above all, he is thankful: thankful that God led him to Uganda, to Maryam, to rethink everything he thought he knew about what he wanted from his life. When he thinks about what he has been blessed with (which he does often now), he feels grateful again and again and again.

They didn't discuss anything before he left – it was too rushed, he was leaving too soon. They met again only once, when she took him to the airport, but Ibrahim and Ruqaya insisted on accompanying them, and there was only one stolen moment alone in the airport, when Ibrahim took Ruqaya to buy some water: a kiss and a promise that he would come back soon. She waved goodbye as he went through security, a hand on Ruqaya's shoulder, and gave him a trembling smile without dimples. In that moment, as he waved back, he knew that she loved him too and that she felt she was somehow weaker for doing so.

At the back of his mind, he is quietly aware that he is going to quit his job and move to Kampala. Maryam will never leave Uganda. She has an obligation to her father and to her country. Sameer, on the other hand, is ready. Ready to quit his job: he feels surprisingly calm about this, as if it is just his conscious catching up with his subconscious. And he is ready to leave the UK: that is what he had been planning in any event, just to Singapore, not Uganda.

But as the plane touches down in Heathrow and he stares out of the face-shaped window onto the calm concrete of London, the steady, reliable grey drizzle, he feels such a rush of comfort that he wonders for a moment whether moving to Uganda is really a good idea. Then, as he passes through baggage reclaim and his feet are almost run over by the trolley of someone, who, in response to Sameer's protests, gives him an 'Oh fuck off', the nostalgia is washed away, just like that. No Ugandan stranger, sweet-natured and smiling, would ever react like that.

The family – aside from Mhota Papa – are waiting for him at the airport. His mother cries when she sees him. 'You've become so dark,' is the first thing she says. His father is tight-lipped, still angry, but he came. Zara laughs at Sameer's complexion. 'You look African, bro,' she jokes.

'How is Mhota Papa?' Sameer asks.

The family exchange sideways glances and he knows it's not good news.

His father begins the lecture in the car on the way home: it is the first time that they have spoken in five weeks, and it's a lecture. Mhota Papa is unwell – he has been admitted to hospital with pneumonia. 'Now, see, this is what happens when you disappear for a month like that, what did you expect?'

I expected you to tell me, Sameer thinks. 'How long has he been in there?'

'Three days.'

Why didn't you tell me? he thinks. He feels like he is being punished, but he's not sure what he's done wrong. It is his father who decided to telephone his employers; it is his father who decided not to speak to him for five weeks. 'If I had known I would have come home earlier,' Sameer says quietly.

'Well, your Amira Ben flew over from America as soon as she found out,' his father retorts. 'She's staying with us.' This is delivered smugly, as if it is a competition and Amira Ben has won – despite the fact that the playing field was not even, because she knew, and he didn't. Mhota Papa's daughter who lives in the US didn't get punished for not living in this country, he thinks bitterly. They reserved punishment only for him.

There is silence. Sameer stares out of the window miserably. There are no questions about his trip, and he volunteers nothing. He closes his eyes and then feels a light touch on his arm. A gentle voice, his ever-loyal sister: 'So, tell us about your trip. What's Kampala all about?' Sameer turns to Zara and smiles. He tells her – just loud enough for his parents, sitting in the front of the car, to hear, if they wish – about staying with the Shahs, about visiting their grandfather's old house, about exploring the national parks of Uganda. His voice drips with affection and Zara comments: 'You've really fallen in love with the country, you're making me want to go! Maybe you can take me with you next time?' Sameer grins. He does not tell them about Maryam. Not yet.

They drive straight to the hospital from the airport. A pang of anxiety greets Sameer at the revolving doors: he does not want all of his memories of Leicester to be of its general infirmary. But seeing Mhota Papa, who is frail and small and distant, is so different to seeing Rahool. Sameer looks at Mhota Papa, a bag of bones, covered in crumpled skin, and ponders the brevity of life. One day – God willing – Sameer will look like that. It is not distressing; it is inevitable and understandable, something to be grateful for. He sits close to Mhota Papa and takes one of his dry, veiny hands, into which a tube has been inartfully inserted. 'I'm sorry I didn't come sooner, Mhota Papa,' he says.

Mhota Papa is slow, but acknowledges Sameer with a smile. *'Toon Kampala giyo hato? Kewoo laygoo?'* You were in Kampala, right? What did you think?

Behind him, Sameer's father paces the floor. Only two people are allowed in the room at any given time, and the family have been operating on a shift basis, with different people coming at scheduled times throughout the day. 'Why don't you guys go home – you must be tired?' Sameer suggests, glancing at his watch. 'There's only half an hour until visiting hours are over. I'll catch an Uber home.'

His father doesn't protest and leaves immediately; Sameer finds himself relieved at his departure.

He sits and talks to Mhota Papa, looking into his rheumy eyes and, when Mhota Papa's eyelids begin to droop, at the layers of sagging skin that roll onto his eyelashes. They talk about his trip to Uganda, about the family's old shop. Each time, Mhota Papa removes his oxygen mask to speak, prompting a series of coughing fits. But he is animated, switching to English for the first time in years that Sameer can remember (then again, he can hardly remember the last time he sat with Mhota Papa and had a conversation this long).

'Did you visit the house, *beta*?' Mhota Papa asks through raspy breaths.

Sameer nods.

'Is the bougainvillea still there at the front?'

'Yes – and it was in full bloom. I've never seen anything like it.'

'And you never will, *beta*. The country is unique. That's why Papa loved it so much, that's why he couldn't let it go. He was blindsided by his love for that country –' but this is too much for him and he begins to cough, aggressive, chesty coughs that cause his whole body to shudder and bring up a thick brown phlegm that he hocks into a tissue. Sameer's own throat starts to feel scratchy as he watches helplessly.

'You rest, Mhota Papa, I'll talk,' he pleads, handing his uncle the glass of water that's on the bedside table.

Mhota Papa begins to nod but can't help himself. 'Was Abdullah's family living there?' he croaks.

'Yes, Mhota Papa.'

Mhota Papa seems satisfied with this answer and leans back in the bed, but then he starts again: 'Your dada loved that man more than anyone else in the world.'

Sameer swallows and says nothing. Mhota Papa wheezes a little, but it doesn't turn into a coughing fit.

'Your dada was not an easy person to understand, Sameer,' he says, closing his eyes. 'But he had a lot of love in his heart.'

Sameer looks at his uncle, thinking back to the Shahzeb of his grandfather's letters. 'Dada talked about you so much,' he whispers. Mhota Papa doesn't respond. 'I brought back the letters,' he adds, still in a whisper. 'I wasn't ready to finish reading them, but I brought them with me – every single one.' He had thought about destroying them, but couldn't bring himself to do it, and he's glad of it now, suddenly curious to know more about the young Shahzeb. Still, Mhota Papa does not respond; he is definitely asleep. It's only at this point that Sameer realises that Mhota Papa is not wearing his hearing aid; that they'd had an entire conversation and Mhota Papa hadn't struggled to hear him speak. Sameer stays a few moments longer, watching the slow but steady rise and fall of his grandfather's oldest surviving child, and thinks: To Him we belong, and to Him we return.

On the way home in the Uber, Sameer finally turns his attention to WhatsApp, firing off a series of messages to Rahool (*Are u around tomorrow? Am in Leicester but going back to London Monday*), Jeremiah (*Yo, I'm back, are you in Leicester?*), and, in response to her last message (*Land safe?*), Maryam (*Yes – will call you later. Going to tell my parents about you tonight*). Nervous tremors of excitement run through him at the thought of it.

But, that evening, the house is full. Amira Ben and her youngest daughter are staying in the spare room, her two sons have been sleeping in Sameer's room; Yasmeen Foi and Haroon Fua's daughter, Samah, and her husband John are in town for the first time in months, and everyone has gathered at Sameer's family's house for dinner. It is noisy and crowded; the dining table is extended to seat its maximum of twelve, but this is not enough because Yasmeen Foi's other daughter, Shabnam, and her family have also arrived. Chairs are pulled from the study, stools brought from the breakfast bar in the kitchen, and everyone squeezes in around the table to be served helpings of Sameer's mother's multi-coloured biryani.

It has been a long time since they were all together like this, and he is reminded of evenings at Maryam's house in Kampala, but it is different when it's his own family and (no matter how long it has been) he doesn't have the privileges of a guest. Shabnam's belly is now enormous and she complains about back pain while her young son Ayaan throws his food on the walls and the floor, only encouraged by his father's hapless attempts to stop him. Sameer's parents are occupied with Amira Ben as they try to persuade her that the US is no place to live, and her two young sons try to draw Sameer into a debate about American football teams that he's never heard of. Zara and Amira Ben's daughter giggle conspiratorially over something on her phone; although Amira Ben's daughter is several years younger than her, Zara, being the type of person she is, will make an effort to get along with just about anyone she is asked to. Samah and John are fussed over incessantly by Yasmeen Foi and Haroon Fua, who seem to be just so grateful that they have made the arduous journey down from Leeds, and when Samah shyly reveals that she is three and a half months pregnant, Yasmeen Foi starts to cry with joy. They barely pay any attention to Sameer at all – he has no chance to tell them about Uganda, let alone Maryam.

After dinner, Sameer manages to grab Samah and bundles her out into the back garden, no shoes. The grass is damp from the drizzle and soaks into their socks.

'I've missed you, *ben*,' he says. 'I haven't seen you since the wedding.'

'I know,' Samah says, her tone almost contrite. And then, half defensively: 'You're always welcome to come and visit us in Leeds, you know.'

'Yeah, thanks,' Sameer says. Now that he is standing in front of her, everything he had wanted to ask seems childish and unnecessary. 'Congratulations on the baby,' he says after a pause. 'You both must be so excited.'

Samah instinctively touches her stomach with one hand. 'The first mixed-race baby in our family,' she whispers. 'I hope it doesn't end up looking completely white.'

'Either way – are you going to call it Sam?'

He flashes her a smile and they start to laugh, quietly at first and then loudly, full-bellied. It is suddenly like no time has passed at all, as if they are the same Samah and Sameer – Sam and Sam – digging holes in the garden with a stick and daring each other to eat worms.

'I wanted to tell you something, actually,' he says. 'I've met someone. Someone I want to marry. You know, a love marriage, like you had. How exactly did you go about it with Foi and Fua?'

'Wow, little bro,' she attempts to ruffle his hair as he ducks out of the way. 'Congratulations. Is she Muslim?'

Yes.

'Sunni?'

Yes.

'Indian?'

No.

'What is she then?'

Ugandan.

'Even better,' Samah grins. 'They'll love that. Where are her parents originally from – Gujarat?'

'No,' Sameer says. 'She's not Ugandan Asian.'

Samah frowns, not understanding.

'She's African,' he explains. 'A black Ugandan. Hijabi.'

Samah's mouth falls open. 'Black and hijabi, Sameer?' she laughs. 'Nice one. That'll really push their buttons – well done.'

He scowls. 'I didn't do it to piss them off, Sam. And I was asking your advice because you married – you know – John –'

'Yeah, but, Sameer, John's *white*.' Samah shakes her head incredulously. 'You really think they're going to treat a black girl the same way they treat a white guy? You do realise they used to have black servants in Uganda, right?' Sameer visibly winces at this comment. 'OK, maybe I'm being unfair,' Samah concedes, 'But I'm just trying to be honest with you – I'm not sure how they're going to take it.'

There is a short silence as they stare out into the depths of the lawn. The kitchen is illuminated against the evening sky and Sameer can see his mother, Yasmeen Foi and Zara cleaning away the dishes. Then, Samah says: 'She must be really special, huh? Tell me, what's she like?'

Later that evening, when everyone has left and Amira Ben's family have gone upstairs (Sameer had reluctantly agreed with his mother that it would make sense for him to take the sofa bed in the living room rather than turf his cousins out of his room), he tries to corner his parents before they go to bed. 'Mum, Dad, can I talk to you?'

'What is it, *beta*?' his mother's eyes are tired, hands raw from the washing up. One hand rests on her back like she is in pain.

He takes a deep breath. 'I want to talk to you about something important.'

'Something important, huh?' his father glances at the clock hanging on the wall. 'Well, now is not really the time. We can speak tomorrow.'

Sameer sighs inwardly – but the arms of the clock do read 1.35 a.m.

He changes into his pyjamas, brushing his teeth in the downstairs bathroom at the same time as scrolling to his messages with Maryam. He had warned her that the dinner would go on late and he wouldn't get a chance to escape and speak to her; they had arranged to speak during his morning, while she was on her lunch break.

It's the first time that they will have spoken to each other on the phone and he is strangely nervous, but when her face, grainy but beautiful, appears on the small screen in the morning, the memory of being with her comes back to him so strongly that it is like a physical ache. They talk for an hour – until someone raps on the bathroom door and Sameer is forced to say goodbye and flush the toilet. Zara is standing outside the door, arms crossed, eyebrows raised. 'You were talking to someone,' she says. 'Who were you talking to?' Sameer shakes his head, a faint smile still on his face, and pushes past her for the kitchen.

But there is no time to talk to his parents over breakfast, and immediately afterwards, they all go to the hospital to visit Mhota Papa. Sameer goes straight from the hospital to see Rahool.

It is the first time in perhaps six or seven months that he has been to Rahool's family home, and standing there outside the front door, he suddenly wishes that Jeremiah was with him. But Jeremiah had not responded to his last message. He raises a hand and presses the bell.

Rahool's mother opens the door and hugs Sameer firmly. She looks tired but happy; underlying her movements and the rhythm of her speech is relief. 'We are so happy to see you,' she says as she leads him to the front room. 'Just head on in, I'm going to prepare you some lunch.' He protests, but she shoves him towards the door and disappears. He stares at the door for a moment, abandoned, and then forces himself to push it open.

Rahool is sitting in a wheelchair, talking to his father, when Sameer enters the room. He looks so small, knees knocking together, hands sitting placidly in his lap, shorn head tilted ever so slightly to the left.

'Hey, Rahool,' Sameer says loudly. 'Hello, Mr Patel.'

Rahool's father pats the seat next to him and Sameer sits opposite Rahool. The wheelchair has such presence, dominating Rahool's small form, the stiff black upholstery visible from every angle, the awkward metal framing holding him together. He wants to pull Rahool out from its constraints – to embrace him, clap him on the back, grab his hand. 'How you been doing?' he asks instead.

'Good,' Rahool says with a lopsided grin – 'Better. Heard I forgot you for a while.' His speech is punctuated with pauses, given context with jerky gesticulation, and his smile makes Sameer wants to cry.

He stays for lunch, and then he stays a little longer. Rahool is slowly learning to walk again and Sameer helps him to practise with a walking frame (the physiotherapist will be coming later and she is apparently quite terrifying when Rahool has not done his homework). When his parents are not in the room, Rahool volunteers that he doesn't remember anything about the night he was attacked – that this was the first thing that Jeremiah had wanted to know and he's sorry to disappoint, but it's a black hole. Sameer is surprised to find that he is unbothered by this news. The trial is over, what has happened has happened, and he's not interested in retribution or reopening wounds that are on their way towards healing. He's interested in Rahool's recovery only. He changes the subject and tells Rahool that he has just come back from Uganda and – unable to keep the excitement out of his voice – that he has met someone. Rahool's smile is so genuine that it lifts the corners of Sameer's own mouth until their faces are matching, both beaming, and for a moment Sameer has his old friend back, the Rahool he grew up with, who celebrated each of Sameer's successes as if they were his own. Sameer stays upbeat the whole visit, nodding and smiling and acting as if everything is completely normal, but it's exhausting and as soon as he leaves, he almost feels depressed.

It's only in the evening that Sameer is finally alone with his parents, when Zara has taken Amira Ben and her children to the hospital for the final visiting slot of the day. He forces his parents to sit in the front room and says: 'I really need to talk to you now.' His mother looks anxious; his father nonchalant, looking around as if the room is far more interesting than anything Sameer has to say.

Sameer is surprised to hear his heart beating loud and fast and his voice is almost shaking when he speaks: 'I've done some serious thinking in my time off.'

His father's arms are crossed and he glances at his watch.

Sameer closes his eyes briefly. 'I'm quitting my job. I'm going to hand my notice in tomorrow.'

Immediately his father's eyes snap up. In an instant, the anger has dissolved, those five weeks of silence mean nothing. His father's eyes are shining: Sameer is forgiven, all is forgiven. 'Well, my son –' his father's voice trembles with emotion – 'you've finally seen sense, I am so proud of you.'

'Dad – no –'

'You are a smart young boy – you always took after me in that way. What you and I, son, will make of this business, we'll be such a success together. To know that there is someone who will take over the legacy that we have worked so hard to create . . .' he breathes, almost overcome. 'I can't put into words how happy you have made me today, Sameer.'

Sameer shakes his head disbelievingly: how is it already going so wrong? But he lets his father finish because there is no use in trying to interrupt him. When his father finally stops, looking at Sameer with anticipation, Sameer looks straight back. He steels himself. 'I'm not quitting to join the family business, Dad,' he says. 'I'm quitting because I'm going to move to Uganda.'

It is as if he has slapped his father in the face; he is now deflated, confused. Sameer's mother's voice pipes up, small and vulnerable: 'What are you saying, *beta*? Is this some kind of joke?'

'No.' He explains that he has seen a gap in the market that he wants to exploit, that he has some capital and he'll use a loan to fund some of it, and if it doesn't work out, there's nothing to stop him from coming back. 'It's not a permanent move,' he says.

'It's a bloody stupid idea,' his father snaps. 'You've spent one short holiday there. You know nothing about that country, nothing about what it put us through. That country is not safe for people like us. They resent us. You think you're so high and mighty now that you would be insulated from all that, huh?'

'Well, there is one other thing,' Sameer says, and this time he averts his eyes, so he's looking beyond his parents and at a spot on the wall. 'I've met someone.' Silence. 'Who I want to marry,' he adds.

His mother's face expands with excitement; the tears have dried instantaneously. 'It's the Shahs' daughter, isn't it?!' she yelps. 'Now, she is a bit young, but she comes from a very good family, a very rich family –' a high-pitched giggle – 'oh, it all makes sense now, but you don't need to move to Uganda for her, she will easily come here. She's already studying in London, at the SOAS.'

Sameer bites his lip. Why do his parents have to do this? 'Mum,' he says, 'it's not Aliyah. It's a lady called Maryam.'

'Maryam?' his mother's eyes narrow with suspicion; the drawbridge is going up.

'Dad,' he turns to his father. 'Do you remember a man

called Abdullah? He was friends with Dada.' His father says nothing. 'Well,' Sameer continues, 'his family are living in our family's old house. Maryam is one of his granddaughters.'

'I don't understand,' his mother says, looking at his father.

There is silence for a few moments and then, abruptly, Sameer's father stands up. 'Abdullah was our house servant,' he spits.

'Yes – *was*,' Sameer begins, but he is cut off again by his father.

'A servant whose family took everything from mine. They took our house, our business. They took my father,' and he chokes on the last word. 'Your grandfather went back to that godforsaken country and died in the care of those people. That's the family your son wants to marry into,' he says to Sameer's mother.

Sameer looks at his father and tries to force himself to feel pity – he imagines what it might feel like to lose your father at the tender age of twenty-one, to lose him to a country that had so clearly rejected him, yet a country to which he had returned. He tries to feel the anger, the hurt. Mhota Papa's voice comes unprompted to his head: *Your dada loved that man more than anyone else in the world.* He exhales slowly. 'Abdullah was Dada's friend above everything,' he says. 'Yes, he was a servant, but then he became a businessman. He worked with Dada. He was a Muslim. Maryam is a Muslim. And yes, she is a black Ugandan.'

He looks at his parents' horrified faces and his heart becomes cold. They look pathetic, almost stupid. 'Is there a problem?'

'*Astaghfirullah,*' his mother whispers. *May Allah forgive us.* 'So this is the real reason you want to move to Uganda, huh?' she lets out a sob. 'Ensnared by some black witch!'

'What the fuck, Mum. What are you saying?'

'Don't you dare use that language with your mother,' his father warns, voice dangerously quiet. He is still standing; perhaps he had made up his mind to leave, but something had stopped him, trapped him to the scene of the unfolding drama. His mother sobs softly in the background. Then his father says calmly: 'Sameer, it is inappropriate. We will not accept it.'

'How is it inappropriate?' Sameer challenges. 'There's nothing inappropriate about it.' He knows that they cannot bring themselves to spell it out, why they disapprove, why they don't want this for their good Asian son. 'And I don't need you to accept it. But I would love for you to be a part of it.'

'We will never be a part of such a thing,' his father says bitterly. 'She will never understand our family, she will never understand our culture. There are plenty of lovely women at the mosque who you could marry. If you're feeling ready, then we can help you satisfy that need. You don't have to go off to Uganda to do that.'

'But I love her,' Sameer says bluntly, annoyed that it has come to this because he knows they will interpret this statement as childish and whining.

'You don't know what love is – you've barely known her a month!'

'Oh, and you both knew, did you, before you had your arranged marriage? You didn't know each other at all!'

There is silence after this comment, and in a way this is worse than any response they could have given him.

'Look,' he tries again softly, 'Samah married John and that was fine –' ignoring the mutter from his mother that *Samah's not our daughter* – 'we live in a multicultural world now, you can't expect me – or Zara – to marry someone from the same village in India that your ancestors were from. And it doesn't make sense anyway.' There is the sound of a car in the driveway, the chatter of voices: Amira Ben and Zara have returned from the hospital. 'Just meet her once,' he says quickly, eyes imploring. 'I'm going to hand in my notice tomorrow and then I'm going back to Uganda. Come with me. Meet her.'

22

To my first love, my beloved

18th July 1974

Shabnam has been on strike for two months now. That beautiful brown package that she would bring home to my eager waiting hands at the end of each month has stopped coming; the money has all but dried up. We are dependent now on the family's general pot, and once the money has filtered through the needy hands and greedy pockets of the younger generation, there is little left to spare for the frivolities of the older generation: six children to put through school, one child soon to go to university, Zakir for whom we must find a wife (the lazy bastard is still not working), and Fatma for whom we need to save up a dowry. I will admit that priority is given to the matter of my medication, but at this stage, I hardly care whether I live or die. (Shabnam, for your information, is well, no health problems so to speak. Indeed, she has never been better it seems.) I have said several times to Shabnam that we should follow my Farah and move to London, where Noor's wealthy family will be able to provide for us. But Shabnam did not want to take our children – 'You really want to make them move again, Hasan? They have only just settled in their schools. And I'm not going without them. My babies need me.' But they are not babies. The lot of them are old enough to be married. 'I'll just go without you then,' I grumbled back. But I have not contacted Farah yet.

Well, there is one thing Shabnam is wrong about. The children are not settled. Rizwan came home with a broken nose last week, blood dripping down his little zip-up jacket, face swollen with snot and tears. Shabnam screamed when she saw him. She stood up from the floor where she had been painting a picket sign and scooped him into her arms, rocking him and asking: 'What did they do to you, *beta*?' I was in my armchair and I called for Shahzeb; then, remembering that of course he would not be in the house, I called for Tasneem. 'See what is wrong with him.' Tasneem took him from Shabnam and tilted his head towards the single yellow bulb. 'His nose looks broken, Papa,' she said to me. 'I will take him to the hospital.' We don't have a car, of course, so off they went in the bus, Shabnam, Tasneem and Rizwan, leaving me with a half-painted picket sign and an uncontrollable itch.

Tasneem told me later that Rizwan had been walking home from the bus stop, minding his own business, when he was kicked in the back of the knees and stumbled. He righted himself, and turned to face two boys, no older than him – perhaps even younger, he said. 'Wogs out!' one of the boys shouted and smacked him so hard in the face that he fell to the floor. Who knew small children could carry such brute force?

When they finally returned from the hospital, it was two o'clock in the morning. They had been gone for ten hours. I had not moved from the armchair; in fact, I had fallen asleep on it in front of the flickering television set. Rizwan's nose was bandaged; in one hand he held on to a boiled sweet.

'I don't want to go to school tomorrow, Papa,' he said in a muffled voice.

'You will go,' I responded curtly.

Shabnam put a hand on his head, and said gently: 'If you do not go to school, you will not become clever like your papa. That's what they want, isn't it, the people who did this to you? They don't want you to become clever. So if you don't go to school, you are letting them win.'

'I d-don't w-want to go!' Rizwan burst into noisy tears and ran up the stairs. Tasneem sighed heavily and followed him. I wanted Shabnam to stay with me; I tried to grab her hand as she walked past my armchair, but I could not reach her. I wanted to tell her that she had found the words I had wanted to say, that she had said the right thing. But she walked straight past me, and I did not say anything at all.

Shabnam despises me now; I am certain of it. That is fine; I also despise her. There is no need for privacy now and there is no room for it anyway: we share a room with two of our children; the other children share with Shahzeb's youngest son; Samir and Tasneem share a room with their two children. Shahzeb, his wife and their two daughters live in the adjoining house, together with Ahmed and his wife and their two children, and Aisha and her husband. I tell no lie! – all twenty-three of us, squeezed into two three-bedroomed houses, squashed together under the same adjoining roof, along the same suffocating road.

Belgrave is a far cry from Nakasero; my heart longs for its trim lawns and wide-open spaces. This street is run-down, England's equivalent of a slum, where, instead of *karia*, brown children run barefoot along the pavements, houses reeking of fried onions. Leicester has many brown areas, and – just like Kampala – has its white areas also. We are in what I am told is the best of the brown areas – because we were fortunate enough to know the Mehtas, whom Shabnam diligently contacted as soon as she arrived. There is already a community here, and yes, they are mainly Hindu, but I do not mind – I would still rather live here than in the depths of Spinney Hill, mixing with immigrants from the Caribbean and elsewhere. At least here we are all Asian.

Signs of the Asian occupation are already starting to show; Belgrave Road has the beginnings of the facade of Old

Kampala, though none of its spirit. Samir and Shahzeb used our export relationships to bring goods from India into the country. They had no money, so they had to borrow it, and they had no credit history, so they had to invent one. But the good news was that rent was cheap. And, in my brief absence, they opened a shop, doing just what Papa did all those years ago when he first arrived in Uganda. Saeed's Saris. I was so proud of them when the store launched. If I have done nothing, Amira, I have succeeded in one thing. Instilling business in the blood of my children.

Oh, how I long for the warm air of Kampala! Sometimes I think that if I can just want it enough, Allah will find a way of taking me there. I suspect Allah may be quite angry with me though. We have not spoken for some time, because I feel too guilty to face him. The Quran says that alcohol has some good and some evil, but the evil is greater than the good and we should therefore abstain. You know me, and I swear to you that until I came to England, I never touched a drop of that *haraam* liquid. But these British public houses are places where you can 'drown your sorrows' and it is easy, so easy, to forget with drink.

'We are worried about you, Papa,' Samir says to me, sitting me down on my armchair and looking me in the eyes. Musty old second-hand armchair in the corner of the small, insipid room. I close my eyes and I remember the grandeur of our house in Kampala, where five families could live comfortably under that roof and not complain for space. 'Are you taking your medication?' Of course I am taking my medication, you idiots. I need to keep myself alive so I can get back to Uganda. I'm just in need of a drink.

Shabnam looks at me with a combination of pity and disgust. I have pulled her hair, grabbed and pinched the flesh of her arms, trying to make her see what I am feeling. When I arrived in England, I noticed that she was different somehow; hardened. Gone were the soft rolls; there was steel in her eyes. She had taken up a job. A woman who had never worked a day in her life, and within a month of being in Leicester, she and Aisha were working in a local factory.

But I tell you, this strike business is a stupid injustice. Like most things now, it makes no sense to me: I am both proud of her and angry at her. We are a desperate people, so we are not in a position to be making demands. Yes, I understand that it is not fair, that she is being paid less than her white counterparts, that she is not getting the promotions or the better roles. But since when was life fair? And since when were Asians in this country in a good bargaining position? We have nothing; now is not the time to be negotiating. For as long as she strikes, she brings me no money, and for as long as I have no money, my throat stays dry. She spends her days painting placards and protesting in front of the factory. It is a dangerous business, I have warned her – there are women who have been arrested by the police, women who have been attacked by the National Front. She thrust a newspaper in front of me with a quote from the trade union official in response to the strike: 'They've got no legitimate grounds for complaint. They've got to learn to fit in with our ways, we haven't got to learn to fit in with theirs. In a civilised society the majority view will prevail.' She says she will not live like this.

From where has she imbibed this stronghold attitude? There is perhaps more of a community here than there was in Kampala; here there are no barbed-wire fences or sky-high hedges, we live atop one another, and there is no way of avoiding having your business known by everyone. Shabnam has formed a friendship with the striking ladies that runs deeper than any friendship she has ever known: they rise together, eat together, strike together. I have told her that we need the money ('To fund your drinking habit, astaghfirullah!' she screamed at me as I grabbed her wrist), that beggars cannot be choosers. But she will not return to work.

There is a part of me that watches her determination every day, her purpose, a part of me that watches the rest of them getting on with their lives whilst I flounder and stumble, and I loathe them all and wish that I had never joined them. I had imagined that they would be lost without me, that they had spent their days waiting for me to join them, that they could not survive without me. But by the time I arrived in Leicester last summer, they were already settled into their new lives. It was as if my arrival was an inconvenience; Shabnam had been living with Aisha, but there was no space for me to live in that house too – Samir offered to take me, but they had to rearrange their sleeping arrangements to accommodate me. The young children were excited to see me at first and I unloaded my pockets with treats from Belgium; but then they quickly forgot about their old papa as they returned to their new world. Samir and Shahzeb had already begun to rent the shop, and I realised that they did not need their papa's help to start their own success stories.

I tried to work, you know. At first, when I arrived, I applied for seven different jobs. And I received seven different rejection letters. No one has the need for a man of my age – I am not fit to work in a factory, nor quick enough to work in an office. I wanted to help Samir and Shahzeb with the store – the thing I know above all else – but pride held me back. They had gone ahead and done it all without me; well, if they did not need me, then I would not impose myself upon them. When Samir asked me if I might be able to watch the shop for the day, I declined – sorry, I told him, but I was meeting an old friend.

It was not a lie. I met Manish Mehta at a public house and had my first alcoholic beverage. To this day, I do not know why

I did it. Yes, I was not working and was waiting to go back to Uganda, but no more so than I had been in Belgium. Yes, I resented my family, the lot of them, but I was also quietly proud of them all. Yes, I was with an old friend, a friend who was not a Muslim, but that did not differ from Kampala. Perhaps it happened because I had stopped praying. There is a Hadith that says that when a man asked the Prophet (peace be upon him) why we pray five times a day, the Prophet replied that if a man is near a stream and washes five times a day, is it possible for the man to remain dirty? Something about this country has dirtied me and now I cannot clean myself.

People here treat us as if we are no different from the *karias*: black, brown or yellow – as long as you are not white – there is no distinguishing between any of us: we are all 'coloured'. I have been called a black bastard and a nigger, words shouted at me across the street as I walked home from the pub, words spat at me on the bus. When a shop sign reads: 'No Blacks. No Irish. No dogs' it means no Asians too.

Sometimes I think upon how we treated the *karias* back home with a tinge of guilt. Is this how they felt? Certainly – surely – we were not openly racist like they are towards us here. This country's National Front has its headquarters in Leicester. There are certain areas of the city that we simply cannot visit. They gather and chant, protesting our presence in their city. The group is led by skinheads with grotesque-looking tattoos and the hardest eyes you have ever seen, but it is not only these types that participate in the marches; there are also otherwise average white people, in their thousands. What have we done to disturb these people? What is it that we have done, by coming here, that so offends them? We are the immigrants, but they are the ones who feel displaced, somehow uprooted by our arrival. I have seen a mother and a child cross the street to avoid us; I have walked into a barber shop to have people wrinkle their noses and say loudly: Can you smell a Paki? My children are being called monkey and nig-nog and wog. My children are coming home from schools where they are not wanted, bruised and bleeding because they have been attacked for no reason other than that they are brown. And there is nothing I can do to protect them.

Tell me: is this country so different from Amin's Uganda? Is there nowhere that we might be safe?

23

Sameer leaves for London without seeing – let alone speaking to – his father. His mother takes him to the train station and the journey is conducted in a steely silence. She parks the car in the usual side road, eyes forward. Finally, still looking ahead, hands clenched on the steering wheel, she says: 'Are you really handing in your notice?'

'Yes.'

'Have you thought about this properly? Everything you've worked so hard for, everything you've achieved and are about to achieve, you want to throw it all away now for some woman you just met?'

'But, Mum,' he begins, and then stops. This is confusing and contradictory; they wanted him to quit his job – better yet, they tried to do it for him; they didn't see his career as an achievement, they saw it as a failure of his familial duties. But now they have seen how much worse it could be – the dilution of their blood – they would rather have him in a job that they hated than with her. He shakes his head. There is no point in trying to explain the internal struggles he had had with his career choices, the emptiness that came with it, the desperate longing to be needed, the stark reality of being bullied. 'I've got to go – I'm going to miss my train.' He gets out of the car and doesn't look back.

As he walks through the station, his fingers find their way to Maryam's name: *Leaving Leicester now, didn't speak to Dad.* It was a new feeling, this desire to share with her the fragments of his days, and to want to know what was happening in hers – it made him feel connected, like she was always with him, and this made him feel better about things; it gave him a confidence he didn't otherwise have. He had worried at first how he would tell her about his parents' reaction but when they'd spoken briefly on the phone the night before, it had all poured out: he had forgotten how easy she made it to talk. 'It's OK,' she'd said. 'I'm not surprised. Your *taata*'s father died here in our house. He has never liked us, of course.' She did not say the other reason, but he knew that they were both thinking it. He'd forced himself to be cheerful, told her that with time they'd come round, and she'd given him such an assured 'Of course they will' that he'd almost believed it himself.

Now that he's on his way to London, he rereads the email he drafted the night before. He'd never done this before; he'd had to google what to say: *Sameer Saeed – Notice of Resignation.* It looks OK. He presses send.

There is no going back now; it zooms irretrievably out of his draft items and is done. Within minutes, there is an email from Deb setting up a meeting with Chris and his partner mentor later that afternoon. That's it then. The time has come. He ponders, briefly, what has led him to this moment; how only a few short months ago he had seen the way his life was going to play out, endlessly reaching for the next goal, and now, it stretches ahead of him, empty – but, strangely, feels fuller than it ever did before. An old man takes a seat across from him, perhaps Mhota Papa's age, perhaps older. There are so many lines in the man's face and hands that it almost looks unnatural. Sameer watches as the man sets down a paper bag on the table and carefully retrieves a takeaway cup of tea, a small plastic spoon, sugar, milk. Each item is dealt with slowly and with great concentration: this is not the making of a cup of tea, but the delicate repair of a watch. Swollen fingers open a sachet of sugar, measure it out into a plastic spoon, and tip it in. Milk next: the foil lid is peeled back, gently, an amount is dribbled, trembling, into the dark liquid. The mixture is stirred thrice clockwise, and twice anticlockwise; the spoon is lifted and tapped softly and very carefully against the side of the cup. There is such dignity and vulnerability in the whole episode that Sameer has to look away.

It's the first time he has been to the flat in over a month; he thought he would have missed it, but it feels like a stranger. His things, just the way he left them – Barker shoes, rudely sitting just behind the front door having not been tucked away neatly before he left; work pass, thrown onto the bed; cufflinks resting on the bedside table – untouched, but he feels like they belong to someone else. He studies himself in the full-length mirror – the suit he is wearing fits extremely well against his body, which is a deep, healthy shade of brown – but he does not recognise himself. His tie is tied too tightly; it is choking him.

In Bagel Express, the eyes of the man behind the counter light up. 'Long time no see,' he says.

Sameer smiles. 'Hey – how much for a fresh orange juice?'

'Four pounds fifty,' the man says, picking up a couple of pale, sad-looking oranges as he moves towards the juicer. Sameer takes a fiver out of his wallet and thinks of the number of oranges it would buy in Uganda.

The man hands him the juice. 'Where've you been then?' This is the first time they have attempted conversation; Sameer is surprised. The man has clearly missed his regular customer – or, more likely, the steady income flow.

'I'm actually moving.'

'Oh, right. Where to?'

'Uganda.'

'Where's that then, Africa?'

Sameer nods. There is a small queue of people behind him now waiting to be served.

'Why you off to Africa for?'

'Long story,' Sameer says apologetically, gesturing towards the queue. 'I better go.'

The man nods. 'Hey – I never knew your name,' he says before Sameer can leave. 'I'm John.'

'Sameer.'

'Good luck to you, Sameer,' John says, beaming.

It is an odd sensation going back to the office after having been away for so long. Sameer expects people to stop him, to say: Sam, welcome back – we've missed you! But people go about their days; no one at the reception looks twice; it is as if he never left. Ryan is sitting hunched over his computer screen, half asleep, and Sameer clears his throat loudly when he enters.

'You're back,' Ryan says, head jerking up. There are huge bags under his eyes. 'How was it?'

'Are you OK?' Sameer asks.

'All-nighter,' Ryan supplies, waving a hand towards the paper strewn across his desk, three mugs of half-drunk coffee, brown ring stains. 'Supposed to sign today though, so . . . hopefully.'

Sameer cannot remember the password to log into his PC. He sits and stares at the screen. His brain has already shut him out. 'It's weird to be back,' he says.

'Feels like you were barely gone – six weeks goes quicker than you think. Been on this fucking deal for six weeks and barely slept, you know?'

'I've actually got some news,' Sameer says, as he types an email to IT from his phone to ask for a password reset.

'Yeah, yeah, I know, Singapore, what, next week? Two weeks?'

'No, actually. I've handed in my notice. I'm not going to Singapore any more.'

'Wait, what?' Ryan's eyes snap up. 'You're serious?'

He nods.

'You're serious!' The look of shock has been replaced by one of intrigue. 'Hang on, who's going in your place?'

'No idea,' Sameer says. Ryan has not asked him why he is leaving, what happened on his break, nothing; he's interested in one thing only – whether he can use Sameer's departure to benefit himself. But Sameer finds himself laughing inside. He really, truly, doesn't care. He has let go of something – he doesn't know what exactly – but he has let go and like a scrap of paper in the wind it has flown away.

The partners don't let Sameer off as easily at the meeting later that afternoon. In fact, Chris is furious. 'It's a bit of a fucking joke,' he says to Deb from human resources and Sameer's partner mentor, David – a man he has spent approximately twenty minutes with in the last few years. Deb scratches her neck uncomfortably. 'You can't accept the Singapore gig, a position other associates would have killed for, telling us for months that you're really up for it, and then turn round just before we're due to send you and tell us you've decided not to go. It's fucking out of order – you've completely left us in the lurch. And getting your parents to resign for you, then taking it back, and now resigning again – what exactly are you playing at, Sam?'

Sameer bites his lip. For some reason he doesn't understand, he has to stifle the urge to laugh.

'Well, he has the right, obviously, to leave,' Deb says hastily, still scratching her neck.

'The question is, why does he want to,' David interjects

softly. 'We need to focus on what we can be doing to help you here, Sam, what we can do to make you stay. I think I can safely say that we would all be very sad to see you go.' There is a snort from Chris. 'Did you get a better offer elsewhere?' David continues. 'Why are you leaving, Sam?'

They all look at him.

He imagines trying to explain it to the group of people in front of him: Chris, a man who he is supposed to spend the next two years in Singapore with, but who has bullied him relentlessly for the past few months; David, a man assigned to be his 'mentor', but someone for whom he has never worked and to whom barely spoken, save for the perfunctory annual meeting to discuss his 'progress and aspirations'; Deb, the pastoral intermediary, always there but hardly ever useful. He thinks about telling them how difficult it has been to work with Chris, a man who has treated him differently to the way he treated everyone else, who spat on him every chance he got, who has made him feel like an outsider. A man who has been, quite frankly, racist. He thinks about telling them how the job had left him unfulfilled, how gruelling he'd found the hours, how it couldn't possibly be sustainable long term. But then he looks at their expectant faces and he remembers the number of colleagues he's watched come and go. The firm had never changed and is never going to change, so what's the point in wasting his energy? Pragmatism takes hold: why burn a bridge for no reason? And, still, at the back of his mind, it remains: the sliver of doubt that maybe there's nothing wrong with Chris; maybe there was something wrong with him.

'I'm leaving the law,' Sameer finally says. 'Going to do something completely different.'

There is a collective sigh of relief (even from Chris). It is always a relief to know that it is not us – we are not the reason he has chosen to leave – it's more that he isn't suited to the job itself. If he isn't going to be a lawyer here, then he certainly can't be a lawyer anywhere else.

Even then, this reaction is somehow disappointing. A part of him had wanted them to beg him to stay; he had wanted the chance to wield power over them for once; he had wanted to leave believing that he was part of the lifeblood of the firm. But the truth was that he was far from indispensable; he was just another fungible resource, like the paper in the printer, or the staples in the stapler, something that was needed and, if absent, would be inconvenient, but was ultimately replaceable. With this thought, he says: 'I don't really think it makes sense for me to work my full notice period, seeing as I was supposed to be going to Singapore in a couple of weeks? But I will do whatever is required, of course.'

There is a short discussion; the matter will need to be signed off by management, but they do not see any reason why he should be required to complete his notice period. Chris's arms are folded, his face stern; they don't leave the room when Sameer does and he knows that they will be talking about him afterwards.

He goes straight from the meeting room to the lift and exits the building. As he steps through the revolving doors, Sameer knows that he won't be returning. The sun has appeared from behind a gap in the clouds and he sees a streak of startling blue backdropped against the grey structures of London. He never knew that this job had weighed so heavily upon him until he let it go; he had never understood.

While he waits for his working visa to come through, Sameer stays in London. There's no one in London (and Jeremiah still hasn't replied to Sameer's last message, despite being seen online) but at least here he can spend his days working on the business and speaking to Maryam without being disturbed. He finds himself desperate to speak to her and worked up if he cannot: his loneliness breeds a neediness that surprises him and that he cannot suppress.

There is one other person with whom Sameer is in regular contact: Mr Shah, who is delighted to hear that Sameer will be returning to Kampala. 'I'm going to help you to set up this juice business, son,' he said over the phone. When Sameer told Mr Shah that his parents were not so happy about his decision, Mr Shah's reaction was: 'Well, I'm sure they'd be happier if they knew you were being well looked after – and at least that is something I can provide.' He had been glad that Mr Shah could not see the colour rising to his face. He had not lied, but at the same time he had not told Mr Shah the entire truth. It didn't seem like the right time to tell him about Maryam.

His mother called him once, begging him to reconsider. Sameer listened as she wailed down the phone. He had asked her not to cry, but he felt cold somehow, empty. Something between them had snapped irreversibly. His parents had lost their power over him.

When Jeremiah finally contacts him, it's a relief: he thought that perhaps he'd been cast aside, that Jeremiah had moved on to cooler, better friends, but no: *So sorry, bro, it's been CRAY. Loads to tell u – drink?* and they arrange to meet at a rooftop bar in London Bridge. Sameer looks forward to the evening with excited anticipation: he's really missed his friend. But Jeremiah arrives at the bar with a woman on his arm, and Sameer has to force a smile to hide his disappointment that he did not come alone.

'Sam, bro, it's been ages,' Jeremiah says, throwing an arm around Sameer's shoulder. Sameer's fingers touch the surface of Jeremiah's jacket, a suede that is so soft it feels like fur. His eyes quickly scan Jeremiah head to toe: new haircut, new watch, the latest Off-Whites. He looks so good – in fact, every time Sameer sees Jeremiah, he looks better. Is this just Jeremiah now: forever improving? He wonders what Jeremiah thinks of how he looks, but he doesn't ask because the woman is there. 'Sam, meet Angela,' Jeremiah nudges the woman. 'Sam is one of my day ones,' he says to her.

'So nice to meet you,' Angela steps forward, embracing him with her bosom, which is tightly packed into a low-cut leopard-print top.

'Good to finally meet you,' he says, recognising her now from the Instagram page Jeremiah had shown him. 'I've heard so much about you,' he adds, thinking that this is a nice thing to say.

They are seated with a view of the Thames snaking its way through the city beneath them, the panorama of London's icons backlit and glowing with yellows and blues. Sameer smiles wistfully as he thinks that perhaps, a year or so ago, the three of them might have been him, Jeremiah and Rahool. He feels a pang of tenderness for his old life in London.

'Shall we get a bottle?' Jeremiah asks, flicking through the wine list.

'I'm not drinking, actually,' Sameer says.

'Oh, really?' Jeremiah looks up. 'Why not?'

'I've stopped.'

'I've heard that one before,' Jeremiah says, grinning. 'But it's not Ramadan again, right? I swear that was only a few months ago . . .'

'Actually I think I'm stopping for good,' Sameer says, surprising himself, as before this evening, he had not consciously decided that this was what he wanted to do. At this realisation, he repeats: 'Yes, I'm stopping for good.'

'You found God in Uganda, huh? Good for you, bro.'

And that is Jeremiah. No judgement, no questions – just acceptance. Sameer wonders if he will ever make a friend like Jeremiah in Uganda.

'Hope you don't mind if we . . . ?' Jeremiah points to the wine list.

'Of course not.'

'I find it so impressive when people don't drink and are still, you know, sociable,' Angela says seriously. 'So much of our professional and social lives are constructed around alcohol. I don't think I could do it.'

Sameer gives her a short smile in response. A social life without alcohol had seemed unimaginable to him too not so long ago, but he no longer wants to be tied to alcohol in this way. He no longer needs it to feel that he is a part of something, or perhaps he no longer cares about feeling a part of whatever it was that alcohol made him feel.

The drinks arrive and they toast, wine glasses clinking against Sameer's pint glass of Diet Coke. They make small talk for a few minutes, Sameer asking Angela where she's doing her PhD (and being very pleased with himself for having remembered she was doing one) and where she lives in London.

'So what else happened out there?' Jeremiah asks when the small talk dies down, one hand taking a slug of the wine, the other snaking around Angela's waist and pulling her close. 'You seem . . . different.'

Sameer shrugs, twirling the straw in his Coke with one hand. '*You* seem different,' he responds. 'Going up in the world?'

Jeremiah laughs, setting down his glass of wine to pick up his phone. 'I'm kinda blowing up, haven't you seen my Instagram lately?'

Sameer shakes his head; he cannot remember the last time he went on Instagram. Jeremiah thrusts the phone under his nose, beaming. 'Thirty thousand followers,' he says proudly.

'Wow! That's a lot.' Sameer takes Jeremiah's phone and begins to scroll through the posts. He stops at a picture of Jeremiah standing next to a very familiar face. 'Wait – is that –'

'Yup,' Jeremiah is glowing. 'He was doing a feature with a British artist for his new album and came to the studio to record it. He heard me mixing and I've been sharing a few of my beats with him ever since.'

Sameer is astounded. 'Mate, that is so cool,' he finally says.

Angela leans into Jeremiah and plants a kiss on his cheek. 'He's going to make it,' she says passionately.

This brief display of affection warms Sameer, makes him crave Maryam.

'So what's up with you?' Jeremiah asks, locking his phone triumphantly and putting it back on the table.

'Well . . .' Sameer pauses, taking a sip of his drink. 'The big news is that I'm moving to Uganda.'

'Uganda?' Jeremiah looks confused. 'Man, I can't keep up with you these days. What happened to Singapore?'

'I quit my job,' he says simply. 'I quit the job, met a girl, and am moving to Uganda.'

'Hold up.' Jeremiah's eyes widen. 'Did you say you met a girl?'

Sameer laughs. 'Yeah,' he says. 'Her name is Maryam,' and the words dance on his tongue and taste sweet.

'Holy shit, you must be in deep. Quitting your job for her?'

'It's not really for her – she's a part of it, but –'

'Pic,' Jeremiah interrupts. 'Let me see a pic.'

Sameer starts to take his phone out of his pocket and then stops. He has never taken a photo of Maryam and – for some reason the thought brings a smile to his lips – she doesn't use Instagram or Facebook. 'I don't have one,' he says.

'You're moving to Uganda for a girl you don't have a picture of?'

'I don't know, I just never took one, I guess. And she doesn't really use social media.'

'How long have you known her?' Jeremiah asks, pouring Angela another glass of wine.

'A couple of months?' and he blushes as he says it, the existence of them, acknowledged by the passing of time, giving him a little flush of pride.

'So what are you going to do out there?' Jeremiah asks, scraping the flesh off a large green olive with his teeth. Sameer had not even noticed that olives had arrived.

'I've got some connections there from my family,' he says. 'I know someone who would probably give me a job, but I'm going to try my hand at starting my own business first. After the wedding, I'll –'

'What wedding?' Jeremiah nearly chokes on an olive pit, which he spits out and into the palm of his hand.

'My wedding,' Sameer says, and now he is stifling laughter, thoroughly enjoying the shockwaves he's sending Jeremiah's way.

'You're marrying this girl?' Jeremiah's mouth drops open. 'Are you fucking with me, bro?'

'Stop acting so surprised, man,' he says, laughing, 'you know that's how we do things in my culture, my religion – we move quickly. My grandfather met his wife for the first time on their wedding night.'

'But culture and religion aren't the same thing,' Jeremiah raises an eyebrow, 'you were the one who always told me that. And not gonna lie, but you and your grandfather are a few generations apart . . .'

'Yeah, but you know, no sex before marriage and all that. So get married quickly, before you end up having sex.'

'Wait, wait, wait, wait. So you haven't even banged the girl?' Jeremiah leans forward, intrigued. He narrows his eyes at Sameer. 'Now I don't care what you say, that can't have been your decision, you're a fucking horny bastard –'

Sameer and Jeremiah are both laughing; Angela is staring at them, looking slightly perplexed. 'Honestly, I can't explain it,' Sameer says eventually. 'It's not like that with this girl. Obviously I want to. But it's so much more than just physical. It's like a spiritual connection?' He looks at Jeremiah, thinking that if there is anyone in the world who would understand what he means, it would be him. 'I know this is a cliché, but I feel like she's my soulmate, do you know what I mean?'

'Do you really believe in soulmates?' Angela says, and her cheeks are flushed. Sameer notices that the bottle of wine is nearly empty. 'It seems like you're giving up a lot for a girl you barely know?'

Sameer bites his tongue. He wants to tell her that the precise measure of time is immaterial; that it has felt much longer than two months; that life before Maryam was no life at all. But he is aware that this will sound ridiculous and he doesn't need to justify himself to her, so he says nothing.

Jeremiah shakes his head. 'You don't know my guy,' he says to Angela gently. 'He's the smartest person I know, and he doesn't make decisions lightly. If he says she's his soulmate, then she's definitely his soulmate.'

These words from Jeremiah, this signalling that his friend will have his back no matter what other people think, tells Sameer that their friendship transcends the countries they live in or the amount of time that has gone by since they last spoke. He wants to say something, but he doesn't know how to convey the importance of what has just passed, and so he simply smiles at Jeremiah who gives him a brief nod in response.

There is a silence that might have been awkward, but Angela shrugs and takes another sip of wine. Jeremiah turns to Sameer. 'So when's the wedding?' he says. 'I've always wanted to visit Uganda.'

He'd told his parents when the flight was leaving; he'd sent a message on the family WhatsApp group. There'd been no reply. Zara had messaged him separately, privately: *You coming home before you go?* and he'd arranged with her when he was going to come – just for a few hours to say goodbye and to collect the suitcase he'd left behind before he rushed back to London. She picks him up from the station and they talk about everything except Uganda on the drive home. His father is not there when he arrives, and his mother hugs him but says nothing about his trip. He had wanted, at the very least, to say goodbye to Mhota Papa, but he is asleep. He knew that there would be no grand send-off, no big goodbye, but even so, it's a little hurtful that no one seems to care. He reminds himself that he will be back and forth in the first few months anyway. They would come round, as Maryam had assured him, and if they wanted to reconcile with him the next time he came back, they could.

As he packs his suitcase, Zara sits on the swivel chair at his desk, pushing herself around with her feet and watching. 'You could come with me, you know,' he says as he throws a T-shirt into the case. Zara shakes her head slowly. 'Chuck me that charger.'

As she hands over the cable, she says evenly: 'You've upset Mum and Dad.'

'I know,' he shrugs, rolling the charging cable into a ball

and slotting it into a pocket in his case. 'They're just being racist.' Zara does not respond to this, so Sameer continues, 'You do realise the only reason they don't like her is because she's black?'

'Did Dada die in her house? That's what they told me.'

'Yes, but he was an old man and he just died in his sleep. There's nothing weird about it. And trust me,' he adds, 'he would have been happy that he died in Uganda.'

'How would you know that?' Zara says, swinging the chair all the way around so that Sameer can't see her face. He stops packing and looks up. 'You don't know that,' she says as the chair comes back around to face Sameer. 'Just try to imagine how they might be feeling right now, when their son is talking about marrying a girl from that house.'

'Zara,' Sameer snaps, 'this has nothing to do with that. This is about the fact that Maryam is black. That's why they don't like it. Did you not hear what I said? They. Are. Being. Racist.'

'I'm not saying that it's not messed up,' Zara says, raising her hands defensively. 'I'm just saying that you should think very carefully about what you're doing. Like, do you really want to disobey them? To get married without their blessing? Come on – surely you agree that's wrong?'

'It's more wrong that they disagree with it because of the colour of her skin,' he is nearly shouting with frustration. Of all people, he thought that she would understand, that she would be on his side.

'*Bhai*,' Zara says softly, 'I get it. They're not always right. I'm not saying they're right about this. But just think about it for a minute – you've only known the girl, what, a few weeks? You've known our parents your entire life. Think about how many sacrifices they've made for us, all the things they've done for us – is it really worth hurting them for a stranger?'

Sameer wants to throw something at her. Nothing she has said makes sense. How had he thought, all these years, that he knew her so well?

'I'm sorry,' Zara says, standing. 'It's just I wouldn't do it if it were me.'

In that moment, he suddenly understands. He looks at her expression, his little sister, awash with the pain of the family she would never let down. His anger dissipates immediately. 'Of course you wouldn't,' he says. 'Please get out of my room.'

'I was leaving anyway,' she says and walks out.

24

To my first love, my beloved

Today, my love, my forgiving, precious love, I write to you from the room that is our study in our beautiful house in Nakasero, Kampala. Yes, Kampala! I am back, and the house has not changed one bit. Bougainvillea still blooms on the porch. The rooms still possess that ineffable scent of home.

But there is no inclination, it seems, to deliver me joy alone. This visit has come unfalteringly with heartbreak. The Quran says that Allah does not burden a person with more than that person's soul can bear. How many times am I to suffer before respite is delivered? Is it so that I am capable of bearing pain again and again?

You should have heard Obote on the television – he was begging for us to return. He has a great deal of admiration for us, my darling. He recognised our contributions – that without us, Uganda had failed to prosper, and that on our return, it would rise to success once again.

We had already begun to make our mark in Leicester. Before we arrived, Belgrave was a run-down slum. It was our small community of East African Asians who improved it beyond recognition. What was once a strip of disused offices and peeling paint is now a glorious stretch of saris and salwars, dosas and chaat, yellow-gold jewellery shining from behind window fronts. People come from all over the country to visit Belgrave Road. There is nowhere else like it in the UK – even London.

Our wonderful sons have built the sari shop from the ground up – packed full of every type of fabric, rolls upon rolls of colours, patterns, textures, all glinting under the shop lights. My children and grandchildren are attending good schools and they will all receive full university educations, free of charge *inshallah*. We are comfortable. But I am not foolish enough to suggest that I can claim any of these successes as my own. It is not me, but my children and my family who have succeeded.

When Amin was overthrown, it was as if a light inside me had been switched back on: my interest in life resumed. I began to pay attention to the newspapers. I stopped drinking – just like that, they call it going 'cold turkey'. I simply did not need it any more. I had been waiting for this moment for nearly ten long years. What had I done in all that time? Sat in my bitter corner of the room, bottle in hand. The past few years have not been kind to me, Amira. I am not the man you would remember. My features are bloated, my liver is poisoned and my heart is failing. I should almost certainly be dead. But somehow I am still going.

I asked Shabnam to come with me, but she did not want to come back. 'Not even just for a week? To see what it's like now?' I had hobbled towards her from the comfort of my armchair, clutching the newspaper in one crooked hand. She was washing dishes in the kitchen sink, sleeves rolled to her elbows.

'Stop this, Hasan,' she said irritably, jaw set. 'We are happy here now.'

'You are happy,' I moaned, standing in the doorway of the kitchen, unwilling to cross the threshold. 'The children are happy. Everyone is happy except me. And how can you be happy if your husband is not happy?'

Shabnam stopped washing for a moment, sighed heavily and turned to face me. 'I understand your frustration,' she said. 'I understand your pain. Do you not think that I miss Uganda too? That I didn't also live my life there? That it didn't hurt me to go from that, everything we had, to this?' she gestured around the small room and soapsuds flew from her hands to the floor. 'But at least here, we are safe, *hai na*? Have you already forgotten what it was like when Obote was in power the first time?'

As I stood hunched in the doorway, watching the deft movements of her hands in the sink, her cheeks flushed from the heat of the water, I became so aware of the twenty-year age gap between us. England has given Shabnam a new lease of life; her blood pumps with youthful vigour. I, on the other hand . . . I looked down at my hands, still clutching the newspaper with Obote's black-and-white face squeezed beneath my swollen arthritic joints. Twenty years is a vast gap. I realised in that moment that Shabnam and I could not be further apart.

My children did not want to come with me either. Samir and Shahzeb had no interest at all: too busy, too focused on the business to leave, even if only for a short visit. The younger ones refused – 'Why would we want to go to Africa, Papa?' – their memories miss the mango sweetness of the fragranced air: they know only hushed voices, low whispers and palpable fear.

My youngest, Rizwan, took me to the airport, the others apparently unable to spare the time. 'You will come back, won't you, Papa?' he asked before I went through security.

I looked at my son's sweet, bright face, fresh out of university with an honour's degree in management, about to embark upon his first foray into business by helping his older brothers to run the shop. My youngest child, my boy, was becoming a man. I smiled. 'Of course,' I said, 'it is only a week's visit. Of course I'll be back.'

I had a plan, you see, that if things were good and I could find a way for us to live in Kampala again, I would convince the family that we should return. And if they did not want to, well, I would go back alone. There is nothing for me in England.

And so it came to be that I arrived in Uganda this morning, alone.

I had not expected the flood of memories to hit me with such force as they did on landing in Entebbe (indeed, I did not know that they were capable of doing so, my wearied old mind forgetting even now, so often, your face), but there it was: flashes of laughter on the shop floor, sitting cross-legged as a skinny child on top of the counter; the cardamom-fennel taste of Abdullah's milky chai; the caress of your slender fingers over my back, windows open, our bodies sticky with sweat.

I asked the taxi driver to take me through the Asian neighbourhoods in Old Kampala, down Rashid Khamis Road and past Madras and Bombay Gardens, where we purchased our first house. The houses looked so different; run-down, unkempt, glass missing from window frames through which multiple pairs of eyes stared at me from the darkness. How many African families were now living in these buildings, crammed into each of the rooms? The driver circled the block, looking at me with suspicion, and I quickly directed him on towards Nakasero. I did not know what I would find of our own house, but I prayed to see Abdullah's face.

As we approached the wrought-iron gates, an immense sense of panic began to descend upon me. I came very close to telling the driver to take me straight back to the airport! But the gates swung open and the bright fuchsia of bougainvillea burst into sight and it calmed my heart. Nothing, my darling, had changed.

To my relief and surprise the door was opened by none other than Abdullah's son, Ibrahim. A man who had disappeared had returned alive and well! I stumbled into his arms, my hands touching his face to check his features were real. His arms, as solid as tree trunks, held me gently. '*Mjombe* Hasan?' he said. 'It is really you.'

'I am so happy, Ibrahim,' I said, unable to stop the tears from running down my cheeks. 'I never thought I would see you again.' Behind him, I could hear the scampering of feet: children, women disappearing into the shadows – this house was full. 'Where is Abdullah?' I asked, pushing past him.

'Uncle,' he said softly, 'come and sit down. Let me make you tea.'

And so I sat with a cup of tea in my old drawing room (different, but the same) with Ibrahim. He could have been Abdullah, sitting there across from me with that knowing, smiling look, as we shared his milky chai. But it was not Abdullah. It was his son.

And so, it is with a heavy heart that I relay to you now the news he delivered. He told me that when he had disappeared, he had fled to Tanzania because he knew that it wouldn't be long until his tribal roots marked him as a target of Amin's regime. He told me that the military began to look for him, and Abdullah – a prominent and well-known figure thanks to Saeed & Sons – was a means to exert pressure. He told me that one day, on 6th January 1973, Abdullah just disappeared.

'I joined the Tanzanian forces in the struggle to overthrow Amin, and we took Kampala in the spring of 1979,' Ibrahim said. 'When I came here, to this house, it had been abandoned by whoever had been living here before the war –' and he avoided my eyes momentarily – 'so we just took it. But it is yours, of course, you are welcome to have it back if that is what you came for.'

'Where is your father?' I repeated.

'Uncle, we do not know,' Ibrahim's voice caught in his throat. 'He never returned. And no body was ever recovered.'

I looked down at my hands, gripping the china mug tightly, saw my nose and chin swimming in the milky surface, and was suddenly seized by the urge to throw the cup across the room, to smash it to pieces against the wall, to let the tea stain everywhere. I had always believed – perhaps somewhat naively, yet, nevertheless wholeheartedly – that I would see him again. We were not finished; I was not yet done with him, like I was not done with you, and I wanted to tell Ibrahim: there was more to be said between us – I had more to say . . .

'May I borrow your car?' I asked Ibrahim. 'I need to go somewhere.'

'I would be happy to take you anywhere you want, Uncle.'

'No,' I said shortly. 'I must go alone.'

It felt good to be behind the wheel and in control. Nothing about the roads had changed, save, perhaps, that they were in a better condition than I remembered. At first I thought I was going to the Muslim cemetery – to visit your grave – to lie myself down on the dirt above your skeleton and weep. But I found myself turning out onto the empty roads that led to Jinja. I drove for an hour before I stopped, in the middle of nowhere, where bush meets exposed volcanic rock, where the formation of the land is reminiscent of prehistoric times. I clambered atop one of the rocks, knelt down and prostrated my unwilling body so that my head touched the stone.

I had only ever been here once before: the night I had found you sitting with Abdullah, your slender hands pressed against his black skin. I had never thought about this place again, and if anyone had ever asked me where it was I would not have been able to tell them.

To this day, I cannot justify to myself why I did not talk to you the week before your death. You will not understand when I say to you that the way a man's mind works is to jump from the visual to the physical. This is tangled up with our sense of possession, our sense of pride and our sense of shame. I am sorry, Amira. I am sorry I did not talk to you.

You see, for so long I have tried to forget that night. Terrible things happen, you process them and you move on. That is our capacity as humans, to forget, so that we do not stop ourselves from living in the present. That is our gift.

Now it comes back to me with a shame I cannot bear. My fingers sweat and the grip on this pen loosens.

I see myself, walking into the house we shared together, after a long day of work, Abdullah lying on the sofa, you, crouched over him with a damp cloth. Your hair was loose – falling on his face, tickling him, he would have been able to smell its aroma, soft and fresh. Why hadn't you tied it back? I watched you both for a moment; you said something softly and he laughed, a deep gurgle from the belly.

I did not say anything. It was as if, after so many years, all the pieces of the puzzle had finally slotted into place. As if I had been a blind man, feeling my way around for my entire life, and suddenly I had been given the gift of sight. That look of tenderness in your eyes, the gentle way in which your fingers touched his skin – it all came crashing together, to me, in that moment. You loved him. You had always loved him.

Perhaps I let out a scream – I must have done something to alert your attention, because you started and looked up at me, eyes wide and innocent, just like they were on our wedding day. 'Hasan?' you said gently. 'Abdullah's been hurt.' Abdullah scrambled to his feet then. Blood was dripping into his eyes. You looked at each other and you looked at me. 'Hasan?' you said, stepping forward. There was concern in your voice. I stumbled backwards, out of the room, out of the house.

I jumped in the car and began to drive. As I drove further and further, all these things started to race through my mind. You need to understand: my mind would not stop. Things that had seemed so innocent, that had meant nothing at the time – they all suddenly took on meaning. The way you always fought his corner; the way you laughed at his jokes; the way you spoke of him and his devotion to his faith; the many, many ways in which you showed you cared. You loved him, and I finally saw it.

I drove a great distance, until I was forced to stop the car to relieve a sudden urge to throw up. I stood at the side of the road to a view of these rock formations and, just as I did today, I knelt on the rock and prayed to Allah that this problem would resolve itself. I prayed for the strength to deal with your betrayal and for justice to be done – for me to prevail over him.

When I eventually returned to Kampala that night, the house was quiet. There was no sign of Abdullah. You greeted me at the door, anxious. I still remember the way your lips trembled, as if you were about to cry. Your soft voice: 'Hasan, what is going on? Where did you go?' I could not look at you. You have to understand, at that time I believed that you had betrayed me. You and him both. And you were feigning innocence, like you had no idea. Before that moment, I did not realise that the way you feel about someone can change in an instant, like the snap of fingers. Before that moment, I had always thought of you as an extension of me; that you were my ultimate source of comfort – and I yours – because we were simply a reflection of each other. But in that moment, I realised that, in the end, we are all on our own. In that moment, I detached you from me.

I wanted nothing to do with Abdullah either. And so I sent a message that he had been dismissed and I did not speak to you for a whole week. I found it difficult to look at you. It was easier for me to pretend that you did not exist; to turn away from you when you tried to speak to me, to walk away when you tried to touch me. You have to believe me when I say, Amira, that I was trying to find the words. After twenty years of marriage, twenty years of words flowing between us, unbroken, I suddenly did not know what to say. This was a new world, one in which you were no longer a part of me: how could I convey to you what was going through my mind? But before I even had the chance to try, you were taken from me.

A freak accident, they said. She was terribly unlucky – never normally happens in Kampala, it's much more common up in the northern parts of the country. Sorry, Hasan, but she was just in the wrong place at the wrong time. Why you went out in a thunderstorm, I don't know. Where you were going, I don't know. And because I had refused to speak to you, I never will.

It was only at that point – when Abdullah came to me at your *janaza*, when we both wept like children, when we embraced like brothers, when he swore upon Allah that nothing had ever happened between you – that I knew that I had to believe him. I had to be humbled, otherwise my jealousy would destroy everything I loved, and I loved him. I had lost you. I could not lose Abdullah too.

So tell me, my darling, who did you love? Was it me, or was it him? Because it cannot have been both of us. All those years after your death, I convinced myself that it was me. Abdullah convinced me that it was me. But it is your souls that have been reunited now, whilst mine remains on Earth.

Do you remember when we first married and I used to have the driver take us out in Papa's old car so we could explore Uganda?

Our first trip together, two months into our marriage, our faces dewy with youth and love, holding hands in the back of the car as we went along that winding dirt road to Sipi Falls. I still remember exactly what you were wearing: a simple yellow salwar, hair pulled back, no make-up. And I remember thinking that you were the most exquisite creature in all the world. Halfway up the mountain road butterflies appeared – hundreds and thousands of them – and you made the driver stop for fear of killing them. We got out, laughing, surrounded by butterflies dancing maniacally in the wind, clinging to your hair and your clothes, leaving your pale yellow salwar streaked with orange dust. We went back to Sipi many times, but we never saw anything like it again.

Remember February of 1925, the hottest summer on record, when I shared with you the secret hiding spot I used to visit as a child? An enormous canopy rock at the top of a hill on the outskirts of the city. We climbed under the rock on our knees and into the cool shelter, avoiding the small pools of water that collected in drops from the low ceiling. Sitting cross-legged and breathing in the cold smell of earth and damp, I still remember how your lips tasted like strawberries behind that curtain of cold air.

Remember our weekend picnics, when Samir was just a toddler, and we would take Papa, and your parents too – we'd all squeeze into one car, seven or eight of us, and drive to Entebbe? Laughing and talking, as we made our way through the ginger lilies and starbur, to sit on the green grassy mounds overlooking Lake Victoria in the shade of the trees, heating red chicken curry on a Primus stove. I still remember how that curry smelled as it rose from the stove, mixed with the scent of the jasmine that surrounded us.

Uganda, my beautiful land. In spite of everything I have lost, it is so good to be home.

25

The first time Sameer returns to Entebbe, Maryam is waiting for him at the airport, alone. He sees her, standing a few steps away from everyone else in the crowd, tall and slender, hands clasped in front of her, wearing a floor-length blue dress. He breathes with a new excitement, but he doesn't run to her and she doesn't move forward. He wants to savour this moment, the return, and so he walks until he is standing an inch from her. She looks unbelievably beautiful. 'Where is everyone?' he asks.

'I didn't tell them you were coming,' she says. He drops his bag and puts his arms around her waist, pulls her close to the smell of strawberries, drops a kiss on her forehead. People are staring openly at them, but they don't notice. She nestles her head into his chest. 'I didn't know if you were really coming,' she admits, almost in a whisper, and he pulls her closer.

Stepping out of the airport and onto the red dust land is like coming home: familiar and comforting all at once. He's booked an Airbnb in Old Kampala, but Maryam insists they go straight from the airport to her family house in Nakasero.

'*Taata* is home and you have to speak to him,' she says, and her voice is strained with urgency. 'I haven't told them anything about us, but it doesn't feel right for you to be here and them not to know.'

'OK,' he says, giving her hand a small squeeze. He was prepared for this; he knows what he is going to say.

Maryam is quiet on the journey towards Kampala and Sameer finds himself doing most of the speaking, chattering away about the progress he has made with his business, telling her about Jeremiah, Rahool. When they eventually arrive and she pulls into the drive and kills the engine, she turns to face him and he can see trepidation in her face. 'Don't worry,' he says gently. 'It's going to be fine. Come on.'

One of Maryam's aunties – Sameer cannot remember her name, although he recognises her face – is standing right behind the door when Maryam turns the key, as if she had just been about to open it. 'Sameer?' she says, surprised. 'Maryam?' An eyebrow is raised.

'*Assalaamualaikum*,' Sameer tries, but the auntie just nods her head and steps back to let the pair of them into the house. Maryam takes him to the drawing room and tells him to wait there.

The minutes pass slowly and he is drawn to the photos sitting in frames along the display cabinet: the young children of the house, grouped together in a dirt yard under a mango tree; a black-and-white photo of two older women he doesn't recognise, with severe expressions and no smiles; a picture of Maryam and her father at her graduation, Maryam smiling with her whole face, a noticeably younger Musa with one arm proudly around her shoulder.

There is a noise behind him and he jumps and the photo falls backwards. He rushes to straighten it (he did not realise he had been touching it) and turns round quickly. Musa and Ibrahim are standing in front of him – no Maryam.

'Hello,' Sameer says, eyes addressing both men.

'*Assalaamualaikum*,' Musa replies, coming forward to embrace him (Sameer rushes a hasty *wassalaam*, annoyed that he has not been able to work out who says *salaam* in this house). Although Ibrahim is older, it is Musa who uses a walking stick; as he walks towards Sameer, his movements are spasmodic, difficult. This reminds Sameer of Rahool and he shakes his head to get the image out of his mind. 'Sit down.' Musa gestures towards the settee and Sameer sits; they take a seat opposite him.

'So,' says Ibrahim, 'you have returned.'

'Uganda is a very beautiful country,' Sameer replies carefully.

'Just Uganda?' Musa asks, leaning forward so that his head rests on his hands, which are placed atop his walking stick. They both stare at him.

'Uncle, as you may know –' Sameer clears his throat – 'I have come to ask you for your daughter's hand in marriage.'

Musa nods, seemingly unsurprised. 'We do not have intermarriage here,' he says. 'I do not know any Asian who has married a Ugandan.'

Sameer doesn't know what to say to this.

'Tell me something, Sameer. Why do you want to marry my daughter?'

Sameer is slightly taken aback; he had not expected such a direct question, but he is aware that pausing for any longer will convey uncertainty, where none exists. 'Well,' he says, 'she's the most incredible person I have ever met. I can't imagine my future without her in it. I want to make her happy.'

'Mmm. And how will you do that, Sameer? How will you make her happy?' The air in the room is clammy and Sameer has started to sweat. He opens his mouth, about to speak, but then Musa says: 'She's only ever known the Ugandan sun,' and his voice falters on the last word as he turns his face towards Ibrahim, searching for comfort.

'Uncle,' Sameer says, almost laughing as he understands, 'I have no intention of asking her to come to England – you know that, right? I intend to move to Kampala.'

'To Kampala?' Musa repeats, eyes narrowing with suspicion. 'You?'

'Yes, Uncle.'

'But what will you do here?'

'I'm going to start my own business, a juice business. I really believe it's got a future,' Sameer says excitedly. 'But if, ultimately, it doesn't work out,' he adds, 'I can always work in my uncle's company.'

'Ah,' Musa says, leaning back. 'I see.' Musa has visibly relaxed; that his daughter will stay in Kampala is a different world to the one he had pictured. 'And this is what you want? To move to this city?'

Sameer can't help smiling when he says yes. He has not just fallen for Maryam, but for her city and her country too.

Musa studies Sameer in silence for a moment. Then he says: 'You know that this may not be easy for you.'

'Your family in particular may find it difficult,' Ibrahim adds delicately. 'It is the Asians who don't like to intermarry.'

Sameer looks at the men squarely. He is not going to skirt about the issue. He is not going to lie. 'They don't approve,' he says bluntly. 'I told them I wanted to marry Maryam, and they didn't approve.'

Ibrahim nods. 'But you still came.'

'I still came,' Sameer repeats.

As he anticipated, during his first few months in Uganda, Sameer returns to the UK to tie up a few loose ends – the lease on his flat, his finances, his belongings.

He'd half expected his family to have missed him; to welcome him with open arms on his return. Time has passed: how much time did they need? But when he had gone back to Leicester, his father was not at home. 'He's visiting Bapa Zakir,' his mother had said. Bapa Zakir, his father's older brother who lived in Birmingham, who Sameer could not remember his father ever visiting before.

334

He could tell by the way she'd held him that his mother was happy to see him, but she refused to talk about his move to Uganda and acted as if it was not happening at all, despite watching him drag a suitcase full of his things from his room into the corridor. In the night, he thought he could hear her sobbing. Mhota Papa was weaker than ever and slept on and off most of the day. Zara was the only one who would talk to him about the move. 'They haven't told Mhota Papa you're leaving,' she said. 'And you mustn't tell him. It will cause him too much distress.'

'So he thinks I'm still in London?' Sameer had asked warily.

'Yes, and it needs to remain that way for his own good.' Zara stared at him and he stared back. 'Please, Sameer, can you at least do this one thing for our family?'

Sameer had swallowed the bitterness rising in his throat and did not respond to this remark, but he did not say anything to Mhota Papa either.

It is England that now feels like the foreign country; perhaps because his family have rejected him, his reasons for calling it home exhausted. In Uganda, Sameer has found family in Maryam – and in Mr Shah. Mr Shah has done a lot for him, putting him in contact with a local lawyer, getting his juices a month-long trial period with well-known retailers, helping him to find commercial kitchen space to rent. He's even invested a not insignificant amount of money into the business as start-up capital.

Sameer doesn't know why Mr Shah has taken him under his wing, but he remembers that he often used to feel like this – at school, at work, people just liked him for no apparent reason – and he is thankful that his good luck seems to have returned. When Mr Shah insists that Sameer should come for dinner at his house at least one night a week, batting away Sameer's counter-offer that he could take them out for dinner instead,

Sameer has no choice but to agree. Mrs Shah is especially happy to see him and makes a huge fuss of the occasion each time, but Aliyah is notably absent and he is quietly grateful. 'Although she'll be back at Christmas,' Mrs Shah reminds him cheerily. 'How funny that just as you came here, she went back to university. But it's no bother, she's not planning on staying in the UK after university,' she adds quickly. 'She's quite taken with Kampala, like you.' Sameer remembers guiltily that he had not replied to Aliyah's last message (*Sam, hi, are you in London? I'm back at uni, would love to see you!*) and he had not told her that he was moving to Kampala; then again, he is sure that her parents have.

When the retail trial period for Sameer's juices begins, he doesn't employ anyone to assist him. He has some inexplicable feeling that he must do this alone; that it should be difficult and that he should feel it. The kitchen is stocked with commercial juicing machinery, but almost all of the processes are manual. Sameer spends the day operating the machinery, blending the juices, filling the bottles and date-stamping them. He finds it almost therapeutic to use his hands to create something tangible – more than tangible, something edible, something sustaining. He recalls with a detached sense of amusement the greengrocer he used to pass on his way to work every morning – if he was early enough, loading a van with crates of fruit and vegetables; otherwise clearing away the scraps of onion peel and carrot leaves from the street outside the shop. He used to wonder what kind of life people who worked jobs like this lived: did the man just go home at the close of the morning, job done for the day? Was it fulfilling, sourcing fruit and vegetables and delivering them across London? Was it challenging?

Waiting for feedback is almost painful; the anxious checking and refreshing of his inbox; the odd sensation of a constant, underlying nausea, a feeling he had almost forgotten since waiting for exam results. For the first time since he has had the idea for this venture, he wonders: what if it doesn't work? But by the end of the first week of the trial, two of the retailers have contacted him to say that they are going to need more bottles for the second week – they have been selling out by lunchtime. Sameer is so grateful that he almost cries.

The additional supply takes total bottle production to more than he can manage alone – after the first day of the second week, when he locks up at 2 a.m., he asks Mr Shah to find him a short-term employee. Whereas before Sameer was unbothered by late nights (and even relished the feeling of being needed, of having something to keep him occupied every evening instead of coming back to an empty flat), now he keeps one eye on his watch, always conscious of when Maryam's shift will be over and he will be able to see her. Mr Shah offers one of the sugar factory interns, a young boy named Patrick, and Sameer gratefully accepts; the work is made all the more pleasant by the fact that Patrick is eager and good-natured despite having been removed from the job he had originally applied for and told that he would now be working at a random start-up. Days spent with him on the kitchen floor are easy and enjoyable. Sameer starts to dream about the future, taking Patrick on as a full-time employee, laughing and joking together as the money rolls in, and is secretly disappointed when Patrick reveals that he will be going to university to study engineering the following year (Sameer can never tell how old Ugandans are).

Whether it is luck, the grace of God, or just the fact of being in Uganda, to Sameer's relief and elation the four-week trial is a success – all of the retailers agree to twelve-month contracts with him. At the weekend, Mr Shah takes Sameer out for dinner to celebrate.

'May we have many more successes together, *inshallah*,' Mr Shah declares, as the waiter brings over two flutes of champagne.

'*Inshallah*,' Sameer responds, declining the champagne with a shake of his head.

'You're not drinking?'

'I've stopped,' he says simply, remembering the tumblers of whisky they had shared in the past. He does not offer any further explanation and Mr Shah does not ask for one; he nods curtly and waves the waiter away with one hand.

'No – please, go ahead,' Sameer says quickly, suddenly aware that he does not want his decision to decline to come across as righteous.

'No, no, don't be silly, I won't drink without you,' Mr Shah smiles, but Sameer cannot help but feel that Mr Shah now likes him a little less.

Over dinner, Mr Shah tells Sameer that other retailers and even some restaurants have expressed an interest in trial contracts. They talk about opening a factory, employees, and automating the processes. Tremors of excitement run the length of Sameer's spine: so this is what it feels like to create something. At the end of the evening, Sameer refuses to allow Mr Shah to pay. 'I just don't know how to thank you for all the help you've given me,' he says, surprised to find his voice thick with emotion. He looks at Mr Shah, who is removing a napkin from his collar with one hand and rubbing his protruding belly with the other; the gold chains nestled in the folds of his neck, the bright purple Versace shirt, the gold rings on nearly every finger – he looks ridiculous. But Sameer watches him with fondness – a man who not so long ago was a stranger and is now like a father.

'Now, now, don't forget I haven't done all of this for free. I'm still a shareholder in that company, albeit a small one. Don't go abusing your majority position on me . . .'

Sameer laughs. 'None of this would have been possible without you,' he says. 'And I know you have a lot of other more important things you could be doing – I really appreciate it.'

'Just because it's a small project doesn't mean it's not important,' Mr Shah looks at Sameer with affection. 'You know, you remind me of myself when I was your age. So full of ideas and energy, I thought I could change the world.'

'You have,' Sameer says, thinking of the impact that Shah's Sugar has had on Uganda's economy.

'And so will you.'

Sameer's chest swells with pride as his face breaks into a huge smile. He feels lighter than air and like he is floating upwards and into the sky.

The feeling of glory lasts a long few weeks – unlike the highs he used to get from a deal completing, which were as short-lived as the days that passed before he was put on the next one. Sometimes he is scared by how well things are going. In just over a month's time, Maryam will be his wife; he has three twelve-month contracts that will bring in a modest income after they return from honeymoon; and in the meantime, he's secured further trial periods with other retailers, which means potentially even more business. Nothing, not even the fact that his family are still not speaking to him, can diminish the pride he feels.

A week or so into the additional trial period, someone comes to the kitchen, knocking on the window rapidly. Patrick goes to the door and calls for Sameer. A Ugandan man is standing in front of him. 'Is this Saeed & Sons?' he demands.

The tone of his voice makes Sameer swallow.

'Why?' he says, wiping a hand on his apron. He is still holding a knife that he had been using to cut papaya and a drop of dark orange juice falls from the blade to the floor; he sheepishly tries to hide the knife behind his back.

The man's lip is trembling. 'You and your people, always stealing business from us – how can we compete with you?'

Sameer's heart starts to pound. 'I'm sorry, what?'

'I am being told my contract is terminated. I go to the supermarket, and all I see is your juice! I looked it up, I found this address. You are with Shah's Sugar, aren't you?' the man says. 'You Asians, always helping each other out, never thinking about the people who are hosting you in the very land on which you are standing!'

The acerbic tone cannot hide the pain that leaks from the corners of the man's eyes; Sameer meets them and is hit with the full force of his anguish. He looks at the man's worn and tired clothing; his stance reveals some discomfort in his leg, or perhaps his back; Sameer imagines the hungry mouths of the family he has to feed at home. He takes a step back. 'Look, Mr – I'm sorry, I don't know your name –'

'What does my name matter to you?' the man says, and now the bitterness has left his voice and only desperation remains. 'Your foreign money and your connections have caused three of the biggest retailers who sell my juice to shift to you. Now what do I do?'

The look on the man's face is one of hopelessness, but more than that, Sameer senses resignation: that for this man, Sameer standing here in front of him like this was inevitable. Before he can say anything, the man sighs, says something in Lugandan that Sameer does not understand, and starts to walk away, limping slightly.

Wait! Sameer wants to call after him, but when he opens his mouth to speak, no sound comes out. He remains in the doorway, stunned, watching the back of the man's stumbling figure. He is suddenly very aware of his own able body, the cost of his shoes, the watch on his wrist.

'Mr Saeed?' Patrick appears behind him, concerned.

'I've told you to call me Sameer,' he responds automatically.

'Sorry, boss,' Patrick wheedles. 'Sameer, are you OK?'

Sameer cannot bring himself to explain to Patrick what has just happened. Not only is he guilty of doing the things of which he has been accused, but worse: he was unaware that he was doing them. 'I need to go,' he says to Patrick. 'Can you finish up?'

On his way out, and he doesn't know where he's going, he reaches for his phone and calls Maryam once, twice, three times. She doesn't pick up.

He finds himself outside Mr Shah's offices. When, agitated, he tells Mr Shah what happened, Mr Shah dismisses it as meaningless and typical. 'The same thing has happened to me before,' he says. 'It's happened to all of us – no doubt it happened to your grandfather. These *karias*, they hate to see us succeed. But let me tell you something, son, there is nothing to feel bad about. This is just capitalism.'

Sameer is sickened by these words, and Mr Shah's face, just moments before these words, so kind and unassuming, now distorted into the image of his grandfather, his grandfather's face distorted into the image of him. They are all the same. Sameer stumbles out of the office – Mr Shah calling after him: 'Are you OK, *beta*? I've heard there's going to be a storm tonight, and it's going to be nasty, please stay out of it. Sameer?'

But Mr Shah did not see the man, standing there in front of him, defenceless and hurt, his livelihood having been snatched from his hands by Sameer; he had not spoken to him. Mr Shah, with his comfortable life, his immense wealth, he didn't care about anyone but himself. And now Sameer was doing exactly the same thing.

Back in the Airbnb and his suitcases are upended – suitcases he has been living out of for weeks now – a visitor to this country, a guest. He'd kept the package of letters somewhere here, a little part of his dark history carried with him everywhere. He hadn't been able to bring himself to read them. But now there is only one thing to do: to know it all, to its bitter end. He takes the bundle and walks out of the Airbnb, walks until he reaches Kololo, struggling in the humidity, scrambling up the steep red hill that leads to the park bordered by the disused airstrip. The sky is perfectly clear – but there are no people, as if everyone knows something he doesn't.

There he sits and reads. Letter after letter, unfolding in his palms, squinting at the cursive, aching at the tenderness, burning at the racial slurs, laughing sometimes at the sheer stupidity and ignorance. He has never sat and read the letters in a row like this and he is spirited away – he is his grandfather now, hunched over his desk, loopy writing in blue ink that bleeds onto the page, while his heart bleeds for Amira and Uganda. He is his grandfather while his rights are stripped, while his passport is taken from him, he is his grandfather as the only place he ever called home expels him. He is his grandfather as he tries and fails to settle in a country where he experiences cold as he's never known it, and he is his father now, getting smacked in the face walking home from school. He is his father as he listens to the drunken slurring of life in Uganda, a country which evokes nothing but anger – how could they do this to us, cast us out here? He is his father now, sleeping like a sardine cuddling up to his brothers and cousins because there are five of them asleep in a room and they can't afford to switch the heating on. He is his father watching his mother serve dinner to her children and husband and realising that after that, there is nothing left. He is his father as he watches his mother smiling and saying cheerfully that it's OK – if it goes into your stomach, it goes into mine. And then, finally, he is his grandfather again – returning to the country in which he will die, admitting that he never knew if his first wife ever loved him.

When he is done, Sameer's face is streaked with tears. Clouds have begun to gather. He is empty now, spent. There is nothing left of him. He will lie, face down in the red ground of Kololo's Independence Park, and allow the rain to wash him into the earth. Suddenly, he is overwhelmed by the strongest urge to call his father. He retrieves his phone from his pocket and dials the number. On the fourth ring, his father picks up and says shortly: 'Sameer?'

'Dad,' he chokes.

'Son?'

Why did he call? 'Dad, I'm sorry. I'm sorry for everything.'

There is a pause in which Sameer wonders whether his father will hang up. But no – 'Are you OK?' his father asks.

'I'm OK, Dad,' he breathes. 'I just wanted to let you know that I'm sorry for everything that I've put you through. I know this is really hard for you.'

His father sighs heavily, making the line crackle. 'You know, all I have ever tried to do is what is best for you. I wanted you to have the life and opportunities I did not have.'

Sameer knows that the usual lecture is about to begin, but he doesn't interrupt. He wants his father to have this one. He wants his father to know that he is listening. There's no security in Africa – it's not like England – there is no respect for rights, you will never be one of them, whereas even if the English won't accept you as one of them, they will respect your basic rights. There's a reason we don't want this for you – and there's a reason we don't want her for you. Yes, you are

English, but we didn't raise you with English values – we raised you with our values. We raised you to put your family above everything else: we didn't raise you to be selfish. We raised you to understand the sacrifices we have made to allow you to be where you are today, and we raised you to understand that you have duties.

Sameer listens. He doesn't agree with all of the things his father is saying, but he understands, perhaps for the first time, why his is father is saying them.

'Sameer, I can't force you to listen to me any more. But you're a good boy at heart. I think you know what the right thing is to do. Come home, son.' – and on these last words, Sameer is nauseatingly homesick and his eyes fill with tears. Maybe he should leave Uganda. Maybe it's time to go home.

But – Maryam . . .

Right on cue, the call with his father is interrupted by a call from Maryam. 'Dad, I've got to go,' he says, and then, hesitatingly, 'but I've heard you. I love you, Dad. I'll call you later.'

'Sorry, I was on the phone to my dad,' he says to Maryam. She is surprised and pleased at this news – what triggered the reconciliation? 'I need to talk to you,' he says.

'Sameer, is everything OK?' and when he doesn't respond immediately: 'Where are you?'

'Kololo Independence Park.'

'There's a storm coming, you should get indoors.'

'It hasn't broken yet.'

'OK, just stay there,' she says. 'I'm coming to get you.'

While he waits, his mind races. They'd never discussed the possibility of living in England – it was always just assumed that he would move to Kampala. But they'd never *actually discussed it*. When he spoke to her, she'd see the turmoil his mind was in, and maybe she would consider it. Practically speaking, getting her to England wouldn't be a problem once they were married – she would be on a married person's visa. But would she ever leave her father?

He scrambles down the hill and waits for her familiar Toyota; it pulls up on the side of the road and he climbs in. The sight of her – as always – delivers relief, like he's come home. He reaches out to touch her face and she nuzzles her cheek into his palm.

'What's going on? Why are you out here?'

'I really need to talk to you.'

'Now?' and there is a hint of fear in her voice.

'Now is as good a time as any,' he takes a deep breath and begins: 'I had a visitor today . . .' He tells her everything: the man at the kitchen, Mr Shah's reaction, what he read in his grandfather's letters, how it made him feel. Like he's an impostor, repeating the mistakes of his grandfather, thinking it's OK to come in and exploit the country like this, a country to which he doesn't belong. He tells her that he spoke to his father – and yes, that was great news, but it made him wonder: was this all moving too fast? They had never talked about England, but she could be happy in England. He would make her happy; he could be enough. England would love to have her – just as it accepted his family after they were expelled from Uganda. He's rambling now, but he can't stop.

She allows him to speak without interruption, but when he is done, she shakes her head, expression pained. 'OK,' she says calmly. 'Is this all about that man who came to your kitchen? His contract wasn't terminated for no reason, you know . . . your products are obviously just better. That's not your fault.'

'No,' he insists. Hasn't she been listening? 'Everything I read in the letters – it's made me wonder, am I doing the right thing by trying to stay here? I just don't know if any of this is right – none of this, except you, feels right. I know that this isn't what we planned, but can we at least talk about maybe going to the UK?'

'I don't understand,' she says, and she cannot keep the emotion out of her voice. 'You think you're causing a problem here, so you want to deal with it by running away?'

'It wouldn't be running away.'

'But what would you do in England, Sameer? Go back to the job you hate? Work for your father? It doesn't make any sense.'

'I don't know yet. I don't need to have a plan. We would work it out.'

'What would I do? I wouldn't be able to work there, my qualifications wouldn't be recognised.'

'Of course they would,' he says unsurely.

'Look,' she tries gently, 'I understand you're feeling strange. But you haven't thought through any of this.'

'Do you think I thought through coming here?' he snaps, and her face recoils with hurt. 'You know what I meant,' he adds, but her eyes have filled with tears and her lip is trembling now.

'How did you not realise any of this before you asked to marry me, Sameer?' she says, and the tears are rolling down her face now – she's agreed to marry an idiot. He reaches out to touch her arm – he shouldn't have brought it up like this. She flinches but doesn't pull away.

'Maryam,' he says, pulling her elbow towards him gently, coaxing her body to turn to face him, 'I know I'm sounding confused. I'm sorry. My mind is fucked up right now – I can't tell you what's going on inside my head.' He takes her face in his hands and wipes the tears with his thumbs. 'But the one thing I'm not confused about is you.'

She gives him a half-smile and he brushes one thumb over her lip; she catches it in her teeth and sucks it gently, surprising him and arousing him. Then she pulls away and looks out of the window. 'I can't leave Kampala, Sameer.'

He leans back in the seat with frustration. Could he really stay? After everything he has done and seen, is it really right for him to stay? Outside, the sky has turned an angry shade of grey, like nightfall has come early. He opens the car door and wind rushes in, diffusing the heat inside the metal shell.

'What are you doing?' she says. 'Let's go home – we can talk to *Taata* about this. We'll work something out.'

He doesn't respond and steps out of the car, leaving the door open. A single, fat drop of rain lands almost immediately on his cheek, a strange relief. It's almost cold. The wind is strong and the rain will be heavy.

'Sameer, what are you doing? It's about to rain – we should head home.' She's come out of the car now, standing in front of him, arms all wrapped around herself as she likes to, and she's having to shout over the sound of the wind.

'I don't know what I'm doing,' he admits. 'You don't understand because you haven't read the letters –' and then, in a moment of madness, he reaches into the car, retrieves the bundle from his backpack and hands them to her. 'You have to read them – all of them.' But he had not secured the twine properly and as she takes the package, the top two letters are picked up by the wind and carried away into the air. 'Shit!' he rushes to take the package back, but it's still in her hands too and as they attempt to prevent the others from flying away, the whole package falls apart and suddenly there are letters everywhere – some on the ground, some in the air. 'No, NO!' Sameer falls to his knees, scrambling around in the red dirt to collect up the letters. Maryam drops automatically to the floor to help, and the rain has started to come now, thick and fast, the heaviest rain he has ever experienced; these are not individual droplets but sheets of rain, slicing through the sky and drenching the two of them.

'We need to go!' Maryam yells, standing with a bunch of crumpled, sodden paper in her hands.

'No – I need to get all of them!' He is still on his knees, which are now swimming in puddles of reddy-brown water. He gathers together what he can, but the ink has run and the paper is disintegrating under the weight of the water. The rain is relentless but she doesn't get back inside the car. When he finally stands, they are both soaked through. The paper in their hands is no longer paper: it is coloured pulp. He is glad for the rain and the cold, masking the tears that are shaking his body. She comes towards him and takes one of his hands, full of paper pulp. 'Let them go, Sameer,' she says gently. 'Let go.'

He shakes his head, but he drops the pulp to the floor, taking her in his arms and pulling her close, so they become a single figure pounded by the rain. Her whole body is shivering and he squeezes her harder, letting his lips rest on her forehead. 'I just don't know how to fix this,' he whispers, trembling.

'Some things just can't be fixed, Sameer,' she says.

26

Orange burns the horizon, jagged with the shape of ashy trees. Although it is mild tonight, Sameer shivers as he watches the last vestiges of the day leave the sky. He's standing on the balcony of his Airbnb for the last time. This one had allowed him to stay longer than he was strictly supposed to – he'd had to pack up the parts of him strewn across the small apartment; it had only ever been intended to be temporary, but as things tend to after a period of time, it had begun to take on his essence. That was it in Kampala: you could get away with bending the rules, no one minded. It wasn't the same in London.

He misses her.

He'd thought a lot about what he could do to try to fix things, but she was right in the end. Perhaps some things were incapable of being fixed. He had thought about setting up a charity to help those struggling, but it wouldn't really have been feasible to run alongside the juice business. He settled for making a donation to assuage his conscience, followed up with a promise that if he ever made it, he would set up a charity. But it all seemed so half-hearted, as everything did with him. Something bothers him still, and it will take time for him to come to terms with it – time is the only solution to this issue. All he knows for certain is that he will be better than those who stood here before him; he has to be.

He thinks of Maryam again, of her lips. The softness of them. But it's not long to wait now.

The wedding has been organised by Maryam and her

aunties. Sameer has no particular interest in the wedding: only the marriage itself. He has insisted (despite Maryam's protests) on contributing financially; he has no idea what a wedding costs and when he asks her what the total is, it seems cheap enough. It will be a low-key affair, with a small number of guests: the *nikkah* will take place in the National Mosque, and afterwards the wedding party will go to the same steakhouse that Sameer and Maryam dined in on his first visit to Uganda, for the reception.

His father had not reacted well to the news that Sameer would not be coming home; but he had sounded resigned more than anything over the phone – this son of his, with his ever-changing mind, the son he raised to indecision, this son without a backbone. What kind of a son was he? But at the same time, with a son like this, there is every chance that he will return to him in the future. He has not given up hope yet.

A handful of Sameer's family members are flying to Uganda for the occasion: Yasmeen Foi and Haroon Fua, Samah and John (Samah insists on coming even though she is in the third trimester of her pregnancy), and – Sameer's heart beats gratefully – Zara. Also on his side, Jeremiah and Angela, Roy and a few of the other boys from his school friendship group, the Shahs and Patrick. When Sameer finally gave the invitation to Mr Shah, only two weeks before the event, Mr Shah had expressed a quiet disappointment at the news that he was getting married (although Sameer had an instinctive feeling that the disappointment would come more from Mrs Shah) and asked casually who the lucky lady was. Sameer could not bring himself to look Mr Shah in the eye when he told him. This was not out of embarrassment, but out of respect. Nevertheless, the whole family – including Aliyah – said they would attend. And that was really it from Sameer's side.

It is decided that, for now, the newly-weds will live in Maryam's family house after the wedding. Sameer finds it funny that he will not have seen all of the rooms in his father's old house until he marries one of its inhabitants, but he will be happy to leave the Airbnbs, this nomadic existence, moving on every few weeks to a new place. The wedding day approaches with surprising speed, coinciding neatly (and to Sameer's amusement) with the end of the notice period he never completed – just over three months from the day he resigned. How much has changed in the space of a notice period.

Two days before the wedding, Sameer catches a taxi to Entebbe to meet the family arriving from the UK. As he stands waiting in front of the arrivals gate, his stomach begins to knot and the hairs on his arms stand to attention. He looks up: his mother is walking through the gate. She comes to him slowly and hugs him. 'I'm so happy to see you, Mum,' he says, and she bursts into tears. Zara, Yasmeen Foi and Haroon Fua, Samah and John – they are all there behind her. But his father is not.

They get two taxis back to Kampala, splitting into their respective families. Zara takes the passenger seat and Sameer sits in the back with his mother, who holds his hand firmly in her own. 'He wanted to come,' his mother lies. 'But he had unavoidable work business. He sends his love, though. And a gift for Maryam – gold.'

Later, when they are in the Airbnb, Zara tells him the truth: 'He's punishing you. And he's pissed at both of us for coming. We're getting the silent treatment.'

Sameer's hands ball into fists. Zara can cope with the silent treatment, but he hates that his mother must suffer this. Zara is young, busy at university and has her whole life in front of her. Sameer has a new family, Maryam, and a new life in front of him. His mother's life has no new beginnings. It has only endings now, and the path to those endings is filled with Sameer's father. 'Don't tell me this,' he says. 'It makes me wish you hadn't come.'

'Don't be silly,' Zara responds, avoiding his gaze for a minute, and what has been unspoken between them is no longer necessary to say. 'And anyway, Mum said you don't know anything about weddings,' Zara is grinning now as she puts on a desi accent: 'We had to come to make sure you didn't make a fool of yourself and bring shame to the family's name.'

True to her word, his mother's suitcases are packed full of gifts for Maryam and her family – an Asian tradition Sameer had no idea existed. She wants to march over there straight away with the family in tow, but Sameer manages to convince her to wait until he has arranged it with Maryam. He messages Maryam (*My mum came . . . and she came with gifts. When can we come over?*) and they arrange for the families to meet for the first time the day before the wedding.

The meeting is a solemn affair; while his mother is impressed with the house ('Much nicer than the area and the place we're staying in, huh?' she says in the taxi on the way back, but not being able to stop herself from adding, 'then again, it is of course your father's old house'), she is reserved almost to the point of coldness with Maryam and her family. Maryam receives four suitcases – two from Sameer's mother, one from Yasmeen Foi and Haroon Fua, and one from Samah and John – packed to the brim with clothes, handbags, shoes and costume jewellery. Sameer cringes as his mother insists that the cases are opened in front of them and, upon seeing layers and layers of heavy salwar kameez and embroidered saris, Maryam says thank you in a small voice that is almost painful to Sameer's ears. The other members of Maryam's family are much more enthusiastic, fawning over the beautiful, intricate details so much so that Sameer wonders if they have gone too far, whether this level of excitement at the gifts is inappropriate. But his mother is wearing a little smile of triumph. He wants to feel proud of her for trying – clearly some effort has gone into choosing the outfits, and each of the accessories match the colours with painstaking detail – but, looking at his mother, he just feels hollow. Samah and John's suitcase is filled with Western clothing – much more like the kind of thing he thinks Maryam would wear, long skirts and dresses, T-shirts and palazzo pants. Maryam flips through it, quickly closing the case just as Sameer spies a bag under all the clothing labelled Victoria's Secrets, and she thanks them, even giving Samah a hug. Sameer glances at his mother and sees her eyes harden.

Maryam's family insist that they stay for dinner; Sameer's mother initially protests, but eventually gives in, and although Sameer is desperate for the meeting to conclude as quickly as possible, he is also glad, because dinner at Maryam's house is always delicious and he wants Zara to experience it. After *isha* (and this is the first time that Sameer's mother looks pleased, to pray in congregation), a table and chairs are brought into the drawing room; there is not enough space in the dining room to seat them all, and refusing to separate their guests, Maryam's family create a buffet on the dining table and ask their guests to eat from their laps. There are a sufficient number of them to fill any potentially awkward silences, but Sameer notices that his mother barely engages with anyone else in the room.

When the dinner is over, Sameer and Maryam are not allowed a single moment in private before he is bundled away into a taxi by his mother who says that they all need to get an early night because it is a big day tomorrow.

•

When Sameer looks back on his wedding day, he will only remember two things: the look on Maryam's face when the *nik-kah* was complete – exultant; and the contrasting image of the Ugandan wedding party, entirely sober, but wildly dancing in all their traditional clothes, while his mother, Yasmeen Foi and Haroon Fua sat on the sidelines, looking miserable and muttering between themselves. The Shahs had left almost immediately after the dinner; Samah was relaxing with her feet up on another chair, head bobbing to the music, while John rubbed her shoulders; Sameer's friends from home were dancing with Maryam's family (Jeremiah having effortlessly mixed with the Ugandans and learned their dance moves); and Zara had made friends with one of Maryam's cousins and was standing by the edge of the dance floor, chatting. Sameer sat with Maryam and surveyed the scene, exhausted. Her hand rested in his, and every so often he would squeeze it and feel surprised at how small it was, how delicate.

When the party is over, they are finally allowed to retire to a hotel for one night. Somewhere in the unspeakable back of his mind, that morning when Sameer had pictured the rest of his life fanning out in front of him under the Ugandan sun, he had wondered whether he would end up resenting her for it – after that horrible day when he had lost his grandfather's letters, there had been several conversations and she had insisted she wouldn't move. That doggedness, uncompromising – it had angered him and he had admired it in equal measure. He knew it made sense: she being the one with the sick father, the steady job which she loved (and which helped people); but he hated that she couldn't even begin to consider any compromise (well, you could live there and I here, was a decidedly stupid suggestion). But at the same time, he couldn't get past the image of the man standing outside his kitchen, the hurt etched in his face. Every time he goes to work, it haunts him.

He can still see his grandfather's slanted writing when he closes his eyes – as he spoke about Abdullah, the betrayal he suffered upon being expelled. If it made so much sense to stay, why did this continue to bother him so much? Would there be a day when he woke up and realised he could not stay any longer?

But in the corridor outside the door of their honeymoon suite, she has never looked more beautiful: the floor-length, fish-tailed orange *gomesi*, cinched in at the waist by a golden sash; headscarf adorned with costume jewellery and flowers; she is wearing more make-up than he has ever seen her wear before: false eyelashes, lipstick, black henna in swirling patterns on her hands, back and front. Her beauty commands him, melting away his worry about the future. He takes both her shoulders – again, surprised to feel the smallness of her – and kisses her on the mouth, fully and deeply.

She goes straight into the bathroom when they enter the room. Sameer goes onto the balcony, looking out over the city, inhales deeply and closes his eyes. At some point, the sound of Maryam exiting the bathroom makes him turn round. She stands in front of him, smiling shyly, completely naked. Sameer has never even seen her with her scarf off and this is almost too much to process – the smooth curves of her figure, the rise and swell of her breasts, climaxing in black, hard nipples, the shape of her collarbone. Her hair is short, scraped back into a low bun, partly curly, partly relaxed. The protruding, wholesome roundness of her backside, the wide shape of her hips, and on the inside of those hips, that soft V shape. He moves towards her slowly, as if he is in a dream.

The next week, spent at a beach hotel in Zanzibar, is the happiest of Sameer's life. They take long strolls along the white shores in the mornings and evenings, spending their days in the bed or outside under the rain shower. For the first time in his life, Sameer understands what it means when people say that sex changes everything. Before, sex was a physical function to satisfy a need – like eating, or sleeping. It felt good and necessary. Now, sex is a way of connecting with Maryam; it is an opening, a way of sharing a part of himself with her, and her with him. There is something almost spiritual about it. It morphs the quality of their relationship; it moulds and binds them to one another. When they are out at dinner and Maryam strokes his thumb with her own, or innocently licks her lips, he flushes at the memory of what they did to each other earlier that day and it gives him a rush of pleasure. They talk endlessly – sometimes interrupting each other, almost tripping over their own tongues in their hurry to get the words out – often digressing down rabbit holes and forgetting what they had initially been talking about and laughing. Being with her – sleeping with her – makes him forget everything else, like a drug. He has a new sense of purpose with her, as if she – and them, together – is ultimately the only thing that really matters. He did not know that it was possible to feel so complete.

'I'm not ready to go back to real life,' he says to her on the last day of the honeymoon, her head resting on his chest while he traces the outline of her nipple with a fingertip.

She turns her head up slightly, tickling his torso with her hair. 'Me neither,' she whispers. 'But there's something amazing about knowing you're going to be there, every day when I wake up and before I go to sleep.'

He grabs her hand and squeezes it. 'I know what you mean,' he lands a kiss on her shoulder. 'That in itself doesn't feel real.'

'After a while it will feel all too real,' she says, laughing. 'We shouldn't forget to take holidays when we go back.'

But they will have no money or time for holidays. She settles back into her life with no change to her routine, just the nice addition of him; for him, everything is different. And it's strange, when they return from honeymoon, not having their own space. Although they do have their own room (Maryam's auntie kindly having vacated to allow the newly married couple some privacy), their nights together are muted, one hand placed over Maryam's mouth to quieten the sound of her moaning, gritting his own teeth as he releases. It is exhilarating at first, sexy even, but he quickly realises that he doesn't want to live in the house on a long-term basis.

He also finds himself spending a lot of time working, which doesn't level with his expectations; perhaps working for Mr Shah had given him the wrong impression; perhaps it is the fact that he had assumed that he had left behind a life of working long hours late into the night. But it is necessary as the factory lease is signed, employees are hired and contracts are concluded. The work is endless, but the difference is that he controls when he leaves and when he chooses to work. When Maryam's shifts finish in time for dinner, he takes a break from work and meets her at a restaurant, or they go home to have dinner with the family, before he returns to his office. Sometimes, hunched over a desk looking at the business plan, he will remember what happened; he will see the face of the man and beads of sweat will materialise on his forehead. It will take him a good few minutes to calm down.

Sameer hears from his father for the first time two months after the wedding. The WhatsApp simply says: *Mhota Papa is dying. Will you come home?* He's in a meeting with a retailer at their offices in downtown Kampala when he receives it. He asks to be excused and steps out, heart leaping into his throat, scrambling for the keypad, finding his father's number and pressing the call button. His father picks up on the fourth ring.

There are no pleasantries. 'It's good you phoned,' he says shortly. He sounds exhausted. 'Mhota Papa has acute heart failure. The doctors are saying he could go any time now. Come if you want to say goodbye.'

Sameer doesn't ask any questions. 'I'll get the next available flight.'

It is nearly six o' clock in the evening and there are no more flights that day: the only flight he can get leaves the following morning from Entebbe. Sameer cannot concentrate when he returns to the meeting and, informing the retailer that he has had a family emergency, he asks if it would be possible to rearrange.

It's not quite sunset and the evening sun basks Kampala city with an orange glow. Sameer's mind is racing uncontrollably. He wants to walk to try to clear it – if he leaves now, he can make it back home before nightfall. He had wanted to speak to Mhota Papa after he'd finished reading his grandfather's letters; he'd wanted to tell him that he'd finally understood what Mhota Papa had said to him in the hospital, the last real conversation they'd had: that his *dada* had a lot of love in his heart. He'd meant to call – he'd really meant to. But the time had gone so quickly; there had always been something more pressing – and the thought of shouting down the phone to Mhota Papa, trying to get him to understand, became ever less of a priority. Sameer's eyes sting with shame, hating him for not even trying.

As he crosses the road next to the golf club, its green-grass grounds filtered golden by the lowering sun, he hears a shout behind him. 'Eh, *muhindi*!'

Sameer looks back – two figures, silhouetted by the dying light, are walking towards him. He doesn't know what they want, but instinct tells him that it is not friendly. Further along the road, at the bottom of the slope of the hill joining the main road, Sameer can see the shadowy figures of people walking and talking, dimly lit. Up here, it is deserted and almost dark. He starts walking towards the main road and the people behind him follow. 'Stop, Saeed!' the men call. 'We just want to talk to you!'

Sameer breaks into a jog, and they start jogging too; he starts to run and they start running. As he is about to approach the main road, he thinks of Maryam. He is nearly home.

Acknowledgements

To my Pirmohamed family, for raising my awareness of this chapter of history and for sharing their stories of their time in Uganda. To Bapa especially, who dedicated not hours but days pouring over the manuscript in painstaking detail to make sure every last word was right – always the Pirmohamed way!

To Akua, Stormzy and the #Merky Books team, for making this dream happen; for giving people like me the opportunity to tell our stories.

To Abi, for the moral support and guidance through a process which was completely new to me.

To Tom, for believing in my novel, for understanding my characters sometimes better than I understood them myself, for the vast improvements you made to the manuscript and for giving up so many evenings and weekends to get it there.

To the incredible country that is Uganda, and to those who welcomed us – to Ssebbowa Dauda Mutimba, for taking us on such a beautiful journey, and for the lifelong friendship; to Tumusiime Wardah Magezi, for your immense help with the modern-day Ugandan narrative, and for your infinite patience. To those who gave up their time to be interviewed – Namulema Haliimah, Kibunga Atidu, Rashidah Nakaweesa, Shadia Rajab, Nanyonga Salmah.

To the scholars who have dedicated their time and shared their research on understanding the causes and consequences of the Asian expulsion, and to the Asian Ugandans who have shared their stories with the world.

To Hanah, for being there from the initial #Merky Books

launch, for your early edit, and for your invaluable advice and support ever since.

To Mummy and Baba, for raising me on fiction and telling me that it was possible to achieve anything; for your unfaltering support and guidance; for just being you.

To Sanaa, for being my biggest cheerleader and for never allowing me to doubt myself; for always listening.

To Riaz, without whom this book would not have been written . . . to Riaz, for everything.

Alhumdulilah.

Reading Group Questions

1. Sameer says to Maryam that 'If you don't understand where you've come from, you'll never really understand who you are or where you're going'. Sameer is a second-generation immigrant, just like Hasan. To what extent do you think this has affected their sense of identity and belonging?

2. When Sameer tells Jeremiah that his grandfather met his wife for the first time on their wedding night, Jeremiah says that Sameer and his grandfather are a few generations apart. Do you think that the concept of duty and cultural expectation has changed from Hasan's generation to Sameer's generation, and if so, how?

3. The novel explores the issue of anti-blackness in South Asian communities. Sameer is horrified by his parents' reaction to his marriage proposal and embarrassed about his grandfather's views when reading the letters. How similar do you think Sameer is to his grandfather? Do you think Sameer's grandchildren would be embarrassed by any of his views?

4. What do you think really happened between Amira and Abdullah? Do you trust Hasan's narrative and does he become more reliable by the final letter?

5. The idea that one race may be superior or inferior because of their physical or biological attributes ('scientific racism') is expressed in various characters' views in both narratives. Where and how do you see this drawn out, and how are these views damaging to those who hold them?

6. Mr Shah says that 'You'll never be anybody if you work for somebody.' How is the concept of success discussed in the novel? Is it ever defined?

7. In both narratives, the Asian protagonist's closest friend is black. How are their relationships similar and in what ways do they differ?

8. Maryam and Zara are the two closest women to Sameer in the novel. To what extent do you think Sameer's views of women are progressive, if at all?

9. Maryam says to Sameer that 'We have all been affected by British colonialism.' To what extent does the legacy of colonialism have an impact on each of the characters in the modern-day narrative?

10. The political history of Uganda, Idi Amin's regime, and the expulsion of Asian Ugandans are all told through Hasan's eyes. How do you think the novel would have differed if the historical narrative had been written from Abdullah's perspective?

11. How does Sameer's relationship with his religion change throughout the novel and what do you think the reason for this is?

12. By the end of the novel Sameer feels like he understands his parents better. What do you think Sameer has learned that has helped him reach this understanding?

Further Reading

There is a vast amount of information publicly available about the history of Uganda and the South Asian expulsion. For those who would like to learn more, some of the resources that were consulted when undertaking the research for writing this book are listed below.

Books

Non-fiction

Alicia C. Decker, *In Idi Amin's Shadow: Women, Gender, and Militarism in Uganda*, Ohio University Press, 2014

Ashley Jackson, *The British Empire and the Second World War*, A&C Black, 2006

Assa Okoth, *A History of Africa: African societies and the establishment of colonial rule, 1800-1915*, Volume 1 of *A History of Africa*, East African Publishers, 2006

David Ernest Apter, *The Political Kingdom in Uganda: A Study in Bureaucratic Nationalism*, Routledge; first edition, 1997

Grace Stuart Ibingira, *African Upheavals Since Independence*, Westview Press, 1980

Jordanna Bailkin, *Unsettled: Refugee Camps and the Making of Multicultural Britain*, Oxford University Press, 2018

Mahmood Mamdani, *From Citizen to Refugee: Uganda Asians Come to Britain*, Pambazuka Press; second edition, 2011

Phares Mukasa Mutibwa, *Uganda Since Independence: A Story of Unfulfilled Hopes*, C. Hurst & Co. Publishers, 1992

Memoir

Andrew Rice, *The Teeth May Smile But the Heart Does Not Forget: Murder and Memory in Uganda*, Picador USA; first edition, 2010

Dolar Popat, *A British Subject: How to Make It as an Immigrant in the Best Country in the World*, Biteback Publishing, 2019

Jamie Govani, *Life Is a Lesson: Never Give Up Hope*, AuthorHouse, 2012

Nergesh Tejani, M.D., *I Hear a Song in My Head: A Memoir in Stories of Love, Fear, Doctoring, and Flight*, SCARITH/New Academia Publishing, 2012

Robeson Bennazoo Otim Engur, *Survival: A Soldier's Story*, AuthorHouse, 2013

Yasmin Alibhai-Brown, *No Place Like Home*, Virago Press Ltd, 1995

Fiction

Shenaaz G. Nanji, *Child of Dandelions*, Second Story Press, 2008

Tasneem Jamal, *Where the Air is Sweet*, HarperCollins Publishers, 2014

Journals

Anneeth Kaur Hundle, 'Exceptions to the expulsion: violence, security and community among Ugandan Asians, 1972–79', *Journal of Eastern African Studies*, Vol. 7, No. 1, 2013, pp. 164–182

Becky Taylor, 'Good Citizens? Ugandan Asians, Volunteers and "Race" Relations in 1970s Britain', *History Workshop Journal*, Vol. 85, 2018, pp. 120–141

Carol Summers and Ahmad Alawad Sikainga, 'Ugandan Politics and World War II (1939–1949)', pp. 480–98, *Africa and World War II*, edited by Judith A. Byfield, Carolyn A. Brown and Timothy Parsons, Cambridge University Press, 2015

Edgar Curtis Taylor, 'Asians and Africans in Ugandan Urban Life, 1959–1972', 2016, available at deepblue.lib.umich.edu

Frances M. Dahlberg, 'The Asian Community with Special Reference to Lira (Uganda)', Neue Folge / New Series, Vol. 26, No. 1, 1976, pp. 29-42

Frank Wooldridge and Vishnu D. Sharma, 'International Law and the Expulsion of Ugandan Asians', *The International Lawyer*, Vol. 9, No. 1, 1975, pp. 30–76

Hasu H. Patel, 'General Amin and the Indian Exodus from Uganda', *A Journal of Opinion*, Vol. 2, No. 4, 1972, pp. 12–22

H. S. Morris, 'The Indian Family in Uganda', *American Anthropologist*, Vol. 61, No. 5, 1959, pp. 779–789

Jack D. Parson, 'Africanizing Trade in Uganda: The Final Solution', *Africa Today*, Vol. 20, No. 1, 1973, pp. 59–72

John L. Bonee III, 'Caesar Augustus and the Flight of the Asians – The International Legal Implications of the Asian Expulsion From Uganda During 1972', *The International Lawyer*, Vol. 8, No. 1, 1974, pp. 136–159

K. C. Kotecha, 'The Shortchanged: Uganda Citizenship Laws and How They Were Applied to Its Asian Minority', *The International Lawyer*, Vol. 9, No. 1, 1975, pp. 1–29

Shezan Muhammedi, ' "Gifts From Amin": The Resettlement, Integration, and Identities of Ugandan Asian Refugees in Canada', 2017, available at ir.lib.uwo.ca

Thomas Fuller, 'African Labor and Training in the Uganda Colonial Economy', *The International Journal of African Historical Studies*, Vol. 10, No. 1, 1977, pp. 77–95

Vali Jamal, 'Asians in Uganda, 1880–1972: Inequality and Expulsion', *The Economic History Review*, Vol. 29, No. 4, 1976, pp. 602–616

William Monteith, 'Heart and Struggle: Life in Nakasero Market 1912–2015', 2016, available at uea.ac.uk

Archives

Ugandan Argus and other archival material, as well as contemporary transcripts, available at asc.library.carleton.ca/exhibits/uganda-collection

Institute of Current World Affairs, The Late Kabaka and First President of Uganda GJ-12 May 15, 1971, available at icwa.org

Other Resources

asiansfromuganda.org.uk

Contemporaneous and recent press reports can be found in the following publications: *Daily Monitor, Daily Nation, The Economist, Forbes, Guardian, Independent, LA Times, New Vision, The New York Times, Telegraph, The Times*; broadcasters: BBC, CNN, Channel 4, PBS; and websites: observer.ug and YouTube.

About the Author

Hafsa Zayyan is a writer and dispute resolution lawyer based in London. She won the inaugural #Merky Books New Writers' Prize in 2019. *We Are All Birds of Uganda* is her debut novel, inspired by the mixed background from which she hails. She studied Law at the University of Cambridge and holds a master's degree from the University of Oxford.